The
SPEAK EASY
Duet

MELANIE HARLOW

They slipped briskly into an intimacy
from which they never recovered.

F. Scott Fitzgerald, **This Side of Paradise**

Part One:

Speak Easy

Chapter One

Friday, July 13th, 1923

The woman approached me at the counter, keeping her eyes low. "A quart of maple syrup," she said, her voice hushed.

I didn't recognize her. "What kind?"

"Canadian." Clutching her purse to her stomach, she peeked at me from beneath the brim of her hat.

"What are you making?"

"Griddlecakes."

I nodded. If she'd answered waffles, or even pancakes, I'd have directed her to the east wall of the store, where tin cans of actual maple syrup were stacked three high on a shelf. But since she knew the password, I named our price and took down the order and her address. She'd get her whisky in a day or so.

Bootlegging was that simple for a small operation like ours. The customers were loyal, the neighborhood grocery store was a legitimate cover, and thanks to the narrow waterway separating Detroit from Canada and its distilleries, our whisky supply seemed endless. Timely payoffs assured us of little trouble from city officials, and the local cops were some of our best customers. So when the bell over

Jefferson Market's front door jangled again that afternoon, I greeted the customer with a smile. But as the well-dressed man removed his light gray fedora and walked toward me at the back of the store, the air took on a strange charge. Gooseflesh rippled across my skin.

It was him. The sheik.

He'd been in twice in the last week. Each time, he'd said practically nothing, bought one pack of Fatima cigarettes, and paid with a fifty-dollar bill. I thought of him as the sheik because he reminded me of a movie star: dark, silent, and handsome in that delighted-villain sort of way, as if he'd just tied a girl to the train tracks and now it was time for a cocktail and a smoke.

"Good afternoon." His voice was deep and smooth, just how I imagined a screen idol's should be. "Are you Miss O'Mara?"

I blinked. *He knows my name.* "Yes. Can I help you?"

"Give this to your father." He pulled an envelope from his coat and laid it on the counter, next to the cash register. When I reached for it, he placed his hand over mine, pinning it to the cool marble. A buzz swept up my arm as our eyes met. His were so dark they appeared black, and a small scar rested at the top of one cheekbone. "Tell him to answer by tonight."

It took me a moment to find my voice. "All right."

Replacing his hat on top of his slick dark hair, he walked out without looking back. The bell jangled once more, and I released the breath I'd been holding, leaning on the counter for support. I jumped when I heard a voice behind me.

"Tiny?" My older sister Bridget poked her head in from the stockroom, her long brown hair coming loose from its knot at her nape. "Daddy's ready for you to make deliveries."

Quickly I swiped the envelope into the front pocket of my middy blouse.

"Just let me put the bread in the oven," Bridget said, disappearing into the stockroom again. She and her children lived in the apartment over the store. At almost twenty-one, I was more than ready to move out of our father's house and get my own apartment, but it would have to wait. There were two more daughters after me who needed tending, and with our mother gone and Bridget widowed with three young boys, I wasn't going anywhere soon.

While I waited, I fingered the envelope in my pocket. The sheik said Daddy had to answer by tonight, but what was the question? Was he a bootlegger too? He looked a little older than me, but still in his twenties, and wealthy, if his clothing was any indication. He wore exquisite three-piece suits.

First black, then blue, and today, gray. I looked at the back of my hand, where he'd touched me, then brought it to my lips.

"What are you doing?" Bridget's voice startled me again, and she laughed.

Cheeks burning, I tucked my hand into my pocket. "Nothing. Can I go?"

She nodded. "I'll bring the grocery sacks out to you in the alley."

I exited through the stock room into the wet heat of a Michigan summer afternoon. In the alley, I pulled the envelope from my pocket and looked at it. Jack O'Mara was written on its ivory face in black ink, the cursive letters small and lean. The seal was tight. No way to tell what its contents were, no clue as to who the sheik might be or whom he worked for.

Not that I much cared about his occupation.

If he comes in again, I'll say hello first, I thought, recalling those dark eyes that smoldered like Valentino's. "Hi, there," I said, practicing. No, too girlish. I cleared my throat and tried again, imagining how a sultry screen vamp like Theda Bara would greet a man like the sheik. "Hello." Yes, that was better. Deeper, more mature.

Next, I tried to even out my walk so that I could slink into a room, cigarette holder in one hand, highball in the other. But slinking was a bit difficult for me because one of my legs is shorter than the other, not that either of them is what you'd call long. My mother was so small she had difficult births, and my hip broke as I was being born. It hadn't healed right, resulting in a one-inch difference, and I have to concentrate if I don't want to limp, especially if I'm tired. But if I smoothed out my gait, kept my weight back and my chin down, bent my knees a little...

Damn. Slinking was harder than it looked.

Giving up, I jogged the rest of the way down the alley and pushed open the door to the garage. Once my eyes adjusted to the dim light, I saw Daddy taking apart the back end of a Cadillac hearse.

Officially, he was an auto repairman, but his real talent was rebuilding cars—creating hidden compartments, phony gas tanks, false floorboards. It was amazing how many bottles of booze could be stashed in the unseen lining of an automobile. Hearses were especially popular with bootleggers because they had wide back ends, but I stuck with my Model T. Those hearses were *creepy*.

"I'm here!" I called over the banging of his hammer.

The noise stopped and he straightened halfway, bracing his hands on the hearse's frame and tilting his chin toward me over one shoulder. His profile revealed the crooked line of his nose, which had been broken several times. "It's over there. Can you load it?" He jerked his head toward two large boxes labeled Royal

Baking Powder sitting on the cement floor near the door.

"Sure."

"Fifteen per bottle, and don't take less."

"I won't. This came for you." I moved closer to him and held out the envelope. "The man who brought it said you should answer by tonight."

He took it from me, barely glancing at it before shoving it into the front pocket of his work overalls.

"To hell with that. I don't answer to him or anybody else."

"What's this about?"

"It's nothing. Now go on, I'll meet you at the boathouse at six sharp. I want to get the whole place cleared out, bring it all here."

I nodded. That could take a while. We had a lot of booze stashed in that boathouse, probably enough to —

"What the hell do you want, a police escort?" He waved his hammer toward the door. "Get moving!"

"OK, OK. Jeez," I muttered, hurrying over to the boxes loaded with whisky bottles. Daddy had a quick temper, but he wasn't usually so short with me. Either it was something about the letter, or he owed money to his bookie. His business ventures made enough to house, clothe, and feed us, but every extra dime fed his ravenous betting habit. *Every man has his temptations*, I supposed, slipping my fingers underneath a box. And every woman too. I could still hear the sheik's low, velvety voice in my head. My stomach tightened as I imagined getting him out of that buttoned-up three-piece suit, removing that crisp white collar, slipping the crimson tie from around his neck. A sweat broke out on my back.

I lugged the boxes just outside the door, then left them sitting there while I retrieved the car. Daddy and I shared a 1921 Model T Sedan he'd rigged with hidden compartments and a trunk with a false floor. Jefferson Market was painted on the side in cheerful white letters, and I always had bags of groceries in the back seat, just in case I got stopped. After pulling alongside the garage door, I turned off the motor and jumped out. I was leaning into the back lifting up the bench seat when I heard a deep voice behind me.

"Excuse me."

My head snapped up, my heart hammering as I backed out. *Please don't be a fed.* I turned around and sucked in my breath.

The sheik was leaning against the brown brick wall, barely three feet from me.

"What are you doing back here?" Definitely not the sultry greeting I'd rehearsed.

"Looking for you." He lit one of his Fatimas and held it between long fingers, the smoke curling above his head.

"Why?"

"I'm wondering if you can help me out. I need some whisky."

A trickle of sweat made its way down my chest. "What makes you think I can help you?"

He put the Fatima to his mouth, inhaling and exhaling in no particular hurry. I stared at his lips as they closed and opened around the cigarette. "I listen carefully in a crowd."

I looked him over, trying to read his eyes, which were shadowed by the brim of his hat. "How much?"

"Maybe ten cases. That too much for you?"

I lifted my chin. "No."

"How much do you charge?"

"Two hundred a case," I said, quickly raising my price.

"And how soon can I get it?"

"As soon as you want it."

He lifted his brow. "Impressive. You bring it over in the car?"

"Leave the details to me. You'll get what you want."

One side of his mouth hooked up. "I always do."

He came off the wall, and I backed into the Ford to steady myself. I wished I hadn't chosen my shabbiest blouse this morning. It used to be red but had faded to a mealy-tomato color. When his feet reached mine, he swayed forward, placing his hands on the car's roof, one on either side of my head. The air hummed between us, and every inch of my skin tingled with awareness of him. I let my lips fall open.

His smile deepened. "I'll be in touch, Miss O'Mara." He straightened up, and with a tip of his hat, walked away.

"Just a moment!" *Think of something—quick!* "May I have a cigarette?"

Retracing his steps, he took a gold case from his coat pocket, opened it, and offered me a Fatima. I put it to my mouth. *His fingers have touched this.* His eyes held mine captive as he pulled out a lighter, and I jumped when the flame burst from its tip. Once the cigarette was lit, I took what I hoped looked like a deep and sultry drag.

With a nod, he walked away again, and I could think of nothing to make him come back. Nothing smart and sophisticated, anyway.

"Wait!" I called, shading my eyes from the sun. "What's your name?"

He looked at me over his shoulder, but only smiled with closed lips before disappearing around the corner.

"Shit," I said, kicking the tire of my car. I'd admitted too much for nothing in return. *And he knows my name.* What the hell? For all I knew he was going to sell my information to a prohi around the corner. I stared at the cigarette he'd given me, dragged on it, and swore again. "Shit, shit, shit."

"She smokes and she curses," said a voice behind me. "Should I bring you a spittoon too?"

I whipped around and saw Joey Lupo standing there with two grocery sacks in his arms and an irritating grin on his face. Joey was my age, some kind of cousin of Bridget's late husband, Vince, and one of those guys whose big mouth is always trying to make up for his short stature. He once stole a pair of underwear from my dresser and charged the neighborhood boys a penny for a peek. Five years had passed, but I still hadn't forgiven him.

"What are you doing here?" I demanded. "I thought you went to Chicago."

"I'm back. You miss me?"

I sucked on my cigarette and blew the smoke at him.

His grin widened. "Still sugar-sweet. Some things never change." He set the grocery sacks down and reached for a box. "Come on, Little Tomato, I'll help you load."

"Don't call me that." I was just about to tell him I didn't need his help when Daddy came out the garage door. Throwing the cigarette to the ground, I tried to fan away the smoke but wasn't quick enough. Daddy let me work for his bootlegging operation but he was strangely old-fashioned about lipstick and smoking, and I didn't want a lecture in front of Joey.

"Frances Kathleen O'Mara, I told you no smoking and I meant it," Daddy growled. "Your mother is turning in her grave, God rest her soul." He crossed himself and looked skyward. "You see what these girls do to me, Mary?"

I rolled my eyes, ignoring Joey's infuriating chuckle. "I'm twenty years old, Daddy, not ten."

He glared at me, pointed a knobby finger at my chest. "You live under my roof, you follow my rules."

How badly I wanted to say, *To hell with your roof and your rules—I'm done with them!* But I couldn't. I chewed my bottom lip instead, my fists tight with frustration.

"And Christ almighty, get going already. Here's the orders." Daddy dug a folded piece of paper from his pocket and shoved it at me before stalking back into the garage.

"Still living at home, huh?" Joey didn't even try to hide his amusement.

"Shut up. If you came here to help, then get to it." I picked up the second box, and we put the booze into the compartment beneath the rear seat, placing the grocery sacks on top. I started the car and looked at the list.

"Where you headed?" Joey asked.

"Smith, side door. Hix, back alley. Then Koehler. Last is Henshaw, and the housekeeper wants the delivery by four." I wrinkled my nose and shoved the list back in my pocket. "The housekeeper. There goes my tip."

Joey laughed, dug in one pocket of his grubby black pants, and tossed me a candy bar. "Here—here's a tip for you. EAT. You haven't grown an inch in three years—in any direction!"

Grimacing, I put the car in gear and moved forward, hoping I might run over his foot. Who the hell was Joey to talk? Maybe he'd filled out some since the last time I'd seen him, but he wasn't that much taller than me. Four inches, tops. And that mop of mangy brown hair on his head made him look bigger than he was.

As I turned out of the alley and headed north on Jefferson into Grosse Pointe, my unease about the conversation with the sheik returned. It was the same creepy-crawly feeling I get when I enter a room and just know there's a spider in it somewhere, watching me. But I sold whisky almost every day of the year. Why should it be any different just because the customer was a little mysterious and a lot gorgeous? Still, I found myself glancing over my shoulder more than usual as I unloaded and collected payment.

At the Smith and Hix houses I made a few dollars in tips, but Mrs. Koehler was five dollars short on her standing order. "Just bring it to the store as soon as you can, Mrs. Koehler," I told her. She was a good customer, and we hated to lose anyone's business.

Some other bootlegger could come along tomorrow and undercut us.

By four o'clock I was headed for the Henshaw estate, and the twitchy feeling was still with me, like an itch that refuses to go away even after it's been scratched. But when you're breaking the law on a daily basis, perhaps a bit of anxiety should come with the territory. Daddy always says good instincts are more important than good friends in our business.

Rather than the stingy housekeeper, it was Mrs. Schmidt, the cook, who answered my knock at the kitchen door of the Henshaws' lakefront mansion. When I greeted her, she welcomed me with a hug. Mrs. Schmidt had been close to my mother, who'd been a housemaid for the Henshaws before marrying my father. For a year after our mother died in childbirth with Mary Grace, Mrs. Schmidt brought meals to our house and spent her days off teaching Bridget and me to cook. As my sisters will attest, Bridget was the superior student.

"How are you today, Mrs. Schmidt?"

"Oh, I don't like to complain," she said, releasing me and rubbing the considerable width of her lower back. "But since you asked..."

I hid a smile as she ran through a list of ailments, nodding and clucking my tongue in sympathy. Finally she paused to draw breath, and I put the grocery bags on the butcher block and carried in the last of the whisky, setting the box on the black and white tiled floor.

"Thanks, love." She brushed my hair off my face when I straightened. "Such a gorgeous color, this hair. Like sunlight through garnet. Why did you ever cut it off?"

"Just easier this way. Less fuss."

"Your mother never minded the fuss of long hair." Mrs. Schmidt crossed her arms. "And I don't mind saying she wouldn't have liked you cutting yours off."

"Yes, you've mentioned that." *About a million times.* I nodded my head of improperly bobbed hair toward the whisky. "Shall I move it to the cellar for you?"

"Leave it be, I'll have the boy do it." She paid me for the groceries, but Mr. Henshaw got his booze for free in exchange for allowing Daddy to use an old dock and boathouse at the edge of his property. "And before you go..." From a canister on a pantry shelf she took a bill and tucked it into my palm. "Mr. Henshaw said to give this to you."

When I saw it was a fifty, I gasped. "He did? Why?"

"I may have let it slip about your paying your way through nursing school."

"Oh, Mrs. Schmidt, thank you!" I threw my arms around her globe-shaped middle and practically squeezed the life from her.

"You're welcome, girl. Now scoot, I've got the groceries to put away." Laughing, she shooed me out the back door, and I skipped to my car.

Fifty dollars! That would go a long way toward tuition and books. Classes would begin again in August, and they weren't cheap. Daddy didn't mind my going to nursing school as long as I kept the house running and my sisters in line, but he couldn't be counted on to pay for anything. He claimed there was no money for it, but I suspected he didn't offer much because the sooner I had my degree, the sooner he'd be on his own with the house and the girls. It took every ounce of restraint I had not to ask him about all the cash that ended up lining Ralph the Bookie's pocket.

Sitting behind the wheel, I looked at the crisp fifty in triumph before tucking it into my pocket along with the wrinkly dollars and spare change the other customers had given me. But as I drove back to the store, I began thinking of all the things I could buy with that much money—a smart new dress, something with beading or fringe. A darling little cloche or headband. A pair of satin shoes for dancing.

And how many months' rent would fifty bucks pay? I clenched my teeth. I didn't need much—just a studio apartment with a little bath. My own space, in which I would do as I pleased, with no rules. I thought about the sheik, and the way he paid for his cigarettes with fifty-dollar bills. My pulse raced when I recalled how he'd leaned close to me, near enough for me to smell the smoke on his breath.

After parking in the alley behind the store, I peeked into the front but saw Joey at the register, so I headed up the steps to Bridget's apartment. The smell of fresh-baked bread hit me in the stairwell and my stomach growled when I saw the two loaves on the kitchen counter. "Bread's done, help yourself," Bridget called from the front room, where the radio played "I'm Nobody's Baby." Humming along, I cut two thick slices and slathered them with butter. Bridget's cooking and baking skills trumped mine by a mile, and I nearly moaned as I sank my teeth into the doughy white softness. She wandered in a minute later with two-year old Eddie on her hip. "Oh, it's you," she said. "I thought it was Joey."

"Does that mean I have to put the bread back?" I mumbled, my mouth full.

She smiled, which always changed her face from plain to pretty. "No, you can have some. Do you want some cold meat for a sandwich? Joey brought some ham from Eastern Market."

I shook my head and polished off the first slice. "I saw him downstairs. I thought he moved to Chicago."

She set Eddie on the yellow linoleum floor and sliced a piece of bread for him. "He did, but his mother took ill, and he's worried about her. Wants to stay closer to home for a while. I know he's not your favorite, but try to be nice. He's family."

"He's not *my* family."

"He's a good guy."

"He's a pain in the ass."

She pursed her lips as she handed Eddie the bread, and I decided to switch topics.

"Look at this." I licked my fingers and pulled the fifty-dollar bill from my pocket.

Bridget wiped her hands on her stained apron and took the bill. "Jaypers cripes! Where'd you get that?"

"From Mr. Henshaw, as a tip." I picked up my second slice of bread and sank my teeth in. "But don't tell Daddy."

Our eyes met, and I knew she understood. Bridget kept my tips for me, stashing them in a big yellow envelope underneath her mattress. It wasn't that I didn't trust Daddy, but I felt safer with my tips out of the house. "Want me to put it with the rest?"

I hesitated, the image of myself in a beaded dress and satin shoes vanishing in a puff of smoke. "I guess so." Slumping into a chair at the round kitchen table, I dropped my chin into my hand. "But boy, I wish I could be spending some of that money on something else. Like a new dress. Or shoes. Or rent."

She patted my shoulder before going into her bedroom, which was off the kitchen. "Is Daddy giving you a rough time?" she asked when she returned.

I shrugged. "I'm twenty years old. I'm just tired of living with my father and having two little sisters underfoot all the time."

Bridget went to the stove and stirred something in a large copper pot. "You've got your own bedroom. That's more than I had when I lived at home."

"So what? The only thing I do in it is read and sleep. And I can hardly even do that without one of the girls barging in on me." I sat up straight and mimicked our sisters' high-pitched voices. "Tiny, can you mend this blouse? Will you make my lunch? Can I wear your blue sweater? She's bothering me! She's following me! She hit me!"

"Well, cheer up." Bridget clacked the spoon on the edge of the pot and set it aside. "Molly will be done with school in three years, and by then Mary Grace will be old enough to look after herself. You'll be free to do as you please." She turned and waggled her brows at me. "Inside your bedroom and out."

"But that's years away! I want a little excitement in my life now." I thumped the table for emphasis.

"Take it from me—a little excitement goes a long way," said Bridget, gesturing toward the front room, where I could hear her two older boys playing. "You don't want to do what I did."

That was true. Bridget had gotten pregnant before her wedding and Daddy had been furious. But still. "For cripes sake, Bridget, when would I have the opportunity? I haven't even kissed anyone in months!"

"So kiss somebody." Bridget grinned and dropped into the chair across from me. "Then give me all the saucy details."

"It's more than that," I insisted. "In the morning I want to get up and go to work without cleaning up a big mess after breakfast. At night, instead of washing all the dinner dishes and making sure everyone has clean clothes for the next day, I want to go dancing and drink champagne. I want to wear a short dress and red lipstick without my father scolding me. I want to hit the best nightclubs with a dashing swain at my side to light my cigarettes. Like the Arrow Shirt man," I said wistfully. "Or the sheik."

Bridget laughed. "The sheik?"

"That guy who comes in for the Fatimas. He was in again today looking for Daddy." I touched my buttery mouth, picturing the sheik's lips on his cigarette.

The light in Bridget's eyes went out. "Oh."

"Any idea who he is?"

She jumped up, grabbed the broom from the

corner and swept the floor with angry strokes, shooing Eddie into the front room. "No. But I don't like the looks of him."

"Since when? The other day we were both swooning over him like he was Valentino."

Bridget seemed to struggle with words. "I don't know…It's only…Something about the way he keeps showing up gives me a bad feeling." She swept harder, not meeting my eyes, and her voice grew quieter. "He reminds me of those guys who used to come around for Vince."

My twitchy feeling returned. I knew the kind of men she was talking about. The day Vince was murdered two years ago, he was picking up a mobster named Big Leo Scarfone from the police station. He'd been shot right there on the sidewalk.

Twenty-one times.

I swallowed. "You think he's connected to Vince's…to what happened to Vince?"

"I don't know, Tiny. I don't recognize him. I just suddenly got a bad feeling, that's all." Finally, she stopped sweeping and looked at me, tears in her eyes. "You need to be careful. A little excitement is one thing, but I don't want to be up at night worrying about you. Understand?"

I nodded, deciding not to mention the episode in the alley. She put the broom away and returned to the stove as I recalled getting the news about Vince, delivered by a Detroit police officer at the store. Three other men were killed that day, including Big Leo and Joey's father. The third guy lived just long enough to break the code of silence and reveal the names of the gunmen, members of a rival crime family. They were arrested and charged with murder, but Bridget said they'd never go to jail, and she was right. It took the jury less than fifty minutes to find them innocent.

So I was hoping her instincts about the sheik were off. Because I wanted to see him again.

I wanted to do more than that.

Chapter Two

The boathouse was a bootlegger's dream.

Sitting right at the edge of Lake St. Clair, it was accessible only by a bumpy dirt path off Jefferson Avenue that was so overgrown it was nearly invisible. Daddy hadn't arrived yet, so after parking beneath a huge weeping willow, I wandered onto the dock. A light breeze ruffled my hair as I looked across the water to Canada, its tree line clearly visible on the opposite shore. The lake appeared unusually calm. *We should have made a run this afternoon.* I glanced at our motorboat bobbing in the water before turning toward the boathouse door. It was partway open, the rusty padlock unlatched and dangling.

Confused, I looked around, but mine was the only car in sight. *Daddy must have taken a streetcar then*, I thought, stepping inside. Despite the hot day, the interior of the boathouse was shadowy and dank, empty but for the sacks of whisky and crates of scotch at the back. I was heading for them when I heard footsteps behind me.

"I made the deliveries," I said, picking up a burlap sack of Canadian Club by its bunny ears. "Mrs. Koehler was a little short."

"I'm not sure *you* should be calling anyone short."

I spun around as someone stepped from the shadows into a narrow beam of sunlight slanting through a high window.

My breath hitched. "How did you get in here?"

The sheik smiled, hands in his pockets, coat unbuttoned. "I have a talent for lock and key."

"How did you find this place?"

"I followed you."

The gooseflesh returned. Was Bridget right about him? "Why?"

"I was curious." He approached me slowly. "And I wanted to see you again."

I glanced at the open door. "You shouldn't be here. If it's whisky you want, I'll bring it to you."

He took the sack from my hands and set it on the floor. "What if I want something besides whisky?" His dark eyes were beautiful, but it was his mouth that fascinated me. My breath came faster as I stared at the sharp peaks of his upper lip.

"Such as?"

He tipped up my chin, but went no further, his mouth so close I could feel his breath. His slow smile sent my pulse skittering out of control.

I was done waiting for it. I grabbed his head and pulled his mouth down to mine.

His arms snaked around my back, the heat of his body enveloping me. When he opened his mouth, I did the same, my entire body humming like a swarm of bees was under my skin. *I'm kissing the sheik! I don't even know his name! Daddy could walk in here any second! Damn, he smells good—like aftershave and tobacco.* My breasts tingled and I rose up on tiptoe, trying to press closer. Wishing his skin was bare, I ran my hands down his vest and twined my arms around his taut waist. My fingers hit a hard object, and I froze.

He has a gun.

I pulled my hands back as if they had been burned. "We have to stop," I said against his mouth.

He lifted his head and loosened his grip a little. "Why's that?"

My blood was pumping way too fast, shock and desire battling inside my veins. *Because you've got a gun in your trousers.* "Because...my father is going to be here any minute." I put my hands on his chest and pushed him away. Some instinct told me not to acknowledge the weapon. Willing my heart rate to return to normal, I tucked a stray piece of hair behind my ear. "What's your name, anyway?"

He began buttoning his coat. "Enzo DiFiore."

"I'd tell you mine, but you already know it."

He smiled as he adjusted his cuffs, and I twisted my hands together to keep from launching myself at him and tearing the clothes from his body.

"Well, Mr. DiFiore, it is a pleasure to make your acquaintance, but I really have to ask you to leave now. My father will not take kindly to a stranger alone in the boathouse with me. Or his liquor." I turned around to pick up the whisky sack, and by the time I straightened and faced him again, he was gone.

I moved to the doorway and looked out.

Nobody. The air was hot and still and silent.

What the hell?

27

Dazed, I walked from the boathouse to my car, opened the trunk, and placed the sack inside it. Staring at the burlap, I brought my hands to my face, my belly tightening at the memory of the sheik's mouth on mine. *Enzo DiFiore.* I thought about his arms around me, the commanding way he'd slanted his open mouth over mine, and the contraction moved lower in my body. Bridget had joked about spilling the details of my next kiss, but I could never tell her about this.

I wandered back into the boathouse, but instead of grabbing another sack, I plunked down on a crate of scotch and stared in disbelief at the pool of sunlight where we'd stood.

"Enzo DiFiore," I whispered. Who was he? All I knew about him was his name. And that he was a good kisser with a talent for lock and key. A laugh bubbled up in me. After all, if he'd wanted to steal from us or harm me in some way, he could have done it. But all he'd done was follow me. Watch me. Kiss me.

My insides trembled with excitement. Would he seek me out again? At the sound of a car sputtering to a stop outside, I stood and smoothed my clothing before heading out to meet Daddy.

My rosy spirits withered when I saw Joey unloading the whisky I'd just put into the trunk. "Why are you doing that?" I snapped, marching toward him.

"Because this is the biggest space you have and we need it for the crates. The sacks should go under the back seat."

He was right, which annoyed me. I yanked the whisky from his arms.

"Got your mind on something else?" Joey opened the back door and lifted the seat.

"Like what?" I shouldered him aside and dropped the sack in.

"You tell me. I saw you talking to a guy in the alley earlier. Who was it?"

I turned to him, hands on my hips. "None of your beeswax."

He smiled at getting a rise out of me, his brown eyes lighting up. "Come on, Tiny, a guy like that, in a suit that fancy?" He looked me up and down. "You're not his type."

I lunged for him, giving him a hard shove with both hands to the chest. Joey wasn't tall but he was solid, so I was surprised when he went over backward. Since I'd thrown all my weight into the push, I went over too, and we landed in a heap of tangled limbs on the dirt. To my chagrin, my body betrayed me by tingling at the feel of our torsos pressed together. For one awkward moment, we paused, our faces inches apart.

"Kiss me, you fool," he said, but then he burst out laughing.

"Go to hell." I rolled off him and stood, brushing the dust off my skirt.

Joey popped up on his feet, still chuckling. "Good hit. Caught me off guard."

"Did I hurt you?" I asked hopefully.

"With what—a pebble to the backside?" He readjusted his floppy cap.

I was tempted to keep sparring with him since I was so worked up, but just then Daddy arrived. We got to work emptying the boathouse into our cars, and then drove back to the garage, where we unloaded the booze into the hidden rooms in the basement. No one spoke more than one-word commands or responses, and Daddy looked over his shoulder more than usual. Not that I blamed him—the events of this afternoon had me on edge too.

By the time we were through, I was sticky and tired and my left hip ached. While Daddy went over the day's take in the office, I sat on the stained cement floor and watched Joey bring in the last of the booze. His black pants hugged his butt as he moved, and a surprising little flutter swept through my belly. He set the whisky down and wiped the sweat from his forehead with the back of his wrist. It left a trail of dirt smudged against his olive skin, but I had to admit he'd gotten better looking in the last couple years, sort of grown into his strong nose and wide mouth.

He caught me staring. "See something you like?"

I made a disgusted noise at the back of my throat, as if he hadn't just read my mind. "No."

"Joe," called Daddy. "Come in here a minute." When Joey stepped into the office, I hopped to my feet, counted to five and followed, stopping just out of sight of the open door.

"Just keep your ears open," Daddy was saying. "And let me know what you hear."

Hear about what? I wondered. Did this have anything to do with the letter from Enzo?

Daddy dropped his voice. "And keep an eye on Tiny, too. She needs it."

I made a face. *Like hell I do. Especially that eye.*

Joey came out of the office, giving me a slug on the shoulder as he headed for the back door. "See you around, Little Tomato."

I ignored him. "Daddy," I said loudly, drawing him out of the office. "What's going on?"

He was still shuffling through the stack of bills and didn't meet my eye. "Nothing I can't handle."

"What was in that letter? The one I gave you earlier."

He didn't even lift his head. "Nothing to worry about."

He was lying, but Daddy was stubborn as a one-eyed mule. If he didn't want me to know what was going on, I wasn't going to get it out of him. Maybe I could snoop around for the letter tomorrow. "I guess I'll walk home then, see what the girls have cooked up."

"A heap of trouble, no doubt." He flashed a quick smile in my direction, but it didn't reach his eyes.

#

Later that night—after making supper, washing the dishes, breaking up a fight between my sisters over whose turn it was to dry them, running the carpet sweeper, and putting out the trash—I took a cool bath, put on my nightgown, and flopped facedown onto my bed. Our home wasn't large by any means, but keeping it clean and running smoothly was exhausting, not to mention keeping two younger sisters fed, clothed, and out of trouble. Daddy did what he could, willing to cook the occasional pot of soup or scrub the tub from time to time, but as the oldest daughter at home, I had the most responsibility. Sometimes the weight of it all threatened to drag me under.

It was probably crazy to attempt nursing school too, but my mother had always talked about how she'd have liked to be a nurse if only she'd had the opportunity. She was a poor Irish girl who grew up on a farm—she hadn't even finished the eighth grade, let alone high school. I felt closer to her, knowing that I was fulfilling a dream she'd had for herself. Plus, a nursing degree would allow me to get a good job and make my own money. My first plan was to get an apartment, but after that I wanted to go places, and I didn't want to be dependent on anyone else to take me.

From my nightstand, I picked up a dog-eared Photoplay magazine. I'd already finished reading it, but I loved looking at the advertisements boasting of grand hotels, luxury rail lines, and exotic locales. Too hot for covers, I flipped to my back and lay atop the sheet, thumbing through the tattered pages, grateful for a moment of peace.

It didn't last long.

"Tiny!" Mary Grace burst into my room without knocking. "Molly's going to Electric Park tomorrow, but she says I can't go along. Tell her she has to take me too!"

Sighing, I tossed the magazine back onto the nightstand and braced for an argument.

"I won't take her," said Molly from the doorway, arms crossed. "Last time she embarrassed me terribly by telling my friends I wet the bed until I was eight."

"Well, you did," insisted Mary Grace, chin jerking. "I can't help it if that's the truth." She looked at me and pouted. "She just doesn't want me there because *boys* are coming."

"You be quiet," snapped Molly, leaning in to slap Mary Grace on the shoulder.

"Girls." I got off the bed to separate them. "It's late, and I'm tired. We'll talk about this tomorrow. Now go to bed before I find some chore that needs to be done yet tonight."

"But she—"

"OUT!" I shoved them both through the door and shut it behind them. Half-expecting them to bang on it again, I waited a moment before switching off the light and crawling under the covers.

Certain they were scared off by the threat of more housework, I closed my eyes. Enzo's face appeared. Breathing deeply, I replayed the scene in the boathouse in my head. When I got to the part where he first touched me, I slowed down to savor every delicious morsel—his fingers under my chin, his smoky breath, his lips on mine, our chests pressed together. Even the memory of discovering the gun gave me a peculiar kick that radiated from my stomach throughout my limbs.

Like the buzz from a cocktail mixed with equal parts fear and fascination.

\#

Several hours later, the ringing telephone jarred me awake. I stumbled down the stairs and into the darkened hallway to answer it.

"Hello?"

"Tiny," a male voice rasped. I thought it might be Daddy, but he'd spoken so softly I couldn't tell for sure.

"Daddy? I can't hear you. Hello?"

"The garage," said a smooth new voice. "Come alone. And bring the money or he's dead."

"Who is this?" The phone went dead before I could get an answer, and my stomach turned over. Trembling, I set the receiver back on the switch hook. What money? Or who's dead—Daddy? Racing up the steps up two at a time, I opened his bedroom door. The moonlight streaming through the window illuminated an empty bed.

I dashed back into my room to dress without turning on any lights. The first outfit I got my hands on was the red blouse and black skirt I'd worn today, which I threw on over my chemise while questions pummeled my brain. Who was that? Should I really go alone? Should I call the police? Is this about a gambling debt? Does it have something to do with the letter?

Damn it, Daddy! What have you done?

I didn't have any money at the house, and my tip envelope was at Bridget's. The last thing I wanted to do was to alarm her or put the kids in danger—I'd have to see who it was and find out what they wanted first. If I ignored the instructions and involved the police, I might put Daddy in more danger than he was already in.

I shoved my bare feet into shoes and moved quietly down the stairs. As I let myself out the front door into the warm night, I tried to place the voice I'd heard. Daddy's usual bookmaker was a cock-eyed sleaze called Ralph the Bookie, but he had a distinctive nasally whine. This voice was deep and smooth, with a slight accent. Was it Italian?

My stomach churned. The cops found unidentified bodies in the Detroit River all the time these days. Almost nightly, said the papers. Guys who'd been shot, beaten, drowned. I fought off the nausea by quickening my pace.

As I ran past darkened houses, a memory surfaced without warning—Daddy surprising me with a new Hawthorne bicycle on my ninth birthday and teaching me how to ride it. Running alongside me down this very street shouting encouragement.

Clenching my fists, I dug my nails into my palms as I reached the end of the block and stopped to catch my breath.

Then, with fear lodged like a hatchet in my chest, I turned the corner and inched through the alley toward the garage, my feet crunching on the gravel. At the back door, I closed my right hand around the handle and twisted—unlocked. I pushed it open and stepped in, hearing nothing but my own quick breaths. Seconds ticked by.

I was beginning to wonder if it was all a joke when I heard a rusty voice behind me. "Glad you could make it."

The door slammed and a meaty hand clamped over my mouth. A thick arm snared my waist. Cackling, the man walked me deeper into the garage, pushing my legs with his own. Too terrified to resist, I moved forward like a rag doll in his grip.

When we reached the office door, he kicked out a leg and it creaked open.

I was struggling to make sense of the shadowy shapes in front of me when someone switched on the lamp—I gasped behind the sweaty, smothering palm.

On the chair was my father, slouched and bloody. At his temple, the barrel of a gun.

Chapter Three

Arms like thick iron chains held me fast when I struggled to get to Daddy. I whimpered against the hand over my mouth.

"Well. No one told me you were so lovely," said the man holding the weapon. Even in the low light I could tell he hadn't been the one to deliver the beating. Daddy's face was a swollen red and purple mess, but not a speck of blood marred this man's white shirt. Not a black hair was out of place.

He nodded to my captor, who released me. I rushed over to my father and put a hand on his neck. His skin was warm, but I couldn't find a pulse. "Is he dead?"

"Looks that way, don't it?" snapped the voice behind me. Over my shoulder, I glared at him. He was younger and stockier than the well-dressed man, and his jaw was shadowed by whiskers where the older man's was clean-shaven. His wrinkled blue shirt stained with blood, making my stomach heave.

"Now, now." The well-dressed man spoke very gently for someone holding a gun to a person's head. "He isn't dead yet. No need to be cruel."

My fingers finally located a pulse. *Thank God.* "What do you want?" I asked, my voice trembling.

"Is she armed, Raymond?"

Raymond started to grope me from behind. "Stop it! I'm not armed!" I shook him off. "Please! Why have you done this?"

The older man put the gun down and picked up his black suit coat from the desk, brushing it off before slipping into it. "Your father has refused to acknowledge my offer of protection." He adjusted his cuffs. "He's testing my patience."

"That's right," put in Raymond.

"Raymond, please." The man tucked the gun inside his coat.

"Protection...protection from what?" My mind reeled.

"From anyone who might wish to harm him or his business, of course. These days it could be anything —bombing, arson, the murder or kidnapping of a family member." He listed these things as if he were reciting the menu at a roadhouse diner. I shivered, even though I was sweating.

"I don't understand. Why would anyone want to harm us or the business?"

"It's nothing personal, *piccolina*. In fact, it's a compliment. Your father is a small fish, but he runs such a good operation, he's caught the attention of bigger fish."

"Sharks," said Raymond.

"Exactly," agreed the man. "And sharks, when they see the fine meal of a small fish, they get greedy. They get hungry. They want a piece of the meal for themselves."

"And you're the shark?"

He laughed, revealing straight white teeth. "Of course not. I'm here to *protect* you from the sharks. I have offered this protection to Jack several times already, but each time, he has ignored my request to meet and discuss it. That's dangerous." His eyes slid sideways to my father.

I swallowed, understanding sinking in. "How much for this...protection?"

"Ten thousand dollars."

My mouth gaped open. "Ten thousand dollars!"

"To let him live tonight, I will accept half."

"I don't have five thousand dollars," I said, my eyes filling.

"That's unfortunate." He reached inside his coat, and I put my hands out. Daddy was going to die if I didn't think of something—fast.

"Wait! Just wait. Maybe I can get it."

"That's a good girl." He took his hand from his coat, empty.

My mind groped for a solution. Was today's take still here in the office? If it was, they'd probably already stolen it. Daddy kept no spare cash at the garage, I knew that much, but we did have booze. *Yes, the booze—whiskey as currency.* "OK. This afternoon my father and I brought at least twenty cases of whisky here. They're in the basement, hidden in some rooms beyond the south wall. You can have them all."

"That ain't five thousand bucks," spat Raymond.

"We also have at least two cases of scotch."

"What kind of scotch?" the man asked.

"Good stuff. Imported from Europe and smuggled through Canada by rail. Expensive—we sell it for one twenty-five per bottle." I'd just offered all our stock; it had to be worth five thousand, probably more, but I wasn't capable of arithmetic just then.

The man thought for a moment, his eyes on me. "I'll accept this offer. On one condition."

"What?"

"You bring me ten thousand dollars in cash this week."

"Ten minus five is only another five!"

He shrugged. "Those are my terms. And my final offer to let him live tonight."

My guts churned—there was no way we could come up with ten grand in a week—but what choice did I have? "Deal. Now will you let us go?"

"I'll let *you* go. He stays with me until I have the money." A smile crept onto his lips. "Why don't you come down to my club tomorrow night, *piccolina*? We'll discuss the details of this arrangement in a more civilized manner, and you'll bring me one hundred dollars as a sign of good faith."

I twisted my clammy hands together. "Where are you taking him?"

"Never mind about that. I won't kill him if you keep your word." Then, as casually as if he were brandishing a stick of chewing gum, he pulled the gun from his coat and aimed it at my chest. "But I won't think twice about killing both of you if you don't."

Fear gashed my heart so sharply I thought he might have pulled the trigger. "I'll be there."

"Splendid." The corners of his mouth tipped up. He looked vaguely familiar in that moment, but I couldn't place his face. He was about Daddy's age, but taller, leaner through the middle. His hair was so dark it appeared black, and his features were narrow and even—no scars or evidence of a broken nose or jaw. "I confess, I didn't like the idea of doing business with a girl," he continued, "but this has been almost enjoyable. I feel certain once your father comes to, he will be more willing to negotiate with me. Now, how do we access those rooms?" The gun was still pointed at me, and I could hardly think. My teeth chattered.

"You—you'll have to move the m-middle cabinet on the west wall first. Then open the phony icebox in the left corner—it has no back—and you'll see a latch. Pull it. It releases the d-door behind the cabinet."

He looked impressed as he slid the gun back inside his coat. "Quite an operation. I can see why the sharks are circling."

They left Daddy and me alone in the office, and I heard my instructions repeated in the garage. I wasn't sure how many men were out there, but I knew the chances for escape were next to nothing. Even if I made a run for it, and I wasn't much of a runner, that left Daddy sitting here alone, his hands tied to the chair. I looked him over, checking for the worst of the injuries. His face was almost unrecognizable—eyes bruised and squeezed shut from the swelling, nose broken again, cheeks and chin nicked with cuts—but I saw no evidence of a mortal wound. I brushed a matted lock of dark hair from his forehead, relieved to see a spot of unbloodied skin.

"My God, Daddy," I whispered. I felt sorry for him, but a little angry too. Why had he ignored this man? Had he thought the threats were idle? For Christ's sake, he read the papers —and look at what had happened to Vince! He knew what these men were capable of; extortion was their *least* worrisome crime. I sank to my knees again and clutched his limp arm. "What if I can't save you?" I whimpered before his battered form went blurry beyond my tears.

While I wept, the men emptied the basement of all our stock. Everything we had would be gone—and now they knew our hiding spot too. I scrambled to my feet when two goons lumbered in, and watched helplessly as they untied Daddy and carried him out by his arms and legs. When they exited into the alley, I leaned against the office doorframe for support.

The older man appeared to my left. "Miss O'Mara. You'll find me at Club 23 tomorrow night." His eyes dropped to my disheveled clothing. "Wear something pretty." Placing a black fedora on his head, he followed the others out the door, shutting it behind him.

I rushed over to lock it, but when I turned around, my skin prickled with the awareness of someone watching me.

I wasn't alone.

Knees trembling, I searched the shadows of the silent garage, gasping when I saw a slender man in a dark suit standing about ten feet away, perfectly still.

Enzo.

I clenched my jaw. "Go to hell."

He moved closer, and the sight of his handsome face both thrilled and appalled me. I stiffened when he stopped right in front of me and smiled. "Tell them Angel sent you."

#

As soon as Enzo was gone, I locked the back door and returned to the office. Sinking into the chair, I put my hands to my head and tugged on my hair. Where were they taking Daddy? And how on earth was I going to come up with ten thousand dollars this week? I had no booze to sell, no talent for rebuilding hearses, and no emergency payoff cash tucked away.

But I had to get it somehow. They knew who I was and how to find me. And if they could find me, they could find my sisters. My nephews. They could bomb not only the garage but the house or the store.

Bridget had been right about Enzo.

Burning with anger, I realized he had to have known about the kidnapping plot when he kissed me in the boathouse. Bastard! Why didn't he say something then? He could have warned me, but instead he'd let me walk right into this trap. Maybe I'd even been *part* of the trap—he'd asked questions, followed me, discovered the boathouse. *Damn him. I should have known he was trouble.* But I'd never been good at resisting temptation. It wasn't in my blood.

I chewed my thumbnail. Ten goddamn grand. I only knew one way to make that kind of cash, and since I'd just given away all our stock, the only resource I'd have to start with was my envelope full of tips. My tuition money. Crossing my arms over my belly, I lay my forehead on the desk in defeat.

Within seconds, a pounding on the back door had me bolting upright. My heart hammered wildly as I switched off the lamp and waited. More pounding, then the thumping of bodyweight being thrown into the door. *Move, you idiot!*

I ran out into the garage and frantically searched for somewhere to hide. My eyes roved right and left—I couldn't open the roll-up door fast enough to escape onto Jefferson, and the only other hiding spots were the basement or—gulp—a hearse. When a gunshot blasted through the back door, busting the lock, I squeaked in terror and took a running dive into the hearse with no back end. I yanked on a curtain from the window and the whole rod came down. Burrowing underneath the black velvet and curling into a ball, I was starting a Hail Mary when I heard slow footsteps. Then creak of the office door.

Silence.

When the footsteps started up again, they seemed to be coming toward me. I curled tighter into myself, my body stiff with terror. The intruder came closer. I stopped breathing.

Then, for five agonizing seconds—nothing.

Finally, I could stand it no longer. I opened my eyes and peeked out.

Joey stood at the back of the hearse, aiming a pistol at me.

"Tiny?" He dropped the gun and gawked. "What the hell are you doing?"

"It's a long story," I said. "Which I might tell you, if I can ever breathe normally again." I hoped I hadn't wet myself. Why the hell did everybody have a gun all of a sudden?

Joey tucked his into the back of his waistband and reached for me. "Well, I'm glad you're not dead. I'm staying at Bridget's tonight and when I heard noise down here, I looked out the window and saw a body being carried out and put into the back seat of a sedan."

I let him drag me to the edge of the hearse by my forearms and pull me out. My rubbery legs threatened to buckle. "Yeah, that was Daddy. He's not dead though. Yet." I put both hands on my stomach, which was still pitching.

"What?" His voice cracked on the word.

I took a breath and explained, starting with the phone call and ending with my swan dive into the back of the hearse.

"Jesus. Your dad mentioned there might be some trouble." He scratched his head. "How many guys? Did you recognize them?"

"There were five at least. The older one who did the talking was well dressed and maybe in his forties. Dark hair. Didn't look like the type to do his own dirty work. Two younger guys were with him, and a couple goons." I decided not to tell him that one of the younger guys was the fancy suit I'd been talking to in the alley.

"Did you get names?"

I hesitated. Naming names was against the rules; it got people into trouble. But I thought I could trust Joey. "One of them might be called Angel."

"Angel DiFiore, that son of a bitch." Joey nodded in recognition. "That's the older one. The younger two were probably his sons, Enzo and Raymond."

My mouth fell open. Enzo was Angel's son?

"Angel is an associate of Tony Provenzano," Joey went on, "and Provenzano is the bastard who put the hit on Big Leo Scarfone and got my father killed."

I sucked in my breath. "Was Angel involved in those murders?"

"He wasn't put on trial, but that don't mean he wasn't." Even in the dark, I saw the fury in Joey's stance. "He came from Brooklyn a while back, and his operation was on the west side of Detroit, but now he's over here with his sons, muscling in on the east side rackets. He's pissing some people off."

"How do you know so much?"

He shrugged. "I got ears."

"Is he a bootlegger?"

Joey shook his head. "Not that I know of. He runs a club, lottery, races, and a bunch of other things you don't want to know about."

A series of clanks from the alley made us both jump. "Let's get out of here." I grabbed his arm. "Can you come home with me?"

"Been waiting years for you to ask me that."

I almost choked. "Please."

We walked back at a fast clip, and I jumped at every cricket chirp and cat yowl. I checked on my sisters the minute we got in, relieved to see them both sound asleep. Mary Grace clutched a small stuffed bear she claimed she didn't like anymore. I brushed the strawberry hair off her pale forehead and tiptoed out, shutting the door behind me.

Joey was in the kitchen. "You got anything to eat?"

"Are you kidding? How can you think about food?"

"A guy can always think about food." He shot me a look over his shoulder. "Among other things."

I gave him a flat look. "Well, all I can think about is that ten thousand dollars." I sat down at the kitchen table with a stubby pencil and piece of paper while Joey foraged for a snack. Some quick math told me I'd have to move about fifty-six cases of whisky to clear ten grand. Scribbling more numbers, I figured I had at least enough in my shoebox to buy twelve cases after taking out the hundred I had to give Angel tomorrow night. If I sold them all, I'd have just over two thousand bucks —a far cry from ten. But maybe it would be enough to buy me some time.

"So. What's your plan?" Joey munched on some Uneeda Biscuits right from the box and straddled the chair across from me.

"My plan is to get the damn money. What choice do I have?"

He was silent a few seconds, then spoke low. "You don't want to go to the cops, do you?"

"Are you kidding me? I know better than that," I scoffed. "Angel'd kill him. And I don't want to tell Bridget about this yet, either. She'll panic."

"Do you think she has the money, though? Maybe she'd give it to you."

I shook my head. "She's on her own with three boys, and she has Martin to pay too."

"Who the hell is Martin?"

"The assistant manager she hired after you left for Chicago. Anyway, after what happened to Vince, I don't want Bridget involved at all."

Joey frowned. "OK, but she's gonna notice your pop's missing."

I thought for a moment. "I'll tell her he went down to Cleveland to deliver a car to somebody. He's done that before."

Joey shoved one last cracker into his mouth and brushed off his hands. "I'm coming with you tomorrow night."

"That's a terrible idea. You might run your mouth and cause trouble. Besides, what harm can they do at a crowded club?"

"You don't want me to answer that question. I'm going, and that's that."

I thought about arguing, but realized it might be smarter to have someone with me, even if it was big-mouth Joey. "OK, fine."

"Now let's talk about getting those ten G's," he said. "That's a lotta dough."

"I need to make a run as soon as possible."

Joey rubbed the stubble on his chin. "Tiny, I think you need...some friends in this."

"What do you mean?"

"I mean, you're a girl alone trying to defend yourself against guys who hustle people for a living, and that's putting it nicely. You need allies."

I blinked at him. "Like who?"

"Well, I got some friends I know from when I was at the Bishop school. They used to be with Big Leo, but they're kinda doing their own thing now. They call themselves the River Gang, and—"

I put my hands up. "No. No way. I'm not getting involved in any Italian gang wars, Joey. All I want is to pay off Angel DiFiore and get Daddy released."

"But DiFiore's not just going to go away. Even your dad is going to need allies after this."

"That'll be his problem, then. I'm not interested in revenge or power or allies or anything else—I just want my father back so I get get on with my life. Now are you going to help me or not?"

Joey exhaled and scratched his head. "We'll need dark. Tomorrow night's out. How about Sunday?"

"OK."

"Do you have the money to buy with?"

I swallowed. "Yes."

"What about a distributor?"

"I'll call our usual guy, Blaise. I just hope he doesn't get prickly about selling to me without Daddy there." My stomach turned over. "And I hope the boat has enough gasoline."

"Leave that to me." He swung his leg over the top of the chair and picked up his cap from the table. "I better go. Delivery truck's coming early in the morning and I told Bridget I'd help unload."

"What time will we meet tomorrow night?" I whispered, following him to the front door. "And should we meet at the club?"

"No. I'll pick you up at nine." He paused, glancing over my shoulder up the stairs. "Do you want me to stay tonight?"

Yes. The word popped into my mind before I had a chance to think about it.

Joey noticed my hesitation. "I don't mind staying here, if it will make you feel safer." His voice was soft and low, and it was the first time I'd ever heard him say something like that without joking. Standing there in the dark, I was tempted to tell him to stay. With his full, familiar lips so close, I was tempted to do more than that.

What the hell is with you today? Say goodnight!

"No," I said, stepping back. "You can go. I'll see you tomorrow."

After he left, I locked the door, crept into my room, and undressed. Wearily I climbed back into bed and lay there, my body numb with fatigue but my brain buzzing with questions. Where were they keeping Daddy? Would they hurt him again? Were we safe here? I chewed on the edge of the sheet. Now that I knew a locked door was no match for Enzo DiFiore, I wasn't sure I'd ever feel safe again. What was his role in all this? And why had he kissed me like that?

My eyes slammed shut. Jesus, you couldn't trust anybody. Not even men with movie star faces whose kisses felt like fire in your veins.

Rolling to my side, I crooked one elbow underneath my head. *I'm a horrible person. How can I even think about kissing Enzo with Daddy being held hostage?* What was the matter with me? And had I really been tempted to kiss *Joey* at the door? That boy had been nothing but trouble my entire life, and now it looked he'd make a career out of it. Was he working for the River Gang? It was hard to believe he'd want the same kind of life his father had—or the same kind of death. But he sure had a lot of information. Could I trust him?

I wanted to trust him.

But I also wanted a gun.

Chapter Four

After settling the argument between my sisters
— Molly lost, I said she had to take Mary Grace to
Electric Park—I told them Daddy had gone to
Cleveland for a few days, and if they stayed out of
trouble while he was gone, they could each pick out a
new skirt or blouse from the Sears Roebuck catalog.
Then I broke up the fight that ensued when Mary
Grace said Molly was hogging the catalog behind the
locked bathroom door, which is where she insists she
has to go if she wants any privacy at all.

I spent the rest of Saturday morning stocking
shelves at the store, jumping out of my skin every time
the bell over the door rang, and wiping my sweaty
palms on my skirt. I managed to avoid Bridget, who
said she needed some fresh produce and took the kids
down to Eastern Market. Since Martin was minding
the store in her absence, I went over to the garage,
where it looked like Joey had attempted to repair the
busted lock but hadn't finished the job. Inside the
office, I dug Daddy's directory out of the desk and

called Blaise at the Cloverly Inn, a Windsor roadhouse near the docks.

"Yeah?" barked a gruff voice.

I cleared my throat. "I'm calling for Jack O'Mara."

"Yeah?"

"Uh, I need to make a pickup. Twelve cases. Tomorrow night, if possible."

"It's possible."

"Can I make the pickup after nine?"

"Thirty-five per. I'll meet you at the docks."

There, I thought, allowing myself a sliver of triumph as I hung up. But when I replaced the directory, I noticed someone had been in the secret compartment at the back of Daddy's bottom desk drawer, the one where he kept the ledgers. I reached in and felt around.

Empty.

"Damn it," I whispered. Money slipped through Daddy's fingers like water but he kept meticulous records of what we sold and to whom. Angel had probably taken them, but why? My blood iced over as I thought about where those ledgers might be —and worse, where they might end up. Daddy was sunk if Angel turned them over to the Prohibition Bureau.

He could go to jail. And I'd be on my own with the girls for years.

Shoving that predicament from my mind, I walked back to the store, focusing on a more immediate problem: I had nothing to wear to a place like Club 23. Two Sunday dresses hung in my closet, but neither was what you'd call smart, and I certainly didn't want to walk in there looking like a girl on her way to Mass. I also didn't want Enzo to think he'd bested me—he'd taken me by surprise, of course, but I wanted him to know I couldn't be broken so easily. The right clothing was essential.

Later that afternoon I approached Bridget as she rang up a purchase for a customer. Behind her, the boys were stacking empty boxes in the stock room and then knocking down their cardboard tower with glee.

"Would it be all right if I left a bit early today?" I asked when the customer had gone.

"Sure, I have Martin here." She smiled at me. "Go do something fun. It's Saturday."

Right. "Uh, I need a little bit of money from my tip envelope. Is your door open?"

"Should be. How much do you need?" She glanced behind her. "Thomas! Don't shut Eddie in that box, he'll suffocate!" While she rescued her youngest child from his brothers, I snuck up the stairs before I had to explain why I was taking every penny I had.

#

My closest girlfriend was Evelyn LaChance. She still lived with her parents too, and their house was only a couple blocks from ours. Evelyn attended nursing school with me, but during the summer she helped out at her family's bakery. On Saturdays, she only worked mornings, so I walked to her house and found her in the bedroom she shared with her twin sister Rosie, folding laundry and stacking it in neat piles on her bed.

"Hey, I was just thinking about you," she said. "Want to go to the movies tonight?"

I perched on the edge of the dresser. "I would, but I actually have plans."

Her plump mouth formed on O. "A date? With who? Where?"

I winced. "Don't call it a date. With Joey. To a place called Club 23." I wondered how much was wise to tell her. I was dying to divulge the entire story about kissing Enzo in the boathouse, but I didn't see how I could without revealing the rest. "It's for my father... he has business there."

She hugged a folded pair of white bloomers to her chest. "God, you're lucky. Joey's so handsome."

"You think so? He drives me crazy with his big mouth."

"Mmm, that mouth drives me crazy too."

I rolled my eyes. "That's not what I meant. I'll put in a word for you, but right now I need you to help me find something to wear."

She tossed the bloomers aside. "Let's go to Hudson's. Rosie's working."

We walked to the streetcar stop and caught a crowded car heading downtown. I kept my purse clutched tight to my side, since I'd stuffed the entire envelope, fat with small bills and change, inside it.

Rosie worked at the cosmetics counter at J.L. Hudson's department store on Woodward. Even at four in the afternoon, her face was painted-on pretty, crowned by curly locks of golden blond hair cut fashionably short. They were twins, but it always struck me how different they were—in both looks and demeanor. Where Rosie was long-legged and slender, Evelyn was almost as short as me, with a rounder face and thicker middle. She wasn't unattractive, just plain —but any girl could look plain next to Rosie, who was as tart as she was beautiful.

"Tiny has a date tonight," Evelyn announced breathlessly. "With Joey Lupo, going dancing at Club 23. She needs help finding something to wear."

"No kidding." Rosie tilted her head, like she might be seeing me in a new light. "Club 23, huh?" Glancing at the huge clock on the wall, she nodded. "I'll take my break now and help you out. God knows you'll need it."

She accompanied us to the dress department on the sixth floor, where she began pulling dresses off the rack for me to try on. "Lord, Tiny, you're so short I don't know what will fit," she complained. "But you are nice and skinny. Let's try these."

"Isn't that a little flimsy?" Evelyn asked when I had the first one on.

I knew what she meant, but I liked it. It was slate blue satin underneath and had a sheer chiffon overlay in the same color. It had a V neck and no sleeves—a first for me—and hung straight to my hips where its satin sash was tied in an intricate knot on the left. The skirt hung in fluttery panels with a zigzag effect. Glancing at my purse in Evelyn's hands, I wondered how much it cost—I'd already be down a hundred bucks tonight, and I needed four hundred twenty to buy whisky with tomorrow. Since I was usually so frugal, even the nicest dress in my closet cost less than ten dollars. Something told me this one would be considerably more. "How much is this?"

"Hmm." Rosie stood back and pursed her lips. "Good color for you, matches your eyes." She circled me like a vulture.

"What does it *cost*?"

"Around twenty, I think. Maybe closer to thirty."

My heart plummeted. But then I imagined someone like Rosie in the club wearing something like this blue number, while I stood next to her in my green-checkered church dress. *To hell with the cost.* "I'll take it."

"Good." She nodded. "You'll need new stockings —sheer black," she said, scrutinizing my lower legs. "With roll garters. Then new shoes, with higher heels."

"And a lipstick," I added.

Rosie pointed at me. "Now you're talkin."

When I boarded the streetcar for home, I carried bags that held the dress, a pair of black stockings and satin-covered roll garters, black satin t-straps with high heels, a tiny silver mesh evening bag, and a pale peach lace-edged step-in—which Rosie had assured me was all I needed to wear under my dress. She also helped me choose a tube of lipstick called Red Velvet and told me she'd be home at seven if I wanted her to help me get ready. My envelope had taken a huge hit, but I still had enough to pay Angel tonight and buy twelve cases tomorrow.

Barely.

Back at my house, I prepared supper—scrambled eggs and bacon, the one meal I didn't habitually screw up—and gave the girls permission to go to the movies. I told them I was going out and wouldn't be home until late, but I warned them to observe their regular curfew or else. Molly's eyes lit up, and I figured she'd be tempted to take advantage of my absence, but I also knew Mary Grace would tattle on her first chance she got. After doing the dishes, I drove over to the LaChance house, my purchases in the back seat.

I felt like a doll as they worked on me up in their room, fastening my dress and fussing over my hair and makeup. "You're so lucky to have this naturally wavy hair," Rosie said, curling it around her fingers. "And such a perfect little body, straight up and down. I know girls who'd kill for that figure. It's just right for all the new dresses."

"I could never wear this." Evelyn fingered the soft chiffon.

"Ya got that right," said Rosie with a snort. "OK, now the powder and rouge." Her fingers fluttered and smudged across my face while I tried to hold still. "There. Now, when you get home, rinse your mouth out with Listerine and then put on the lipstick, like this." She took my new lipstick and put it on her own lips. "Try to make a little bow on the top, like I did." She puckered and preened in the mirror over their dresser.

"Got it." I stood to look at my own reflection. My hair was styled neatly around my made-up face, and Rosie had lent me a black beaded headband, which hid half my forehead. The blue of the dress brought out the color of my eyes, and I loved the way the sheer black stockings peeked out from under the zig-zag hem. Even more, I adored what I couldn't see

—the way the stockings were rolled to just above my knee and held there by the garters, the decadent feel of satin against my unbound breasts, the looseness of the step-in compared to the usual body-binding corselette.

"You look like a million bucks," Rosie said, a rare compliment from her.

"Thanks. I owe you."

"Can you get me into Club 23?" One penciled brow peaked above her hopeful eyes.

"Maybe next time," I told her, although the last thing I wanted to do was make an entrance into a club next to Rosie.

Back at home, I brushed my teeth and did some final primping in my bedroom mirror, thankful for the privacy while I practiced walking in my new heels. It took me a few tries to get the bow lips right, but I thought I had a reasonable imitation by the time I heard a knock on the front door.

When he saw me, Joey's eyebrows shot up. "Damn, Tiny. If I didn't know it was you, I'd say you were beautiful." He was wearing a dark brown suit, white shirt open at the collar, no tie or hat. The suit looked a bit worse for wear, but he'd tamed his hair and shaved, revealing clear skin and a strong jaw. My insides performed a funny little flip.

"You're a riot. But I'll thank you to just keep quiet tonight." I pulled the door shut behind me and walked to his car, a black Ford much like mine.

"Don't you want me to get the door for you?"

Was he joking? I waved him off. "This isn't a date, Joey. Just get in and drive. Do you know where we're going?"

"Yeah." He slid into the driver's seat, stealing a glance at my legs before starting the car. I smoothed the dress over my thighs and pressed my knees together.

Neither of us spoke on the way downtown.

The block he parked on looked perfectly ordinary, lined with darkened sandwich and coffee shops, a florist, a shoe store, and a photography studio. Steam rose from grates on the cement, and the electric streetlights cast a yellowish glow.

"Where's the club?" I asked as we got out of the car.

"Right over there, I think." We walked down the street and he pointed to the florist's door, which had the number 23 painted on it. "See that opening in the sidewalk? That's a stairwell to the cellar, where the entrance is."

We descended the cement steps. At the foot of the staircase was a massive metal door, which Joey knocked on.

No answer.

He pounded a little harder.

Nothing.

I was about to tell him to forget it, this couldn't be the place, when we heard a few clicking sounds, like the door was being unlocked from inside. I pushed it open, and we stepped inside a dark, closet-like space with a second door ahead of us.

"That wasn't so hard," I said. But when the big metal door slammed behind us, we were trapped in blackness. Immediately my heart began thudding, but within seconds, a tiny slot at eye level—well, more Joey's eye level than mine—opened up.

A pair of eyes appeared. "Yeah?"

"Is this Club 23?" Joey asked.

"Get lost." The slot closed.

"Angel sent me," I said loudly.

The slot opened again. "Who said that?"

"Me. Down here."

The eyes found me and the voice attached to them laughed.

"Listen, can we come in or not?" I asked irritably.

"Sure, you can come in," the voice said. "If Angel sent you, you're in." The door opened, and we were directed down a dark, low-ceilinged hallway with a red-tiled floor and black-painted cement walls toward the club's main room. The music grew louder as we approached. At the end of the hall were two red velvet curtains, tied back on either side.

My heart raced as I took in the club's cozy underground opulence. The front third of the room was dominated by an elevated stage, where a dozen musicians shook the walls with a hard-driving rhythm. The rectangular dance floor in front of it was two tiers lower than where I was standing and packed with dancers. Cocktail tables edged the floor, and crescent-shaped booths with plush red velvet seating rimmed the next two tiers. The walls were also lined with a few intimate, red-curtained booths, and the room was crowded with elegantly dressed men and women, many of them dancing or smoking, all of them drinking. The dark wood bar ran the length of the back wall, and the cocktails were served in real glasses, not mugs or teacups like I'd seen in other joints. White linen dressed the tables, and the waiters wore tuxedoes.

A hostess seated us at a small cocktail table near the dance floor. Joey ordered a whisky and asked if I wanted one. "I'll have Canadian Club. With ice." In speakeasies it was important to order your poison by name—otherwise you couldn't be sure what was in it. The hostess disappeared and we sat listening to the music for a few minutes, my eyes scanning the room for Angel or one of his sons.

Our drinks arrived, and Joey handed the waitress some cash. She winked at him, and I didn't blame her, which irked me.

I sipped my whisky. "Swell suit. Too bad you couldn't afford a tie."

He took two big swallows and set down the glass with a clunk. "I don't prefer neckties. And now, hard as it may be, I think you should tear your eyes from me and look over your shoulder. Is that Angel DiFiore watching you?"

A spidery chill crawled up my back. I turned in my chair, and there he was, in a black tuxedo, raising a glass to me in a silent toast. He drank, set the glass down, and headed my way.

I took a gulp of whisky. "Yes. That's him."

Joey watched him approach with his chin lifted, eyes sharp.

In a moment, Angel appeared at my side. "Miss O'Mara. What a pleasure to see you again, and how beautiful you look." He offered his hand and I saw no choice but to take it. Turning to Joey, he said, "Angel DiFiore."

"Joe Lupo."

Angel held out his hand again but cocked his head at hearing Joey's name. Did he recognize it? "Perhaps you will enjoy a cigar in the lounge behind that curtain, Mr. Lupo." He took a cigar from inside his coat and handed it to Joey. "The Miss Detroit is excellent." He signaled a goon on the room's periphery. The goon nodded and pulled a black curtain aside, revealing a room beyond it from which pale blue smoke billowed.

Joey took the cigar from Angel and looked at me. "You all right?"

"Sure." I swallowed my fear along with another mouthful of whisky. At least we were surrounded by a crowd.

Joey stood, adjusted his coat, and disappeared behind the curtain. Angel gestured toward his seat. "May I?"

"It's your club."

"It is, indeed. But manners are manners." While I marveled at his concern for ettiquette in this situation, he lowered himself into the chair, pulling a cigarette from a small gold case. A girl in a short-skirted Club 23 uniform rushed to light it. "*Grazie. Allora, Signorina* O'Mara," he began, exhaling smoke. "Your coming here tonight tells me you are cooperative as well as lovely. A nice combination, I think." His black eyes shone as he looked over my hair and clothing.

I met his gaze but said nothing.

"Did you bring the money?"

Keeping my purse on my lap, I opened it up and removed the bills. Then I placed them on the table, covered them with my hand, and pushed them toward him.

"Splendid," he said, pocketing weeks of my hard work within seconds. "I should have come to you in the first place." He tapped ashes from his cigarette into the small tray on the table. "So let's talk business. I want five thousand dollars by Tuesday night."

My heart plummeted to my heels, and took my cool demeanor with it. "Tuesday night! That's in three days—that's impossible!"

"Nothing is impossible."

I clutched my purse tight. "I need more time."

"You don't have it. Now, you can bring the cash here, or leave it up to me to find you." He smiled as he stood. "But I believe you'll prefer the first option. Until then, Miss O'Mara. I do hope you enjoy yourself this evening." Placing the cigarette between his lips, he offered me his hand again.

I felt like spitting on it and bolting, but one glance beyond him reminded me of the men stationed at every doorway. When he was gone, I sat stiffly, unblinking. Hearing neither the crowd nor the music.

Five grand. By Tuesday night.

I closed my eyes.

Deadline—the word took on a whole new meaning.

I felt a hand on my shoulder and looked up to find Enzo beside me, a drink in his hand. My traitorous heart thumped double time at the sight of him.

"Good evening." He sat in the chair his father had just vacated—without asking—and I stared coldly, angry that his good looks were matched by his duplicity. He wore his usual three-piece suit. Dark blue tonight, with a light blue shirt and a deep red tie. His hair was brilliantined to a shine. Taking several swallows of whisky, I wondered about the scar on his cheekbone and hoped some girl had scratched him trying to gouge his eyeballs out.

"How are you tonight, Miss O'Mara?"

"As if you care."

"Why wouldn't I?"

The *gall* of this man. "You pretended to be a customer, you spied on me, you followed me, and you broke into our boathouse." Fuming, I leaned forward. "You kissed me."

"You kissed me, actually."

Heat flooded my face. "That's not the point. You knew the whole time what your father was planning to do. It was a dirty trick."

He drank, looking at me over the rim of the glass, and set the glass down. "It's a dirty business we're in."

I put my hands on the table. "Listen, I'm no crook. I make an honest dollar supplying a harmless demand. What you're doing is called extortion."

"Every racket's legit when it's all illegal. Don't kid yourself that you're above it." My blood boiled harder as he took a Fatima from his case. "You're a bootlegger, Tiny. You work the black market, and the black market has its own rules." Pulling a silver lighter from his breast pocket, he lit the cigarette between his lips. "You follow them, no harm comes."

I raised my eyebrows. "No harm? That's not what it looked like last night."

"Well, your father didn't follow the rules, did he?" He took the Fatima from his mouth and exhaled. "But you're a smart girl. You do what you're supposed to, and I promise—no harm comes."

He promises. Ha. Just watching the smoke slip from his lips was enough to do me harm.

"You don't believe me."

I sat back. "No. I don't."

"What can I do to convince you?"

"I want to see my father."

"Impossible."

"Then let me talk to him."

He looked at me a moment before speaking. "Are you alone tonight?"

Heat pooled in my lower body. "Does it matter?"

"If we're going to use the telephone, you'll have to come upstairs with me. Alone."

At first, I wanted to tell him I wasn't dumb enough to go anywhere alone with him. But then I remembered something my mother used to say: *You catch more flies with honey than vinegar.* If my goal was to get them to give me more time to come up with the money, then perhaps I should play nice.

But I should also play smart.

"Just let me tell my friend where I'm going." As I stood, Enzo's hand shot out, gripping my forearm.

"I'll take care of that." Without letting go, he got up and steered me toward the bar. When we reached the long counter running the back of the room, he released me. "Wait here."

As he walked away, I looked down at my arm — his fingers had left red marks that wound around my pale wrist like rope.

It should have frightened me.

Chapter Five

For several minutes, I waited alone at the bar, shifting my weight from one foot to the other and rubbing my lips together. Was I screwy to go somewhere alone with Enzo? What would he say to Joey? How did he even know who Joey was? Had he been watching us?

"Can I buy you a drink, doll?" said a voice to my left. The guy was blond, round-shouldered and burly, with pink pimply skin.

"No, thanks. I'm waiting for someone."

"I'm someone."

"Just leave me alone." I turned away from him.

"You can't come to Club 23 and be alone. At least let me get you a drink."

"Fine," I said, mostly to get rid of him. He snapped to get the bartender's attention while I kept my eyes on the crowd, watching for Enzo.

In a moment, my pimply admirer tapped my shoulder and handed me an ominously clear martini. "Here ya go. Best juice in the house."

"Thanks." I took it from him but didn't drink.

He lit a cigarette. "Your fella didn't show yet, huh? He shouldn't leave a pretty young thing like you unattended." Leaning toward me, he exhaled in my face.

I coughed and fanned the air between us. "Listen. I don't want to be rude, but I've told you already to leave me alone."

He laughed again, an annoying little heh-heh-heh that sounded like my car when it wouldn't start. "Why don't ya get to know me before you give me the boot? Name's Harry."

"Now I know you. I still want you to beat it."

"Not too friendly, are ya, kid?" Harry reached out and traced a line from my neck down one shoulder.

Recoiling with a scowl, I threw my drink in his face. While he sputtered in shock, a hand came down on his arm and spun him around.

"Get the fuck out of here," Enzo growled.

Harry mopped his face with his sleeve. "Enzo. I didn't realize." He scowled at me before backing up and losing himself in the crowd.

Enzo took the empty glass from my hand. "Can I get you another drink?"

"No, thank you." Between the whisky I'd imbibed at the table and the difficulty I had walking in these high heels, I was impaired enough. Not to mention the way Enzo's dark eyes and slow smiles threw me off balance. I leaned against the bar for support. "Did you speak to my friend?"

"It's all taken care of."

I found it hard to believe Joey had let him off so easily. And a little disappointing, frankly. "What did he say?"

"Oh, he threatened my general well-being, as well as some specific body parts, if any harm should come to you." He took my arm, more gently this time, and led me around the bar. "I promised to return you to him in twenty minutes, unmolested."

I was beginning to regret turning down a drink.

He pushed open a door behind the bar, and we entered a room filled with crates, boxes and sacks of alcohol. "Is all this yours?" I asked, impressed.

"Yes." He guided me to the back and opened another door.

I hesitated before entering the dark, narrow space. "What's this?"

"It's the quickest way to the office."

"Whose office?"

"My father's."

"Will he be there too?"

Enzo looked at me sideways. "I'm a grown man, Tiny. My father doesn't need to know everything I do." He pulled me into the tunnel, closing the door behind us. Gasping at the complete darkness, I grabbed his arm.

He laughed, and a second later, I heard the flick of his lighter. The little flame created a small sphere of light, illuminating his sculpted features from below. "Better?"

No. You're too handsome. And too close. "Yes." I released his arm. Stepping gingerly on the balls of my feet, I walked beside him down the long, narrow passageway. The walls were raw planks of wood, and the ground was hard-packed dirt. Our footsteps made no sound. *No one knows where I am.*

"So what's your real name, anyway?" His tone was friendly and curious, as if we were out for an evening stroll in the park and not sneaking through a subterranean passage beneath an illegal club.

"Uh, it's Frances, but I've always been called Tiny." *Pay attention to your surroundings. Keep it friendly.* "When I was born, I was so small I fit into a cigar box."

He chuckled again, chipping away at my antagonism. "Really?"

I nodded as we veered left; another tunnel snaked to the right. *They must run beneath the entire building.* "These tunnels must come in handy."

"Always good to have more than one way out these days. Do you supply any clubs?"

"A few. Mostly Al Murphy's places. But his speaks don't have this kind of hidden access. I wish they did. It would make deliveries a lot easier."

"I imagine so. Watch your step here." Enzo's voice was steady as he took my arm, guiding me through a door into a narrow stairwell. From there I followed him up rough-hewn steps on shaky legs, wishing there was a rail to hold onto.

At the top of the stairs we emerged into a dimly lit wood-paneled hallway. "This way." Enzo tugged my arm to the right. A quick look behind me revealed that the door we'd come through blended into the wall so well, I wasn't sure I could find it again. At the end of the hall, Enzo unlocked a door and stood back so I could enter. He locked it again behind us, and my skin tingled when he brushed by me. A moment later, he switched on a lamp across the room.

The office looked like any businessman's—a large mahogany desk with two red leather chairs in front of it, thick gold velvet curtains over the windows, and a sideboard along the back wall functioning as a bar.

"We'd best be quick about this." He picked up the telephone on the desk.

To my dismay, he spoke in Italian when the call was put through. I caught only a few words—*ragazza, padre, parlare*. When Vince was alive, he'd tried to teach me a few things, but I hadn't paid close attention, a fact I now regretted.

"Tiny?" Enzo held the phone out to me.

My stomach tightened as I took the earpiece from him. I laid my purse on the desk and picked up the candlestick base. "Hello?"

"Tiny. Is that you?" It was Daddy's voice. I was sure of it, although it was weak and raw.

"Yes, it's me." Willing myself not to dissolve into tears, I asked, "Are you all right?"

Silence. "Yes. I'm sorry, Tiny—"

"I'm taking care of everything, Daddy. I—"

"Enough!" barked a new voice in my ear.

84

"No! Put him back on," I begged. I looked helplessly at Enzo, who took the phone and finished up the call in Italian.

"Satisfied?" He set the phone down and raised his eyebrows at me.

"I guess." At least I knew Daddy was still alive, and conscious enough to speak on the phone. My job now was to get the money. But even if I sold the twelve cases I'd pick up tomorrow night, I'd need to sell seventeen more to come up with five grand by Tuesday. It couldn't be done—I needed more time. But what leverage did I have to bargain with?

I looked at Enzo, my mind and heart racing.

No. You can't.

"We should go. I promised to return you within twenty minutes." Enzo gave me that slow smile, which made my belly go hollow. "And I do rather value those body parts your friend threatened."

"Right." I licked my lips as I walked to the door, and Enzo waited until I reached it before turning off the lamp. His silhouette came closer in the darkness, and my insides tightened.

Oh yes, I can.

"If you'll move, I'll unlock the door," he said.

85

Fear and some other untamable feeling buzzed through me. "No."

"No?"

"We still have five minutes." I rushed forward and threw my arms around his neck, crushing my lips to his. For a moment he was stunned; I heard his keys hit the floor. Then strong arms locked around my back, and his mouth opened wide over mine, his tongue lashing inside with deep, demanding strokes. My body ignited in a way I hadn't anticipated. *Keep your senses. This is just a ploy. You're angry with him.* Our mouths battled each other with such ferocity I couldn't breathe, and I imagined the fire between us consuming all the oxygen in the room. He tasted like temptation— whisky and smoke.

Pressing my forearms against his shoulders, I jumped up and wrapped my legs around his waist. Enzo pushed my back up against the door, his hands slipping beneath my dress to the undersides of my legs, his fingers gripping the bare skin above my stockings. Gasping, I squeezed his torso between my thighs as his mouth traveled across my face and down my neck. His fingers edged inside the lace of my step-in, teasing the soft pink folds at my center while his tongue lingered in the hollow at the base of my throat.

Something deep and powerful surged within me. Threading my fingers through his dark hair, I pulled his head back and we stared hard at each other before our mouths slammed together once more. He shifted my weight under one arm and found the side fasteners of my dress with the other.

Somehow, he undid seven hooks and eyes with one hand.

His fingers slipped inside my dress and pressed against the bare skin on my lower back. Then he swung me away from the door and moved to the desk, setting me on its edge with my dress bunched up around my hips. Standing between my knees, he ran his hands up my pale white thighs, which glowed in the dark above my stockings. My chest heaved with ragged breaths as he shrugged off his coat and loosened his tie. My hands itched to touch him, to travel under starched cotton and over hot skin, to reach low and feel exactly how he wanted me. To know for certain what he could to do to me, if I let him. For a moment, I forgot every circumstance that brought me here and nearly reached for the buttons on his trousers.

But only for a moment.

"Enzo," I whispered instead, gripping the edge of the desk. "We can't."

He put his hands on my buttocks and pulled me flush against him. "You said we had five minutes." He pressed the hard length of his cock between my legs.

Oh God, that feels so good. I struggled for control. "It's been five minutes. And neither of us wants to get caught here."

He paused. "You're right. Besides, what I'd like to do to you takes more than five minutes."

My heart thumped wildly as he backed off. I brought my knees together and tried to gather my wits. *Ask him. Now.* I took a deep breath. "I need more time too."

"Oh?" He sounded amused as he picked up his coat and slipped it back on, as if he thought I'd been referring to sex.

Dropping to my feet, I fastened my dress with trembling fingers. "Yes. More time to come up with the first five grand."

He froze for a second before adjusting his collar. "Is that what we're doing here?"

"Couldn't you intervene for me? Ask for more time?"

"Why would I do that?" His words were cool and even.

My spine stiffened. "I thought you liked me."

He didn't answer right away. "I'll admit there's something I find hard to resist about you," he finally said, pulling a handkerchief from a pocket inside his coat. He wiped the lipstick off his mouth before handing it to me. "So I'll tell you that as long as you do what's asked of you, no one gets hurt." The look in his eyes was razor-sharp. "But don't mistake attraction for affection."

His words infuriated me, but fear tempered my reaction. "What if I can't do what's asked of me?"

He walked away, picked up his keys from where they'd dropped and unlocked the door. When he pulled it open, the light from the hallway spilled in, washing him in gold. He watched as I quickly wiped my mouth and smoothed my hair, uncomfortable under his scrutiny. "Don't underestimate yourself, Tiny. Nobody else is."

#

Joey was waiting for me near the club entrance. Chin jutted. Eyebrows furrowed. At the sight of us, he released his crossed arms and puffed up his chest a bit, but relief eased his features.

"I see that your date is glad to have you back in one piece," said Enzo from behind me. Since I'd asked for more time, his disposition had been all business. No wink-and-smile banter, no flirty innuendo, and no touching. Was he actually angry, thinking I'd kissed him under false pretenses? Maybe he did like me—at least more than he was willing to admit.

I glanced over my shoulder. "I never said he was my date."

"In any case, I've returned you as promised, and —"

"Not exactly." I turned and walked backward a few steps. "I believe you promised to return me *unmolested*." The barest flicker of fire crossed his face.

"You ready to go, Tiny?" Joey did his best to stand tall, although Enzo had a couple inches on him. In a fight, though, I might bet on Joey. He just looked hungrier.

"Yes." I locked eyes with Enzo. "We're through. For tonight anyway."

"Enjoy the rest of your evening." Enzo nodded at us before turning on his heel and striding away.

"What the hell was that about?" Joey demanded.

"Just business." I watched Enzo go behind the bar, pour himself two fingers of whisky and down it. Then he poured another.

Ha, so I did get to you.

He looked over at me then, and when our eyes met, I vividly recalled his fingers on my bare legs, sliding higher. My thighs clenched involuntarily, and I sucked in my breath.

"Doesn't look that way to me." Joey grabbed my elbow. "Let's get out of here. Now." He was rough, tugging me toward the exit as if I were an unruly child.

I jerked my arm from his. "Quit it! I said I was ready to go, you don't have to grab me."

Joey's lower jaw slid forward but he said nothing—not a word until we were halfway home. "So are you going to tell me what he said or not?"

"What who said?"

"Angel!" Joey thumped the steering wheel with the heel of his hand.

"Oh. Right." With difficulty I shoved the memory of Enzo's torso between my legs from my mind. "Uh, he said I have three days to bring him five thousand dollars."

"What? That's crazy."

"I know it's crazy," I snapped. "That's why I was trying to play nice with Enzo."

"Ha." He turned the car so abruptly I had to grab the dash to stay upright.

"It is! He let me speak with Daddy on the telephone. Then I asked him if he would intervene for me with his father, ask for more time."

"Why would he do that?"

I bristled. "Maybe he likes me."

Joey snorted. "Sure he does. So will he do it? Intervene, I mean?"

I turned my face to the window.

"That's what I thought."

Somehow I was as angry with Joey for saying that as I was with Enzo for denying my request. I tried to think up a sharp remark but failed.

Joey turned onto my street. "Did you talk to Blaise?"

"Yes. Twelve cases, after dark tomorrow night."
"And you've got the money?"

"Yes. It's everything I've made this summer so far." The words tasted bitter in my mouth.

"I'll meet you at the docks at nine thirty." He pulled into my driveway, and I faced him.

"I don't need you, you know. I can do this myself," I lied.

"I *said*, I'll meet you at nine." He stared straight ahead.

"Fine."

"Fine!"

"Good night, then!" I opened the door and slid out. I was about to slam it shut when he looked over at me.

"Tiny."

"What."

"You can't trust him."

I lifted an eyebrow. "This from the boy who stole my underwear for profit."

"That was a long time ago."

"Yeah, well, I have a good memory."

Joey focused his attention out the front window again.

I slammed the car door and went inside.

After checking on the girls, I undressed and washed off my makeup. When I was in my nightgown and under the covers, I lay awake, staring at the ceiling. Angel's deadline loomed above me like the blade of a guillotine. And Enzo's refusal to intercede on my behalf cut deep, especially after what had happened between us.

Don't trust him, Joey said. And I didn't, not one bit. But I couldn't stop thinking about him.

I didn't even try.

Chapter Six

After attending Mass with my sisters, I walked to the store to pick up the notebook I kept of our customer phone numbers and addresses. This afternoon I'd make some calls, see how much whisky I could sell over the phone before I even picked it up. I said hello to Martin and scooped up the notebook from a drawer behind the counter while he rang up a shopper.

Since I was there, I decided to face Bridget. My feet felt heavy as I plodded up the stairs. I wasn't looking forward to lying to her, but there was nothing she could do to help, and she'd only worry herself sick about Daddy. On her apartment door was a note for me.

Took the kids to the park for the afternoon. Come for dinner if you like. B.

My shoulders released some tension as I exhaled. Saved—at least for now.

When I got home, I placed a call to Al Murphy, an old friend of Daddy's who ran several small speakeasies nearby and always bought his whisky from us. His wife answered, but she said they were getting a little low on Canadian Club and placed an order for eight cases. If she'd have been in the room, I'd have kissed her.

Next, I started making phone calls to customers on the list, concentrating on the wealthier homes first. By late afternoon, I figured I had about ten cases sold all together. *See? You can do this. Chin up.* About five o'clock, my stomach began growling, and I remembered Bridget's dinner invitation.

It gave me an idea.

"Girls!" I shouted out the kitchen window into the yard. "We're going to Bridget's for dinner! Come in and wash up!"

We cleaned up and walked over to Bridget's, where she served us meatloaf, green beans, and mashed potatoes. A basket of fresh-made bread was on the table, and a plate of chocolate chip cookies sat on the counter. Watching Mary Grace gobble it all up, a wave of guilt washed over me. I never served meals like this—how the hell did you turn meat into a loaf anyway?

After dinner, Molly and Mary Grace took the boys outside while Bridget and I cleaned the kitchen. "Bridge," I began, rinsing off a plate, "could the girls sleep here tonight?" They were always glad to stay with her because she let them wander down the street to the ice cream parlor, where local kids lingered on summer nights.

"Sure. Why?"

"You remember how I said I hadn't kissed a boy in a long time?"

Bridget set down the plate she was drying and looked at me. "Ye-e-e-s."

My face got hot under her stare. "Well, I have a date tonight. And I'd like the house to myself."

She squealed and snapped my behind with her dishtowel. "Who is it? Anyone I know?"

"No. Just someone I met recently." I kept my eyes on the bowl I was scrubbing. "So it's OK?"

"Absolutely. I love having them here to help with the boys."

"Thanks." Relieved, I finished washing the dishes and kept the chat on safer topics. Bridget didn't even question the story about Daddy going to Cleveland. She was much more interested in what I was going to wear on my date, where he was taking me, and what we'd do afterward. I told more lies than I could count.

After saying goodbye to the girls, I walked back home in the fading light. I had about an hour to change out of my church clothes, pull the four hundred twenty bucks from my stash, and get to the boathouse. *At least the weather is good*, I thought as I climbed the steps to the front door.

But my hands were shaking, and I dropped the key twice before getting it in the lock.

#

Joey was already on the boat when I arrived. He reached for me with one hand. "Need help?"

Shaking my head, I jumped on board, but I stumbled a little, bumping into him. "Sorry."

He caught my upper arms to steady me, and his chest looked so broad and comforting, I almost laid my forehead on it. "Nervous?"

"A little," I admitted.

"If you don't want to go, I can manage this alone."

"No. It's my operation. My responsibility." Too much depended on this to leave Joey in charge.

I sat down on the bench at the center of the boat while Joey untied the rope tethering us to the dock. Like me, he was dressed in shabby dark clothing, and the floppy cap was back on his head. We didn't talk the entire way across the lake, but he did hand me his jacket when he noticed I was shivering. I shook my head, but he held the jacket out until I took it and draped it across my shoulders. It was warm with his body heat.

At the Canadian docks we met Blaise, a jowly, pot-bellied French-Canadian who took the cash I offered and never looked up from it. He shuffled through the bills and tucked the wad out of sight, and as the money disappeared into his pocket, I fought the urge to throw myself at him and demand it back. How long had it taken me to save four hundred twenty dollars? How many cases had I smuggled, hauled, and delivered, knowing at any moment I could be questioned or arrested? And what were the chances I could earn it back by the end of the summer? Would I have to put off school for another semester? Or year? My insides knotted with anger as Joey and I loaded the whisky into the boat.

"Don't turn sharply or go too fast," I ordered as he started the motor.

He gave me a look that said *shut your trap*.

"Listen, the last thing I need is booze I've just paid for to go right to the bottom of the lake."

"Sit down, Tiny. I know how to drive the damn boat."

I opened my mouth to argue, but then I remembered my mother's advice about honey. Since I wanted to ask him about getting me a gun, I bit my tongue and sat. As we moved slowly away from the docks, I tried to think of the best way to approach him about it. I hated to keep asking him for help, but I had no one else to ask.

"Joey...I want a gun. Can you help me get one?"

He looked at me without speaking, and I couldn't read his expression in the dark.

"Please?"

"Why do you want a gun? Do you even know how to use one?"

"You could show me. I'd feel safer with one."

"There's nothing safe about a girl carrying a gun. Plus, you'd never shoot it. I know you."

"What? You do not! I would too!" The wind picked up, whipping my hair around my face, and I tried to hold it away from my eyes so I could glare at him.

"I'll think about it. Now hold on, looks like the lake got choppy."

He was right—the rough, black water tossed the boat relentlessly, and I held my breath practically the whole the way across the lake. Once, I looked back at Joey and found him staring at me, which sent an unfamiliar shiver up my spine. After that I forced myself to keep my eyes straight ahead. Finally we arrived at the boathouse, and as he worked to secure us to the dock, I watched his hands in the moonlight. He had nice hands, actually. Strong but not meaty, with solid wrists and dexterous fingers. Something fluttered in my belly again. *Quit it. It's goddamn Joey.* I jumped up onto the dock before he could offer to help me.

"I'll hand up the sacks to you, and then we'll take them into the boathouse," he said.

I nodded. When he held out the first case, our fingers touched, and I took it quickly to avoid prolonging contact. Then I lashed out, because that was more comfortable than acknowledging an attraction to him. "Did you fix the lock on the garage yet? It's been three days."

"Don't nag. I bought a new door this afternoon, and I'll put it in tomorrow." He handed me another burlap sack, and I grabbed it from the bottom.

"Well, you're the one who busted it up."

He paused before holding out the next case.

I pressed my lips together. "Sorry. I'm just—wound up. Thanks for fixing the door. I don't want those hearses stolen."

Joey was quiet a minute. "You have the keys for those hearses?"

"Yeah. Why?" I took the last case from him and he hopped onto the dock next to me.

"We might need them." He grabbed two sacks and headed for the boathouse.

"Oh, no," I said, close on his heels. "I'm not driving one of those death wagons around."

"You're awfully particular for someone so desperate."

"Well, it's my desperation, not yours. I'll do things the way I always have." We reached the door and I set down the whisky to dig the key from my skirt pocket.

"You can't do things the way you always have," Joey said. "No one can."

I tugged the padlock open. "What's that supposed to mean?"

"This is just the beginning, what happened to your pop. Now that he's caught the attention of bigger guys, his days as a lone whisky hauler are over." He shouldered by me.

"Says who?" I picked up my whisky and followed him in. Moonlight filtered in through the high window and suffused the boathouse with silver-gray light.

"Says the big guys." Joey set his sacks down, lifted his cap and ran a hand through his hair. "Things are changing around here, Tiny, and small-timers like him aren't gonna be allowed to run booze free and clear like they have been."

Part of me knew he could be right, but I didn't want to admit it. And I had no energy left to argue with him. "I guess that will be *his* problem. But right now, all I care about is getting all this sold tomorrow."

We loaded Al Murphy's whiskey into the boathouse and put four cases in the Ford for the neighborhood deliveries. "I'll follow you home," Joey said after opening the driver side door for me. "We need to talk."

I didn't see why it was necessary, and I was completely exhausted, but I said OK. *Maybe I can try again about the gun,* I thought as I started the car.

Clouds had moved in, so moonlight was scant as I bumped along the drive toward Jefferson, but I couldn't risk turning on the headlamps until I was a safe distance from the boathouse. The whisky bottles clanked in the back.

At my house, we unloaded in silence, hiding the whisky behind a false panel Daddy had put in the pantry. Afterward, Joey followed me into the front room and sank onto the sofa. "Are your sisters here?" he asked as I switched on a lamp.

"No. They're at Bridget's." I sat at the opposite end of the sofa. "What is it you want to talk about?"

Joey took off his hat and tossed it between us. "You remember I told you about those guys I knew from school, the River Gang?"

"Yeah."

"Well, they're taking over all booze smuggling on the water, starting now, north and south of the city."

I crossed my arms. "What the hell does that mean, taking over?"

"It means from now on, you want to run booze from Canada by boat, you gotta contract them as kind of a...taxi service. They buy and transport the load for you."

I tilted my head. "How sweet of them. And what do they charge for this service?"

"A percentage of the load, whether the cargo makes it or not."

"I don't understand."

"Well, say the cops catch them. You gotta pay the River Gang even if the load has to be dumped or gets confiscated."

My jaw dropped. "Are you kidding me? That's nuts, Joey! Nobody is going to pay them!"

"Then there's gonna be a lot of bodies at the bottom of the river." He looked me in the eye, but it felt like he'd kicked me in the gut.

"So there's no risk to them whatsoever! Brilliant, these guys. And you said they went to the Bishop school?" The Bishop School was where you ended up after being tossed out of too many regular schools. Joey used to run craps games in the yard there.

"It was bound to happen, Tiny. There's too much money to be made, and with war coming..."

"What war?"

Joey rubbed a finger back and forth under his bottom lip, saying nothing.

I threw my hands in the air. "Christ, Joey!"

He dropped his hand. "All right, here's your history lesson. The Scarfone and Provenzano families have been fighting each other for control of the Italian criminal rackets for years—tons of guys shot, knifed, blown up, whatever. Then about four years ago, they each get a big hit—Provenzano's sister and brother-in-law are shot coming out of their house, both killed. Then two days later, Scarfone's brother's body is found in a beer barrel on Riopelle. He'd been shot through the head and butchered."

My stomach heaved.

"Anyways, at that point the two sides apparently decide enough's enough with the killing. A sit-down is called, and they draw up this peace pact."

"A peace pact?"

"Yep. My pop told me about it. Signed in blood and everything. Territories in the city and surrounding area are mapped out and each faction is given a slice of the pie. Some small gangs are recognized, but the big players are still Scarfone and Provenzano. Things are calm for a few months. And then"—he paused —"Prohibition passes, and the stakes go way up. We're talking millions in bootleg liquor since Detroit can funnel in so much Canadian whisky and beer."

I had a pretty good idea how this story ended. "So let me guess. Two years ago Provenzano decides to hell with the peace pact and has Big Leo Scarfone taken out at the police station." I looked over at him; he was staring straight ahead, jaw set. "I'm sorry," I said softly, remembering his dad was killed that day too.

He cleared his throat. "Yeah. And after that, what's left of the Scarfone group kinda re-organizes, but it isn't real tight. The older guys don't like the younger ones, so they're not respecting the pact, neither. They're moving in on other territories, taking over rackets that don't belong to them. Like Angel coming over here and shaking down guys like your dad."

I'd never thought of our operation as a criminal racket, just a business. Before all this, my biggest fear had been a bust by the cops. "So now what?"

"So now the younger guys have decided to break from the old gang altogether," Joey went on. "We're gonna do our own thing on the river."

I grabbed his arm. "We! Joey, have you lost your mind? After what happened to your father, how can you get involved in this gang stuff?"

He shook me off. "Forget about me. The point is, Angel doesn't have any right to be over here, running booze or anything else."

"Oh, but it's OK for the River Gang to come out of nowhere and start demanding a percentage from any bootlegger on the water!"

"That's the way it goes."

"Jesus." I collapsed back onto the sofa. "I just want out of this. And how the hell am I going to do that when I can't even make my own runs anymore? I don't have any money to spare for your *friends*." I spat the last word. "And I'm sorry to say, I don't see a damn bit of difference between what they're doing and what Angel's doing. He just happened to nab Daddy first."

"Well, there *is* a difference. And if you're smart, you'll respect the way they want things done. The only reason they didn't bother us tonight is because I told them what happened with Angel. Sam wants to make a deal with you."

"Who the hell is Sam?"

"Sam the Barber. He's head of the River Gang."

"Swell. What kind of deal?"

Joey cleared his throat. "Well, they'll allow you to run your own small loads to pay Angel off, and in return, you give them the hearses and...some information."

I narrowed my eyes at him. "Information about what?"

"About Angel's operation. About the club. About any big shipments they have coming in."

My spine snapped straight. "They want me to be their spy? No chance, Joey!" I splayed my hands on my chest. "You think I'm crazy? Angel would kill me or Daddy or maybe both of us if he found out! And it's not like the DiFiores are my friends—they have my father hostage!"

Joey remained infuriatingly calm. "Still. You're able to get closer than they can." He paused. "And you said Enzo likes you."

I glared at him. Of course he'd bring that up, now that he needed it to be true. "What if I say no?"

"I'm not sure you have a choice. It's either work with them or pay for their services. I can't promise I'll be able to hold them off."

"Oh my God." Struggling to breathe, I lowered my face to my knees, covering my head with my hands. "How did I get into so much trouble?"

"You never could stay out of it."

"It was always your fault." Resting there for a moment, I was surprised when I felt a hand on my back. Joey and I didn't touch each other like that.

"Hey."

I looked over at him. He'd moved closer to me, and his expression was serious and almost tender. I sat up. "What?"

"You're not alone in this. I mean, you don't have to be."

His tone was cajoling, but his asking price was too high. "No. I don't want to be a soldier in any gang war, Joey. I just want to get the money, get Daddy released, and turn this problem over to him." Heaving a big sigh, I stood. "And after that, I need to get a new job. Secretary. Telephone operator. Dog catcher."

"That's probably a good idea." He picked up his cap from the couch. "You got the twelve cases sold?"

"Nearly. Tomorrow I just have to deliver and collect. Then I need to buy more whisky."

"Tomorrow night?"

"Yeah." I met his eyes. "Will your friends bother us?"

He shrugged. "I guess we can take our chances, stay well north of the city." He rubbed the stubble on his jaw, and for one insane second I wondered what it would feel like against my cheek. "Lock the door behind me, and I'll see you tomorrow."

I stood in the doorway and watched him go down the front porch steps. "Hey, Joey?"

He turned around.

"Why are you doing this? I mean, I'm grateful," I added quickly, "but I'm also curious. You'd cross those guys for me?"

"Hmm." He came back up the steps and stretched his hands to the walls on either side of the door. "Maybe it's because your dad was good to me when I needed help after my dad died. Or maybe it's because I always felt bad about stealing your underwear." He leaned forward, putting us nearly nose to nose. "Maybe I'm planning to steal all that whisky from the boathouse tonight."

I rolled my eyes. "Fine. Be sure to shoot me when you're done."

"Maybe I'm just a nice guy, Tiny."

"Maybe." His full lips were so close, I couldn't help staring at them, wondering what kind of kisser he was. They tipped up in a wicked grin.

"So how's about a goodnight kiss?"

I shut the door in his face before my lips could answer otherwise.

Chapter Seven

Monday dawned cloudy and humid. Trying not to think about all the money I could be putting in my tuition stash after a day like today, I loaded the four cases from my house into the Ford and made my rounds. I sold all forty-eight bottles by telling our customers I wasn't sure when I'd get another load since running near the river was getting dangerous and expensive. No one wanted to be without, so people were willing to buy a little extra to stock up.

By one o' clock, I'd collected all money owed plus twelve dollars and fifty cents in tips. I went home, shoved the money under my mattress, and made lunch. After that, the girls headed to the library for the afternoon, and I drove over to the boathouse to load up Al Murphy's cases. Joey was right about using a hearse —in my car, several of the sacks were visible because there wasn't enough hidden space. Thankfully I only had one destination, and I was hoping Al would be around to help me unload. My back and my hip were hurting like mad.

The Murphys lived in a large old Victorian hidden behind a thick grove of pines, and they ran a speakeasy in the old carriage house at the back of their property. I parked in the drive, knocked on the massive front door, and Gladys Murphy answered it a moment later. A former showgirl, she was a tall middle-aged woman with unnaturally black hair, and she always penciled in her eyebrows overly-arched. It gave her a look of constant surprise, which my sisters and I giggled about whenever she came into the store.

"Tiny," she said in her slight Southern accent. "Al's been trying to reach your father." Her forehead was wrinkled with concern.

"He's out of town. Is there a problem?"

She wrung her hands and looked down the street in each direction, setting off a warning bell in my head. "Come in." The hair at the back of my neck stood on end as I stepped into their elaborately furnished living room. I'd never seen the Murphys nervous about deliveries before. "Wait here. I'll get Al," Gladys told me. She peeked out the window before disappearing up the wide staircase.

I perched on a clawfoot chair and bit my thumbnail. The air in the room was stuffy and still, and the heavy drapes were pulled. Gladys returned a minute later, followed by Al, a portly guy with a thick head of red-brown hair and a mustache. He must have been shaving, because he had a speck of shaving cream on his neck and his collar was open.

"Tiny," he said, coming forward with his hand out. "How's your pop?"

"He's fine." I stood and shook Al's hand but gave him a wary eye. "I've got your whisky. Eight cases."

Al and Gladys exchanged glances and his Adam's apple bobbed. "Uh...the thing is, Tiny, I can't buy whisky from you anymore."

"Why not? You always buy whisky from us! Has somebody offered it cheaper?"

"No, no. It's not that. It's—" He swallowed again. "I have to buy it from somebody else now."

It took me a few seconds to comprehend what he was saying. "Or that somebody else will get mad?"

He nodded. "Your pop's been my friend a long time, done a lot for me, but..."

"They threatened us." Gladys's voice shook. "They showed up here with guns last night and said they'd bring in feds, or maybe just blow the place up if we bought from anyone else."

"Of course they did." My skin itched with fury. Enzo—that son of a bitch. He asked me what speaks we supplied and I'd flat-out told him. This was my fault. And now I was stuck with eight cases of whisky, which I'd never be able to sell by tonight, so I'd have no cash to buy the rest of the whisky I needed to make five grand by tomorrow night. Daddy was as good as dead.

And maybe I was too.

Without a word to the Murphys, I bolted to the door and yanked it open, then flew down the steps to my car. Tears spilled over as I backed out of the drive and took off down the street.

"Shit!" I pounded the steering wheel. "Shit, shit, shit!" Now what was I going to do? Wiping my nose with the back of my hand, I drove to the boathouse and unloaded everything again. I barely noticed any pain in my hip; I was too busy panicking about Daddy and fuming about Enzo. How dare he trick me that way? And then kiss me that way?

You kissed him, remember?

"That is not the goddamn point!" I yelled to no one.

I shoved my own culpability to the back of my mind and drove to Bridget's. To my relief, Joey's car was parked behind the store. Breathless, I rushed in the back door and found him unpacking boxes in the stock room. "Thank God you're here."

Joey lifted his brow. "Did I hear that right?"

"This is serious." I took the carton of Armour's Oats he was holding and threw it back into the box. "Come with me." Dragging him by the arm into the alley, I shut the back door and threw my hands in the air. "They screwed me!"

"Who?"

"The DiFiores! At least, I assume that's who it is." I told him what had happened at Al Murphy's house.

Joey crossed his arms. "How'd they know your pop supplied Murphy?"

My neck got hot. "I mighta let that slip when I was with Enzo the other night."

He pressed his lips together. "So now what?"

"Now I hang myself, Joey! I don't know what to do." I slapped a hand to my sticky forehead. The air was hot and steamy, and I figured it would probably storm tonight, making a run across the lake much more difficult, if not impossible. I kicked the brick wall, which hurt my foot, and then slumped back against it.

"All right now, just relax. Let me think."

"If I don't get five grand by tomorrow night…"

"I *said*, let me think." Joey looked down the alley for a moment. "I gotta make some calls."

"Wait." I grabbed his bicep. "No gang stuff."

He held up his hands. "No promises, Tiny. You want your dad back, you might have to trade some favors." He pointed at the store. "You go in there and help Bridget. I'll call you here later."

I hopped from one foot to the other. "When? It's almost three, and if I don't unload those eight cases of whisky today…" I hated how panicky and small my voice sounded, but all my confidence in myself was shot.

"I got it. Now go in there and make yourself useful." Finally he attempted a grin. "Although I know that's hard for you."

#

Joey finally called the store around six, just as Bridget and I were closing up. When the telephone rang, I was sweeping near the front door, but I dropped the broom and vaulted over the counter to grab it, ignoring Bridget's surprised stare. "Hello?"

"It's me."

"Yes?"

"I got it worked out. Meet me tonight, ten o'clock, at the boathouse."

I turned away from Bridget. "And?"

"And bring the keys for the hearses. Any of them that run."

#

After supper, Mary Grace went outside to play, but I pulled Molly aside before she could follow. "I need to talk to you."

She took her arm from my grasp. "Well, I'm meeting someone, so hurry up."

"I have to make a late run tonight." I'd decided to be up front with her. In case anything happened, someone should know where I went.

"Why?" She narrowed her eyes. "Where's Daddy anyway? He's not usually gone so long."

Jesus. She has to pick tonight to get wise? "He's working on some business connections in Cleveland. We might...run some whisky down there."

"Oh." Molly appeared satisfied by that. "So what time will you be home?"

"I'm not sure. But I want you both in bed at a decent hour, and no one comes over. Is that understood? Or do I have to ask Mrs. Mulder to check up on you?" Mrs. Mulder was our two-doors-down neighbor. When we were younger we used to call her "Meanie Mulder" because she was always crabbing at kids who ran across her lawn.

"Ugh, no. But all this late night running around is strange, Tiny." She began to walk out, then turned around, one eyebrow arched like Gladys Murphy's. "Is there a *boy* involved?" She tapped a finger on her chin. "Now that I think of it, I believe I did see a new dress in your closet, perhaps even new shoes—and a lipstick in your dresser." She blinked coquettishly.

My cheeks burned. "Stay out of my room."

Her mouth dropped open. "There *is* a boy! And you better tell me who it is, or I'll tell Daddy about the lipstick and all these late nights!"

I grabbed her by the ear, which I knew she hated more than anything. We were about the same height, and she probably had a few pounds on me, but when I got her like that, she knew she'd better listen good. "You cross me," I whispered fiercely, "and I'll tell him what I know about you and Jimmy Haskell on the back porch."

She gasped. "Mary Grace, that little tattle tale!"

I let go of her ear. "I don't want to hear another word out of you, is that understood?"

"You're not my mother," she spat, rubbing her ear. "And I'm sick of you acting like it."

I almost laughed. "You know what, Molly? I'm sick of it too."

#

When I pulled up at the boathouse at ten, I saw two cars—Joey's Ford and a beautiful red Buick Touring. I parked next to the Ford and took a few deep breaths before opening my door. A group of guys stood on the dock, cigarette tips glowing orange in the blackness. No moon tonight.

I picked out Joey right away. He wasn't the shortest or the tallest, but his silhouette in the dark was familiar to me now. It made me feel a little safer.

Walking toward the group, I held the hearse keys in one hand and an envelope of cash in the other.

"Tiny." Joey's deep voice cut through the slap of waves against the seawall. "This is Sam and Angelo and Whitey." All three of them wore suits, no ties. Angelo and Whitey wore floppy caps like Joey, but Sam's head was bare. He was short, thick-necked, and bald, which surprised me—for some reason I'd pictured a barber with a full head of hair.

"Hello," I said.

They said nothing. One might have nodded.

Joey cleared his throat. "Did you bring the keys like I asked?"

I held them out, and he gave them to Sam.

"Where are they?" Sam asked, tossing his cigarette butt into the water.

"They're at the garage I told you about," Joey said. "Here's the key." For a minute I was confused as to why Joey would have a garage key, but then I remembered that he had replaced the back door today.

"At least two are running right now." I swallowed hard when they all looked at me. "There's a third my father was still working on."

"I can get it running," Joey said quickly. He turned to me. "In exchange for the hearses, Sam here's gonna buy all the cases in the boathouse."

"One fifty per," Sam said.

I bit my lip. That was thirty bucks less per case than usual, but what was I going to do? It was sell to Sam at a discount or kiss Daddy goodbye. I nodded. "OK."

"And he's also going to let us make a run tonight without paying his percentage," Joey added. His tone implied I should be grateful.

"Thank you," I said. Sam took a wad of bills from his pocket and handed it to me. I tucked it into the envelope, too scared to count it in front of him.

Joey spoke up again. "One more thing."

"Yes?" My voice cracked.

"We heard—well, Sam heard—that Angel's expecting a huge rum shipment this week by rail from the East Coast. You know anything?"

Was he serious? "No. And there's no way for me to find out." Rain began to fall. Fat, heavy drops that hit the dock with soft thups.

"All you have to do is listen," said Sam.

"Someone always talks." His voice was so low and gravelly I could hardly hear it. "We want to know what night it's coming."

"I—I don't..." I flashed Joey a look that said *help me*. There was no way any of the DiFiores would let something like that slip—especially in front of me.

"Just keep your eyes and ears open, Tiny. That's all we're asking." Joey's expression pleaded with me to accept the terms.

"OK," I whispered.

"We better go." Joey sounded relieved. "We got seventeen cases waiting to be picked up. Tiny, unlock the boathouse for them."

I did as he said, and the guys loaded the whisky into the red Buick. Once they'd driven away, Joey and I hurried to the boat. Although the rain was intermittent, the wind had picked up and the lake was even choppier than last night. I held on tight as we headed out on the open water.

"You all right?" Joey asked.

"No, I'm not all right! Not only did I just give away three hearses and the keys to the garage, but I sold eight cases of whisky at a discount when I need every penny I can get!"

"I know, but that was his price. And you don't have a lot of time to turn a profit here, Tiny. You're better off selling fast than selling high right now."

"Yeah, but—"

"But nothing. You got a thousand bucks in your pocket that you wouldn't have if I hadn't negotiated the deal with Sam. Now forget about what's already sold and start thinking about the next load you're gonna have to sell—*by tomorrow night.*"

He was right. It wouldn't do any good to agonize over what was already done. Nauseated, I focused my attention on the lights across the lake as the waves tossed us up and down.

At the Canadian docks, I paid the distributor— a younger guy I didn't recognize—five hundred ninety-five dollars. The seventeen cases barely fit into the boat, which sat frighteningly low in the water. "Come on, hurry," Joey said. "The rain's starting again." He was veering out to the lake before I could even sit down. Halfway across, he stiffened and sat up tall.

"What?" My pulse quickened.

"Come here," he said quietly, slowing the boat and shutting off the engine.

"Joey, it's raining! Turn the motor back on and get us back!"

"Just come here," he said, more insistent this time. He thumped the space next to him on the bench. As we drifted on the swells, I carefully stepped between the sacks to sit beside him. He put his hands on my shoulders and looked me in the eye. "Kiss me."

My stomach cartwheeled. "Are you nuts?"

"Kiss me," he said again, but he didn't wait for me to do it. He squeezed my upper arms and pressed his mouth to mine. His fingers dug into my skin as my heart careened out of control. *What the hell is going on? He picks this moment to get romantic?* He took his lips off mine and buried his face in my hair by my ear. "Inspectors," he whispered. "Now act like you love me."

My eyes darted around the lake, and sure enough, what looked like a Prohibition Navy boat was passing us about ten yards off. I saw men in rain slickers lining the deck, guns at their sides. With my pulse roaring in my ears, I threw my arms around Joey and kissed him as if we were just a couple out for a romantic boat ride in the rain. But fear had me frozen stiff; it must have been like kissing a statue. "Relax," murmured Joey against my closed lips. "I've got you."

His low voice loosened my limbs and my inhibitions, and when he pulled me onto his lap, I went willingly.

His mouth was hot, and his soft lips teased mine open. The rock and sway of the boat lulled us into a rhythm, and I melted into it, into him. One of his hands began kneading my hip, and the other inched up the side of my ribcage, his thumb nearly grazing my breast. My nipples tightened. I wanted his hands on them.

Oh my God, I'm kissing Joey. And I like it.

The inspectors had to be past us by now, but I didn't want to stop. Raindrops splashed our faces and mingled with our kiss, but they did nothing to cool me down. Without thinking, I slipped my tongue between Joey's lips, and he sucked it gently before stroking it with his own. Picturing his familiar lush mouth, I held his head in my hands and plucked softly at his top lip, then his bottom lip, and then I pulled away slightly to rub my lips back and forth against his. His breath was hot on my mouth, and coming faster. A pleasant ache began between my legs and I arched my back, moving my hips a little. For a moment his arm tightened and I felt his flesh stirring beneath me—but in the next second he pulled away.

"They're gone." He set me beside him and turned on the motor.

I sat still, breathing heavily and trying to recover my senses. My whole body shook.

"You OK?" Joey asked. I was irritated to see a smile on his lips.

"No." I stumbled over the whisky back to the other bench seat. "I can't believe you did that." *I can't believe how much I liked it.* Had he been pretending the whole time?

He laughed. "Sorry. But I can't say I didn't enjoy it."

I cocked my head, grateful he couldn't see my cheeks flaming in the dark. "Glad I could amuse you."

"Listen, I don't know if those guys cared about us or not, but I didn't feel like discussing things with them tonight, seeing as we're unarmed, have no cash to spare, and smuggling seventeen cases of whisky across the lake."

As we zipped through the drizzle, I kept my eyes on the shore, resisting the urge to peek at Joey. It didn't seem as if the kiss had affected him the way it had me, but maybe I was making too much of it. Maybe it was just fear and adrenaline fueling that kiss, rather than any chemistry between us. And all the

fooling around with Enzo had me wound so tightly, I
was about to burst.

It isn't Joey. It can't be.

Besides, I had a much bigger problem—at my
feet was a hell of a lot of booze that I had to sell in
twenty-four hours. In addition, I owed Sam the Barber
any information I could get about that rail shipment.
How was I supposed to do that? Could I get it out of
Enzo? That meant being sweet to him again, and I
wasn't certain my acting ability was up to par—I was
furious that he'd stolen Al Murphy's business,
especially since he *knew* I needed money this week.
Bastard, I thought for the hundredth time today. If I
could get that information, it would sure feel good to
pay him back for double-crossing me. It would make
Joey happy as well.

Finally I risked a peek at him, and he was
looking at me too. For a few seconds, we stared at each
other, neither one speaking, until the tension between
us had every muscle in my body clenched so tight I
had to look away.

Once we docked, Joey and I ran the whisky into
the boathouse while lightning flashed over the lake.
The wind howled and rain fell harder, pelting our
faces. Thunder rumbled in the distance as I picked up

the last case and hurried toward the boathouse, where Joey stood just inside the doorway.

"I'll buy three cases from you," Joey said as I set the sack down. From his pocket he took a wad of cash and handed it to me. I stared at it, and then at him.

"What the hell, Moneybags? You rob a bank this afternoon?" The roaring wind slammed the door shut behind us, and I jumped.

"No, I earned it. You're not the only one who works, you know." Joey tucked the money into the front pocket of my blouse. Then he moved for the door, but I scooted in front of it.

"Hold on a second."

"What?"

"What exactly are you doing for Sam the Barber to make that kind of money? And why doesn't he have hair, anyway?"

"What's his hair got to do with anything?"

"I don't know. I just thought a barber would have hair."

"He's not a barber."

"He's not? Well, why do they call him—"

"Because he's good with a razor."

Lightning cracked, illuminating Joey's grave face.

"Oh, God." My legs threatened to buckle as the thunder rolled. It sounded as if the storm was right above us.

"Look, Sam's not a bad guy," Joey said as rain pummeled the roof. "He's fair, at least. You get him what he wants, and he'll return the favor without double-crossing you."

I shook my head. "I can't get him what he wants. Angel's not going to tell me anything."

"I agree. You'll have to get your fancy suit to talk."

"How am I supposed to do that?"

"You'll find a way." Lightning flashed again, allowing me to see the ghost of a smile on his face as he came toward me. For a second I thought he might kiss me, but he didn't. He just rubbed his lips back and forth against my ear and whispered, "You've got hidden talent."

Chapter Eight

That night I tossed and turned in sheets damp with sweat and humidity. I listened to the storm through my open window and fretted about selling enough whisky to buy Daddy's life and protect my sisters. My stomach ached, and I curled into a ball on my side. Had I done the right thing by going to Joey and not the police? Was I wrong to hide this from Bridget? Would I regret making a deal with Sam the Barber in which I promised to trade information for protection?

If anything went wrong, it would be my fault.

And Joey—I'd kissed Joey. Slamming my eyes shut, I tried to block the memory, to forget how much I'd enjoyed it. What the hell was wrong with me? Was I just starving for physical attention? Desperate for a release of the tension? Between Joey and Enzo, I'd had more sexual excitement in the last three days than I'd had all year. And none of it was real; someone was always acting.

Flopping onto my back, I tried to think of things I could say or do to entice Enzo to tell me about the rail shipment. He was too smart to let something slip, so my only hope was using the attraction between us. I'd failed last time, but maybe if I let things go further...

My heart thumped hard. Just how far was I willing to go? I wasn't completely unspoiled, but my sexual prowess was fairly untested beyond the usual heavy petting. Despite my Catholic upbringing, I knew how to give myself an orgasm—and George Gerrity, the one boy I'd dated seriously in high school, had certainly been no great challenge—but Enzo was another entity altogether. He wasn't a schoolboy ready to go off at the sight of a girl's knees. He was a man, and he seemed like a man with experience. Would I know what to do to get him to yield? And how would I keep my temper in check? Every time I thought about the way he'd stolen Al Murphy's business, foiling my chance to get the ransom money, my skin got hot with rage. It would take a huge effort not to accuse him of deliberately playing dirty with me, not that he'd care.

It's a dirty business, Tiny.

It sure as hell was. Dirty and dangerous and full of constant temptation.

As I remembered his fingers beneath my dress, on my bare skin, touching the most sensitive parts of me, my body thrummed with desire. I flexed and fisted my hands in the sheet, imagining what his body was like underneath those custom suits. Suddenly I had all kinds of ideas for getting him to talk.

He said he found me hard to resist. I was going to test him on that.

#

"I *might* be able to help you," Rosie said coyly, leaning toward her reflection as she applied her lipstick. With her social life, I thought she might know some people interested in buying whisky, so I'd stopped by the LaChance house, hoping to see her before she left for work. She met my eyes in the bedroom mirror. "But what's in it for me?"

I couldn't offer her cash—I needed every dollar to pay Angel. But there was something else I thought she'd go for. "How'd you like to go to Club 23 tonight?"

She straightened. "You serious?"

"Yes."

She capped her lipstick and rubbed her ruby lips together. "Why do you need the money so bad?"

"My father's in trouble. I'm helping him cover a debt, and I have to pay it immediately." I'd decided to be sort of up front with Rosie because she liked Daddy. Mr. LaChance had an eye for other women and a tendency to disappear for weeks at a time, and more than once Daddy had helped Mrs. LaChance pay the rent.

Rosie nodded. "What's the price?"

"Fifteen per bottle."

She admired her reflection again. "Club 23, huh? I bet there's a lot of high class daddies in there." In the mirror, her eyes wandered around the room she shared with Evelyn. "Maybe I could get out of this play pen."

"So it's a deal?"

"It's a deal." She went to the closet and pulled down a brown leather suitcase. "Pack as many bottles as you can in here, and I'll take 'em down to the store. I know a few suits I can sweet talk."

I ran out to my car and hustled in one sack of whisky. We managed to tuck all twelve bottles inside the case. "I bet I'll have it all sold before lunch," she bragged, flipping the latches closed.

"If you do, I'll buy your first drink at the club."

She pursed her perfect bow lips as she slipped into her shoes. "Honey, once we're through that door, you can go chase yourself. I won't need you."

#

That day, I called or visited every customer on our list. I braved sales calls to restaurants where I knew the owners and even ventured into the Country Club to speak with a waiter I'd gone to high school with. Short of standing on a street corner and shouting to the world that I had whisky for sale, I'd done everything possible to move every last drop, but at five o'clock I still had forty unsold bottles. That meant I'd be six hundred dollars short when I faced Angel tonight, and *that* was assuming Rosie managed to sell all twelve bottles she'd taken to work.

I drove home, racking my brain. Who could I borrow from? Bridget was out—I was avoiding even talking to her because I felt so guilty about lying. And she was bound to start asking questions about Daddy's absence. He'd never left us this long.

We had no other close family. Evelyn didn't make much at the bakery, and Rosie was already doing me a favor.

That left Joey. Again.

Inside the house, I stared at the phone in the front hall, tugging at my hair. I hated to ask Joey for anything more since he'd given me over five hundred bucks yesterday. But I had nowhere else to turn, and Daddy was depending on me. My sisters were depending on me, even if they didn't know it. I looked up his mother's number in the directory and dialed, but she said she hadn't seen him all day and didn't expect him back any time soon. Normally I laughed when I heard anyone refer to him as Giuseppe, but not today. After thanking her, I hung up and yanked on my hair again. "Shit!"

I paced back and forth in the hall, utterly panicked. I had no idea where Joey was. I still hadn't heard from Rosie. I hadn't seen my sisters all day and God only knew what they were up to. My father was being held in some gang hideout somewhere, maybe being tortured or beaten, and I was short six hundred bucks on the ransom payment due at the end of the day. And that was only half the cash I needed to free him! My nerves were so raw that when the phone rang, I shrieked before grabbing it.

"Hello?"

"Heya, Frances," Rosie chirped. "The deed's done."

I held my breath. "It is?"

"No foolin. I got the cash right here."

"And you got the price I asked for?"

"Are you doubting me? Seems to me a person in your...predickerment should be a little nicer."

Closing my eyes, I exhaled. "I'm sorry. I know how hard you had to work, and I'm very grateful."

"I never said it was hard, Frances. I said it was done."

I paused. Took a breath. *Honey, not vinegar.* "Thank you, Rosie. I'll pick you up at nine tonight." After hanging up, I put my hands over my stomach. The church bells down the street rang out six times, sending chills down my arms. I closed my eyes and began to pray.

#

The girls wandered in shortly after seven, and I threw supper together—bacon and eggs again, which caused both girls to roll their eyes. "I really should learn to cook," Molly said as she scraped eggs onto her plate and slapped the spatula back into the pan.

"Me too," added Mary Grace. "Even I could do better than this." She held up a piece of bacon I'd blackened to a crisp.

"I'll eat that one. I like it that way." I grabbed it from her and took a charred bite.

When the phone rang a minute later, I jumped up from my chair so abruptly it tipped over backward.

"Hello?"

"It's me."

"Joey, what the hell? I've been looking for you all day!" I didn't even care if the girls heard me curse.

"Calm down. I had business to take care of. Did you get the money?"

"No, I'm short." I glanced over my shoulder.

"How much?"

I was silent, the amount stuck in my throat like a wad of chewing gum. I didn't want to say it within earshot of the girls.

"Are your sisters there?"

Bless you, Joey. "Uh huh."

"A hundred?"

"More."

"Three?"

"More."

"Jesus. Five?"

"Six."

Joey exhaled. "OK. I can't pick you up tonight because I have something to do, but I'll meet you in front of the club at ten with the money."

Relief cascaded over me like a waterfall. "How are you going to get it?"

"Don't worry about that. Just be outside at ten."

"OK. And thanks...I owe you."

"Owing *me* is the least of your problems." He hung up.

#

"I don't get it," Evelyn said as she watched Rosie and I dress for Club 23 in their bedroom. "Why does she get to go with you and I don't?"

The hurt on her face wrenched my heart, but I refused to put Evelyn in danger. Rosie could handle herself. "I'm only giving her a ride there, Evvy. I have to drop something off for my father again, and I don't intend to stay. Can you fasten this?" I was wearing an old black dress of Rosie's, which had a small tear at the side seam and was too big for me, but was still better than being seen again in the blue. She let me wear the headband once more too. If I ever had money to spend on myself again, I'd buy my own.

"I've never seen you wear black," said Rosie, darkening her caramel lashes to soot. "It looks good on you."

Evelyn helped me with the tiny snaps at the side of the dress, but continued to grumble. "I've hardly even seen you this week."

I hugged her. "I want to get in and out of there quickly," I said. *Alive*, I left out. "And the men I have to deal with are not the sort of men you want to meet. It's too dangerous."

"I might like dangerous men."

"Oh, please," put in Rosie from the mirror. Her rouge matched her satin dress—the shortest dress I'd ever seen off a movie screen. "You don't drink much, you don't smoke at all, and you don't know how to dance. What would you do there?"

"I'm a better dancer than Tiny, and *she's* going."

"Tiny's got connections." I detected the note of admiration in Rosie's voice. "When you get some of those, you can go too." She gave Evelyn a patronizing little pat on the head. If I was Evelyn, I'd have kicked her.

"Next time, I promise." I squeezed her shoulder. "You *are* a better dancer than me, and we'll go to a club together soon, OK? Maybe Joey will take us."

She brightened a little at his name. "All right."

"I'll call you tomorrow."

Leaving a disappointed Evelyn at the door, Rosie and I climbed into my Ford. "I do wish we had a better mode of transportation." She wrinkled her pert little nose. "This jalopy really isn't my style."

"Want to walk?" I asked tersely. "I can give you directions, but you're on your own for the password."

"I'm only joking. Don't have a kitten." Rosie patted my shoulder.

My fingers tightened around the steering wheel.

"You mentioned Joey. He coming tonight?" Rosie batted her spidery lashes at me.

"No."

"Too bad. I like those big brown eyes. But there will be plenty of other eyes there."

Mine slid sideways to her bare knees. "All on you in that dress."

She shimmied her shoulders. "That's the way I like it."

I took the same route Joey had driven Saturday night and parked along the quiet downtown side street. My password worked again, and we were sent through the winding basement hallway that ended at the club's main room, where Rosie stood slack-jawed for a full ten seconds. Finally she whistled, slung an arm around me, and spoke loudly over the raucous music. "I take back everything I've ever said about ya, Frances. You're the cat's meow." She dug a cigarette out of her purse and eyed a table full of young men near the dance floor. Glancing over her shoulder as she headed for them, she said, "See ya."

Left alone, I gulped back my nerves and looked around the room. I didn't see Enzo or Angel, and I didn't want them to spot me until I had all the money. It was nine-thirty, which meant I had to kill half an hour before Joey arrived. Keeping my eyes low, I went to the far end of the bar and stood with my back to the crowd, hoping to be invisible.

No such luck.

"What'ja do, bring your homework?" Pimple-faced Harry parked himself on my left and gestured at the envelope I clutched to my side.

"Get lost." I kept my eyes down.

"Why do all the pretty ones gotta be so unfriendly, Raymond?"

I stiffened at the name of Angel's other son, the one who'd dragged me through the garage.

"Dunno, Harry." Raymond's voice came from my right. "But this one's pretty all right. And she's got nice little round tits too. I copped a feel of 'em when I was holding her down."

I looked at him sharply, considering a knee to the groin. "You did not."

He leered at me and licked his lips. "I did, and I liked it."

Clenching my fists, I stared up at him, breathing hard through my nostrils. It wasn't difficult to see the resemblance in the DiFiore family—like Enzo, Raymond had the classically attractive features of their father, although his eyes were slightly wider set, and his jaw was a shade weaker. I felt like spitting in his handsome face. But if I caused a scene, I'd only draw attention to myself. *Keep calm. Don't move. Don't speak. It's almost ten.*

"Maybe you think you're too good for a drink with us. Is that it?" Harry's tone was menacing.

"No," I said. "It's just...I don't see anything I want."

"What do you mean by that?" Raymond demanded. He moved closer, poking a meaty finger toward the bottles lining the back wall. "We got all the good stuff, way better than what you and your lousy pop are running."

A little bell pinged in my head. I pretended to look over the offerings behind the bar. "Nah. You don't have what I'm looking for."

Raymond huffed. "Like what?"

"Well, I'd like to try some rum. The real thing, from the islands. Not some coffin varnish made from industrial alcohol and prune juice." Taking a cue from Rosie, I batted my lashes at Harry. "You got any rum?"

As I'd suspected, Raymond scooted around and elbowed his way between us. "I'm the one who's got the goods, not him."

Looking his wrinkled suit up and down, I sniffed. "I doubt it."

"I do!" He thumped his chest. "I'm the rum runner here, not Harry. I can get it for you."

I cocked an eyebrow at him. "Right now?"

"No, it ain't here yet."

I shrugged and turned back to the bar, my heart pounding. If my instincts were correct, Raymond wasn't terribly sharp. Painful as this was, I had a much better chance of getting him to talk than his brother. "Then like I said, you don't have what I want."

"But it's coming," he went on. "I'm big time now. I got a shipment coming in that's the real Malloy."

"McCoy, you idiot," snapped Harry.

I faced Raymond again. "Well, how long's that gonna take, Big Time?" I smiled and winked before straightening his crooked tie. "I'm not a girl who likes to wait around. I could find a little rum someplace else."

He nearly bounced with excitement. "Not this rum. You come back in two days, and I'll give you all the tasting you want."

Two days—did that mean the shipment would come in tomorrow night? Or could it be tonight? "I'm busy Thursday night. How about tomorrow?"

"Uh uh. It ain't gonna be here till late tomorrow night."

"Oh. Maybe I'll change my plans, then." I winked at him again, but inside I was screaming, *I did it! I did it!* When I went out to meet Joey, I could tell him the shipment would arrive late tomorrow night. Then maybe I wouldn't feel so guilty about taking more of his money.

"So how's about you and me go someplace quiet?" Raymond asked, running a hand up my arm.

"Hey, I spotted her first, you know." Harry grabbed Raymond's shoulder and spun him around. His face was red with anger. "And if your brother sees you touching her, he's gonna throttle ya."

"What's my brother got to do with it?" Raymond jerked a thumb toward the dance floor. "He's got his own girl."

Bug-eyed, I craned my neck toward the dancers, scanning the room until I spotted him. The floor seemed to tilt beneath me, and I reached for the bar to steady myself. He stood with a cocktail at the edge of the dance floor, looking deliciously at ease in a black suit, white shirt, and a bow tie. His hair was pushed into a wave above his forehead. I watched him bring the glass to his lips, heat flushing my neck and chest.

Before he saw me, a squealing smarty in a gold dress as shiny and short as Rosie's accosted him, demanding attention. His kissed her cheek and took her arm, leading her to a booth nearby. Lightning bolts of jealousy ricocheted throughout my body while she preened at his side, looking around to make sure everyone noticed her. From my vantage point, she was cute but not beautiful, with dark hair, a wide forehead, and big red lips.

"Excuse me." I pushed both Harry and Raymond aside to get to the exit. I wasn't sure what time it was, but I needed some air.

Thankfully, neither of them followed me as I raced through the curtains and down the long hallway toward the metal door. I told the guard I was meeting someone and sweet-talked him into letting me back inside once my friend arrived.

"She as cute as you?" He wore a black suit and white shirt that had a tomato sauce spill down the front. At least I hoped it was tomato sauce.

I lowered my chin and looked up at him with a flirty wink. "Not nearly."

He laughed and opened the door.

"Thanks. Hey, can you tell me what time it is?"

"Sure thing, doll. It's five to ten."

"Perfect." Flashing one more smile at him, I went through the vestibule and up the cement steps. Once I was outside, I almost collapsed. My heart was racing so fast, I thought it might gallop right out of my chest. Fanning my face with one hand, I leaned against a light post. I'd done it. I'd discovered when the rum shipment would come in without having to come on to Enzo.

So why did I feel a little disappointed?

I should be even angrier with him. Not only had he stolen business from me, he had a girl, for Christ's sake. He'd kissed me and touched me, and all the while he had some little chippie waiting for him! Had she been at the club Saturday night? Maybe that's why he dragged me through the underground tunnels—he didn't want to be seen with me. Maybe he knew all along what would happen when he got me behind a locked door, and he didn't want anyone to know about it. Then he'd gone behind my back with Al Murphy.

Bastard. No man that despicable deserved to be that handsome.

A dark sedan pulled up to the curb, and thinking it was Joey, I moved toward it. But instead, a young couple got out of the back seat, laughing as they stumbled toward the stairwell. Clearly they'd been at the bottle already. *I wouldn't mind a sip or two myself*, I thought, backing up to the post again. *Come on, Joey. Get here, why don't you?* I looked up and down the street, but saw no sign of him. A few pairs of headlamps approached and passed. My stomach began to ache as a question I hadn't considered popped into my head.

What would I do if he didn't show?

Another car slowed, and the lone driver looked me over, but he sped up again without stopping. Shit. I couldn't stay out here alone like this much longer; it wasn't safe. But going back in there without all five grand wasn't safe either. A string of the foulest curse words I knew ripped through my brain. I had no idea what time it was, but I knew it was well past ten.

My knees started to tremble. And then my hands. A searing pain worked its way from the back of my skull to the front, settling right between my eyes.

Maybe that's where they'll shoot me.

Goddammit! I shouldn't have trusted Joey! I should have gone to Bridget. Maybe she would've panicked, but she might have had six hundred dollars to lend me. Then again, she might have insisted on cops too, and that wouldn't have done me any good.

Joey was my only hope, but that hope was draining away to dregs.

When my feet started to ache, I knew that I had probably been standing for close to an hour. I had run out of curse words to think.

"Fuck," I said. I'd never spoken the word aloud before. Actually it was kind of helpful to physically utter the word; it relieved some tension. "Fuck, fuck, fuck." Just the feel of it bursting from my lips felt sinfully good. *And if I'm going to die, I might as well sin a little before I do.*

Exhaling, I looked down the street once more. *I could make a run for it. I could leave here and go to the cops. Fuck it, I could leave here and go to Paris!* I had more than four thousand dollars tucked under my arm. They'd never find me. No one would ever know I'd been a coward and abandoned my family.

But I'd know.

"Fuck it," I said. Loudly. Then I turned around, took a deep breath, and headed down the stairs into the club.

Chapter Nine

Once inside, I wasted no time. Spotting Enzo alone near the bar, I squared my shoulders and tried to walk like he did—long, confident strides with purpose. When I reached him, I tapped his shoulder, and he turned.

"You made it." His eyes traveled down my body and back up again.

"Did you doubt me?"

A hint of a smile. "Not for a moment. Follow me." He led me toward the far right wall, where a tall, stern-faced guard stood in front of a red curtain. He nodded at Enzo before allowing us to slip behind it.

The sound of the music receded as we walked down a dim corridor. The air smelled like cigar smoke, and I heard laughter and shouting behind several closed doors, each of them guarded. At the end of the corridor, I followed him up two flights of stairs. From there we entered the paneled hallway I recognized from Saturday night, and I knew he was leading me to Angel's office. My heart tripped faster, and I ransacked my brain for the right words to say as I handed Angel an envelope that was six hundred dollars short. Should I admit it up front? Should I accuse them of stealing my business? Should I trade the information I had about the River Gang planning a heist of their rum? The thought of betraying Joey made bile rise in my throat, but I was on my own. I had to do whatever it took to protect my family.

The door was open but guarded by two men, and Enzo gestured for me to enter first. Angel sat behind the desk, and at the sight of it, my stomach flipped repeatedly, like a coin through the air. Three nights ago, Enzo had set me on it and stood between my knees, loosening his collar. *What I wouldn't give to be in that moment instead of this one.*

"Good evening, Miss O'Mara. Please sit." Angel rose to his feet as I approached. Big Time Raymond stood in a corner and had the nerve to wink at me.

I sat stiffly on the edge of a chair and placed the envelope on the desk.

"Enzo?" Without taking his eyes off me, Angel indicated his older son should take the money. When Raymond stepped forward and tried to take the envelope, Angel snatched it out of his reach. "I said Enzo. Count this."

Enzo came from behind me to take the envelope while Raymond retreated to the corner and sulked. "He always gets the money. He's probably skimming," he mumbled.

"Raymond, please."

"I'm sick of him bossing me. When's it my turn to —"

"Never," Enzo interrupted. He fell silent, presumably counting the cash.

I braced myself for the discovery, my heart like gunfire in my ears.

"It's all here."

Huh? I whipped my head around to stare at him, my mouth open. The envelope and cash were hidden somewhere already.

"May I offer you something?" Enzo asked, his face impassive. "A drink? Some champagne perhaps?"

"Don't let her say no, Enzo." Angel walked over to the sideboard laid out with glassware and bottles of booze.

"No, thank you." My voice shook. What the hell kind of game was Enzo playing? *He refuses to help me, he steals business from me — now he covers for me?*

154

"Nonsense," said Angel. "I have the best champagne in town, the real thing. Imported from France."

"She prolly never drank shampoo before," said Raymond, lumbering out of the corner.

"Champagne," Enzo corrected. "No more talking out of you."

Angel popped the cork, the noise startling me. He poured three glasses, handed one to me and one to Enzo, and kept the third for himself.

"Hey, Pop, what about me?"

"Go ask Matilda to cook me a steak dinner, Raymond. Rare. I'm ravenous."

"But how come—"

"Now, please."

Raymond shot his brother and father a nasty look as he left the room. Angel raised his glass. "A toast. To Miss O'Mara. I'm most impressed." He sipped his champagne and stared at me. After an uncomfortable pause, I sipped mine too, the bubbles fizzing down my throat. It tasted so good, I took three more quick swallows.

"Now," Angel continued, returning to his chair. "I've got business to attend to. Enzo will escort you back to the club, where I hope you and your companion will enjoy the evening."

"I believe she's unattended tonight," said Enzo.

Angel regarded me. "A pretty girl like you?"

"Yes," I said, getting to my feet. My mind was still spinning. "Uh, I want to ask about my father."

"What about him?" Angel's eyebrows rose.

"Is he all right?"

"He will be very glad to know you paid me tonight, and even gladder once you bring me the rest of the money on Friday."

My heart stopped. "Friday?" I repeated in disbelief.

"Friday." His tone was final, and his stare told me not to argue.

I was tempted to gulp down the rest of my champagne, but I left the half-drunk glass on the desk and headed for the door. Enzo followed me down the hall and into the stairwell, saying nothing as we descended one flight. His silence was maddening. Was he not going to offer an explanation? What the hell was he thinking? Finally I couldn't stand it any longer.

I whirled to face him. "Why did you lie?"

He went around me and continued down the steps, and I clambered after him, grabbing his arm.

"Why did you lie? The money wasn't all there."

He met my eyes. "Because I'm not ready for this to end. Not tonight."

I swallowed. Not ready for what to end? Was he talking about the kidnapping or something between us? "Then why wouldn't you agree to help me before?"

One side of his mouth rose. "That wouldn't have been any fun."

I dropped his arm. "This is fun for you?"

"Well, certain parts of it are fun." He came up one step so that his face hovered near mine. "Don't you think?"

I can't think with you so close to me. His dark eyes glittered, and I forgot all about ransom money, whisky, and deadlines. My breath came faster, and I felt the silk of my dress whispering across the tight, hard peaks of my breasts. Enzo lowered his gaze to watch my chest rising and falling. Then, meeting my eyes again, he lifted one hand and slowly brushed the back of his fingers over one taut nipple, poking visibly through the thin bodice of Rosie's dress. Desire sparked at the center of me and zipped through my veins like fire along a fuse.

But I wouldn't explode.

I can play this game too. With one hand I reached for the button of his coat. Slipped it through the hole. Without breaking the stare, I ran the back of my hand down the front of his trousers in the same deliberate way. But I didn't stop there—I turned my hand over and slowly moved my palm up and down, enjoying the way he sucked in his breath, the way he swayed toward me, unsteady on his feet. The way I could feel his flesh growing beneath my touch. *Now who has the power?*

I brought my lips close to his. "We should get back," I said softly as I stroked him. "Someone is waiting for you."

"Fuck," Enzo whispered, eyes closing.

My thoughts exactly.

I stepped to the side and continued down the stairs without him.

#

When I had cleared the curtain into the main room, I stopped for a second, bracing myself against the back of a chair. *Oh my God.* It felt as if steam would

rise from my skin, I was so hot. *I need to get out of here.*
Not only was I in danger of losing complete control if
Enzo and I were alone again, I had to find out what
happened to Joey and tell him about the rum shipment
tomorrow night.

I saw Rosie at the bar and headed for her,
smoothing my dress. "Hey." I tapped her shoulder.
"I'm leaving."

She turned slightly, barely enough to make eye
contact. "Oh. OK, see ya." She was about to ignore me
once more when her eyes went wide. "Criminy, who is
that?"

I wasn't surprised to hear Enzo's voice in my
ear seconds later. "Don't go." He placed a hand on the
small of my back, sending heat buzzing down my legs.
"I've decided you can't leave. Is this a friend of yours?
You should both join my party."

"Sure we will," said Rosie, turning her charm
on Enzo. "What's your name, sweetie?"

"Tiny? Will you stay?" It sounded like a
question, but the way he pinned me with his eyes and
pressed his fingers into my back made me feel
differently.

Say no. Say no. "All right. But not for too long."

He nodded to Rosie. "I'm Enzo DiFiore. You are?"

"Rosie LaChance," she said sweetly. "A real pleasure to meet you, honey."

"Ladies, follow me." We trailed him to a group of tables at the front, where a group of young people sat drinking, smoking, and hollering at their friends on the dance floor. As we approached, the brown-haired smarty from earlier narrowed her eyes at us.

"Have a seat." Enzo pulled out two empty chairs, and I lowered myself onto one, the smarty's eyes burning holes in my skin.

"Who's this, Enzo?" She had a voice like squeaky chalk on a slate.

"Ladies, this is Gina Meloni," he said, gesturing to her. "And Gina, this is Tiny O'Mara and Rosie LaChance. Tiny is doing some business with my father. These girls are our guests tonight."

Gina scowled at that. Rosie leaned over to me and winked. "Oooh. You've got competition."

"Can I have a cigarette?" I asked her. She opened her purse, took out a silver cigarette case, and handed me one. Within seconds, Enzo leaned across the table to light it for me. I almost laughed when the little flame ignited between us. Then he lowered himself into the chair next to Gina and lit his own. I watched the first curl of smoke escape his lips and crossed my legs. My thighs were damp.

"So, Tiny," Gina squeaked, looking me over as if I smelled like rotten tomatoes. "What line of business are you in?"

I puffed on my cigarette and blew smoke in her direction. "Bootleg liquor. You interested?" Enzo's lips tipped up slightly.

Gina smirked. "Ain't we all?"

"Tiny's father is a supplier for the club," said Enzo. "She works for him."

Gina's painted eyebrows went up. "Oh yeah? A working girl, huh? I don't know what I would do if I had to work. It sounds posi-lutely awful."

"Lucky for you, your dad's loaded," piped up her friend, a skinny blond with an overbite. "And now you've got a sugar daddy."

"He's twenty-five, he's not old enough to be a sugar daddy, Valerie," scolded Gina.

"Right—your last one was a lot older." They both giggled and Gina mouthed something to Valerie behind her hand. Jesus, was this high school or a nightclub? And why had he asked me to stay here, anyway? So he could keep an eye on me while he kept an arm around his girlfriend?

Bastard.

Throughout their exchange, Enzo watched me. We didn't speak, but the shared knowledge of our secret kisses and caresses hummed between us like a conversation. It was enough to start up an aching throb between my legs. *This is madness. He's just looking at me —from across the damn table!* But the longer I sat there watching him, the more I wanted him. I could still feel him thickening through his trousers in my palm. Was he hard now? Oh, God. I crossed my legs tighter and shifted in my seat, and just the friction of the movement and his penetrating stare nearly brought me to orgasm. Tapping my cigarette out in an ashtray on the table, I stood. "Thanks for the invitation to stay, but I really have to leave now."

Immediately Enzo was on his feet. "I'll walk you out."

An unwelcome frisson of excitement shot up my spine.

Gina pouted, and he put a hand on her shoulder. "Order another round of drinks for everyone, and how about some oysters too? I know they're your favorites." She squealed and clapped her hands like a child while he placed his lit Fatima in the ashtray, as if he'd be back momentarily. Then the bastard leaned down and kissed her cheek.

Rosie barely glanced away from her mark and waved me off with a flip of the wrist. I trailed Enzo through the club and down the long hallway toward the heavy metal door. Our footsteps echoed on the tiles as the sound of the music receded.

The guard seated at the entrance nodded at Enzo and pressed a button, which unlocked the inner door. To my surprise, after opening it, Enzo followed me into the tiny vestibule. Then he let the door close, leaving us in the pitch-dark.

Silence.

Adrenaline shot through me as I waited for him to open the door to the stairwell. Instead, I heard the slam of a deadbolt.

"You don't really want to leave, do you?" His voice was low and lilting.

He's teasing me. "Yes. I do."

"Liar." He moved closer.

Every inch of my skin pricked with heat. "Look who's calling who names. I can think of a few to call you, you know."

His body met mine and he pressed my back into the brick wall. "So do it."

I dropped my evening bag to the floor. "Thief."

He took one wrist and pinned it above my head.

"Cheat," I snarled.

He pinned the other across the first.

"Bastard." The word lashed from my lips just before he kissed me, and I could have sworn it made him smile.

Out of my mind with desire, I kissed him hungrily, straining against him, desperate to have my arms free. But he held my wrists tight, torturing me with deep thrusts of his tongue between my lips. "Let me go," I rasped when he dragged his mouth across my cheek and down my neck.

"Why would I do that?"

"Because I want to touch you."

He paused for a second before letting my right arm go. The left he kept pinned above my head.

"How's that?"

Breathing hard, I swept my right hand up the inside of his leg and smiled—he was hard. I stroked him like I had in the stairwell, my pulse kicking up as he brought his mouth back to mine. Determined to have the real thing, I opened his coat, pulled his shirt from his trousers, and slipped enough buttons through their holes to slide my hand down against tight, hot skin. Wrapping my hand around his cock, I kept my grasp loose at first, allowing him to slip easily through my fingers. When I felt his breath coming harder and faster on my lips, I tightened my grip, further aroused by his moan of pleasure. His hold on my wrist weakened, and he braced himself against the wall. *I'm doing this. I'm bringing him to this.* The surge of power was intoxicating.

But just when I thought he was over the edge, Enzo pulled up my dress and hitched up my right leg, hooking my knee around his hip and holding it there. I had to throw my arms across his shoulders to stay balanced on the toes of my left foot. Our insatiable mouths came together again as his other hand snuck under the loose edge of my step-in. I gasped when he brushed the sensitive skin beneath the lace, and panted softly when he slipped one fingertip inside me. Shallow, feather-light strokes left me breathless and immobile. Clutching the back of his neck, I thought my left leg would give out with the unbearable pleasure of his touch. My breath stilled as he slid the fingertip up to rub the tiny spot that made my belly tighten and my legs tremble. His tongue slipped into my open mouth as his wet finger traced soft little circles. A divine pressure began building deep within me.

Oh my God oh my God oh my God...

"Still want to leave?" he asked.

"I'm going to scream," I whimpered, fisting my hands in his coat.

He bit my lower lip. "Good."

He wants me to scream. He wants me to lose control first. He wants all the power.

Summoning every ounce of strength I had, I dropped my leg to the floor and let go of him. "On second thought, I don't think I'll give you the satisfaction." Because I was panting so hard, my words didn't have quite the sting I wanted.

"Oh no? And why's that?" He brought his arms to the wall again, boxing me in.

"Because this is all a game to you. And it's my life."

I waited for him to spout some nonsense about life being a game, but he didn't. After a pause, he dropped his arms and backed off. Although I still couldn't see anything, I sensed movement and figured he was buttoning his pants.

"I'll pay you the six hundred dollars as soon as I get it."

"Fine."

"Are you going to tell your father I was short?"

"Not tonight."

My heart thumped an irregular beat. "What does that mean? You might tell him tomorrow?"

Enzo sighed. "I do a lot of things well, Tiny, which you would know if you ever let us finish what we start, but not even I am good at divining the future. I have no idea how I'll feel about this tomorrow."

Rage shook my body. "You can't keep doing this! Kissing me one minute and then making threats the next! You went behind my back and stole Al Murphy's business from me, making it impossible for me to get the ransom money, and tonight you play the hero?"

"It seems to me you're playing some games of your own as well." His tone had gone serious, and he threw the deadbolt with a loud, angry thwack. When he opened the outer door, streetlight spilled into our private little space. "Now if you'll excuse me, I should get back to my table."

I scooped up my purse where it had fallen and rushed up the steps two at a time. My heels clicked on the cement as I hurried through steam rising from the street without turning my head.

The metal door closed behind me with a bang.

Chapter Ten

I drove home in a fog, my hands shaking on the steering wheel and my legs nearly numb with shock. What had I done? What was I thinking? No good could possibly come of fooling around with Enzo like that. My father was trapped somewhere at the mercy of the DiFiores—had I lost my mind? What was wrong with me? One minute I hated Enzo, and the next minute I couldn't keep my hands off him. Yes, he'd lied to protect me tonight, but I had the feeling that was more about his desire and amusement than his guilt or sympathy. He could rat me out any time he felt like it. And handsome as he was, I had no idea if he was one of the good guys. He was partly responsible for my father's suffering, wasn't he? He'd lured me into Angel's trap, hadn't he? Stolen my business? And he had a girl he was betraying every time we were alone, whether I liked her or not.

But when I was in bed later that night, it wasn't his faults or transgressions I thought about as my hands wandered over my yearning body. No one had ever made me feel so free and yet so restrained, so powerful and yet vulnerable, so delirious with pleasure and ache all at once. It was too much—his magnetism clouded my judgment worse than any alcohol I'd ever tasted. I had to stay away from him. I had to pay him back, and forget his existence. Forget about how he touched me here—I brushed my fingers over one breast—and here—I ran a hand up my inner thigh —and here—I placed my palm between my legs and pressed with the heel of my hand, trying to relieve the tension that had settled there since I'd pushed Enzo away.

Stop it! This isn't helping!

But I couldn't stop—I thought about his broad shoulders and hooded eyes and sculpted lips and whisky kisses and talented fingers and the way my hands wrapped around his hard—

Crack!

I sat upright, my heart pounding. What the hell was that?

Crack!

Crack!

Something was hitting my windowpane. In the few seconds of silence that followed, I swung my legs over the side of the bed and got to my hands and knees.

Crack!

Someone is throwing rocks at the glass, I realized as I crawled toward the wall. *Damn Joey for not getting me a gun!* The window was open at the bottom. Curling my fingers over the ledge, I pulled myself up and peeked through the screen into the dark yard. A sliver of moon lit the figure on the grass beneath me.

I recognized it.

"Stop!" I yelled in the angriest whisper I could muster.

"Tiny, thank God." Joey's shoulders slumped.

"You're a little late!"

"I'm sorry—can I come in?"

"No. The girls will wake up."

"Please. I have to talk to you." He touched his forehead. "And I think I need something for my head."

Squinting, I realized that blood was dripping down one of his cheeks. "Jesus! OK. Go to the kitchen door."

I threw on my robe and tiptoed into the hall, making sure my sisters' bedroom door was shut tight before descending the stairs two at a time. In the kitchen I unlocked the door and opened it, sucking in my breath at the sight of Joey on the stoop, battered to hell and holding his hand to his head. Angry as I was at him for leaving me to the wolves, pity squeezed my heart.

I pulled him into the kitchen, which still smelled like burnt bacon. Turning on the light over the table, I set him in a chair and looked him over with a critical eye. His face was marked with a couple minor scrapes and a nasty cut under one eye. A big ugly welt was swelling at his temple, and a jagged slice just above it oozed blood. His hair on that side was matted with blood, and his clothing was soiled too. But the wounds appeared superficial, and I didn't believe he needed stitches. "What happened to you?"

"I ran into some trouble." He grabbed my forearms. "What happened with Angel?"

I pursed my lips and pulled my arms away. "After waiting an hour for you on the street, I had to give Angel an envelope that was six hundred light." I went to the sink and scrubbed my hands to the elbow, soaking the sleeves of my thin summer robe. Briefly I considered taking it off, but I was only wearing a flimsy chemise underneath. And no underwear. *It stays on.*

"And?"

I dried my hands on a dishtowel and went to the pantry for the first aid kit. "And I handled it."

Eventually I'd tell him what happened—with the money, anyway—but I wanted to look at his injuries first.

Setting the small metal box on the table, I retrieved a clean towel and wet it. "Now hold still." Gently, I tilted his head and dabbed at the blood on his face.

"Ow. I can do it myself." He tried to grab the towel, but I held it away from him.

"Be quiet! I'll do it." Staring him down until he dropped his arm, I returned the wet cloth to his cheek.

He sniffed. "You burn something in here?"

"Yeah. Dinner." When he grinned, I frowned at him. "I said hold still. Where were you tonight?"

"I went with Sam and a few guys to collect at a couple different places. One asshole didn't want to pay, and he had some friends. Ow!"

"Sorry." Easing up on the pressure, I wiped his skin clean of blood, holding his thick matted hair back with the other hand. I leaned closer to examine the slice on his temple. "What was the weapon?"

"A broken bottle."

I sighed. "That'll do it." Reaching into the kit for a cotton swab and some iodine, I dotted some along each of the cuts on his face, rolling my eyes when he winced at the sting. After putting a bandage over the bottle cut, I rinsed the towel. Wringing it out, I returned to him and wiped some of the dirt and blood from his hair and neck. "You're a mess."

"Thanks. You know, I could do this myself."

"Shut up already. Coat off."

He shrugged out of his brown jacket and pulled his gun from the back of his pants, laying it on the table. Gooseflesh spread across my arms.

"My God, Joey. You're lucky *they* didn't have guns! I've got no experience with bullet wounds."

"They did have guns," he said. "But nobody was willing to shoot first tonight."

Tomorrow night could be another story.

I clenched my jaw. Would Joey have to participate in the rum heist? I hoped he wouldn't, but something told me he would insist on it, the idiot. I moved in front of him and stood between his open knees, running the wet cloth under his chin and behind his ears. His shirt was already loose at the collar, but I undid another button to wipe the back of his neck.

"Somehow I pictured this moment differently, you undressing me. But I do like your outfit." He was staring at my chest, his wicked grin in place.

I looked down and noticed my belt had come loose and my robe was hanging open. "Enough." I slapped the cloth onto the table and tightened my robe again. "Or I'll beat you myself."

He laughed, clutching his ribs. "Ouch. Don't make me laugh."

"Take a few punches in the gut, did you?"

"One or two." He looked up at me quickly. "But I gave as good as I got."

"I'm sure you did." I backed up. "Now take off your shirt."

"Removing my pants would be more fun, don't you think?" He stood and slipped both braces from his shoulders at once.

"Jesus. Will you stop? I want to check for bruises."

"Sorry." He tugged his shirt from his pants and began unbuttoning it. "It's actually a relief to hear you razzing me. I was worried about you tonight."

I ignored the tug in my chest at his words and the quickening in my stomach when he took off his shirt. Underneath it he wore a white, athletic-style tank that hugged his chest and torso. His shoulders and biceps were thick and defined with hard curves, and I was tempted to touch them.

Stop it, you're the nurse here. And this is pain-in-the-ass Joey, not Enzo.

But I was still worked up from tonight's episodes of sexual frustration, and Joey was right here in my kitchen. And probably willing.

The thought unnerved me. "Take off your undershirt too," I snapped.

"Yes, ma'am." He grabbed it from the back and yanked it over his head. "Are you going to be this crabby when you're a real nurse?" he asked as I circled him, checking for bruises or other abrasions.

"Only with problem patients like yourself." But the problem was me—or at least my reaction to him. His chest was as muscular as his arms, and the lines on his abdomen made my insides flutter. I resisted the craving to run my hands over them and instead examined a red and purple patch of skin on his left shoulder blade. "Deep breaths." He did as I asked, without wincing. "OK. You'll hurt for a while, but nothing looks serious. Let me see your hands."

He held them out, and oddly, it was the sight of his hands that finally proved too much—I had to touch them. I ran my fingers over each one, saddened at the cuts and swollen knuckles. Images of them working in the moonlight flickered in my mind. "Wash them." I pointed toward the sink. He soaped and rinsed his hands while I stared at his naked back, watching the muscles flex. *It would be so easy. I could go up behind him, press my breasts against his back, run my hands around to his stomach, lay my cheek on his warm skin.* I swayed to the side before catching my balance and grimacing.

What was with me tonight?

Turning around as he dried off, he asked, "Now can you tell me what happened at the club?" He set the towel aside and picked up his undershirt from the table, and I was grateful when his chest disappeared under the white cotton. The last thing I needed was to mess around with Joey right in the middle of this. Even if his body was swoon-inducing.

"Like I said, I walked into Angel's office with an envelope that was six hundred bucks short." I sat as far as I could from him, on the opposite side of the table.

"What did he do?" He grabbed his blue shirt and shrugged into the sleeves, but left it unbuttoned when he sat down.

"He handed it to Enzo, who counted it and said it was all there."

Joey's wide mouth fell open. "You're kidding me. Enzo covered for you?" He grimaced. "Now you owe him. You don't ever want to owe these guys a favor," he scolded, like it was my fault Enzo had lied about the money.

"Thanks for the tip, but I didn't ask him for a favor. He just did it."

"Nobody just does a favor like that in this business. He must want something."

Damn right he does. I blushed under Joey's menacing stare but said nothing.

"Who else was there? Did it look like Angel had a lot of muscle?"

"Guarding every room," I said, glad to move off the topic of Enzo's want. "The only other guy I recognized was his son Raymond. And Raymond's friend Harry. Don't know his last name."

Joey scowled. "Coupla idiots, both of them. Nasty mean streaks, though." He rubbed his chin, which was shadowed with whiskers. "You hear anything about the rum?"

"Yeah. Raymond said it's tomorrow night."

Joey blinked at me. "Raymond? How'd you get him to do that?"

"Hidden talent, remember?" At his shocked expression, I said, "Don't worry. I didn't have to do anything drastic. A little flattery goes a long way with a guy like that."

He didn't look convinced but let it go. "All right." Standing, he buttoned his shirt. "I gotta go tell Sam."

"Right now?" I checked the kitchen clock. "It's two in the morning! You're hurt and you need rest!"

He tucked in the shirt and stuck his gun back into his pants. "I'm fine. Thanks for the help, and I'm sorry I didn't show tonight."

"Turns out I didn't need you." Anger bubbled to the surface of my skin, hot and itchy. Why was he choosing to put himself at the center of this mess when he didn't have to? It's not like he didn't have other options—his mother ran a boarding house with a restaurant. He could work for her, or for Henry fucking Ford, or for anyone with a legitimate business where he wouldn't have to carry a gun above his ass!

He reached for his jacket. "Are you all right here by yourself?"

"What difference does it make?"

As he shoved his left arm through the sleeve, he winced a little. "Because I can come back."

I crossed my arms, jerking my chin at him. "Forget it. I don't need you."

He looked at me, his expression a mix of apology and irritation. "Yes, you do. I'll negotiate with Sam so you can make your money this week." Digging into his coat pocket, he pulled out a stack of bills and tossed it on the table. "Here. Pay Enzo back. Immediately."

I stared at the money on the table, wishing I didn't have to accept it. How badly I wanted to tell him to take his cash and his gun and his stupidity and go jump in the lake! But I had no promise from Enzo that he wouldn't tell his father I'd been short. Better to pay him than to risk Daddy's life. "The whisky I couldn't sell is at the boathouse," I told Joey. "It's yours."

"No. You need to sell that whisky. This money's just a loan until your pop's back." I opened my mouth to argue but he held up his hand and raised his voice. "Enough backtalk. You're gonna take that and pay Enzo off, and then we'll figure out how to get the next five G's, *capisce*?"

Without thinking, I raised my voice too. "I really hate it when you tell me what to do like that. I'm not a child!"

He dropped his hand. "I don't think you're a child."

"Tiny?" The small voice at the kitchen doorway made us both jump.

"Hey, kiddo," Joey said softly.

"Mary Grace, what are you doing up?"

"I heard noises, and I was scared." She rubbed one side of her head, where her hair was twisty and matted. When she's nervous about something or can't sleep, she twirls her hair in the same spot, which gives her tangles that take forever to comb out. "What happened to your face, Joey?"

"I'm clumsy as heck, that's what happened. I opened the door of my car too quickly, and smack!" He mimed the door hitting him in the face. "Right in the kisser!" Mary Grace giggled. "Your big sister the nurse was helping me get it bandaged up." He leaned toward her and whispered. "But she's awful bossy about it."

Mary Grace smiled. "She *is* bossy."

"OK, that's enough. Back to bed now." Taking Mary Grace by the shoulders, I turned her toward the hall.

She looked up at Joey. "My Daddy isn't here. Are you staying for the rest of the night?" The hope in her voice was undeniable, and I realized she wanted him to stay—she probably felt better having a man in the house. My heart sank to the bottom of my chest.

He glanced at me. "Well, I have to go someplace right now, but maybe I'll come back."

"Good," she said. Then she looked at me. "I miss Daddy."

"He'll be home soon, honey." God, I hoped that was the truth. "Now go on upstairs. I'll be up in a minute."

"Can I sleep in your bed tonight?" With her worried blue eyes on me, I couldn't say no.

"OK, just this once. Scoot." I swatted her backside lightly and sent her down the hall. The stairs creaked as she went up.

"She's scared, poor thing," Joey said softly.

I nodded and turned off the light, my throat closing. "She's not the only one." When I started for the back door, Joey stopped me with a hand on the shoulder. My heart began to beat faster. *I shouldn't have turned off the light.*

"I won't let anything happen to you," he whispered. "Or to them."

How badly I wanted to believe him. "You can't tell the future."

"I'm not talking about telling the future. I'm making you a promise."

My throat was too tight for words.

"I'll be back tonight."

I struggled to speak. "Do you...do you want a key?"

"Yes."

I retrieved our extra house key from a pantry shelf. When I handed it to him, our fingers brushed, and I pulled mine away quickly.

"Thanks. Now try to get some sleep."

"Won't be easy with Mary Grace in my bed. She kicks," I said, feeling the need to make a joke.

"You can always come down and sleep on the sofa with me. I can't promise to keep my hands to myself, but I won't kick you."

I love your hands. "Joey?"

"Yeah?" He swayed slightly closer to me.

"You better go."

Chapter Eleven

I woke the next morning to the sound of music and the smell of frying sausage. Breathing deeply, I stretched, checked the clock, and blinked in surprise. After nine already? It was hard to believe I'd slept that long, considering everything that happened last night, but for the first time this week I felt somewhat rested. The spot next to me was empty except for Mary Grace's stuffed bear, so I pulled on my robe and headed down the stairs, hoping Molly had put coffee on with whatever they were scrounging up for breakfast.

First thing, I need to get those forty bottles sold, place another order, and--

I stopped short at the doorway to the kitchen, my mouth falling open.

Joey stood at the counter with a red apron over his clothes, stirring something in a mixing bowl. Molly was pouring coffee, and Mary Grace sat on top of the kitchen table nibbling a sausage patty. Someone had turned up the radio in the front room, and Henry

Burr's throaty Irish tenor filled the air. I pulled my robe tighter around me.

"She wakes!" shouted Joey. He wiped his hands on the apron and faced me. "And she looks funny in the morning. I didn't know a girl's hair could stick out that way."

The girls giggled as I tried to smooth my wayward hair. "What are you doing?"

"I'm making breakfast, although it's not easy with the scarcity of groceries in this house. For cryin' out loud, Tiny, no wonder your growth is stunted!" My sisters screeched with laughter while I frowned.

"So what are you making then?"

"Well, when I saw the bare cupboards and the poor hungry children living here, I ran down to Bridget's and begged for food. Mary Grace helped me fry the sausage, Molly made coffee, and now I'm making pancakes." He gestured toward the mixing bowl.

"You know how to make pancakes?"

He rolled his eyes. "It's not hard, Tiny. You measure, mix, and throw them on the griddle." He'd removed the bandage from his temple. The welt had gone down but the jagged cut above it looked red and angry. He was still wearing his clothing from last night, although he'd wet his hair in an effort to neaten it.

"Joey said he'd teach me how to make spaghetti sauce this afternoon," said Molly, beaming as she sat down at the table.

"Gravy," he corrected. "And I have to get some ingredients first, so that won't be till later. We'll make supper." He turned on the gas under a cast iron skillet and threw a hunk of butter in it. As it melted and sizzled, Joey stirred the batter and sang along with Henry, loudly and totally off key.

"Lord, Joey, that's awful." Molly put her hands to her ears. "You're worse than Tiny, and she's pretty bad."

I shot her an evil eye and crossed my arms. Something about the scene was throwing me off-kilter, but I couldn't put my finger on what it was.

"Can I pour the batter on?" Mary Grace pleaded, hopping off the table. She grabbed the ladle from a drawer.

"Sure. Come here." Joey let her stand in front of him and put his hands over hers, one on the ladle and one on the edge of the bowl. "Now, scoop some...and carefully bring it over to the skillet...then dump it in." He guided her arms and she managed to do it without dripping any batter on the floor or counter. I watched his hands over hers and felt a ridiculous pang of envy, but I also felt a ripple of warmth. It was good to see my sisters laughing, unaware of the trouble brewing outside their door.

"I need to get dressed," I said, backing out of the room. Ascending the stairs slowly, I put a hand over my stomach and wondered why it felt so unsettled. The girls were safe, they didn't know anything was amiss with Daddy, and I was halfway to making the ransom. I'd gotten the information Sam wanted, and Joey had said he'd negotiate with Sam. Maybe he'd even let me buy some of the stolen rum. I dropped my hand, my shoulders straightening up. *Yes, that's it.* Authentic rum was a rarity around here—our regular customers might not need more whisky yet, but perhaps they'd be willing to buy something more exotic.

Relieved for the moment, I decided I'd take a bath and wash my hair before dressing. I locked the bathroom door and turned on the water, letting it run over my hand as it warmed up. Tonight I'd go back to the club and deliver the six hundred to Enzo. I was thinking about buying a new dress to wear when a jolt of good sense struck me.

You're supposed to stay away from him, remember? It shouldn't matter what you look like—you're going to give him the money and get out.

I put the stopper in the drain and let the tub fill. Dropping my robe and nightgown to the floor, I climbed in and stretched out in the warm water. I could still hear the music from downstairs, and Joey's off-key baritone carried too. Humming along, I ran my hands over my stomach and small breasts. They'd taken forever to grow beyond walnut-size but they were a little bigger now, maybe half-an-orange-sized. I squeezed them gently, and when my nipples beaded I circled my palms over them lightly. *I'm going to hell for this.* But I closed my eyes and imagined the hands were someone else's.

#

By the time I was dressed, my hair neat and dry, the girls had finished eating and the dishes were done. "I don't believe it," I said, pouring myself a cup of coffee. "I didn't even hear any yelling down here."

"They never complained once." Joey had taken off the apron and was seated in a chair at the table, tilting its legs back. "Just did them without being asked, then disappeared out the back door."

"Where'd they go?"

He looked blank and let the chair's front legs hit the floor. "Oops—I didn't ask."

"It's all right. They can't get far." I took a seat next to him.

"Are you hungry?" He slid a plate of pancakes and sausage across the checkered tablecloth.

"Mmm, thanks." I picked up the maple syrup and poured some on. "How's your head this morning?"

"It's OK."

"What did Sam say last night?" I asked, cutting into the pancakes.

"He won't bother you this week."

"Good." I swallowed a syrupy bite, savoring its sweetness. "What about the rum?"

He brought his cup to his lips and took a long swallow before answering. "We wait at the tracks for the shipment and steal it. Or maybe hijack them on the road back. Sam hasn't decided yet."

Laying down the fork, I pushed the plate away from me, appetite gone. "Should I expect you back here at two in the morning again? Perhaps with a bullet in your chest?"

He kept his eyes on his coffee. "Don't worry about it. You gonna give that money to the cake-eater tonight?"

"I suppose so."

"Don't go to the club alone." He drank again. "I wish we knew where they were keeping your pop. You think he's there in the building somewhere?"

"Enzo said he wasn't."

Joey rolled his eyes. "And we all know Enzo's on the level."

My face got hot. "I'm just telling you what he said."

"Well, as far as I'm concerned, that guy's word is worth less than a load of pig shit. I told you not to trust him."

"I don't trust anybody!"

"Not even me?" His tone dared me to admit it.

I swallowed.

"You don't."

Staring at his scraped-up hands holding the cup, I said, "I'm just scared."

"Look at me."

I lifted my eyes to his.

"I made you a promise last night. I intend to keep it."

"But you're going to that hijacking tonight, and if you're shot or—"

"Nothing will happen to me."

"Vince probably said the same thing to Bridget before he left for the police station that day." It was out before I even realized I was comparing us to my sister and her husband.

He took a deep breath before speaking. "That was different. Vince and those guys were totally unprepared. They got ambushed. We're planning things carefully and they don't know we're coming."

"That's an ambush," I pointed out. "Just as many people could wind up dead. And what if Angel somehow figures out it was me who told you guys when the rum would be here?"

Joey shook his head. "He won't. Far as he knows, there's no connection between you and the River Gang."

"*You're* the connection. He met you at the club, remember?" I recalled how Angel had reacted upon hearing Joey's name. "Maybe he remembers your father."

"Angel's not gonna be at the tracks tonight," Joey said irritably, getting up from the table. "You think he drives his own trucks?" He set his coffee cup in the sink.

"Enzo met you too."

He spun around. "Enzo won't be driving the trucks either," he snapped, his face reddening with anger. "Those two fucking dandies don't do the heavy lifting. And even if he is there, we'll have masks on, so he won't be able to recognize me."

Masks. Oh, God. "Joey, please let them steal the rum without you. You don't have to do this gang stuff —you could get a regular job."

"A regular job?" He said it as if I'd suggested he ingest mustard gas for fun. "A regular job? You know who drives the nice cars in my neighborhood, Tiny? You know who has the fancy clothes, the big bankroll, the nicest houses?"

Of course I did—men with Cadillacs and bodyguards who carried machine guns. Men who had apartments in high-rises. Slick custom suits. *Hooded eyes and beautiful lips.* "Yes."

"Well, I'll be damned if I spend sixty hours a week on an assembly line for a few bucks a day just to make rent. Other schmucks can sweat blood working those jobs, but not me." The cut on his temple started to bleed. "And you wouldn't do it either."

"Yes, I would. It's honest work. And anyone can make his way up." Standing, I picked up a clean napkin and reached to dab the blood on his head, but he backed away from my hand.

"Ha. That's a movie. And here's the thing about the movies, Tiny. They make you want things." He poked his chest. "I'm gonna get those things."

I pitched the napkin onto the table. "You're gonna end up like your father, Joey! These aren't toy guns you guys carry around. It's dangerous!"

"Now who's treating who like a child?"

I opened my mouth and snapped it shut again. Why the hell was I arguing with him? What was the point? And why was I suddenly so terrified for his safety, for his future?

"I'm sorry you're scared." His voice was low but firm. "But I'm going. And whatever I make off the heist tonight, I'll share with you. You need me to be there."

My gaze leveled his. "Don't say you're doing this for me."

"I'm not doing this for you."

I'd sort of hoped he might argue with me.

#

I usually worked for Bridget on Wednesdays since it was Martin's day off, but when I checked in with her at the store, she said she could get along without me for the day. Something in her expression stopped me from rushing out, though. I waited until the store was clear of shoppers to ask about it.

"What's with the shifty eyes? Are there cops sniffing around?"

"No." She chewed her lip as she straightened boxes of chewing gum and penny candy on the counter.

"Then what?"

She faced me. "Where's Daddy? Has he even called?"

My stomach dropped. "Yeah, last night. He got some work down in Ohio, fixing up cars. I told him he might as well stay and make the money. The girls and I are fine."

"Joey spent the night at the house, I hear."

"Yeah. He hurt his head on his car door and thought I'd play nurse for him. I didn't think he should drive home with the injury. He was feeling dizzy." The lies rolled from my tongue like Model T's off the line.

"I saw his head. Looks like it hurts." She picked up a dust cloth and began wiping down the wood, eyebrows lifted.

"What, Bridget?"

"Well, one day you can't stand him, a few days later he's sleeping at your house with Daddy out of town. If the neighbors saw..."

I rolled my eyes. "Who the hell cares about the neighbors? We're friends."

"Last week he was a pain in the ass, now he's your friend." She looked up at me out of the corner of one eye. "He's not the boy you told me about kissing, is he?"

"No!" I shouted. But my cheeks burned as I recalled kissing him on the boat. "He's Joey, for cryin' out loud!"

She put her palms toward me. "OK, OK. If you say so. It's just that I've noticed a difference in him when he talks about you, that's all."

"Well, you can forget it. He annoys me just as much as he always has, maybe more. Now if you're done with the inquisition into my virtue, which I assure you is still intact, I'm going to box up a few groceries for home and run some errands."

She set the cloth aside and grabbed a box for me, but I felt her watchful eye while I chose some things to bring home. *Please, God, let this be over soon*, I prayed. The longer Daddy was gone, the harder it was for me to keep the truth from my sisters.

And what the hell did she mean about noticing a difference in the way Joey talks about me?

#

After dropping the food off at home, I went to the bakery to see Evelyn. I felt awful about leaving her behind last night and wanted to make it up to her. She took a break and sat with me at a small wrought iron café table on the sidewalk in front, bringing me a cinnamon bun and cup of coffee. For once the temperature wasn't so high, and the humidity was down. Sitting out in the sunshine actually felt good. "Thanks. This looks delicious."

"It is," she assured me.

I dug in, polishing off the entire bun in a few minutes. "So," I said, licking the icing from my fingers, "how would you like to go to Club 23 tonight?" I figured I'd have a better chance of staying out of trouble with Enzo if she was there.

Her face lit up. "Really? I'd love to!"

"Great. Hey, do you want to come over for supper too?"

She looked dubious. "What are you making?"

"Joey's making spaghetti. He's giving Molly a cooking lesson, supposedly."

"Joey cooks?"

"His mother runs a restaurant, so maybe she taught him." I dotted my finger in the crumbs on my plate and brought them to my mouth. "Hey Evvy, you don't know anyone that needs any whisky, do you? I'm sitting on forty bottles I need to get rid of."

"Hmmmm." She thought for a moment, chewing on her full bottom lip. "You know, the

Andersons just picked up a huge order here for their daughter's wedding. Maybe they need some."

"Would you...would you mind giving me their phone number or address so I can contact them?" I hated asking her, but I was desperate.

"I'll do better than that. Mother is pretty friendly with Mrs. Anderson, and I know she'd be glad to do you the favor."

"Really? Oh, Evelyn! Tell your mother how grateful we are." I glanced through the front window of the bakery, where Mrs. LaChance was ringing up a customer. "Did Rosie tell you about Daddy?"

"No." She looked concerned. "Is everything OK?"

I paused. "Can you keep a secret?"

It felt good to confide in Evelyn. I trusted her, and I needed someone besides Joey to tell me things would be all right. Leaving out only the parts where I got romantic with Enzo, I told her everything. Her eyes got wider and wider, and finally she grabbed my hand and squeezed, tears filling her eyes. "Oh, Tiny," she moaned softly. "How awful!"

"It is," I agreed. "But they promised not to hurt him as long as I got the ransom to them by their deadline."

She sniffed. "You can do it. I know you can. And I'll help you."

"Thanks."

"I should get back to work, but I'll call you as soon as I talk to Mother. There might be other parties needing liquor too. Should I ask her?"

Hope flooded my veins. "Yes. Evvy, you're the best. Thank you."

#

Evelyn called not two hours after I got home. She said the Andersons would take two cases, and if I'd part with the rest of the bottles for two hundred dollars, her mother would buy them from me and sell them out the back door of the bakery. She was sure she could get rid of them quickly with all the June weddings and parties, and while she didn't want to go into the bootlegging business, she was glad to do a favor for Daddy just this once.

"Sold," I said, my heart swelling with gratitude. I went to the boathouse, loaded up, and delivered to the Andersons' home on Beverly Road as well as the bakery's back door. With over five hundred dollars in my pocket, I felt almost light-hearted as we drove back to my house.

"I can't believe I'm going to that club tonight," Evelyn said, twisting her hands together. "We'll need to go to my house after supper so I can pick out something to wear. Your clothes aren't going to fit me."

"We'll have time, don't worry."

Joey's car was on the street in front of my house. When we walked in the front door, the aroma that greeted us sent my head spinning. Onions and garlic and tomatoes and sausage and something else—maybe oregano or rosemary? I wasn't good at identifying herbs, but whatever it was, my stomach groaned in anticipation. In the kitchen, Joey stood with an apron-clad Molly at the stove, watching her stir. "Yeah, break up those tomatoes a little bit. Good." He looked up when we entered the room. "Hope you're hungry, girls."

"Joey, that smells delicious!" said Evelyn. "Can we help you?"

"Why don't you two put together a salad from the vegetables I brought? They're in bags on the table."

"We'd be glad to." Evelyn smiled at Joey in a way that reminded me of Rosie, and when he turned back to the stove, she looked at me and fanned her face. I rolled my eyes, even though I secretly agreed. There was something very attractive about a man who knew what he was doing in the kitchen. Especially when he looked like Joey.

While Evelyn unpacked the bags, I washed my hands and listened as Joey instructed Molly to get the cinnamon and sugar from the pantry.

"You put cinnamon in spaghetti sauce?" I asked, surprised.

"Yes. And we call it *gravy*," he said, swatting my behind with a spatula, "which none of you Irish girls seem to understand."

I smiled, glad he was back to teasing me. "Gravy goes on meat and potatoes. What you're making is for noodles, so we call it sauce." I bumped his hip with mine.

"Noodles!" he exclaimed. "My ma's homemade mostaccioli ain't noodles. Do you know what I had to say to get her to let me have some?"

I laughed as I dried my hands. "No, what?"

"Let's just say I had to make a promise I'm not sure I can keep."

"About what?"

"Grandchildren." He shook his head and muttered something in Italian. "And she says she's gonna light candles for me at church, so if I lied to her, the Virgin Mary will punish me."

"Then I'll pray for you." Crossing myself, I set the towel down and looked at Evelyn, who was watching us with a confused expression on her face. I turned to the cabinets and pulled a large mixing bowl down so she wouldn't see me blush. "Here, let's use this for the salad."

"All right." Evelyn's voice was hesitant, as if she felt unsure of herself. "I'll...I'll peel the carrots if you want to tear up the lettuce."

"Sure." I got to work at the table while she stood at the counter. While I worked I snuck a few glances at Joey's back as he talked Molly through adding a little red wine—which he'd brought—and then salt, pepper, oregano, basil, cinnamon, and sugar to the sauce. He was fully clothed, of course, but I couldn't help picturing his back like I'd seen it last night, naked and muscular. As I tossed the lettuce into the bowl, I thought about some girl's hands clutching at those muscles, maybe sliding down to grip his hips as he moved over her. My belly hollowed just thinking of it, and I brought my feet primly together. But I wondered...what would that feel like? Would Joey be gentle or rough? What would his skin smell like? *Probably garlic and tomatoes tonight.* I lowered my face to hide a smile, but when I imagined how he might put his hands on the girl, it slid right off my lips. I didn't like thinking about his hands on anyone. I didn't want to know about their capacity for tenderness, or for violence.

Liar.

I looked at him again and found him studying me. He averted his eyes quickly and cleared his throat. "Do you want a glass of wine?"

"Yes. Pour one for Evelyn too. She deserves it for helping me sell forty bottles of whiskey today." I smiled gratefully at her. "Actually, she practically sold them by herself."

"Yeah?" Joey smiled as he handed her a tumbler of wine. "Good for you."

Evelyn's cheeks pinkened. "It was nothing."

Joey poured two more and handed one to me. "Salut." Lifting his glass, he leaned toward me and spoke low. "Here's to a big night."

We tipped our glasses, eyes on one another.

Chapter Twelve

We ate by candlelight, with an ivory linen tablecloth underneath matching plates and the radio playing softly in the front room. The meal was delicious, and I was more ravenous than I'd been in weeks, maybe months. The wine took the edge off my nerves, but I kept finding it difficult not to look at Joey, who sat across from me. I'd never noticed how long his eyelashes were, or the sweet way he closed his eyes during grace before meals.

That is the wine talking. Eat your goddamn dinner and get upstairs.

But I could have sworn I caught him looking at me once or twice too.

When everyone had finished, the girls and Evelyn started on the dishes while I said goodbye to Joey. "Be careful tonight," I told him at the door. "And let me know as soon as you can how everything went."

"You be careful too. I know he's good-looking, Tiny, but he's one of them."

I narrowed my eyes. "Look who's talking. I don't need any lectures from you, pal. Except maybe on cooking."

"Ain't that the truth." He pulled his cap from his back pocket and slapped my shoulder with it before setting it on his head. "See you."

I watched him jog to his car and said a quick prayer for his safety.

#

When the dishes were done, Evelyn and I went up to my bedroom so I could change. "Tiny, what the hell?" she burst out as soon as I shut the door.

"What?" From my closet I took out the blue dress, holding it at arm's length to check for wrinkles.

"You and Joey, that's what!" She plopped down on my bed. "It's completely obvious."

I pressed the dress to my body and looked in the mirror over my dresser. My cheeks were flushed from the wine. "There is no me and Joey."

"Yet."

"Ever."

She looked at me in the mirror. "Why not? He's gorgeous. He's sweet. He cooks."

Because I've already had my hands on another gangster's cock. "Mmmm, supper was good, wasn't it? I don't remember when I've eaten so much."

"Yes, it was, although I don't know how you two got any eating done the way you kept stopping to stare at each other."

I turned to her, lowering the dress. "Evelyn, stop it. I'm not interested in Joey."

"You think you're not, but I know you. You are." She crossed her arms, watching me lay the dress on the bed. "And I think you should do it."

"Do what?" I opened a dresser drawer and began pulling out my undergarments.

"You know what. I would."

I glanced at her over my shoulder. "So you do it."

She sighed. "I would do it with him in a heartbeat if I thought he was interested. But he's only got eyes for you."

"You're mistaken." I lifted my black stockings from the drawer. "We can hardly stand each other. And besides, I've got eyes for someone else right now." I held up my step-in and gave it a little shake. "Someone who knows what I wear underneath that blue dress."

Evelyn gasped. "Tell!"

"I will, and I'll even introduce you to him tonight, if he's there." I tossed everything onto the bed. "But the situation is a little strange."

"Why?"

"Well, he's got a girl, for one. And he's sort of got my father too—he's Angel DiFiore's son."

Evelyn's jaw dropped open. "Tiny, are you crazy? Don't you think it's a little dangerous to be fooling around with him?"

"More than a little," I said, unbuttoning my blouse. "But you'll understand when you see him. And you'll know why I'm not interested in Joey."

Because I wasn't. Not at all.

I simply needed to remind myself of that from time to time.

#

At Evelyn's house, I helped her choose an outfit —a pale pink sleeveless dress with a dropped waist and white satin-ribbon sash. The hem fell nearly to her ankles, but the color was good for her and she wore a beautiful strand of pearls with it. She raided Rosie's vanity for a gold headband, which set off her fair hair, but I didn't want to borrow one without asking. Instead Evelyn plucked a gardenia from her mother's garden and I pinned it above my ear.

Once we arrived at the club, we stood near the bar and I ordered champagne cocktails for both of us. Sipping the bubbly concoction from a stemmed glass, I tried to appear casual as I scoured the crowd for Enzo. Inside my evening bag was the six hundred dollars from Joey.

"Do you think we'll be asked to dance?" Evelyn was looking over the crowd too.

"Maybe. If you see someone you like, meet his eye," I encouraged. "You have to let him know you're interested."

"I'll try. But you're always so much better at this than I am."

I rolled my eyes. "Better at what? Just look at him. You don't even have to say anything."

She giggled. "OK. Hey, that one's cute over there, don't you think?"

"Where?" I followed her eye to where a heavyset young man with sandy hair stood talking to friends. He didn't look like a gangster, so I relaxed a bit. "Yes, he is. And he's looking this way, so smile."

She did, and I could tell he noticed her. But as he took a step in our direction, I felt a hand on my shoulder.

"Couldn't stay away?"

I turned, going breathless at Enzo's body so near mine. "I came to pay you back."

"Already? I'm impressed."

I lowered my voice so Evelyn couldn't hear. "Shall we do it here?"

He raised his eyebrows. "Oh—you mean the money." Looking to our left, his eyes lingered on the crowd down front. Gina gawked at us as she stood at their table, hands on her hips.

"You're being watched."

He sighed and I could smell the whisky on his breath, even stronger than usual. "Her father's here tonight. It's a complete drag. If he didn't own a distillery in Kentucky, I'd take you back into the stairwell so I could finish what you started."

My stomach flipped madly. "Maybe I should just give you the cash now."

"Probably." He drained the glass before leaning in to whisper in my ear. "Because if I get you alone one more time, I won't stop until you let me have my way. First with my fingers. Then with my tongue. Then with my big, hard cock. And Tiny—you *will* let me."

Heat rushed my face, and I knew my cheeks must be painted scarlet. Fumbling, I dug into my bag and handed Enzo the money without meeting his eyes. Then I reached for my drink. Taking three long swallows, I finished it and set down the empty glass.

Enzo laughed, deep and low. "Would you like another?"

"Yes."

I felt a tug on my elbow. "Tiny? I'm going to dance, OK?" I turned and saw Evelyn holding the arm of the sandy-haired man, an eager expression on her face. The man smiled and said hello, but I barely heard him. I managed to give Evelyn a half-smile.

"Enjoy the music," Enzo told them, his words slurring a little. He flagged down the bartender while I pressed a hand to my stomach. *Get out of here. He's drunk.* But when he handed me the second cocktail and held up his glass to me, my resolve faltered.

He's so damn gorgeous. I'll just look at him while I have one more drink. No harm in looking, right?

"I'd invite you to join me at my table, but I don't think it would go over well," he said.

"Probably not."

"And having you so close might be more than I can bear, anyway."

I glugged my champagne like it was water and said nothing.

"So then, I bid you farewell for tonight." He picked up my left hand and kissed the back of it before sauntering away. I watched him walk to his table, where Gina tugged him into a chair and sat on his lap.

Bitch.

"Hey," came a menacing whine from behind me. "What's the big idea with my brother?"

Fucking Raymond. I turned and glued a smile to my face. "I just needed Enzo for a moment."

"You and every other dumb Dora in this town." A toothpick hung out of his mouth and he grabbed it, poking at the air between us. "You should be talkin' to me. I'm the one that's getting you what you want, ain't I?"

"That's right. You are," I said, doing my best Rosie routine. "I don't know why I was wasting my time with him."

Raymond nodded and stuck the toothpick back in his mouth. "That's better. Say, want to go up to a room?"

I sipped my drink and smiled with tight lips. "I have a friend here. I shouldn't leave her alone."

"You could bring her too. I got some booze stashed away up there."

"How clever of you."

He puffed out his chest. "I am clever. They don't believe it, but I am." He looked toward Enzo's table. "And pretty soon I'm gonna make my move."

"What move?"

He whipped his eyes back to me. "Don't you worry about it none, doll. You'll know it when I do. Everybody will."

My stomach lurched, and I set down the drink. What was he talking about? How would I know anything about his move? Unless something was going down tonight? *Jesus, I have to get out of here. I'll just go home and wait for Joey to bring me good news about the rum heist. I hope those guys rob the fucking DiFiores blind.* "You know, I'm suddenly not feeling too well," I said. "I think I should find my friend and head home. Excuse me."

"Don't forget about tomorrow night and the rum," he called as I walked away. "It's the real malloy." *McCoy, you asshole.* Spotting Evelyn on the dance floor, I waited for the song to finish before approaching. I tapped her shoulder, and when she turned to me her face was flushed and radiant. It fell when I asked if she'd mind leaving now.

"I can take her home later," her partner volunteered. "I'd like to, in fact." He smiled at her, and he looked like a decent guy, but I felt strange about leaving her.

"But we have that early shift tomorrow." I made sharp eye contact with Evelyn, giving her the chance to let him down easy if she'd prefer to go with me.

"I switched mine, remember?" She patted my hand. "It's all right. Ted can drive me. And Rosie's here too." She pointed to a table near the dance floor, where Rosie was cuddling up to a tall man in a tuxedo.

"All right. Well, have fun." I hugged her and headed for the exit, refusing to look in the direction of Enzo and Gina's table.

If I had, I would've seen that Enzo wasn't there.

Just as I reached the hallway leading to the exit, he stepped in front of me, his eyes snapping with anger. "Why were you talking to Raymond?"

"None of your business." I matched his hateful tone.

"He's an idiot," Enzo spat, and I realized he wasn't so much suspicious as jealous.

Ha! How do you like it? "You're drunk," I hissed. "Go back to your girl and her Kentucky distillery." I tried to step around him, but he wrapped his fingers around my forearm, his eyes darkening with fury.

"No."

I attempted to shake him off. "Let me go."

"I want you to stay."

"And I'm sure you're used to getting what you want from women, but the answer is no." I clenched my teeth and my thighs together. "Now let go of my arm."

He only gripped me harder, pulled me closer. "I know you want me."

I wanted to deny it, but my insides were aching for him. I lifted my chin. "I want you to beg."

A smile spread across his lips before he yanked me behind a red curtain into the dim hatcheck room. "Leave us," he said to the girl working in there. She slipped out without a word, and Enzo swung the curtain closed. Then he spun me around, twisting my right arm behind my back and crushing my chest to the wall. I gasped as he pressed into me, heating the side of my face with heavy breaths. His tongue traced the shell of my ear. "You want me to beg?"

I could feel how hard he was against the small of my back. Every inch of me buzzed with fearsome desire. "Yes."

"You drive a hard bargain, Miss O'Mara." Grinding against me, he whispered in my ear. "I'm begging you. Stay."

In that moment I knew nothing but want—for his body, for total abandon, for the mindless ecstasy I knew he could bring. "Yes," I said. "Yes."

"In five minutes, give my name to the bartender and he'll let you into the storage room. I'll meet you at the entrance to the tunnel." Releasing me, he disappeared through the curtain.

I stood there, mouth open, my breath coming quick and heavy. The hatcheck girl returned and I avoided meeting her eyes. *Don't look at anyone*, I told myself as I slipped through the curtain. *Keep your eyes low, put one foot in front of the other, and for God's sake, don't think!* Hurrying to the bar on surprisingly steady legs, I pictured him in his black three-piece suit. Imagined those pieces coming off, one by one.

Yes, I wanted his clothes off. I wanted to feel his bare, hot skin on mine. I wanted to make him weak with desire and bring him to heel. I wanted to hear him say he wanted me, couldn't resist me. Keeping my back to the room, I counted off five minutes, growing more agitated with every passing second. Speaking low, I gave the bartender his name and was granted access to the storage room. I walked to the far wall, and two seconds later the door opened and Enzo pulled me into the tunnel. As soon as he shut the door behind me, I lunged for him. His arms lashed around my back and his whisky-flavored tongue drove into my mouth, igniting a flame at my center that flared throughout my body like wildfire. I tried to push his coat from his shoulders.

"Not here." He took my arm and pulled me quickly through the blindingly dark tunnel. We exited into a stairwell, and I stumbled going up. He caught me by the elbows, dragging me to my feet, and five seconds later we burst into the paneled hallway, which was dark and empty of guards.

Was he taking me to the office again? We raced down the hall, and for one fleeting moment, I had the fear that it was all a setup and Angel would be waiting for me behind his desk, ready to impose a new deadline or demand more money.

At the office door, Enzo took out his keys and unlocked it before shoving me inside. Then he shut the door behind us and locked it again with a loud click. In the silence that followed, I was glad to hear his breathing was as labored as mine. His keys and my purse hit the floor. My heart felt as if it would crack my ribs, it rattled against them so hard.

"My father is away tonight." Enzo moved toward me in the darkness.

"Is he?" I took a step back, wanting him to chase me.

"Yes. So this is my office right now. Everything in it is mine." As my eyes adjusted, I watched him remove his coat and unbutton his vest. My insides jittered in anticipation, and I backed up further. He dropped the vest and loosened his tie as my back hit the sideboard, rattling the decanters and glassware on top. I made a quarter turn and kept moving backward. A patient predator, he pursued me slowly, releasing his arms from his braces, ditching his collar and tie, and unbuttoning his shirt. My tailbone hit something hard.

"Stay there," he said. "I want to fuck you on that desk."

He closed the distance between us, pulling his shirt from his trousers. Caging me in with a hand on either side of my hips, he devoured his way down my neck to my shoulder. My nipples peaked in response to the nearness of his mouth. I wanted it. I wanted everything. Right now. "Do it," I whispered.

His voice was raw with want. "I've thought of nothing else since I last saw you. I can't even look at this fucking piece of furniture without seeing your legs open for me." As I sucked in air, he caught me underneath the arms and set me on top of the desk.

Pulse pounding, I pulled my dress up to my hips, revealing the lace between my legs. Then I opened my knees. Wide. "Like this?" Finally my voice was low and sultry, like I always wished it would be.

"Yes." Running his palms up my thighs, he unsnapped the step-in with deft fingers. "Just like that." I trembled as he dipped one finger inside me, opening my legs even more. I wanted that finger deeper, wanted to move against it. But he removed it and rubbed its wetness over my clitoris, making everything inside me twist and tighten. Then he slipped the finger back in, deeper this time.

"Oh my God," I murmured, falling back onto my elbows. Deep inside me, a slow pull began, rendering me thoughtless and needy beyond expression but for a single word—yes.

Yes. Yes. Yes.

Suddenly yes was the most beautiful word in the English language, and I couldn't stop thinking it. And when he dropped to his knees and put his lips on the inside of my thigh above the garter, I began breathing it, speaking it, the word breaking out in gasps through my open mouth.

Keeping my legs apart with his hands, he kissed his way up one thigh, and then the other. Soft kisses with warm lips and hot breath that made my limbs quiver. With his velvet tongue, he traced a line up the seam at my fiery hot center and then slid a fingertip back inside me. Barely.

I whimpered in protest.

"Beg," he said.

Before I could release my lower lip from between my teeth to plead with him, he retraced the upward sweep with his tongue, using more pressure. One long, slow stroke that had me writhing in need.

Then he did it again, and again.

After the third time, which had me moaning his name along with God's, he lingered at the top, torturing me with decadent swirls. Every nerve ending in my body was on fire, and the tight ache beneath his tongue was growing too difficult to bear.

"Please," I rasped. "Oh God, Enzo, just—"

But I lost the ability to speak then, because he plunged two fingers deep inside me, all the way this time. And as he moved them in a steady rhythm, he continued tantalizing me with his mouth, licking and kissing and gently sucking. I threw my head back and the world went liquid and golden as the tightness peaked and every muscle in my body clenched. The orgasm built quickly and roared through me in glorious waves of ecstasy and relief.

While I gasped for air, Enzo stood and undid the cuffs of his shirt. The masculine task had me panting even harder. He dropped the shirt from his shoulders and pulled his undershirt over his head. The sight of his bare sculpted chest sent me reeling.

"Fuck," I whispered, sitting up to run my hands over his hot skin. He unbuckled his belt, and my insides quickened again. "Why do I want you so badly?" I swept his hands aside and unbuttoned his trousers myself, pushing them and his underwear down just enough to get my hands on him. Shivers rocketed through me as I recalled his promise at the bar... *First with my fingers. Then with my tongue. Then with my big, hard cock.*

Oh yes, I will let you.

Squeezing the solid column of flesh in both hands, one atop the other, I dragged them up and down, slow at first, and then faster. He grew slicker beneath my fingers, and I loved watching his face as I made him grow harder and thicker and more desperate for me. He closed his eyes, struggling for control. "You want me the same reason I want you," he growled, taking my hands by the wrists and pinning them back on the desk. Then he wrapped one arm around my hip, pulled me toward him and slowly eased his cock into the tight, wet space inside me. "We always want what we can't have."

I clutched his shoulders, expecting pain, but I felt none at first, only the sensation of being stretched, and then an exquisite fullness. But just when I thought he was all the way in, he pushed further, making me gasp at the quick, sharp stab deep within. "God, you're so tight," he moaned. "It feels so fucking good."

His words riled me even more, and I moved my hands to his hips to pull him deeper into me. He groaned as if in pain and finally thrust all the way in, both of us crying out at the shock and pleasure of it. Setting a measured rhythm against me, he whispered, "I knew it would feel this good. I told myself not to fuck you, because I've never been this hungry for anyone. But when I look at you, I am fucking insatiable. It's dangerous."

"What's so dangerous about me?" I breathed, barely able to talk but reveling in the sound of his voice, the words he was saying.

"A man...should never reveal his...weakness to his enemies." He struggled to speak, battling against his body's need to lose control.

"So which am I—weakness or enemy?" I dug my nails into his skin.

"Both," he answered, thrusting faster. Sirens went off in my head as my body responded by growing even wetter. We'd have to stop soon, or else—

He froze.

"Fuck." Pulling out of me, he yanked up his pants. "Fix yourself up, hurry."

I shook my head, sputtering in disbelief. "What? What?"

"It's a raid. We have to get out of here."

I suddenly realized the sirens in my head were actual sirens, probably some kind of alarm system in the club. With shaking hands, I pushed my dress down and hopped to the floor without even doing up the snaps between my legs.

"Listen carefully," Enzo said, buttoning his shirt. "I'm going to take you out a back door and put you in a car. As soon as I find my driver, he'll come out to take you home. Damn it, why tonight, of all nights!"

I was thinking the same thing, but it wasn't just me I was worried about. "What about all the people down there? I can't leave my friend!"

"Hopefully, our lookout sounded the alarm in time for people to dump their drinks onto the rugs, and the shelves behind the bar are designed to rotate so the bottles won't show. As long as we have enough time, we should be fine, depending on who's doing the raid—DPD or feds." He crossed the room and scooped his keys off the floor, unlocked the door and motioned for me to hurry. "Come on."

I rushed to the door, where he took my hand, looked both ways and pulled me down the hall. He wore only his trousers and white shirt, buttoned halfway and not tucked in. Despite the circumstances, the glimpse of his bare chest between the undone buttons made my pulse race even faster. He opened the hidden door and we flew down the stairs and into the tunnel. After scurrying like rats down long, twisting passages, we came to the end. Enzo unlocked the door, and I followed him through it. I couldn't see anything, but it smelled wet and musty. Our shoes made no sounds on the dirt floor.

"Shit, I don't have my lighter. It was in my coat pocket," he said. "But I think the stairs are over here." With tentative steps, he led me over to a staircase, and we went up, feeling our way with our hands along a brick wall. The door at the top opened into a garage. Thanks to pale moonlight streaming through high windows, I could see several luxury cars parked side by side, along with a black truck and a couple utilitarian Fords like mine.

Leading me to a white Cadillac, Enzo opened the door and shoved me inside. "Get down in the back." Then he shut me in and took off without even a kiss goodnight. I watched him disappear into the stairwell before sinking into the plush back seat. Police sirens screamed in the distance, but I barely heard them over the riotous banging of my heart. With jittery fingers, I quickly snapped up my step-in, then clamped my knees together, smoothing my dress over my legs. I put my hands over my face. They smelled like Enzo.

My God. What have I done?

Chapter Thirteen

I don't know how long I sat there in the dark, numb with shock. After a while, I began berating myself for all the mindless things I'd done tonight— left Evelyn with a stranger, gone upstairs with Enzo, had sex with a gangster who didn't care a whit for me beyond his erection, and who also happened to have my father locked up somewhere. To top it off, I'd abandoned my friend at an illegal club just as the police raided it, and now I sat in the back of said gangster's Cadillac, waiting for some man I didn't know to drive me home. I had no purse, no money, no weapon to defend myself.

And what the hell would you defend? Your virtue? Your body? Your honor? Ha! You gave all that away earlier tonight. And for what? To escape? To gain a shred of control where you have none? To feel powerful?

Tears filled my eyes. I didn't feel powerful now. I felt alone, frightened, and foolish. Sniffing, I wiped my cheeks and whispered a prayer that Evelyn and Rosie had gotten out before the cops got in, and that we'd all make it home safely tonight. When the car door opened I gasped, flattening myself against the back seat.

A man slid behind the wheel without looking at me. "Where to?" he barked, starting the engine. He was tall and thick in the neck, and he wore a cap like Joey.

My voice shook as I gave him my address. I'd have to wake up the girls to let me in the house because my key was in my purse on the floor of Angel's office. *God, I hope Enzo sees it there when he goes back for his clothes.* I didn't want his father to find it. The thought of Enzo returning to the scene of our tryst caused a quickening in my stomach. *Don't you dare,* I commanded my body. But even my mind betrayed me by replaying the entire scene in salacious detail as the car exited the garage and drove away from the club. Outside the window, Detroit's riverfront flashed by, but I was back in the office with my dress around my waist, head thrown back, waves of delirium crashing through me. I bit my bottom lip.

God help me, I had felt powerful. And sexy. And alive. So alive it was almost worth it.

#

My pounding on the front door roused the girls within minutes. The Cadillac lingered at the curb until the lights went on in the house, and I wondered if Enzo had told the driver to make sure I got in. *So what are you, Enzo, good guy or thug? I wish you'd choose!*

"Tiny, what on earth is going on? You scared us half to death!" Molly yelled as I entered the house. Mary Grace cowered on the stairs, clutching her bear.

"I'm sorry, girls." I closed and locked the door. "I lost my purse, which had my keys in it."

Molly parked her hands on her hips. "How'd you get home? Where's the car?"

"It's still downtown. I'll have to get it tomorrow." I started up the stairs, patting Mary Grace on the head, the other hand gripping the banister for support. "I'm all right, someone drove me home. Now go back to bed. It's late."

"Damn right, it's late!"

I whirled to face Molly. "Mind your tongue!"

She crossed her arms. "No! I don't have to listen to you anymore. You're constantly telling me to behave, do this, don't do that, and you're out till all hours of the night doing whatever you please!"

"Let's talk about this in the morning." I flicked my eyes toward Mary Grace.

"Fine, but I'm telling you right now, things are gonna change around here. I'm tired of being the babysitter all the time! I'm tired of dragging Mary Grace with me everywhere I go! I have my own friends and I want to spend time with them." She gritted her teeth. "Alone! I want a later curfew, and I want a bigger allowance."

"I want! I want! I want!" I screamed, grateful that I was halfway up the steps and therefore taller than Molly. "I want a lot of things too, you know. I want my own apartment. I want to spend the money I earn on myself. I want the freedom to go where I want when I want, and do what I want without answering to my father or my little sisters! I want to live life now and not wait until I'm too old to enjoy it anymore!" I came down one step and leaned toward her. "But you know what? We always want what we can't have." Then I marched up the stairs and into my bedroom, slamming the door behind me.

#

No laughter or frying breakfast greeted me the following morning. Just a dull headache, a dry mouth, and a soreness between my legs. Dragging myself out of bed, I went down to the empty kitchen and called Evelyn's house. Her mother answered and said Evelyn was already at work, but I could reach her at the bakery if I needed to. I thanked her and hung up, relieved that Evelyn had gotten home all right. If I had a normal life, I'd go see her so we could talk about what happened. But instead I had to clean up after my sisters, who'd left their dirty breakfast dishes in the sink, try to reach Joey to find out about the heist, and figure out how to get back the purse and automobile I'd left at the club.

In the bathroom upstairs, I brushed my teeth and stared at myself in the mirror. Did I look different, now that I wasn't a virgin? I turned my head and shoulders this way and that, but I couldn't see that sex had altered my outward appearance. My insides—that was a different story. Every time I thought about it, my belly responded with a giant swoosh.

I dressed in a red skirt and the embroidered blouse I'd worn yesterday, which was the cleanest one I could find. *The girls are probably running short on clean clothes too.* Tears threatened as I stuffed a bunch of dirty things into a laundry basket. It was too much, trying to be a parent to them while all this was going on. Guilt over the way I'd yelled at Molly sat heavily on my shoulders. This wasn't her fault.

After I had everything from my room that needed washing, I let myself into my sisters' room. Picking through clothing scattered across the bed, floor, and dresser, I tried to determine what was clean and what wasn't. As I worked, I fretted about the heist, knitting my eyebrows together. Had it gone as planned? I prayed that Joey was unharmed, but realized I wasn't looking forward to facing him, having been with Enzo...that way.

He's not your boyfriend. You've got no reason to feel guilty where Joey is concerned. But the thought of meeting his eyes made my stomach churn.

The door to the girls' room swung wide. "Get out of here," Molly said. "This is our room." She glared at me and I put my hands up in surrender.

"I'm just getting the laundry."

"I'll do it myself."

Sighing, I sank onto Mary Grace's bed. "Can we talk a minute? I want to apologize."

"Well, I don't." She crossed her arms.

Stay calm. You're the adult. I took a deep breath. "Molly, I know how you feel. I remember feeling the same way when I was your age. Bridget had just gotten married, and Daddy was depending on me at home. You were only ten, Mary Grace was six, and there I was, fifteen and suddenly the mother of two, running a house of my own. I wanted the same things you want now, but it was impossible. In fact, I still want them. But we have to make do with what we're handed in life."

"No, we don't. That's stupid."

I stared at her. "What?"

"Joey says that if you want something in life, you should go after it."

"*Joey*," I said, my patience waning, "is the last person you should be taking advice from right now."

"But he's right," Molly went on. "If people just waited around for life to happen instead of going after things, where would we be? Women wouldn't even have the vote!"

I opened my mouth to argue, but I couldn't. Instead I asked, "How late?"

"Huh?"

"Your curfew. How late do you want to stay out?"

"Oh." She chewed one fingernail, considering. "How about eleven?"

I leveled my gaze at her. "Ten."

"Ten thirty," she insisted. "That's what all my friends have. And two dollars more a week for chores. I'll start doing the laundry, and I can help out with the cooking too."

I'm too young for this. Closing my eyes, I nodded. "Deal."

#

Downstairs, I made a pot of coffee and sat at the kitchen table drumming my nails. *Come on, Joey. Call already!* But the telephone stayed silent all morning.

By early afternoon, my knees were trembling as I helped Molly hang clothes on the line outside. What if the heist had gone wrong? What if Joey was hurt...or dead? Fighting the need to weep, I began forming a plan. *I'll go to Enzo and beg for mercy. I'll make a deal with him, work for him, give him the garage and all our business if he'll just let Daddy go.*

My thoughts were interrupted by the ring of the telephone. I raced into the house, grabbed the base and whipped the receiver to my ear. "Hello?"

"It's me," Joey said. He spoke quietly, as if he didn't want to be overheard.

"Thank God you're OK! Did you get it?"

"We got it. We're taking the load to Chicago."

"Chicago! But—"

"I'm having a package delivered to you at the store. Don't let Bridget open it, under any circumstances. And be careful." The line went dead.

"Joey, wait!" I pressed the switch hook repeatedly, to no avail. "Shit!" I hung up the receiver and put my fingers to my head, which had begun to pound. A package—what did that mean? Had he gotten the money for me? When was it coming and who was bringing it? I groaned in frustration, but what I really wanted to do was scream. Forcing myself to stay calm for Molly's sake, I took a few deep breaths and walked back outside. "I have to go to the store for a while," I said. "I'll take Mary Grace with me to play with the boys. Can you finish the laundry on your own?"

She took a clothespin from between her teeth and pinned up a pair of bloomers. "Sure. Do you think... maybe I could go to the movies tonight? Without Mary Grace?"

I wanted to say yes, although I couldn't take Mary Grace with me to get the car, either. Maybe Bridget would watch her. "All right."

"Thanks." She smiled, the first genuine one she'd sent in my direction in a long time. It struck me how she resembled Daddy, and I realized how much I missed him and his playful grins, his gruff affection, the way he pleaded to our mother in heaven when we were driving him crazy. A lump swelled in my throat, and I turned away from Molly so she wouldn't see the tears in my eyes. If I failed...

No. Don't even think about it.

I collected Mary Grace from a friend's house down the street, and we walked to the store. I chewed my thumbnail, listening with half an ear to my sister's steady stream of chatter about her friend's new kitten. At the store, I sent her up the stairs to Bridget's apartment and poked my head in the front. Martin was at the register.

"Well, hello, stranger," he said to me. "Haven't seen you working much this week. Come to help out?" Martin was a perfectly nice young man with kind eyes and a ready smile, but I was in no mood to chat.

You have to stay here. So make nice.

"Uh, sure. What can I do?"

"How about make room on the south wall for a new Lysol display?"

"All right. Say, Martin," I began, as if I'd just thought of it, "has anyone brought a package here for me today?"

"Not that I know of, and I've been here since nine." He snapped his fingers. "Come to think of it, there was a woman in here looking for you yesterday. But I think she wanted some whisky."

"Did she leave her name?"

"No, she wouldn't. Said she'd try again tomorrow."

Nodding glumly, I headed for the south wall and began rearranging floor wax and soap flakes to make room for the Lysol display. Every time the bell over the door rang, I jumped, but it was never anyone for me. When I finished with the display, I restocked the dry goods shelves, made a pyramid of soup cans, swept the sidewalk, wiped the back counter, and washed the front windows. Anything to keep my hands busy.

"You're a regular dynamo today," said Martin. "Bridget should give you a raise."

I smiled weakly, feeling light-headed as I wiped one last streak from the glass. What if Joey didn't come through? What if he left me stranded, like he did the other night at the club? A sweat broke out on my forehead. *I'll go to Enzo and* —

The bell over the door rang, and a young boy entered. He looked about ten, a scruffy, undernourished thing wearing torn brown knee pants, black suspenders over a dirty white shirt, and a black cap. The kind of kid hanging around on street corners willing to run errands for a nickel. He reminded me of Joey at that age.

"Can I help you?" I asked.

"Package for somebody named Tiny."

I could swear I heard a choir of angels. "That's me."

He handed me a box clumsily wrapped in brown paper, and I turned it over in my hands, inspecting it. It was rectangular in shape and flatter than a shoebox. "Did Joey send you?" When the boy didn't answer, I looked up.

He was gone. I hadn't even heard the bell ring again.

"Gift from an admirer?" asked Martin from behind the register.

"No, just something from a friend." Heart pounding, I tucked the box under my arm and went into the stock room. Out of sight, I pulled off the dirty string and removed the rumpled brown paper. Underneath was a blue box that said Tiffany & Co. Tiffany? What the hell was this? Slowly, I lifted the top off the box. My eyes bulged.

It was a necklace.

Breathless, I picked it up and let it dangle from my fingers. It looks like something from a movie! Five tiny strands of pearls, held together by little diamond-encrusted bars at the sides, came together at the front in a huge, jaw-dropping brooch made up of tiny diamonds in concentric circles. My hands shook as I lifted it to my throat, feeling its weight above my collarbone.

My chest began to pump a little life into my body. I had no idea how Joey had gotten his grubby hands on a Tiffany necklace, but I could sell it, assuming it was real. Even if it wasn't worth five grand, which it very well could be, it would still bring me a pretty penny. I put it back into the box, did my best to rewrap it, and hid it on a high shelf. Skimming on the periphery of my excitement was the knowledge that the necklace was probably stolen, but I banished that thought from my head. I couldn't afford to worry about it.

I went upstairs and put on a phony smile for Bridget, who was peeling potatoes at the sink. "Bridge," I said, twisting my hands together, "I have to run downtown and pick up the car—I lost my keys last night and had to leave it parked there. And I already promised Molly she could go to the movies. Could you watch Mary Grace?"

Bridget nodded. "Sure. She can stay all night if she wants to. She's had them quiet in that front room playing school for an hour now. The silence is miraculous."

I threw my arms around her from behind. "Thank you! I owe you a thousand favors when Daddy gets back." She smelled good, like lavender and Ivory soap.

She patted my arm. "I'm just glad to see you getting out a little more. You were so down last week. Are you feeling better?"

"Yes," I lied, letting her go.

"You know, eventually you're going to have to tell me about him." She winked at me over her shoulder. "Maybe it's not Joey, but there certainly is someone. I can smell it."

My heart stopped. Could she really smell Enzo on me? I sniffed my arm.

Bridget burst out laughing. "I wasn't being literal, Tiny. I meant, I can tell you have feelings for someone."

"Oh." Relieved, I shook my head. "I thought you meant—never mind. I gotta go." I could hear her laugh again as I ran down the stairs. In the stock room, I took the necklace box from the shelf and held it under my arm. Calling goodbye to Martin, I went out the back door and began walking home.

With every step another question rattled my brain. Where could I sell the necklace? What was it worth? Should I try to sell it this afternoon? Bring the money to Angel tonight? Should I go alone to the club?

Then I had a thought that halted my steps.

What if Club 23 had been shut down by the police after the raid? How would I find the DiFiores to pay them? I didn't want them seeking me out at my house or the store or anywhere near my sisters.

Chewing my bottom lip, I turned around and walked back to Jefferson and then down two blocks. Sometimes a boy sold newspapers on the corner of Jefferson and Fielding in the afternoon, and I said a quick prayer he would be there today. If such a popular place had been shuttered, surely the paper would be full of it.

When I saw the ragtag newsboy in the usual spot, I picked up my pace. "Hello," I called, jogging up with a friendly smile. "May I see a paper please?" He handed one to me and I scanned the front page quickly, looking for any mention of a raid at Club 23.

Nothing.

My heart tripped with excitement.

"You gonna buy that paper, miss?" the boy asked me, scratching his scalp under his cap.

"No, I'm sorry." I was just about to give it back to him when a headline caught my eye. GANG KILLS FOUR IN EAST SIDE HEIST. Underneath that, *Police seek link with mob led by Sam Scarfone.* My stomach suffered an uneasy twinge as I skimmed the article, which stated that Big Leo Scarfone's nephew and former lieutenant Sam the Barber Scarfone was suspected in leading another liquor heist in the city last night. Two trucks full of booze had been hijacked not far from the train station, and three men were killed at the scene. Another man survived the shooting, but police found him a short distance away, mortally wounded. Before he died, he identified Sam and gave a few other details about the crime.

But the line that made my vision cloud with white dots was the article's last sentence. *Police are searching for a black funeral coach in connection with the crime, which was driven by a young gunman, possibly a new recruit of the Scarfone gang.*

#

Back at home, I told Molly I was unwell and needed to lie down. I shut myself in my room and sat on my bed, clutching my hands together. One thought tore through my brain over and over again. *Joey killed someone. Joey killed someone. Joey killed someone.* Hell, he might've killed more than one! Four men were dead! I put my face in my hands. There was no doubt in my mind that he was the new recruit of the Scarfone gang —the River Gang. *And the cops are looking for him.* I wondered if he was on his way to Chicago by now and hoped he was. Actually I hoped he'd stay there. The cops were the least of his problems—four men in the DiFiore camp were dead, and they wouldn't let that go.

Retribution was coming.

I have to get out of this mess. I have to sell the necklace, get the rest of the cash, and spring Daddy before Angel realizes I have any ties to Scarfone or his gang. I looked at the blue box next to me on the bed, my legs twitching with nervous energy. I didn't know of any pawn shops nearby, and the only person I could think of who would was Joey. *Come on, think.* I held my head in my hands and squeezed my eyes shut. *What would Daddy do?* Grimacing, I realized he'd probably bet the damn thing at the tables.

Then it hit me—Ralph the Bookie.

Never in my life had I smiled thinking about Ralph, and I wanted to seek him out about as much as I wanted to let a hairy black spider crawl up my arm, but he was the seediest person I knew. The kind of man who'd know how to get cash fast. I went to my dresser and tugged a comb through my hair. I'll jump on the streetcar and head into the city. I could probably find him at the Sunnyside, Daddy's usual hangout, a crummy old saloon with tables in the back room.

"Tiny?" Molly knocked twice before opening my bedroom door. "Are you all right?" She looked surprised when she saw me combing my hair.

I set the comb down quickly and glanced at my bed, where the necklace box was in plain sight. "Yes. What is it?"

"There's someone here to see youuuuu," she sing-songed.

My heart thumped an extra beat. "Who is it?"

"He didn't say." She grinned. "And I was so flustered by his face that I didn't think to ask. He looks like a movie star!"

The room tilted, and I grabbed the dresser top. *He's here. At my house.* "I'll be right down. Molly, I want you to go to your room, shut the door, and stay in there until I come up and get you. OK?"

She gave me a knowing look. "You could just ask for privacy, you know."

I grabbed her by the shoulders. Hard. "This is serious. Do as I say," I ordered through clenched teeth.

Her teasing expression vanished and her eyes went wide. "What's going on?"

"Just stay in your room."

"OK. But hurry, all right?" She bit her lip and left the room without further protest, and I heard her bedroom door close.

I looked in the mirror. Swallowed. *Maybe he just wants to see me again. Maybe he's returning my purse. Maybe he even brought the car.*

Somehow I knew better.

I walked out of my room and descended the stairs slowly, one hand on the banister for support. First I saw his polished black shoes. Then his legs in dark gray trousers. Then his torso, which had been naked before me last night, but was now buttoned up in a shirt, vest, and coat. His white collar was snug, his blood-red tie knotted as tightly as my stomach. Finally, I saw his chiseled face, shadowed by a gray fedora.

Reaching the bottom, I looked into his eyes, which betrayed nothing.

He put his hand on my arm. "Let's go for a ride."

Chapter Fourteen

"Now isn't really the best time," I said, my heart thudding in my throat.

"Now. And bring the key to the boathouse." He reached into his coat and pulled out my small purse from last night, tossing it on the hall table next to the phone.

I looked at it sideways. "Gee, thanks. But my sister is here, and I—"

His grip tightened on my forearm. Threading his other hand into my hair, he made a fist at the base of my skull and tipped my head back. "I don't think you'll want your sister to hear the conversation we're going to have." He spoke softly, venom oozing between his words. My scalp stung as he tightened his fingers.

You asshole, I gave you my virginity last night! I wanted to shout. But I had no idea what he knew about my role in the heist and thought I'd better play nice. "All right," I said, my legs wobbling. "Can I at least tell her I'm leaving?"

246

He released me. Straightened his coat. "Yell up to her."

I paused a second as we eyed each other, distrust thickening the tension between us. *He doesn't want me to leave his sight.* Suddenly I was irritated. He had my father held hostage, and *I* was the untrustworthy one? Would he really stop me from going up the stairs? "Her door is closed. She won't hear me." I tried to move past him, but he blocked me.

"I said yell." His eyes snapped with anger, and the stubborn set of his jaw made me hesitate.

But not for long. "No. If you want to come with me, fine. But I'm going up those stairs."

We remained in a silent standoff for a moment, and then he jerked me by my elbow up the steps. I scrambled ahead so I'd be first, but he wouldn't let go of me. When we reached the top, I glared at him. "Let go," I whispered through gritted teeth.

"No." He walked us toward the closed bedroom door and put me in front of him, circling both elbows with his fingers. "Tell her you're leaving." His tone was dead calm in my ear.

"Molly? I'll be right back. Just stay in your room, OK?" My voice sounded unnaturally high-pitched, and I prayed she wouldn't open the door to see why.

"OK," came her muffled reply. My throat tightened as I imagined her curled up in her bedclothes, hugging the pillow in fear. I looked at Enzo over my shoulder, raising my eyebrows, and he let my arms go.

He followed me down the stairs and watched me grab my key ring from inside the purse he'd returned, although I couldn't imagine what he wanted in the boathouse. We went out the front door, and I saw his white Cadillac parked at the curb. "No driver today?"

"No."

No witness then. The words popped into my brain, unwelcome as a swarm of mosquitoes. He opened the passenger door for me, and I climbed in, letting him close it. I looked out the window, half tempted to make a run for it. Enzo slid into the driver's seat and started the engine.

"What is this about?"

He didn't answer. When I looked over at him, his profile betrayed nothing. *Goddamn your handsome face and your silent games! If you're angry about something, just yell it like I would!* As crazy as Joey made me, at least I always knew where we stood.

At the end of my street, Enzo turned into the alley and slowed down. My back stiffened when he put the car in park directly behind the store. "My family owns a construction company," he said, putting his arm across the back of my seat.

"Oh?" Baffled, I glanced at his hand near my shoulder. "I didn't know that."

"Yes. Although in the construction business, you do just as much demolition as you do building."

Something clicked. *Oh, no.*

"In fact, we demolished a few old houses last week to make way for a new apartment building. And we happened to have some extra explosives, but wouldn't you know, we ran out of storage space."

Chills broke out over my entire body. "Enzo. Don't."

"So I arranged to store some explosives beneath this building right here," he said, pointing toward the store.

"Please," I begged, turning to him. "Why are you doing this?"

He grabbed the back of my head again, forcing my face closer to his. "You wanted to fuck me last night? Well, you did."

"I don't understand."

"The hearses, Tiny. The fucking hearses. I saw them in the garage that night. I know they belong to your father. Then the next time I hear about them, they're full of booze that belongs to me, being driven by the men who stole it."

Those fucking hearses. I hated them! Why hadn't I thought about that when I gave them to Sam? "Those hearses could belong to anyone. Daddy sells them to bootleggers all the time."

"They were yours, Tiny. Now who was it? Sam Scarfone? Is he working for you? Are you fucking him too?" With the last sentence, he tightened his grip on my hair.

I winced. "No! Goddammit, Enzo, you're hurting me! Let me go."

"Why should I? So you can run to Sam and tell him everything?" But he let go of my hair, and I rubbed my scalp as tears began to drip down my cheeks. "Well, here's something you might not know. My father was going to give me the club," he went on, looking straight ahead. "And turn the bootlegging over to me. So I arrange this big shipment from the east coast, fifteen thousand dollars worth of rum, packed in cases with hidden compartments, in which is stored forty thousand dollars worth of opium. And then it's fucking hijacked." He hit the wheel with the heel of his hand. "Now my father is furious and thinks I'm goddamn incompetent. We're out more than fifty grand, I'm in the middle of another whisky deal with the distillery in Kentucky that I can no longer fucking afford, and I'm left here with my dick in my hand while your boys enjoy the spoils." He looked over at me. "So where is it?"

His eyes had a savage look in them I'd only seen once before, when he was nearly uncontrollable with lust in the office. But it wasn't lust now; it was rage. And if I wasn't careful, he was going to direct it not only at me, but at my family too. "I don't know," I said weakly. "I didn't steal it, please believe me. And I had no idea about the opium."

"Goddammit, Tiny!" He thumped the steering wheel again. "I've been up front with you."

"No, you haven't!" I yelled, forgetting about being careful. "What about going behind my back to Al Murphy? Asking whom I supplied and then stealing his business from under me! You knew I needed it to get the ransom money."

Enzo looked out the front window again. "When my father saw the ledgers, he wanted Murphy's business, so I arranged it. And that's fucking peanuts compared to my shipment."

"Oh, poor you! Well, I don't have it!"

Suddenly he put the car into reverse and backed up, the tires spitting gravel. When he turned onto Jefferson, I knew where we were headed.

"It's not there," I told him. *Please, please, God, let them not have anything stored in the boathouse. Let them have taken it all to Chicago.*

"Then you have nothing to worry about."

Worry wasn't the word for what was going on inside me. I was sweating as if I'd run ten miles, my heart hammering against my chest like it might split my body wide open. As the Cadillac bumped along the dirt road leading down to the water, I grabbed onto the dash to steady myself. Enzo turned off the engine and got out; reluctantly, I opened the passenger door and trailed him to the boathouse door.

"Open it," demanded Enzo.

My fingers fumbled with the padlock, and I recalled how he'd snuck in before. "You don't need me to open this. Why did you drag me here?"

"Maybe I like your company."

I froze and looked at him, but his face remained stony. Once I had the padlock in my hands, Enzo pushed the door open.

"After you."

I stepped into the cool, damp space and looked into every shadowy corner, my body shuddering with relief—nothing but the forty bottles of whisky I'd left on Tuesday. "I told you it wasn't here. That whisky's mine."

Enzo examined the cases and then faced me. "I'm going to ask you some questions now, Tiny. And you're going to answer them. Do you understand?"

I nodded, the tears returning. *Is he wearing his gun? Will he pull it on me?* Glancing toward the open door, I wondered how long it would take someone to find my body in here.

"I want to know who hijacked me and where they took the load. I want to know how you knew about it and who pulled the raid alarm at the club."

I gaped at him. "The raid wasn't real?"

"No, it was merely a distraction." He paused. "Almost as good as the one you presented me with."

"That wasn't a distraction! I mean, I didn't plan that! You're the one who had the idea to go upstairs."

"Just answer my questions."

"I...I can't." Naming names meant certain death —for me, for Joey, for everyone.

"Damn it, I don't want to threaten you, but you're not giving me a choice here." Enzo unbuttoned his coat and reached inside.

I threw both hands out toward him. "No, wait! Please—no gun. I'll tell you...what I know."

He waited, the arm still inside his coat. "I'm listening."

"The load went to Chicago," I blurted. That wasn't really giving up a name, was it?

"And who took it there?"

"I—I'm not sure…"

"Fucking hell. Listen to me, Tiny." He came at me, but instead of pulling his gun, he wrapped his hands around my skull and squeezed. "I don't want to hurt you. But you're making me fucking crazy, day and night. Tell me what you know." In the silence that followed I heard birds chirping outside the door, and the sound was so incongruous I thought maybe I was delirious.

Should I give up Sam's name? Enzo already suspected he was behind the heist, as did the cops. And my loyalty was to Joey, not Sam. "Sam Scarfone bought the hearses from me. I needed the money to make the first payment to your father." I spit out the words quickly, breathing deeply afterward but feeling as if I couldn't get enough air, like it was my lungs he was compressing instead of my head.

Enzo nodded. "How did he know about the load? Did you tell him?"

"No! I don't know how he found out." That was the truth, at least. Sam had told me about the shipment in the first place. I'd only told him when it would arrive.

"No one but family and a few trusted men knew when it was coming. That means there's a leak, Tiny. And I want to know who it is. You're going to find out."

Just like that, I thought of another name I didn't mind giving up. "Wait, I think I know who it was—your brother."

"Raymond?" His brow wrinkled in confusion.

"Yes." No need to mention I'd played a role in the relaying of information. "He's jealous of you. He told me at the bar last night he was going to make his move. I guess this was it."

Enzo released my head from his hands. "That idiot." He looked away from me, staring at the floor. "What the fuck is he thinking?"

"I don't know. He didn't tell me much." I glanced toward the door again—I wanted to get out of here. Molly was probably sick with worry, and I needed to get Bridget, Mary Grace and the boys out of her apartment. "Are you going to remove the dynamite from the store?"

He looked at me again. "There's nothing there. Yet. But my father is unpredictable. I asked him to wait before doing anything, and he gave me this afternoon to speak with you, but that's it." Then he took out his wallet and handed me three hundred-dollar bills. "Take this, give it to your sisters, and tell them to leave town. They aren't safe."

I reached for it automatically, shaking my throbbing head back and forth. He was helping me again? "Why are you doing this? I don't understand you at all—you kidnap my father, you come on to me, you steal business from me, you...do what you did to me, you lie and threaten me, and now this!" I held up the money. "It makes no sense!"

He put his hands on my shoulders and pulled me toward him. "Like I said, you drive me fucking crazy." Before I could protest, he kissed me hard on the lips. Then he let me go and turned toward the whisky. "Now let's get these bottles into my trunk."

#

As soon as Enzo dropped me off, I ran into the house and up the stairs. I found Molly cowering on the floor in her closet, arms wrapped around her legs. When I pulled her up, she burst into tears and threw her arms around me. "I was so scared," she sobbed. "What's going on?"

"Shhhhh." I held her, patting her back and stroking her hair. "It's all right. I'm here, and I won't let anything happen to you." After a moment she stilled, and I sat her down on the bed next to me. "Good girl. Now I need your help." Taking her hands, I told her that Daddy had gotten in over his head at the tables, and I was helping him cover the debt. "But until I pay these men, they'll keep threatening us."

"It's too dangerous!" she cried. "You could be hurt."

I squared my shoulders. "Listen. I can handle this. You can help me."

She took a deep breath and nodded. "Tell me what to do."

"Pack a bag for you and Mary Grace. We're going to Bridget's, where you're going to help me convince her to take you girls and the boys away for a few days —just until I get word to you that it's safe to return. Daddy should be back by the end of the weekend," I said, praying that was true. I couldn't keep this up much longer. "If he isn't, I'll go to the police."

"OK," she said. "Give me five minutes."

I hugged her again. "This wasn't what you meant when you agreed to take on more responsibility, huh?"

She choked out a laugh against my shoulder. "Not exactly."

#

We walked down to Bridget's as the sun began to set. Neither of us spoke. Molly was probably in shock, and I was busy trying to think of a way to convince Bridget to take the kids out of town without telling her the whole truth. After what happened to Vince, I didn't want her to panic and do something rash, like call the cops. *I'll give her the money from Enzo and tell her what I told Molly. That should be enough.*

The store was closed when we arrived at the back door, but I had my key. "Let's hope she listens to me," I whispered to Molly as we took the stairs up to Bridget's apartment. "I may need your help."

When we walked in, the kitchen was empty and the dinner dishes were left on the table, which was odd. Bridget always did the dishes right after supper because she can't stand a messy kitchen. My uneasy feeling intensified when we entered the front room. The kids were playing on the floor, and Bridget sat stiffly on the edge of the sofa, her face drained of color, her hands around her rosary.

"Hello," I said. She looked at me blankly, almost as if she didn't recognize me. Molly and I exchanged nervous glances. "Molly, why don't you play with the kids a minute? I want to talk to Bridget."

"Sure." Molly dropped to her knees next to the kids, who were running tiny fire engines and trucks over the floor and table.

"Yes." Bridget's voice sounded strange to me. "We need to talk." She stood and picked up a glass from the side table, which looked to me as if it contained whisky. That was even stranger, because Bridget rarely touched the stuff. She emptied it into her mouth and set the glass down again. "Come with me."

Swallowing hard, I followed her into her bedroom and watched as she locked the door. "What's going on, Bridget?"

Without answering, she went to her bed and pulled a package from underneath the mattress. It was a large, lumpy brown envelope.

"What is that?"

"Someone dropped it off for you." Her voice shook. "He said it was from Joey."

My blood roared violently through my veins. "*That's* the package from Joey?"

She nodded. "I opened it."

"You *what?*" I moved toward her and grabbed it. It was much heavier than I expected. "Why did you do that?"

Anger flashed in her eyes, a spark of the real Bridget. She grabbed it back from me and dumped the contents on the bed.

A huge mound of cash fell out.

Along with a shiny black pistol.

Chapter Fifteen

"Nothing to say?" Bridget hissed.

"I'm—I'm thinking." But I couldn't think. My mind whirled as I stared at the money and gun. *This* was the package from Joey? So who the hell gave me the necklace? And why? I sank onto the bed and picked up the pistol.

"Tiny, put that down!" Bridget knocked my wrist and the weapon fell back onto the spread. "You want to kill yourself? Or me?"

I stared at it. "Is it loaded?"

"How should I know? The question is, why would Joey leave it for you? And what is all this money for?"

"Give me a second." Putting my fingers to my forehead, I closed my eyes and racked my brain. But no amount of sifting through the events of the past week gave me any indication of who would gift me with that necklace. *What is going on?*

My sister's voice cut through the confusion.

"Tiny, you better tell me what this is or I'm taking all this to the police right now."

"No, don't!" I jumped to my feet and clutched her shoulders, clarity returning with a slap. *I have to get them out of here.* "All right, listen to me. Daddy's in trouble."

Her brow furrowed. "What kind of trouble?"

I hesitated—how should I put this? "He owes money to some...men who don't take kindly to being owed."

"What men?"

I shook my head. "Doesn't matter. The important thing is that Joey helped me get the money together and we're going to deliver it as soon as possible." No need to tell her Joey had gone to Chicago with a load of stolen rum and opium. No need at all.

"Where is Joey? Where the hell is Daddy, for that matter?" She knocked my hands from her shoulders. "Have you been lying to me this whole time about where he is? And why would Joey think you need a gun?"

"Bridget, please." I grabbed her by one hand and tugged. "I'm sorry I lied. I thought I was doing the right thing by protecting you, but I haven't done a very good job." My eyes filled and I took a shaky breath. "Now you have to do what I say, *please.* Take Molly, Mary Grace, and the boys and get out of town for a few days. Go see your friend Helen in East Jordan, or take the kids to the beach and stay in a hotel. Use this." I pulled Enzo's hundreds from my skirt pocket and gave them to her.

Her eyes widened as she stared at the cash. "What on earth..." She looked at me. "Where are you guys getting all this money?"

"Just take it and go. You're not safe here right now. They've made threats...to the store."

She began to cry. "But this is my home, my store. I can't just leave."

"You can, and you must." I went to her closet, pulled down a battered suitcase from the shelf and opened it on the bed. "Martin and I will take care of things here. Call me when you're settled somewhere and stay there until you hear from me. It'll only take a couple days." I gathered up the cash and gun from Joey, shoving it back inside the package. There were a ton of bills, and I wondered if somehow Joey had gotten me all five grand.

Bridget stared at the money in her fingers and then looked at me with wet cheeks. "Maybe," she began slowly, "I should call Vince's family. They might be able to—"

"No! Trust me—we don't need any more gangsters involved in this." I laced my fingers together. "Please, I beg you. You'll only make things worse for Daddy and me if you try to get involved. The kids need you to keep them safe." I didn't want to tell her about the explosives, but I would if I had to.

She chewed on her lower lip. "Does Molly know?"

I nodded. "As much as you do. She can help you with the kids." A breeze blew in the open window, and I realized how sweaty I was. My cotton blouse was sticking to me. *I need a bath. I need a drink. I need a new life.* "Please, Bridget. Say you'll go."

She stared out the window a moment as the bells from nearby St. Ambrose tolled seven times. "All right. We'll go."

Chills of relief swept across my skin with the breeze. When I drew in a deep breath, I could've sworn I smelled my mother's lilac scent, as if she were in the room. I closed my eyes. *Thank you, Mama.* "I can drive you to the station in your car if you want."

She blinked. "Do we have to leave tonight?"

"Yes. You do."

Understanding flitted across her face. "Help me, then. Get the boys' suitcase from their closet and throw some things into it. Underwear, socks, anything clean you can find." She began opening drawers, pulling out underclothes and stockings, and tossing them into her suitcase.

I was on my way out of her room when she spoke again. "Three days, Tiny. That's what you have. Until Sunday. After that, I go to the police."

"Deal." It would all be over in two days, anyhow—one way or another.

#

By eight o'clock, we'd loaded the car and hugged goodbye. The kids were sad I couldn't join them at the beach, but Bridget covered brilliantly, saying Martin would need me at the store in her absence. She turned down my offer to drive them to the station, and I watched her car chug down the alley and turn right, then lifted my eyes to the sky in gratitude.

Walking home on tired feet, carrying the envelope from Joey in both hands, I returned to the puzzling question of who had given me that necklace.

The boy who delivered it had used my name, so I knew it wasn't a case of mistaken identity, but why on earth would someone give me such an expensive piece of jewelry? I didn't know anyone with that kind of money except Enzo, and he'd have mentioned it this afternoon. And why would he shower me with diamonds anyway? It's not as if I was his girlfriend. Plus, he'd been so furious with me.

Letting myself in the front door, I realized there was another mystery—who'd pulled the raid alarm at Club 23, and why? Maybe the River Gang had done it somehow, or paid someone to do it, in order to keep the DiFiores occupied at the club. I locked the front door behind me and double-checked it was secure, wishing we had a deadbolt. Then I rushed up to my room and dumped the contents of Joey's package on the bed next to the necklace. I ignored the gun momentarily while I gathered the cash and counted it.

It was all there. Five grand.

I counted it again. And again. Every time, the small bills, nothing larger than a twenty, added up to five thousand dollars. "Oh, Joey," I sighed, scooping up armloads of cash and lifting them in the air. The money fluttered down to my white bedspread. "I adore you." And at that moment, I really did.

273

Dropping to my knees, elbows on the bed, I clasped my hands together. *God, please let him be safe in Chicago. Don't let the cops or the DiFiores catch him.*

I crossed myself and stacked the bills, grateful I wouldn't have to sell the necklace right away. I knew I'd have to do it eventually in order to pay Joey back, but as of this moment, I had enough money to get Daddy released without Ralph the Bookie's help. I'd clean up, take a streetcar down to the club, and pay off Angel tonight.

It's almost over, I thought, my insides jittery with nerves and excitement. Daddy would be released, and my life would return to normal.

Never had I wanted my normal life so badly.

I put the cash back into the envelope and took it with me into the bathroom. I considered taking the gun too, but I didn't know if it was loaded and had no idea how to use it anyway. Instead I'd shoved it into my underwear drawer. It looked so strange—black metal peeking through white cotton and lace.

I bathed quickly, washing my hair with one eye on the money. When I was done, I wrapped myself in a towel and scooped up the envelope of cash from the sink. My hair dripped on my shoulders as I walked back to my room, which was dark. *That's strange. Did I turn off the light? I could swear I didn't.* Suddenly the lamp across the room clicked on, and I gasped.

Enzo leaned back against the dresser, arms crossed.

I dropped the money and slapped a hand to my chest. "My God! You scared me half to death! How did you get in here?" My pulse drummed in my ears.

"Like any civilized person. Through the door."

"The doors were locked."

He shrugged. "I told you I was good with them."

I tightened the towel around me, wishing I'd grabbed a bigger one. It barely came down over my butt, and if I inched it any lower, my breasts would peek over the top. No way could I bend down to pick up the cash at my feet. *What the hell is he doing here?* "I believe a civilized person would have knocked. For God's sake, I'm not even dressed."

"I don't mind." Electricity crackled in the air between us. He wasn't wearing his fedora or full three-piece suit anymore, just the trousers and a white shirt without a collar or tie. It was unbuttoned at the top, loose enough to see his collarbone. Something stirred inside me.

Don't even think about it. "What are you doing here anyway?"

"Originally, I came to apologize."

"You did?" That was a surprise. I'd never heard a man like him apologize, especially to a woman.

"Yes. I thought you might be right about Raymond. I haven't been able to find him today." He paused. "And perhaps I shouldn't have been so rough with you earlier."

"You should be sorry about that." My skin prickled, and a dozen questions formed in my mind. Was he being sincere? Had he made calls to Chicago? More immediately, was he going to leave so I could dress? And why had he said, *originally?*

Then I noticed the necklace dangling from one hand.

He lifted it up. "Where did this come from?" I froze. "It was a gift."

"From who?"

"From my father. For graduation."

He lifted one eyebrow. "A three thousand dollar Tiffany necklace for high school graduation?"

My insides twisted uncomfortably. How did he know what the necklace was worth?

"What do you want, Enzo? To apologize? Fine, I accept. You want the rest of the ransom money? I've got it right here." Carefully, I dipped at the knee and picked up the stack of bills, keeping the towel together with one hand. "I was planning on bringing it to the club as soon as I was dressed. In exchange, you'll release my father. Tonight." I tried to appear tough, but it was difficult in bare feet and wet hair.

He answered my demand with a laugh.

"What's so funny?" My face burned.

"You. Standing there in a towel, issuing orders to me after I catch you in a lie."

"What lie?"

He nodded at the necklace. "I bought this for Gina almost a week ago, but I hadn't given it to her yet. Then last night, probably during the raid that wasn't really a raid, it disappeared from my apartment at the club, which had been broken into. Because of all the chaos over the hijacking, I didn't notice it until this afternoon. And now it's here, in your possession."

I stared at him. "You can't think I stole it. I was with you the whole time."

"Maybe it was your little friend, Joe Lupo. I hear he works for Scarfone now. Where was he last night?"

"He wasn't at the club."

"Of course not. He was busy hijacking my shipment and shooting my men. Is he in Chicago too?"

Get off the subject of Joey. My voice shook when I spoke. "Listen, I don't know where that necklace came from. It was just handed to me at the store by some kid off the street today."

"You said before it was a gift. There's the lie."

Exasperated, I nearly threw my hands up until I remembered they were holding the towel. "Well, I didn't know what to say! How was I supposed to know it was yours? None of this makes any sense to me." I shivered. "I'm just trying to get that ransom money, Enzo. I know nothing about anything else."

He came toward me, still holding the necklace. "I want to believe you, but I think you know more than you're telling me." Reaching behind me, he pushed my bedroom door shut, and I winced at the noise.

Nervous, I sidestepped him and moved deeper into the room, remembering how he'd grabbed me earlier today. "Enzo, please. I didn't steal the necklace. And I don't know who did."

He backed me into the dresser and put his hands on my shoulders, but instead of getting rough, he turned me gently toward the mirror and draped the necklace around my neck. Our eyes met in the glass, and my breath caught as he fastened the clasp. Chills spilled down my arms when he brushed my wet hair aside and lowered his lips to the skin behind my ear.

"Oh, God." My room tilted and whirled like a carnival ride.

"Sometimes I think," he whispered, sweeping his lips down the curve of my neck, "that you were sent to me as punishment for the things I've done. For the things I've prayed for." He put his hands on the dresser, one on either side of me.

"What have you prayed for?" I barely got the words out. A cyclone of desire and fear swirled within me.

He kissed my shoulder before answering. "When I was an altar boy back in Brooklyn, I used to bow my head when the priest said to pray, but instead of thinking about the sick or the poor or the departed souls, I'd think about my father and other men like him, and ask God for the things they had—money, power, control." With each word, he dropped a kiss across my shoulder blades, setting my back on fire. "And you know how they got it? By giving the people what they wanted. I knew what they did behind closed doors, the deals they made, the rivals they took out.

But on the streets, they were adored—women holding up babies for them to kiss, men falling to their knees to beg for favors, children scrambling for nickels they'd hand out. It was pure adoration." His teeth raked against my other shoulder, followed by the softness of his tongue. "And it meant complete control."

The movies make you want things, Tiny.

Joey's words echoed in my mind, although for Enzo it hadn't been a movie that inspired want, but real life. And unlike Joey, Enzo wasn't talking about wanting the cars or the clothes or the fancy apartment. He wanted the power. The adoration. The respect.

"And me?" I whispered. "Where do I fit in?"

"I've come a long way since those days. I no longer pray for the things I want. I just do what it takes to get them." His arms wrapped around me, one hand stretched taut over my stomach and the other capturing a breast. "Then I meet you, and that control begins slipping through my fingers." He pulled me back against him, and I could feel the hard length of his erection through the thin towel. "I don't like it."

The hell you don't. I met his eyes in the mirror. "Your body feels differently."

His breath warmed my neck. "Yes." He moved his hands over me, squeezing my breasts and hips.

Don't trust him, warned a voice in my head. But my nipples peaked under his touch, and my head lolled backward as he pulled me even tighter against him. The ransom money slipped from my fingers and hit the floor again. "This is all wrong," I said, my voice as weak as my resolve.

"Maybe." He slid one hand down over my pelvic bone and reached under my towel with searching fingers. "Maybe not. I've been thinking today that we could help each other. We each have something the other wants."

Lord almighty, does he have something I want. As he slipped one finger inside me, I remembered how he'd awakened every nerve ending in my body, the way he'd filled me to bursting with need.

"You're wet already," he whispered.

"I—I just took a bath," I said, unwilling to give him the satisfaction of knowing what he did to my body without even touching it.

He laughed softly as his fingers stroked the silky folds between my legs. "Does that mean you don't want to get dirty again?"

Resistance was leeching itself from my bones. If I didn't stop him now, I knew I never would. Pushing his arms aside, I moved away from him, holding the towel tight. I spoke firmly, and I meant the words. "The only thing I want is for your family to leave mine alone."

He looked at me, his breath coming heavy. "I could arrange that. But I want something in return."

"Take the necklace. I don't want it."

"That's not what I meant."

"I'll pay the rest of the ransom."

One side of his mouth hooked up as he moved toward me again. "That's between you and my father. I want something for me." He reached for my hips, and set them against his.

"What?" I asked, struggling not to moan at the feel of him pressing on me. *If I just rise on tiptoe, it would be the perfect spot.*

"I want you to work for me."

"Work for you?"

"Your pal Joe is in with Scarfone's gang now, and he'll have all kinds of information I could use. All you have to do is pay attention when they talk." He put his hands on my buttocks and squeezed, grinding against me. "And then come to me."

272

Oh my God, that feels so good. But he was asking me to switch sides, to turn my back on Joey, the only person who'd helped me. I felt no particular allegiance to Sam Scarfone or the River Gang, but I couldn't betray Joey.

Even if it means getting Daddy released?

I swallowed and tried to find my voice. "You can't hurt my friend. You have to promise me that."

Enzo kissed my forehead, my temple, my chin. "I won't touch him, unless I find out he stole the necklace."

"He didn't," I insisted, although I was less sure of that by the moment. What other explanation was there? "How long do I have to...work for you?" The friction between us was melting all thoughts in my brain into one—*I want him. Now.*

His mouth lingered on my ear. "Just for a little while, long enough for me to get back what Scarfone owes me. That's fair, don't you think?" I felt the towel being loosened and closed my eyes as it fell to the floor. Enzo ran his hands up underneath my breasts, rubbing my nipples lightly with his thumbs.

"I can't think when you touch me like that."

"Good. Then we have a deal."

This is how he operates. He likes to be in control, and then he makes you promise things when you're weak for him. I knew his strategy by now.

But he had a weakness too. I knew that as well.

I opened my eyes. "We might have a deal." Unbuttoning his pants, I took great pleasure in both his quick inhale and his solid erection, which swelled further in my hands as I stroked him. "But maybe I should punish you a little bit first, for sneaking in here while I was bathing. For scaring me." I squeezed his cock a little harder, rubbed a little faster.

His mouth fell open and a quick laugh escaped as he braced himself with his hands on the dresser behind me. "Yes. Ah, God, yes." His eyes closed and his breaths became raspy and fast. A heady feeling surged through me as I brought him closer to release. I smiled hearing his low moans, seeing how he leaned into the dresser to keep his balance. Wearing only the necklace as I made this gorgeous, powerful man groan and tremble with my hands, I knew the seductive nature of power and control. *I can have what I want.*

My eyes widened as his jaw clenched and he fell forward against me, thrusting into my grasp, against my stomach. He clutched my lower back with one hand, fingers digging into my skin, and I felt something hot and wet on my belly and slipping through my fingers. A smile crept onto my lips. "And you an altar boy," I whispered, clucking my tongue.

2He shuddered once more and held me tighter. "I want to fuck you. Now."

I hadn't thought it would be possible, but sure enough, he was still hard in my hand. "Don't you at least want to catch your breath?"

"No," he said, bringing one hand to my breast and squeezing hard. "I don't."

"Hold on a minute." I had to stop him before I lost my senses. Bending down, I picked up the towel and brought it to my stomach. "I want something first."

He smiled. "I know what you want."

"No, not that. I mean, yes, that, but—" I pushed him back, feeling heat in my face. "First you're going to make a phone call." I used the towel to clean up a little and handed it to him. Then I went to the closet and pulled out my robe. "You're going to tell your father I gave you the rest of the money and this kidnapping business is over," I said with finality, slipping my arms through the sleeves and belting it around me. Tight.

"And then?"

When I turned, I saw that he was put back together, pants buttoned and shirt tucked in. But his skin was still flushed with desire, his thick hair tousled, and it made me even wetter between the legs. "And then we can...negotiate further."

He reached for me, and this time my heart thudded only in anticipation. When he slipped his arms around my waist, I put my hands on his chest and kissed his lips for the first time that night. They were warm and soft, and they opened over mine as he teased me with his tongue. "I like negotiating with you," he said, trying to untie my robe. I pushed him back.

"Later. The phone is in the front hall."

He raised his brows. "Don't you want to supervise me? Make sure I say exactly what I'm supposed to?"

"I trust you." The words were out of my mouth before I could think. Enzo stared at me a moment, his expression curious, but he said nothing before leaving me alone in my room.

When he was gone, I looked in the mirror. My damp hair was a tangled mess, and my face was as flushed as Enzo's, but what caught my eye was the necklace. The stones at the base of my throat glittered in the lamplight. *He bought this for her.* Why—because he loved her? Because her father owned a distillery? Was this a token of affection or a bribe to sweeten a deal? What was she to him? And where the hell did I fit into his life?

I didn't. I wouldn't.

Reaching behind my neck, I unclasped the necklace, furious with myself. *What are you thinking, getting all rosy-cheeked and puckering up for him? Don't be a fool. You don't trust him and he doesn't trust you. What he said was right—you each have something the other wants, and that's where the relationship begins and ends. You want to fool around, fine, but don't fool yourself into thinking this "partnership" is anything more than another business deal.*

I put the necklace in the box, my bare neck hot with shame. I never should have worn it. I never should have told him I trusted him—he would only take advantage of it. Putting the top on the box, I pressed it shut and vowed I'd never wear the damn thing again. *I'm giving it back. And if I ever see it on that lousy little tart, I'll laugh in her pug-nosed face about where it's been.*

Grabbing the box, I switched off the lamp and left my room. I was heading down the stairs when Enzo started to yell.

Hurrying into the kitchen, I saw him shouting obscenities into the phone—at least I assumed that's what they were, since he was yelling in Italian. He smashed the receiver onto the hook and ran a hand through his hair, seething. It was the most unhinged I'd ever seen him.

"What's going on?"

"I have to go." With barely a look at me, he headed for the front door.

"Hey!" I grabbed him by the elbow. "Just a minute. Is your father releasing him tonight or not?"

Enzo closed his eyes and exhaled. "Something is going on. I just can't figure out what the fuck it is." He looked at me again. "Your father is missing."

Chapter Sixteen

My jaw dropped. "Missing?"

Enzo nodded, staring me down. "As of this morning, although this is the first I've heard of it."

"You mean, he escaped?"

"Impossible. Not without help."

I didn't know whether to be excited that he'd escaped or worried that he was gone without a trace. Then I realized why Enzo was looking at me so intently. "It wasn't me, Enzo."

"I don't think it was you. At least, I don't think you physically removed him."

I narrowed my eyes. "But you think it was my idea. That I arranged it."

He said nothing for a moment, and I slammed the necklace box into his torso. He grabbed it with both hands and grimaced.

"Search the house, Enzo! He's not here. Search the fucking garage, the store, I don't care!" I pointed a finger in his face. "Only stop acting like you're going to seduce me one minute and then strangle me the next."

He glared at me, seething. "That is, in fact, exactly how I feel about you."

I slapped him. Hard, right across his handsome face, fury pounding through my veins.

I wanted to do it again, but he grabbed my wrist on the second swing, and when I brought the other hand up he got that one too, the necklace box hitting the floor with a smack. We grappled for a few seconds, knocking the phone off the hall table. I was overpowered quickly and backed up against the wall, my wrists pinned on either side of my ear. His breath bathed my lips, and his eyes flashed with rage and passion.

"So which is it now?" I asked through clenched teeth.

"Both." Smashing his mouth to mine, he released one wrist and wrapped his hand around the front of my neck, his fingertips digging into my skin without actually cutting off air. I should have brought my knee up hard, or at least bit him, but instead I licked his lips, searching for his tongue with my own, desperate to drive him as mad as he drove me.

He stepped back, dropping his arms. Our chests rose and fell.

"Go find him, and bring him back here," I demanded. "You'll get the money when I see he's unharmed. And take that goddamn necklace with you."

Without another word, he picked up the jewelry box, turned on his heel and stormed out the front door.

I locked it behind him, for all the good it would do.

#

Upstairs, I sat still as stone on my bed and tried to think through this new twist. *Daddy is missing? Where the hell is he?* And if he showed up here, what would I do? It would look like I'd lied to Enzo, and then he wouldn't hold up his end of our deal—to leave my family alone. Tipping over, I lay my head on my pillow and curled into a ball. His scent still lingered in my bedroom, and I inhaled deeply.

No, no, no. What am I doing with him?

Despite our inability to keep our hands to ourselves, the two of us would always be suspicious of each other. His passion for me was matched by his need for power and a capacity for violence. I was torn between not wanting to betray a friend and protecting my family against further harm—not to mention my all-consuming attraction to him. But our desire could not dissolve our distrust, and our distrust poisoned our desire.

We were toxic from start to finish.

#

Somehow I must have fallen asleep, because I woke with a start when I heard the shatter of breaking glass. Heart pounding, I bolted out of bed and dashed to the dresser, yanked open my underwear drawer and pulled out the gun. I'd never fired a gun before but my hands instinctively closed around the hilt, one finger on the trigger. I froze at my bedroom door, listening for an intruder.

Nothing.

I counted to ten, my heart thumping in my throat, and ventured through the doorway.

Nothing.

Holding my breath, I took the steps down slowly, both hands on the gun. The light was still on in the front hall. I looked left toward the kitchen and saw nothing amiss, and to my right the front door was still shut tight. Straight ahead, the front room was dark, but as I entered it, the hairs on the back of my neck stood up.

One front windowpane was busted, and a brick lay on the floor between the sofa and the coffee table. Looking wildly around the room, pointing the gun in every direction, I listened for the hiss of a fuse, recalling what Enzo had said about explosives. But I heard nothing except crickets through the broken window. Lowering the gun, I turned my attention to the brick, which had a piece of paper tied to it with twine. I set the gun down on the table and snatched the paper free.

It was Daddy's writing.

Bring the money to the boat house at midnite tonite or they will kill me

Midnight! What time was it? I raced into the kitchen to check the clock. It was almost eleven. I put my hand over my stomach. *Breathe*, I reminded myself. *In and out. Make a plan.*

I had the money. I had no car, but I could go down to the boathouse on foot, although it would take me about half an hour. The bigger problem was that I didn't have Joey to go with me, and I had no idea who I'd encounter there. Whoever it was had Daddy for sure—I knew by his chicken scratch handwriting and the way he spelled midnite and tonite.

Midnight. Tonight.

I had one hour.

I raced up the stairs, ripped off my robe and threw on a chemise and dark blue dress. My hair had dried before I had a chance to even comb it, so I hid it under an oversized cloche. Forgoing stockings, I stepped into my shoes and shoved the money inside a large purse.

Right next to the pistol.

#

By the time I reached the boathouse drive, my hip was aching, my feet hurt, and my dress was sticking to my skin. I peered through the dense shrubs and undergrowth, reluctant to leave the comforting

284

glow of the lights on Jefferson behind. But I had no choice. Carefully I made my way down the dirt road, trying to avoid turning my ankle in a rut, and jumping at every snapped twig.

When the boathouse came into view, lit only by a crescent moon, I stopped. A breeze rustled the trees around me, cooling my skin. I saw no cars. Heard no human voices. Closing my eyes, I exhaled and waited for my hammering pulse to slow down. I wondered how many of them were in the boathouse, and whether Daddy was with them too. How had they gotten here—by boat? I couldn't see the dock from where I stood, and I'd have to get past the boathouse to check. A few more minutes ticked by while I put off stepping from the trees and facing whoever waited for me inside.

Enough stalling. It's got to be close to midnight.

Squaring my shoulders, I left my hiding spot and headed toward the boathouse with one hand in my purse, my fingers on the reassuring metal of the gun. I was three feet from the door when a shadow came at me from the direction of the dock. My hand closed around the gun just has a heavy object slammed against my left temple.

285

The shadow eclipsed the moon, and everything went dark.

#

As the fog lifted, a man in a burlap sack mask with eyeholes stood over me, coiling a rope. When I could see, I realized I was lying down in the bottom of a boat, my wrists tied together in front. Lifting my arms, I touched my sore temple with the back of one hand. The pain reverberated throughout my skull. My hat was gone, but it had probably saved my skin from breaking open. I attempted to sit up, but my head throbbed, making me woozy and nauseous. I fell right back down again, moaning in pain.

"Not so fast, doll." That voice...it was familiar, but I couldn't place it. Confusion clouded all my senses.

My purse—I need my purse, I thought through the haze. *There's something in there that will help me.* I felt around for it the best I could, but my efforts garnered only a squawk of laughter.

"Don't bother, toots. I got the goods right here
— the money and the heater. Quite a piece you were
packing. Not as good as mine, though." He jerked his
head toward the machine gun on the seat behind him.
"But I'm gonna pat you down anyway. Been waiting to
get my hands on you." He knelt and groped me
roughly, taking perverse pleasure in running his hands
all over me, laughing continuously, an annoying,
scratchy heh-heh-heh that prompted my brain to make
a connection.

The pimply-faced goon, Raymond's friend.

I licked my dry lips. "Harry?"

"You remember me, huh?" He pulled off the
mask.

"Unfortunately."

He squeezed my upper arm and snarled.
"Kinda brave for a little girl without her gun. If I hear
another insult, you might end up without more than
that. Like your pretty face."

"What do you want with me? You got the
money, so just let me go."

"No chance. Now stay put." He started the
engine, and we took off, heading downriver. Looking
back, I could see Daddy's boat bobbing next to the
dock. Clarity was returning with painful jabs to the

head. *Am I being kidnapped? Where's Daddy? Are the DiFiores behind this?* But it didn't make sense—unless Enzo had lied about my father being missing and set me up. Was the entire phone conversation a ruse? It was possible, but why would Angel need to trick me into giving him the money a day early? Why wouldn't Enzo have just taken it earlier tonight?

I tried to piece everything together as the boat picked up speed. The heist, the false alarm, the necklace, Enzo and I at the boathouse, the package from Joey, Enzo and I in my bedroom, the phone call, the brick through the window, the blow to the temple, being tied up and taken somewhere by Harry.

But I was completely baffled.

The boat swooped through the chop, as unsteady as my stomach. *Stay calm and think. Was it possible Harry was working alone?* "Where are we going?" I shouted over the motor, tucking my knees inside my elbows. Suddenly I was chilled to the bone.

"Niagara Falls, doll. For our honeymoon." He cackled with glee.

"Did you take my father?"

He looked at me. "Maybe."

"Where is he?"

"At the bottom of the river, waiting for you."

288

"You son of a bitch!" I yelled, kicking at his ankles and seething when he laughed. Frantic to escape, I looked at the rough black water. I considered jumping in and swimming for it, but knew I'd be no match for a machine gun, especially with my hands tied. I'd be dead in seconds, my bullet-riddled body found days later by some unsuspecting bootlegger or fisherman, the account written up in the papers. *Girl Caught in Crossfire of Bootleg Wars.* I didn't want my sisters to suffer that. Hunkering down, I hugged my knees to my chest again and kept my face averted from Harry. If I had to look at him, I'd be sick. *Where is he taking me? Did he really kill Daddy? And why doesn't he just kill me, if that's what he's going to do?* Finally, I laid my forehead on my knees and wept.

Eventually, we reached some unlit docks along the river. I saw no one around. Harry pulled up and tied the boat to a post. After jumping onto the wooden platform, he reached down for me and I was forced to give him my arms. He yanked me roughly to my feet like a small child and marched me to a dark-colored Chevrolet. Opening the door, he shoved me in the back seat. "Lie down back there and be quiet. I don't have any problem taking you out of this, so you better behave." He slid into the driver's seat, placing his gun and my purse beside him, and started the car.

Could I reach the gun? Not without his catching on to me. I lay back across the seat, wiping my nose on my sleeve.

I was trapped.

#

After an endless drive on horribly bumpy roads that made my head feel as if someone was beating it with a crowbar, Harry slowed the car. I sat up and looked out the window at a small dilapidated cabin, lit only by the Chevrolet's headlamps. Panicked, I searched for other houses but saw nothing—just woods. The headlamps went off, and blackness enveloped us. Harry spoke over his shoulder. "No use screaming, so keep your mouth shut. I don't like girl noise."

He put his gun in his coat and got out. When he opened my door, he locked his fingers around my upper arm and dragged me toward the cabin. I'd have a bruise tomorrow for sure. If I had a tomorrow. He led me up a few creaky wooden steps to a lopsided porch and knocked on the front door—a rhythmic series of long and short staccato beats.

"That's not the knock," complained a voice from inside.

"Shut your mouth and open the fucking door, you idiot," shouted Harry. "I've got her."

The door opened, revealing a sparsely furnished room with a plank floor. Ahead of me, a beat-up brown sofa was against the wall. A square table and two mismatched kitchen chairs were off to the left, and in the low light of a few kerosene lanterns, I saw the dim outline of crude bathtub gin equipment in the corner. The door slammed behind us, and lurking there in the shadows was Raymond DiFiore. "Hiya, doll. Glad to see me?"

"No." I narrowed my eyes at him, then looked around for Enzo. If he'd set me up, I was going to kick him in the balls, and then kill him. I was pretty sure Raymond would let me.

"Where do you want her?" Harry released his grip on my arm and pulled the wad of bills out of his pants pocket.

"How much she have on her?"

"Didn't count it yet."

Raymond snatched it from Harry's hands. "I wanna count it."

Harry rolled his eyes but allowed Raymond to shuffle through the bills.

"Fifty-six hundred," Raymond announced proudly.

"Wrong," I said. "There's only five grand there, you idiot. It's what I owe your father."

"Don't make funna me!" he yelled in my face. "You should be nice. I told Harry not to hurt you. And I sent you a present." He huffed. "I'll count it again."

A present? The realization turned my stomach to lead. The necklace. Raymond had stolen the necklace from Enzo's apartment and sent it to me. But why?

He parsed through the stack of bills with an agonizing lack of haste as I shuddered, disgusted that I had worn a gift from this jerk. And I didn't see how it made sense. He'd stolen from his own brother? *Maybe Enzo isn't involved.*

"Yep. About Five G's." Raymond looked pleased with himself and pocketed some cash.

"Hey, gimme some too," demanded Harry.

Raymond looked put out, but he handed Harry a few bills and tamped the rest of it together. "Should I put this behind the pishmission?"

"Partition! Partition! How many goddamn times I gotta tell you how to say that word!" shouted Harry. "And it's not a partition, it's just a wall. You drive me fuckin' crazy." He grabbed the money from Raymond. "Move the sofa."

Raymond did as he was told, revealing a removable panel in the wall. Behind it was a stash of guns, booze, and cash. My insides twisted painfully— this was an elaborate setup. What did they want with me?

Harry shut the panel and moved the sofa back in place. "Now where should I put her? In the bedroom?"

"Yeah. For now." Raymond looked at me, a glint in his eye. "I think you'll like it there, got a little surprise for you."

"Wait a minute." I dug my heels in before Harry could drag me away. "Why are you keeping me here? What do you want?"

"What everyone wants, doll," said Raymond with a ghoulish leer. "A piece of the pie."

"And since no one was gonna give us any, we decided to serve ourselves." Harry laughed obnoxiously before giving me a shove down a short hallway to our left. He opened a door and pushed me through it, pulling it closed behind him.

The room was dark and fetid. As my eyes adjusted, I saw a bed in front of me.

Someone was on it.

I gasped, and the person moved. *At least it's not a dead body*, I thought with temporary relief. But was it one of them? Pressing my back to the door, I stiffened. "Who's there?"

The person sat up. "Tiny?"

Chapter Seventeen

It was Daddy.

Relief flooded me and I rushed toward him, my throat closing up. Our reunion wasn't joyful, exactly, but it was as happy as we had ever been to see one another. We embraced the best we could with one of his hands cuffed to a metal bed frame and my wrists tied together. I leaned into him, weeping on his chest, and he squeezed me with one arm. His shirt smelled terrible, but I didn't care.

"They kept telling me they were going to hurt you," he said, sniffling a little. I hadn't seen him cry since my mother died. "Are the girls all right?"

"They didn't hurt me," I lied, hoping it was too dark for him to see the bruise on my head. When I sat up, I let my hair fall over it, just in case. "And everyone is fine. I had Bridget take them out of town. But what's going on? Why'd they bring us here?" I attempted to wipe my nose with the back of one bound hand.

"I've no idea. For days I was kept in a basement room somewhere, and then in the middle of last night I was blindfolded, cuffed, and brought here. Who are they?"

"The dark one is Raymond DiFiore, Angel's son. The other is his pal, Harry." I glanced toward the door and lowered my voice. "Do you think they did this behind Angel's back?"

"Why do it this way otherwise?"

"I don't know. Maybe they just wanted the rest of the ransom money for themselves. But why kidnap *me*?"

Daddy's shoulders slumped. "I'm sorry, Tiny. This is all my fault. I should've never ignored those black hand letters asking for payment."

"No. You shouldn't have." A spark of anger shot through me. "Especially not after Vince. You know what these guys are capable of."

He straightened up a little. "I know, but it's never been like this! A man could make his money the way he wanted to, without paying up to anybody."

"Those days are over, Daddy," I said, recalling what Joey told me about independent bootleggers. "Everybody pays up now." A glance out the lone window revealed no sign of dawn. My eyes had adjusted to the dark, and the four walls closed in on me. How had things gone so wrong so fast? Just hours ago I was standing naked in my bedroom next to Enzo.

Enzo. A little hope nibbled at my despair. *Maybe he can help us.* "Angel's older son, Enzo, came to see me today."

"Why?"

"Because a gang hijacked a shipment of rum he had sent from New York, and he wondered if I was behind it."

"Why would he think that?"

"Because the guy who *was* behind it, Sam Scarfone and the River Gang, used *your* hearses to transport the load. A few men were killed."

"What! Jesus Christ, Tiny!" The cuffs rattled against the metal bed frame as Daddy got agitated. "Why the hell did he have my hearses?"

The ropes chaffed my wrists as I jerked my arms around in frustration. "Because I gave them to him! I had to, so he'd allow me to get the whisky I needed to make the ransom money. See, Sam and the River Gang control bootlegging on the water now," I said bitterly. "You want to smuggle whisky from Canada, you're gonna pay him for the privilege."

His shoulders squared. "The hell with that!"

297

Unbelievable. "That attitude is what got us into trouble in the first place! This is how it is now—you want to run booze, you're gonna have to pick a side and pay up." I had to whisper, but my tone was raw with ferocity.

Daddy scratched his face, which was covered with days-old beard growth. "What's Joey say?"

"Joey made his choice. He's working for Scarfone, and right now he's in Chicago trying to unload that stolen rum. He's the one who gave me the last five grand to spring you, which is now in Harry and Raymond's stash."

"Jesus. Musta been a big load."

"It was. Not only of rum, but opium too, which I don't think Scarfone knew." But just then I realized he might have known the whole time. Maybe that's why he wanted that shipment so badly. "But we're not lining up behind the River Gang. I made a deal with Enzo."

Daddy jerked his chin at me. "What kind of deal?"

"In exchange for their leaving our family alone, I promised to get some information out of Joey, just enough for Enzo to get back what he lost in that heist."

He was silent a minute. "So then we should line up behind Scarfone—at least, we should make it look like it."

Was he right? I supposed so, although the duplicity involved made my skin crawl. One false move in either direction could land Daddy—or me—in big trouble.

"But we've got to get out of here first," he went on. "If we can escape the cabin, do you know how to get back to the city?"

"No. We'd need a car. We're way out of town." Sitting up taller, I made a decision. "I'm gonna ask them what they want. I can't stay trapped like this."

"No!" The cuffs rattled on the bed frame. "Don't go out there alone. They might hurt you."

"They could have done it already. I don't think that's what they want." I stood up and tried the door. Unlocked. Squinting at the light, I walked into the front room.

"Hey, who told ya you could come out?" asked Raymond. He and Harry were sitting at the table, counting all the cash I'd seen behind the panel.

"Enjoy the reunion?" Harry snickered.

"Listen," I said. "You got the money. What else do you want?"

"We're still thinking about that." Raymond got to his feet and stretched. His bulky chest strained against his shirt, which probably used to be white but was now grayish with yellowed underarms. It was amazing how someone who looked so much like Enzo could disgust me so much. "My first idea was to take your money and buy some dope to sell. I'm tired of being cut out of all the deals my father and brother make."

"But you're stealing from your own family."

Raymond shrugged. "I was gonna give it back — after I doubled it. They're gonna see how I can be a... asset to the operation."

I marveled at the backward logic. "I'm not sure this is the right way to do it."

"Nobody asked you, slut," said Harry. "So shut the fuck up."

"Don't call her that!" Raymond snapped. He moved toward me and I backed up. "Things are different now," he continued. "Harry told me about the hijacking, and we figure that those hearses were the very same ones we saw at your pop's garage. So now that I've got you too, I'll make a new plan. Figure out how to use you to my best perantage."

"Advantage." Harry shook his head. "Jesus, you're fuckin' stupid."

"Shut up!" screamed Raymond, his face mottling with rage. He put his hands to his head and grabbed two fistfuls of black hair. "Stop calling me stupid all the time!"

"Then quit saying stupid fucking things," Harry said calmly. He didn't even look up from the cash.

"You know what," seethed Raymond, nostrils flaring. "I'm fuckin' done with you." With that, he picked up a pistol lying on the table and fired five shots into Harry's chest and head before I could even blink.

The noise was *deafening*. I screamed as Harry's body jerked and his chair went over backward. Daddy yelled "Tiny!" as my feet pounded down the hallway to the bedroom. Kicking the door shut behind me, I collapsed on the floor and crawled to the farthest wall, popping stitches in my dress. I opened my mouth to tell Daddy what happened but couldn't speak. It was like someone was sitting on my chest—I couldn't get enough air in my lungs, and my ears were ringing from the shots.

"What?" Daddy kept saying. "What happened?"

The bedroom door opened, and Raymond appeared. "I had to shut Harry up. I was sick of him." He held up one finger. "And, he was mean. But this wasn't in my plans, so now I have to think." He shut the door, leaving us alone.

I was numb. "He killed him. Shot him. Right there in the front room. I saw it," I whispered. "I saw it."

"Listen, Tiny," Daddy said, his voice steady. "I know this is hard, but don't panic. I think you're right —if he wanted us dead, he could have done it already. And now there's only one of them but two of us. Let me think."

I was a quivering blob of jelly—I couldn't think about anything but watching the life being jolted out of a human being. Sitting back against the wall, I hugged my arms to my chest and shivered. Daddy asked me about the roads we took to get here, the area outside, the distance I thought we'd driven, but I couldn't answer any of his questions. From the front room we heard thumping and scraping and something being dragged across the floor. *He's getting rid of the body*, I thought, bile rising in my throat. *What if we're next?*

My teeth began to chatter. *I'm too young to die. I haven't even lived yet. I never got to see New York or Paris or Enzo with all his clothes off.* Would the silent, murky depths of this stinking cabin be the last place I'd see on earth?

We had to get out. I didn't care what it took.

"Daddy," I said quietly. "If I can convince Raymond to let you go and keep me, will you go?"

"No! I'm not leaving you with that animal!" Daddy's whisper was vicious.

With difficulty, I got off the floor and sat next to him on the bed. "Listen to me. If he agrees, you go back to the city and find Enzo."

"Why?"

"Because he's not involved in this, and he'll know what to do."

Daddy went silent, scratching his face again. "You trust him?"

"I do right now." It could all change tomorrow, but at this moment he was my only hope. "I just wish I could think of a way to get Raymond to trust me."

"You have to give him something he wants, make him think you're on his side."

I shuddered.

"You're smarter than he is." Daddy nudged my leg. "Talk to him. Figure him out."

I chewed on my lip for a few minutes, thinking it over. I knew what he wanted and how his mind worked. All I had to do was convince him I had a way for him to impress his father and outdo his brother. After a while, a plan formed in my head, but it was risky. How far was I willing to go? "I've got an idea. If it works, you know what to do. I'm going to call him in here."

"What are you going to say?"

"Just go with it. And if it works, find Enzo as soon as possible." I took a deep breath. "Raymond! Are you out there?"

Heavy footfalls thumped down the hall. The bedroom door burst open. "Yeah?" Lit from behind with sickly yellow gaslight, he looked ominous, like a Hollywood monster. His shirt was even more disgusting now, smeared with Harry's blood. My stomach turned.

"I want to talk to you."

He cocked his head. "About what?"

"About what you were saying...you know, making your own deals. Getting your own rackets and proving to your pop you can be an asset to him."

"Yeah?"

"Well, we have an idea."

He ran a hand through his hair, a gesture I'd seen Enzo make before, and crossed his arms. "I'm listening."

With a silent apology to Joey, I said, "I know who hijacked your shipment. I think you could get it back."

"How?"

"Well, my friend Joe is working for Scarfone now. He was bragging to me just today that he's guarding those loaded hearses in a warehouse until Sunday, and then they're going to take them to Chicago. But I know where the warehouse is. We could steal back those hearses with the rum still in them. Imagine showing up at the club with all that booze. You'd be a hero."

"Yeah, I would." He dropped his arms and stood straighter. "So where's the warehouse?"

"It's near Eastern Market. But Joe's not going to talk to you—you'd be shot if you even got close. However, he *would* talk to my father. You let him go, and he'll approach Joe and convince him to steal it back for you."

"Why would your friend do that?" Raymond asked. "Scarfone will kill him."

"Because," said Daddy. "He's not going to have a choice. I know a lot of cops, and I'll show up there with a few of them. They'll do me the favor of cuffing him in exchange for a few cases of rum. Then me and a few guys drive the hearses to the club for you."

"Your pop will give you your own rackets for sure," I said quickly, my voice oozing admiration, "maybe even the whole club." I stood and sidled closer to him. "I heard he was going to give it to Enzo, but now that you're the big time bootlegger, I bet he gives it to you. Then we'll have that drink you promised me."

Raymond considered this. "I want more out of it."

I panicked, but Daddy spoke up. "How about a share in my bootleg business and the garage? I'll give you the percentage your pop wanted—I'll even raise it. He'll be impressed you managed to get more out of me than he could."

"Yeah, he will." Raymond was coming around, I could sense it. My skin tingled with the possibility of victory. "What percentage?" he asked.

"Fifty," I said. "You can have half."

"That's good." He nodded. "But I still want more."

"What else is there?" I fidgeted, trying to keep from screaming at him.

His eyes raked over me. "You."

"She's not part of the offer," Daddy said firmly. I was so repulsed I couldn't find a voice.

"Then no deal." Raymond crossed his arms again. "I get her, or you get to spend your remaining days out in the woods with Harry and I'll take your business anyway."

I heard the ching of the cuffs on the bed as Daddy struggled with his temper and knew I'd better speak up. Swallowing my fear, I said, "OK, Raymond. You can have me too. Whatever you want. Do we have a deal?"

"Tiny, no!" Daddy yelled.

"Deal." Raymond grabbed my arm and dragged me from the bedroom.

"Wait! Where are you taking me?" I demanded. "What about letting my father go?"

"He's staying here for now."

My blood froze. What had I done? "Daddy!"

"You be quiet, girlie. Don't make me mad." He extinguished the lanterns and opened the cabin's front door. Then he picked up a gun from the table and poked it into my side. "We're going back to the city. No funny business."

In the driveway, I considered making a run for it, but I had no idea where I was and guessed he could probably shoot me pretty easily in the open space. Not to mention what he'd do to Daddy, a sitting duck in there, cuffed to the bed. I looked in every direction but saw no sign of sunrise. No way to even tell which way was east or west.

Raymond opened the car door, pushed me into the back seat, and told me to get down. He drove while I wept, bumping around in the back seat on pocked rural roads. *Please, God*, I begged silently. *Help me.* When the ride smoothed out, I picked up my head. We were on city streets now, and the first signs of dawn lit the sky. I recognized the garage where he parked—it was the same one Enzo took me to during the raid. *We're going to Club 23.* The idea pumped some life into me—maybe Enzo was there. Raymond yanked me out of the car and stuck the pistol in my side again.

We went through the tunnel into the club, up several flights of stairs, and emerged in an unfamiliar hallway dimly lit with ornate brass wall sconces. A dark red carpet runner lay in the center of the polished wood floor, giving the appearance of a hotel. Were these private rooms, or apartments? Was Enzo here somewhere? If I called out for him, would Raymond shoot me? Recalling the speed and accuracy with which he shot Harry, I decided not to risk it.

Raymond took a jumble of keys from his coat pocket and fumbled with them. After two unsuccessful tries, he located the correct key and opened the door to a bedroom. Some light spilled in from the hallway, illuminating a large mahogany bed made up with white linens. A dresser was opposite the bed, an tall lamp whose shade dripped with dark purple fringe stood next to a mirror in one corner, and white lace curtains stretched from floor to ceiling over the windows. A narrow door opened onto a tiny bathroom, which I eyed thankfully.

Raymond pushed me in. "Now you be good and quiet in here. If you do everything I say, we still got our deal."

"Wait." I held up my wrists. "Can you please cut this rope? I have to use the bathroom."

"Oh. Yeah, I guess I could." Pulling a knife from his muddy boot, he slashed the rope, and my arms were blissfully free.

"Thanks." I felt like adding *you asshole*, but I bit my tongue.

He stuck the knife back in his boot and left, shutting the door behind him. The lock clicked. I went to the cheval mirror in the corner, wincing at the blackish purple bruise at my temple. My head ached brutally. *I wish I had some aspirin.* After I used the bathroom and washed up, I fell back across the foot of the bed. Closing my eyes, I waited for the tears to flow again, but they didn't. In my mind, a thousand little spiders spun webs of fear, anger, confusion, and pain. But I refused to give up. Tangled in there somewhere was a little thread of hope.

If only I could think clearly, make a plan. *Don't fall asleep. Stay awake. Stay awake.* But my heavy eyelids refused to open. *OK, I'll just rest for a minute or two. I'll think better if I'm refreshed.*

Numb with exhaustion, I slept.

I awoke to someone touching my face.

Chapter Eighteen

I opened my eyes and rolled away when I realized it was Raymond's sweaty palm on my cheek. "Getting your beauty sleep? That's good. I like my girl to be fresh."

"I'm not your girl." I scrambled backward on the bed.

His face darkened. "Hey, we made a deal. So you don't question me."

I twisted my fingers together. "But—but you're so handsome, Raymond. You could have any girl you wanted, I bet." The words made my skin crawl.

He nodded. "You're right about that. I could. And that girl is you." He slid off the bed and stood. "We got an important meeting today."

"What meeting? With who?"

"With my father. So's he can see what I'm doing." He pouted. "I'm sick of being on the side all the time. I want my piece of the pie. Enzo's been eatin' my share all my life."

"The greedy bastard," I commiserated.

Raymond looked pleased. "Yeah." He rocked back on his heels, opening his arms wide. "But now look—I'll be way bigger than Enzo. I'm gettin' the hijacked booze back, I arranged to get a percentage of Jack O'Mara's rackets, and I got a hot little fancy, just like him."

I wondered what he meant by that last bit, but I was too scared to ask. At this point, I'd agree to almost anything—as long as he didn't try to touch me again.

"I can't wait to see their faces when they realize," he went on. "I just hope they permeciate all the work it took."

"Appreciate."

He grimaced. "You better...'preciate it too, doll. I coulda hurt both you and your pop a hunnerd times already. But no." He hooked his thumbs in his braces. "I been a gentleman about it."

I was tempted to shove him to the floor and make a run for it, but I didn't think I could take him down—he wasn't as tall as Enzo, but he was a lot bulkier.

He waved a hand at me. "Now go clean yourself up. I gotta go get your pop and work out the details of our arrangement. I'll be back later." He turned to leave but halted abruptly, lurching back around to reach for me. Before I could protest he grabbed me by the shoulders, pushed me backward on the bed, and smashed his face to mine. I could barely breathe against his smothering lips, and his chest was unbearably heavy. I did my best to squirm out from under him, twisting my face from side to side, but he had my arms pinned. Finally, he let go and backed off, and I wiped my mouth with my sleeve.

Raymond harrumphed. "You better get used to that. A man's got a right to kiss his girl." He adjusted the crotch of his pants.

I'm not your girl! I wanted to scream. But Daddy wasn't safe yet, so I pressed my lips together.

"That's better." He smoothed the front of his shirt and exited, closing the door behind him.

I wiped my mouth again. My head still hurt, but my mind was much clearer now that I'd gotten a little rest. I slid off the bed and went to the window.

The day was overcast but it looked like late morning, maybe early afternoon. The window opened a little, but not enough for me to get through and it was too high to jump anyway; the concrete below looked terribly unforgiving. The window faced the alley behind the building, and I didn't see anyone to shout to.

A telephone—maybe there was a telephone in here somewhere! I searched every inch of the room but came up with nothing. *And who would you call anyway? The police?* I bit my lip. There was only one person who could help at this point, and that was Enzo. How could I find him? Scream? Bang on the door?

The door. My eyes slid sideways to it. Raymond hadn't been holding keys in his hands when he left. Slowly, a prayer on my lips, I went to the door, grasped the knob, and twisted.

Unlocked.

I gasped in happy surprise. Poking my head out, I saw no one, so I stepped into the hall and closed the door softly behind me. I slipped down the carpeted hall into the stairwell, where I paused to catch my breath and think for a moment. Where could Enzo be? I figured I had at least two hours while Raymond drove to that cabin and back, but still I moved quickly, my feet a blur as I descended three flights of stairs.

At the bottom, I paused for a moment. Hearing nothing, I pushed the door open and peeked out onto a narrow, low-ceilinged hallway with a beige-tiled floor and cinderblock walls. It didn't look familiar. I tried to orient myself in the building but couldn't, and my heart was beating so loud it was hard to think—or were those footsteps coming down the stairs behind me? With no time to deliberate, I chose to go left, scurrying down the passage and pushing open the heavy metal door at the end. I caught it before it could make noise slamming shut.

Turning around, I found myself in a large, dark space. As my vision adjusted, I realized where I was—the room behind the bar at Club 23.

This was familiar ground, at least. I ran through the swinging door and out from behind the bar. A moment later I heard the heavy metal door in the storage room slam.

Shit!

I dove to the floor and crawled under a table at one of the curved booths. Some lights came on, and someone began moving bottles behind the bar. *If I can move quietly enough, the clanking will cover my steps.* I removed my shoes—bare feet would be quietest. But where would I go? Any door I chose, I'd have to cross a stretch of open space where I'd be visible from the bar. After what seemed like an interminable length of time, I decided to go for it and hope the person's back was turned. My legs were going numb underneath me.

I popped up, knocking the table with the top of my head. My hand flew to my crown and the bottle noise stopped.

"Hello?" a deep voice called. "Is somebody there?"

It was Enzo. I was sure of it.

Crawling out from under the table, I brought my feet underneath me. "Enzo!" I called, darting toward him on bare toes.

He whipped around and had his gun drawn so quickly I gasped and put my hands up.

"Tiny?" He dropped his arm and looked at me in shock. "Do you realize I could have shot you? Jesus." He put his gun back inside his gray coat and came toward me. "What the hell are you doing in here? And what happened to you?" He put his hand on my chin and tilted my head, examining the bruise on my temple. I pushed his arm away.

"I'm here because your brother had me kidnapped."

"What?" Enzo's forehead wrinkled in confusion.

"I got a note written by my father telling me to bring the ransom money to the boathouse at midnight last night or he was dead. When I got there, Harry jumped me, clocked me on the head, and took the money. Then he tossed me in a boat and we went downriver, but we ended up at some cabin in the woods, where—by the way—he has my father stashed too."

"Raymond has your father? Impossible."

"Are you listening to me?" I stuck my hands on my hips. "He was just planning on stealing the money and buying some dope to sell. But then he shot and killed Harry for calling him stupid one too many times and decided to rethink his plan."

Enzo looked away, dumbfounded. "Why would Raymond do all this?"

I threw my hands in the air. "Because he wants to prove himself to your father! He's jealous of you and wants what you have. I lied and told him I knew how he could get the stolen rum shipment back so he would agree to let my father go. He said yes to the deal once Daddy threw in a percentage of his business and I said he could have me too."

"You said what?" Enzo looked at me in shock.

Heat rushed my face. "I said whatever I had to! Oh—and he's the one that stole the necklace and sent it to me."

317

Enzo touched his forehead between his brows and closed his eyes. "Jesus Christ. Where is he now?"

"He's driving back to the cabin to pick up my father, I think. He took off after pawing at me a little while ago."

"He pawed you?" He picked up his head, anger darkening his face.

"Yes. In the room upstairs where he stashed me early this morning." I shivered.

Enzo put his hands on my shoulders and looked me in the eye, his handsome jaw set. "I won't let him hurt you. I promise. Now—"

"You take your fucking hands off my girl!" shouted Raymond, coming out from behind the bar and pointing a sawed-off shotgun at us.

Enzo shielded me with his body. "Put that down! Have you lost your goddamn mind?"

Raymond fired into a chandelier and I screamed. Crystal and glass fragments rained down from above, clattering onto the tables and floor.

Enzo's hand reached into his coat, but Raymond quickly trained the gun on him. "Not gonna happen that way, brother. I'm done letting you take everything. That girl and her pop's operation are mine now. And I'm getting the rum shipment back. So you can just stick to your own rackets and your own girl for once." He moved toward us and grabbed my arm, pulling me from behind Enzo and then shielding his own body with mine as he backed up. "Call Pop. Get him down here."

"Let her go first."

"Do it!" screamed Raymond.

"Raymond, calm down," said Enzo quietly. "Don't be stupid."

I cringed at the word.

"I'm not stupid!" Raymond gripped my arm even harder. "And I'm sick of everyone treating me like I am. If you call me names again, I'll kill you right here."

"No!" I met Enzo's eyes and silently begged him to play Raymond's game.

Enzo looked at us a moment longer and went behind the bar to make the call. Raymond's breath was hot on my neck. "This ain't the way I wanted it, doll. You shouldn'ta run off."

"I'm sorry," I whimpered. "I was just scared. Please don't shoot anyone."

In a moment, Enzo appeared again. "He's on his way down. Now let her go, Raymond. You made your point." He put one hand in the air and with the other, reached into his coat and removed his gun, which he laid on the bar.

"Fine." Raymond released me and I could breathe again. "You sit there," he ordered, pushing me onto a nearby chair. Enzo met my eyes and nodded slightly, as if to reassure me, but my bones were rattling in my skin. After a minute, the door behind the bar opened again, and Angel strode through, followed by two guards. He looked furious.

"*Raimondo, che diavolo hai combinato*? Enzo says you removed Jack O'Mara and abducted his daughter?"

Raymond's chin jutted as he gestured at me with the gun. "She was in cahoots with Scarfone. I'm using her to get the booze back."

"That's funny, since you're the one who told him about it in the first place," Enzo snapped.

"I did not! You don't know nothin' about it!" Raymond jabbed me in the shoulder. "She knows where it is. She's gonna help me get it back. And I made a deal with her pop for a percent of his operation."

Angel's anger simmered beneath the surface, his face ruddy but his tone calm. "Raymond, you acted without thinking and without talking to me. What have I told you about that?"

"I figured you'd be glad I was taking matters into my own hands."

"Do I look glad?"

Raymond, looking less sure of himself, shifted his weight from one foot to the other. "No. But I can get the shipment back. She said—"

"Of course she did." Angel glanced at me. "I'm sure she said any number of things to convince you to let her go."

"But I didn't let her go." Raymond perked up. "I still got her pop too. And the ransom money."

"Congratulations," spat Enzo. "You did one fucking thing right."

"That's enough from you," Angel said, holding his palm up to Enzo and then glaring at him. "You made mistakes too." He turned back to Raymond. "You said you made a deal for a percentage of Jack O'Mara's operation?"

"Yeah." Raymond rocked forward on his toes and jabbed my shoulder again. "She said fifty percent. Half." He nodded at me, as if I was supposed to back him up.

"Is this true, Miss O'Mara?" Angel asked.

My throat was so dry I could barely speak. "I— I'm sure my father will make a deal with you once he's released."

"That ain't what you said before!" Raymond exploded. "She said we'd be partners! And her pop wouldn't cross me because she's gonna be my fancy!"

"You're out of your fuckin' mind," seethed Enzo.

"You shut up!" Raymond marched over to his brother, and it stunned me how alike they looked in their fury, face to face that way. "And you stay away from her! You got your own fancy. Now I'm getting everything I want!"

I couldn't stand it anymore. "What's a fancy?"

"He means fiancée." Enzo stared Raymond down, fists balled.

"I know what I mean!" Raymond yelled. But his voice came at me through a tunnel as his words registered. *Enzo has a fiancée?* The whole time I'd known him, he'd been engaged to that squeaky little girl? The club spun around me.

When I focused again, Angel was speaking. "Where is he, Raymond?"

"The cabin outside Pontiac. The one with the still out back."

Enzo looked at me then, and I injected my stare with pure venom. He shook his head, as if to say I didn't understand. But I understood. He was a bastard, just like the rest of them, only better looking. I set my face in stone and looked away. I wasn't sure why it shocked me so much, but it did.

Angel motioned to his guards. "Bring Jack O'Mara back to the city. I have a prior engagement tonight, but I'll speak with him tomorrow." He turned to Raymond. "He'd better still be there. And the money too."

Raymond colored again. "It's there."

"Good. Until we're sure, we'll just keep his daughter safe and sound here. Someone take her to a nice room and let her relax. See that she has everything she needs to be comfortable." He came toward me and I shrank back.

"No need to be frightened, *cara*. We're going to work together now." He leaned over and kissed each cheek. His lips were cold.

#

323

I refused to look at Enzo as he followed his father out of the club. After I retrieved my shoes, a guard led me to a room much like the one I'd been in before— still no phone and no way to get out the window. I sat on the bed, my head pounding. After a short time, a maid brought a tray of roasted chicken and vegetables. She set it on the dresser and left without speaking, and I stared at the food for a few minutes. It looked and smelled so delicious, it wore down my determination not to accept any favors from the DiFiores. I ate every bite. And licked the plate.

A few minutes later, the maid brought a stack of white towels and some soap, a toothbrush, and a tube of Colgate. I looked at the maid in disbelief, a timid woman probably in her forties, wearing a black uniform with a white apron. "So what am I, then, guest or prisoner?"

"Miss," she said, leaving the room without ever meeting my eyes.

I sighed. The truth was probably somewhere in between.

After I cleaned up, I put on my chemise but left the dirty blue dress on the chair. Once I got home, I planned on burning it. Crawling into the bed, I got under the covers and looked out the window. My mind was reeling as I tried to digest the horrors I'd experienced.

I'd been kidnapped at gunpoint. Robbed. I'd seen a man shot to death. I'd made a deal with Raymond to free Daddy and been taken hostage myself. I'd learned that Enzo has a fiancée.

Somehow, it was that final thought that tore the first sob from my chest.

Why? I thought angrily, tears leaking from my eyes. Why the hell should it matter? It wasn't as if I'd thought I would marry him. We never should have fooled around in the first place. Had he owed me the whole truth? Admittedly, part of our spark was how forbidden it was. And I'd already known about Gina, although I'd assumed she was only his girlfriend. So what was I so mad about?

Wiping my eyes, I flopped onto my side and curled into a ball, considering a new wrinkle. Did I have feelings for him I hadn't admitted to myself, or even recognized? But that was ridiculous! An intense physical attraction like ours didn't mean anything. He told me himself I drove him crazy. *We don't even really like each other, for God's sake.* Maybe Gina's the one to feel sorry for, a future with a man like that.

But I couldn't bring myself to pity her.

#

A while later—a glance out my window showed a black sky—I heard a soft knock. It wasn't Raymond's hamfisted pounding, so I went to the door. "Yes?"

"It's me." The voice was Enzo's. "Can I come in?"

My legs went rubbery. Half of me was furious with him; the other half knew I shared the blame. So he'd hidden some truth—I had too. "I suppose." I opened the door, and saw the flicker of desire in his eyes as he took in my bare shoulders and legs.

"How are you?" he asked quietly, hands in his pockets. His hair was slightly tousled and his collar was loose, making him look much like he had leaving my bedroom last night. All that plus the soft, warm expression on his face was enough to make my breath come quicker. *Don't look at me that way, you son of a bitch.*

"OK." I stepped back, allowing him to enter, and closed the door.

336

"Have you eaten?" He crossed to the windowsill and leaned against it. "I asked them to bring you dinner."

"I ate." Perching stiffly at the edge of the bed, I stared at the floor. "Has my father been released?"

"Yes. I saw to it myself."

I looked sharply at him. "Then why am I still —"

"My father wants to keep you here until the terms of the deal are decided, which will be sometime tomorrow. I assured Jack you would be under my protection tonight."

"How convenient," I snapped. We stared at each other as the tension ratcheted up another notch.

"Tiny, about what Raymond said. I—"

"I don't want to talk about anything he said. None of it matters."

He nodded. "Fair enough."

A hot laugh escaped me. "Fair. What's fair?" I glared at him. "It isn't fair that my mother died giving birth ten years ago. Or that my little sisters are growing up with me for a mother. It isn't fair that my brother-in-law was shot twenty-one times protecting some fat boss who probably didn't give a shit about him. It isn't fair that my nephews will grow up without a father." I

327

stood up, the heat of indignation rushing through my veins. "It isn't fair that I used up all my tuition money to pay the ransom your father demanded. And it isn't fair that I'm trapped here—in this room, in this city, in this life." I turned away from him, my arms tight across my chest. "And it definitely isn't fair that I still want you. So stop looking at me that way."

Silence. "I can't. I wish I could."

I heard his footsteps on the wood floor. When he put his hands on my shoulders, it sent gooseflesh down my arms. I sighed. "Go away, Enzo."

He slipped aside one strap of my chemise and rubbed his lips on my skin.

I stepped out of his reach and met his eyes. "You could have told me you were engaged to be married."

"Why? Would it have made a difference?"

"Yes. I wouldn't have...done those things with you."

"I'm not getting married any time soon, Tiny. It was more of a business deal than anything else. I told you, Gina's father owns a distillery, and I want to—"

"Please." I held up one hand. "You're making it worse."

He was quiet a moment. "You know, you still owe me some information."

I narrowed my eyes. "We need to renegotiate our terms. The situation has changed."

"Oh?"

"Yes. If my father still has to give up a percentage of his business to you, and I'm going to put myself at risk so you can get your revenge on Scarfone, I want a piece of the action. Enough to pay my tuition this fall."

He raised an eyebrow. "You do a good job for me, I'll see that you have what you need. More even."

"And you'll keep your brother away from me." I shuddered.

Enzo set his mouth in a line. "He won't bother you."

"Good. Then we have a deal." I held out my hand, and he looked at it.

"That's how you want to seal it?"

"Of course it isn't. But you have a fancy, remember?"

He smiled ruefully but took my hand and squeezed it. "If you change your mind, I'm going to stay in the room next door tonight." He let himself out and I locked the door a moment later, my heart tripping faster. *He shouldn't have told me he was staying next door.*

I wished there was a way to lock myself in.

Chapter Nineteen

The clock on the bedside table told me it was just after ten when Enzo left. For a moment, I forgot what day it was, and then realized it was Friday—the club downstairs was probably packed. I was amazed I couldn't hear the music up here and wondered if Evelyn had come back with her new friend. How nice would it be just to meet a handsome guy at a club? Share a drink, a dance, a laugh, a kiss, maybe more... My head still ached and my limbs felt heavy as I crawled between the cool white sheets again and closed my eyes. I was exhausted.

But I couldn't sleep.

He's right next door. One wall away.

Did he wear pajamas or sleep naked? I felt that weightless swoosh in my belly, the one I got every time I thought about Enzo's body.

So don't think about it.

I punched the pillow a few times and put my face in it. How absurd that I still wanted him even now that I knew he had a fiancée. How awful of me. But I did. *Maybe we can be together just once more*, I thought, desire seeping beneath my resolve. *One more time won't hurt anybody. And I'll never stay here overnight again, so I won't be tempted like this in the future.*

I sat up and swung my legs over the edge of the bed.

Should I?

Of course not!

"But I want to," I whined softly.

A clicking noise at the door sent a chill up my spine. It opened and slammed. Before I had time to react, someone was upon me in the blackness, thrashing around and fumbling with my chemise. I couldn't see anything, but the bulky chest told me who it was before he even spoke.

"You little whore." Raymond shoved me onto my back. "I know Enzo was in here. For once he wants what I have and I'm not gonna let him take it." He dragged my slip up to my hips. One hand clamped down on my mouth and he used the other one to undo his pants. Frantically I fought him off, bringing one knee up sharply into his groin. "Bitch!" He slapped me across the face and grabbed his crotch, and I used the momentary pause in his aggression to wriggle out from underneath him. I just needed one good breath to get a scream out, but he was back on me in a second, bearing down with a force I couldn't overcome. I twisted and kicked and pummeled him with my fists, anything to keep him from touching me where he wanted to. When he leaned over me, I butted my head into his chin.

"Ow!" he yelled, lifting his chest off me slightly. But he managed to get his knees between my legs and pry them open. The hand returned to my mouth. I needed him to stop moving if I was going to get another solid knee to his balls, so I went still, as if I were giving up.

It worked—he was surprised and stopped moving. "There, see?" He put his hand on my thigh. "I bet you'll like this." Suddenly a ray of light streamed into the room and weight was lifted from me.

"Bastard!" Enzo threw Raymond into the dresser and punched him in the face so fiercely blood spurted from his nose.

I scrambled to my knees and scooted backward on the bed. The two brothers fought hard, punching and kicking and tumbling to the floor. Someone bumped the lamp and it went over with a crash. I hated watching, but I couldn't tear my eyes away. Raymond had the advantage of his hefty size, but Enzo was in better shape and quicker with his hands. At one point, Raymond was knocked backward onto the bed and I squealed, jumping to the floor. When I spied a smaller lamp on the bedside table, I shocked myself by having the wherewithal to grab it, yanking the cord from the socket. I hurried to the foot of the bed, where Enzo had Raymond pinned, his head toward me.

Then I did the only thing I could think of— clocked Raymond in the temple with the metal base of the lamp as hard as I could, on both sides of his big fat head. Then I backed up until I hit the wall, and black clouds swarmed my vision.

#

I opened my eyes and the kneeling figure of Enzo emerged from a gray haze.

"No." I was still holding the lamp.

"Come on. Let's get you out of here." He took the lamp from my hand, pulled me up and led me to the room next door, where he gently pushed me onto the bed and told me to stay put. He left, shutting the door behind him. I sat in the darkness, listening to myself breathe. My entire body shook violently.

Bringing my knees to my chin, I wrapped my arms around my legs. Men's voices in the next room filtered through the wall, and the door thumped several times.

After a while, Enzo re-entered the room and switched on the light. His sleeveless white undershirt was spattered with blood. So were his hands. He washed up in the bathroom, behind a closed door. When he emerged, his skin was clean and his hair was damp. A bruise was forming on his right cheekbone, and he had red marks on his throat, but his face still made my insides tighten. He sat next to me on the bed.

"Did he hurt you?"

I shivered. "He wanted to."

He reached for the tender spot on my cheek. "That looks painful."

"It's fine," I said, leaning away from his touch.

"No, it isn't. I'm sorry, Tiny. I don't know what the fuck he was thinking. I never have."

"He said he heard you were in my room. That's what set him off."

"One of the men must have seen me."

"Why would they tell him?"

He shrugged. "Everyone's for sale."

I closed my eyes, the weight of his words sinking deep. "Where is he now?"

"He was put in a car and driven to the hospital." Amusement crept into his voice. "You knocked him out cold, and he needs stitches."

I opened my eyes and stared hard at him. "He deserved it."

"He deserved worse." For a second I thought he might try to touch me again, but he didn't.

It's better this way. I sighed. "Enzo, I want to go home. I want an end to this—I'm tired of danger at every turn. I just want to be a regular girl."

He was quiet a moment. "No, you don't."

My feet dropped to the floor. "What?"

"You don't want to be a regular girl. You like danger. You wouldn't be in the bootleg business otherwise."

I jumped up from the bed, my hands shaking. "You don't know anything about me," I said through clenched teeth.

"Yes, I do."

His ability to stay calm while getting under my skin made me itchy with rage. "Go to hell, Enzo! You're nothing but a liar and a cheat and—"

He was on his feet with his mouth on mine in a heartbeat, hands wrapped around my head. Momentarily stunned, my body went slack. "I love when you get angry with me," he whispered against my lips, hands running down my arms. "Your body is all heat."

"Stop!" I pushed against his chest. "I was attacked tonight!"

"Let me make it up to you." He caught my waist and pulled me near, touching his lips to my forehead. "I'll make you forget everything, even your name."

"No," I said, my heart pounding with alternate beats of fury and desire. I pushed him away again and crossed my arms over my breasts, which were tingling. "You can't have me."

He whipped his stained t-shirt over his head in one smooth motion and let it drop. My belly warmed at the sight of his bare chest and golden skin. A slow smile crept onto his lips as he came toward me. "You want me to go?" he asked. "Because I will. I can't let you leave tonight, but if you'd rather be alone..."

I backed away from him.

Tell him to go. Tell him to go. Tell him to go.

But I couldn't say the words.

"Go on, Tiny," he said, coming toward me as my back hit the door. "Tell me to leave." He put his arms on either side of my head, bringing his face close to mine. "Say you don't want me."

A groan escaped me as he swept his lips across my forehead, bent his knees and pressed his hips against mine, letting me know he was hard and ready. *He always wins. I hate him.* "No." Ducking down, I escaped the cage of his arms and ran for the bed, hopping up on it and standing above him for once.

He faced me. "No, what?"

"I won't say I don't want you. I can't."

He came forward and wrapped his arms around my legs, pressing his mouth to the spot that ached for him most. Through the thin cotton of my slip and underwear, his lips and tongue devoured me, and my knees trembled.

"Oh my God," I whimpered, putting my hands on his shoulders to stay upright.

His hands slid from my calves up the back of my thighs and squeezed my buttocks, pulling me tighter to his mouth. When he moaned, I felt the vibrations go through me like an electric shock. He slipped my underwear down to my ankles and I stepped out of it. "Take your slip off," he whispered. I grabbed my chemise at the hem and lifted it over my head. He took my breasts in his hands and massaged them gently before rubbing the back of his fingers over their hard tips. My desire rocketed. "Enzo. I want you. Right now."

"Wait." Taking my hips in his hands, he pushed me back slightly so he could kneel on the bed in front of me. One hand reached for my breast, while two fingers of the other slipped inside me, slowly, easily. I tried to breathe, but need was choking me. He took my nipple between his thumb and finger, and when he pinched it, somehow I felt it deep within my belly. His other hand penetrated me rhythmically as he kissed the insides of each thigh. When he swept his tongue between my legs, lingering at the top, I felt myself swaying and knew I couldn't remain standing.

Dropping to my knees, I ran my hands and lips over the hard lines of his chest and shoulders as he unbuttoned his trousers. Then I sat on my heels while he undressed, my heart racing in anticipation. Every article of clothing that came off kicked my pulse up higher. By the time he was naked and reaching for me, I was panting.

I fell backward as our bodies and mouths came together. His weight on me was glorious and exhilarating, and I wrapped both my legs around one of his. He propped himself up on his elbows and kissed me ravenously, his tongue driving into my mouth. I reached down and took his thick flesh in my hand, sheathing and stroking it the way I had in my room. *I know what he likes.* The thought aroused me beyond belief. I needed to say it out loud, needed him to hear it.

"I know what you want," I said, looking him in the eye. "I know what you like." His cock grew harder in my grip, and I moved my hand faster.

"Not yet," he said, his voice gravelly. I arched my back as he kissed his way down my throat and chest, taking one nipple in his mouth and sucking it. My knees fell wide open, and long fingers pushed inside me, once, twice, three times. I lifted my hips, desperate for more.

"Enzo," I begged, digging my fingers into his shoulders. "Now. Please."

He moved to the other breast, circling the nipple with his tongue before kissing his way back up my neck. "What do you want?" he asked, his breath tickling my ear. He bit my earlobe gently. "You have to tell me." He lifted his hips and set them on mine, rubbing his cock against me in just the right spot. "Tell me you want me to fuck you. Say it."

"I want you to fuck me," I rasped, clutching his biceps and straining up against him. "Now."

He kissed me hard before rolling to the edge of the bed and grabbing his coat off the floor. Taking a small box from the inside pocket, he opened it up and pulled out a condom. When he was finished putting it on, he rolled back to me, and I slipped beneath him, spreading my knees wide. He reached down to position himself between my legs, and I gasped at his entrance. Leaning on his elbows, he pushed in slowly, giving me time to relax into the way he stretched and filled me. My hands flattened on his back and glided down over taut muscle. Our eyes met, and I nearly lost control right then.

"Oh my God," he whispered. "It's even better than I remembered. You feel so fucking good."

I pulled at him, wanting more despite the quick stabbing pains I felt as he began thrusting deeper. My skin was on fire, and his back grew slick with sweat. He propped himself up on his hands near my shoulders, increasing the pressure where our bodies joined together and pushing me closer to oblivion. I looked at his gorgeous face above me. *He's so goddamn beautiful. How can any man be that beautiful? How can I ever possess him as fully as I desire him?*

I wanted more control.

"Turn over." I pushed against his chest, and somehow I got him onto his back and straddled him. He groaned as I sank all the way down, his long, hard cock gliding so deep it hurt. I adjusted my angle to feel the pressure where I wanted it and take in as much of him as I could.

He dug his fingers into my thighs. I clenched my muscles around him and rocked forward and back, placing my hands on his hard, hot stomach. "Fucking unbelievable," he growled, eyes closed.

"Yes," I whispered, undulating my hips faster. Colors swirled behind my closed eyelids.

Yes, yes, yes...

Suddenly he grabbed my hips and held me still, his jaw thrust forward. "You're seriously testing my self-control here, sweetheart. If you want this to go on any longer—"

I widened my eyes. "Sweetheart?"

One side of his mouth hooked up. "Fair warning. If you don't stop moving that way..."

Flashing a wicked grin, I swiveled my hips. I felt him twitch once inside me.

"That's it." His stomach muscles flexed beneath my palms as he sat up and flipped me onto my back, our heads toward the foot of the bed. "Now listen to me," he said, thrusting into me again and again, harder and deeper every time. "You're going to come for me, now. You're going to scream."

"Yes!" I cried, not caring whether I was in control or not. In fact, the complete abandon was pure bliss. Clawing his back, I rocked my hips to match his rhythm. We were all frantic push and racing breath as we climbed toward ecstasy, and then time slowed as everything in my body tightened. "Yes," I moaned. "Yes, yes!"

He came first, momentarily paralyzed as he thickened and throbbed, and I pulled him into me and writhed against him, crying out again and again as the orgasm crashed through my body and lingered in delicious little tremors.

He collapsed onto my chest, and we stayed that way for a moment, each of us gasping for air.

"Oh my God." I blinked. Repeated myself.

After a moment, he propped himself up on his hands and looked down at me. "Are you all right?"

"I'm not sure."

Smiling, he lifted himself off me. "Good."

I rolled to the edge of the bed, scooped up my chemise, and pulled it on. Dazed, I stumbled to the bathroom, shutting the door behind me. I turned on the light and looked in the mirror.

Jesus, is that me? I had bruises on my face and tangles in my hair. My cheeks were flushed and my lips were swollen. But I liked the way my eyes looked —knowing and satisfied, as if I was in on a secret. I couldn't help the smile that inched onto my face. *Yes. I look like a woman who's been to bed with the sheik.*

The problem was, now that I knew the feverish thrill of it, I wanted to do it again. Right now.

No.

My last shred of sense took over. This had to be a one-time-only experience. The smile slid off my face. I used the bathroom and cleaned up, my mood souring.

When I opened the door, Enzo was lounging in his underwear on the bed, smoking a cigarette. He'd lit one for me as well, and handed it to me wordlessly.

We smoked in silence for a few minutes, watching each other through the drifting haze. "I wish I'd brought some whisky up here," he said. "I could use a drink."

"Me too." I dragged deep and hard on the cigarette, searing my lungs. "Although I'm not sure my body can take any more sin tonight."

He cocked a brow. "Let's find out."

"No. We can't do that again."

"Why not? Didn't you enjoy it?" He tilted his head. "Looked like you did. Sounded like you did." He leaned toward me. "Felt like you did."

Heat rushed my extremities. "That's not the point." I put out my cigarette in the ashtray he'd set on the bed and leaned back against the headboard, my legs crossed. *And they're going to stay crossed.* "You're engaged to be married. I don't want to be some little toy on the side you take out and play with whenever you feel like it."

"We can play whenever you feel like it too."

"No. I'll help you get your money back from Sam the Barber—as long as my friend doesn't get hurt —but that's all." I spoke with finality and hoped I sounded more sure than I felt. And why didn't he get dressed again? His bare skin was tying my stomach in knots.

He put out his cigarette and moved the ashtray to the dresser. "I think you're overestimating your willpower." Returning to the bed, he put his hand on my knee and ran it up my thigh. "And I know you're overestimating mine."

345

God, he was unfairly handsome. He lowered his lips to my shoulder as his fingers crept between my legs, nudging them apart. His other hand brushed the strap of my chemise aside and pulled it down, exposing a breast. I knew before he even put his mouth on it I was lost. Closing my eyes, I let the languorous hum take over my body. "This is a bad idea."

"Why? I think we could be good for each other. We just have to keep it a secret. Our very own..." He licked my nipple with one warm stroke. "Dirty little..." He blew cool air across it, and I shivered. "Secret." He took it between his teeth and bit down.

I gasped in pain, but also with the shock of pleasure it brought me. He picked his head up, a fiendish smile on his lips. "Want to bite me back?"

Instead of answering, I got to my knees, pushed him back against the headboard and yanked his underwear down. Without breaking eye contact, I crawled up his body, one leg on either side of him, until my knees bracketed his hips. After tearing off my chemise, I licked my fingers, reached down and touched myself. His mouth fell open.

Slick with desire, I slid down the rigid length of his cock, smiling when he sucked in his breath.

"Don't come," I ordered, delirious with the power I had over my own pleasure—and his. At his strangled groan, I dug my nails into his shoulders. "I mean it."

"You—are—a wicked little girl." He struggled to get the words out, his dark eyes shooting angry fire. This was way too dangerous, and I knew it.

But I didn't care.

And I wasn't a little girl.

"Put your hands on me," I said.

He did as he was told, running his hands up my legs, then over my stomach and breasts. I rotated my hips, and he moved his hands back to my thighs, digging his fingers into my skin. "Easy," he begged.

So I did it again. This time he put a hand to my throat, his eyes warning me not to push him.

I did it a third time, and his fingers snaked up the back of my neck and fisted in my hair. We stared at each other, breathing hard and trying not to erupt with the madness boiling beneath our skin.

"Pull it," I demanded. As I began rocking my hips, his fingers tightened. The faster I moved, the louder I sighed, the harder he pulled. Sharp needles of pain pricked my scalp, the perfect contrast to the unbearable pleasure that exploded in me at the very same moment. I knew right then that I couldn't stay away from him, no matter what the consequences.

And I knew there would be consequences.

Chapter Twenty

When I woke the next morning, Enzo was gone, but I could smell him on my skin. Bringing an arm to my face, I inhaled, and the scent put a smile on my lips and a flutter in my belly. I got out of bed and stretched, discovering I was sore—not only in the expected places, but in my stomach and leg muscles too. I located my underwear and chemise on the floor and pulled them on, wondering what time it was. Actually I wasn't even sure what day it was.

In the bathroom, I looked at myself in the mirror and experienced the same giddy rush I had last night. The eyelet of my chemise was torn at one shoulder, but I had no idea when that had happened. My night with Enzo could be called a lot of things— fiery, explosive, passionate, shocking—but sweet and tender?

Nope.

Really, I was surprised the thing wasn't shredded completely.

Examining my reflection closer, I touched the bruise at my temple. It reminded me of Joey's injury, and I swallowed hard, guilt slamming me like a fist in the gut. I had to deceive him into providing me with information for Enzo, and Joey didn't deserve deception. I owed him Daddy's life, and probably mine too. Squeezing my eyes shut, I exhaled slowly. *Don't think about that now. Figure out how you're going to get your clothes from the next room and get out of here.*

I went back into the bedroom and noticed an envelope had been slid under the door. When I picked it up, I shivered. It was identical to the one Enzo had handed me at the store last Friday afternoon. I tore it open.

Your things will be delivered shortly by a maid. Your father is expected at one o' clock today, after which you will be free to go and my driver will take you home. We should not be seen together in public, although I do look forward to seeing you again. You are mouthy and demanding, and your temper rivals Vesuvius, but so does your passion.

Until then,
Enzo

While I fumed at his backward compliment and the fact that I was still being held here against my will,

I looked for something to cover up with. What would the maid think if I answered the door in a ripped chemise? I was thinking of wrapping myself in the sheet when I saw Enzo's gray coat on the dresser. I shrugged into it, the sleeves hanging far below my hands, and the length sufficient to cover me nearly to the knee. Tightening it around me, I buried my nose in the collar and breathed him in. The sexy smoke-and-tobacco scent made me dizzy.

But my anger still simmered. Why should he be the one deciding when I could leave? And what did he mean, *in public*? That my company was welcome for a romp in his bed but not for a drink at his club? *Go to hell, Enzo.*

A knock sounded on the door and I heard it being unlocked, but no one entered. The knock sounded again. I rolled my eyes—this prisoner/guest business was wearing on my nerves. I opened the door and the same maid from yesterday brought in my dress and shoes, along with towels and toiletries. She laid everything on the bed and left without saying a word, for which I was grateful. Although she didn't make direct eye contact, she had to have noticed I wore nothing but a man's coat.

Banishing that thought, I washed up, brushed my teeth, and dressed. I wished I had a comb or even a hat, but I did the best I could with a little water and my fingers. When I was finished, I returned to the bed and sat. How long would I have to wait here? Drumming my fingers on the spread, I stewed that even after last night, Enzo still wouldn't allow me to go. Was this any better than having a father who controlled my every move? On a whim, I tried the door, but it was locked from the outside.

Grimacing, I moved to the window. *My car is still down there somewhere*, I realized, although my keys were long gone. Harry had taken the money from my purse Thursday night, but who knew what he'd done with the rest of its contents? I shivered, recalling Harry's death in the cabin—I'd seen some surprisingly gruesome things in nursing school, but nothing so immediate in its violence. And Raymond—what would he do now? He'd be furious with me and with Enzo, looking to get revenge. Would his father be able to rein him in? I turned from the window just as Enzo unlocked and opened the door.

Despite my anger, the sight of him still wound me up. His hair was perfectly coiffed, his collar tight, the bruise on his cheek not dark enough to mar his handsome face. "You really need to learn to knock," I snapped.

A smile tipped his lips as he closed the door behind him. "You're not happy to see me?"

I crossed my arms. "What are you doing here? I thought you were sending your driver for me, so we wouldn't be seen together in public."

He came toward me, detangled my arms and slipped his around my waist. His lips pressed to mine, setting my heart pounding, but I didn't open my mouth. How badly I wanted to give in and fall back into bed with him, but this wasn't the pattern I wanted to set. Our affair had to be secret, but he didn't get to make all the rules, deciding how and when we could see each other.

I pulled back. "I'd like to go home now, Enzo. I haven't been there since Thursday night. I need to let my sisters know it's safe to return, and I want a bath and some new clothes." Tilting my head, I added, "Or am I being too mouthy and demanding?"

He put his face in my neck and kissed my throat. "Mmmmm. You smell good. But a bath could be arranged."

I twisted out of his embrace. "No. Not here."

"Why not?"

Gesturing toward him, I said, "I see you've managed to get cleaned up—I don't even have a comb, let alone clean clothes." I pulled my navy dress from my body. "You do realize I was wearing this the night Harry kidnapped me. Is it too much to ask that I be allowed to change out of it?"

He smiled. "I'll help you out of it."

I sighed and shut my eyes, my shoulders slumping. "You're impossible."

"For God's sake, Tiny, you're more fun when you're mad."

My eyes snapped open and my voice took on a hard edge. "You want me to get mad? Now there's something that could be arranged."

"Ah. There she is." He straightened his coat. "I'm afraid you'll just have to wait. I can't let you leave until your father arrives and some kind of agreement is reached, or my father will have my head." He was so cool about it, as if last night hadn't happened at all.

"You once said our fathers' business had nothing to do with us."

"Yes. I believe that was before you sold Sam Scarfone the hearses which he then used to hijack a very pricey shipment of mine."

"I told you, I didn't know what he was—"

35 4

"Shhh." He reached for me again. Wrapping one arm around my back, he brushed my tangled hair back from my face. "Things are what they are between us, Tiny," he whispered, digging his fingers into my waist. "But let's not tarnish them with more lies."

My lower lip quivered. His eyes were black as night and his expression was tight—whether he was controlling his rage or his passion, I couldn't tell. I said nothing as he traced my lips with one finger.

"I believe this affair could be mutually beneficial," he went on, "but in order for that to happen, you and I are going to have to trust each other a little bit. Don't you agree?"

"Yes." My voice cracked.

"So tell me the truth." The arm around me tightened further, bowing my back. "Did you know Scarfone was planning the heist?" He rubbed one finger back and forth across my lower lip.

Suddenly I was tired of lying about what I'd done. There hadn't been a choice. I looked him in the eye and lifted my chin. "I did what I had to do to protect my family."

His brow twitched, as if he were surprised I had admitted it. "Yes, you did. I like that about you." His finger slipped inside my mouth, and without thinking I ran the tip of my tongue across it. He smiled. "You have a talent for deception, Tiny. And I'm glad, because you're going to need it. This is only the beginning."

He removed his finger and put his lips on mine again, more insistent this time, his tongue slashing into my mouth. Despite my earlier decision not to give in, I craved the pleasure and pain our bodies could bring to one another, and I wanted the powerful abandon I felt making him lose control. When the kiss grew reckless, I struggled to get my arms free and reached for the buttons on his coat.

He shocked me by grabbing my shoulders and setting me at arm's length from him.

"What?"

After a moment, he said, "You can go."

"Huh?"

"You can go home." He lowered his arms and adjusted his collar. "I'll have my driver come for you in ten minutes."

I stuck my hands on my hips, tempted to slap him again. "I hate your games."

He pulled his wallet from his back pocket. "How much do you owe him?"

"Who?"

356

"Your friend. Lupo. How much did he give you to pay my father off?"

My jaw tightened. Something about this scene was too familiar. "None of your business."

"Goddammit, Tiny." He pointed a finger at me. "You're not to owe him anything—not money, not information, not favors. This is part of our deal, now tell me what he gave you."

I had to think about it, Joey had given me so much. "Fifty-six hundred."

"Fine." He counted some bills in his wallet— five one-thousand dollar bills and six hundreds—then held them out.

I looked down at the money in his hand. "Why are you doing this? You think you can buy me?" Straightening my shoulders, I stood a little taller. "I'm not for sale."

He picked up my hand, smashed the money into my palm, and curled my fingers around it. "Sweetheart, everyone's for sale."

As he stormed out, I took off one shoe and hurled it at him, but it hit the door just as it slammed shut.

I got home in time to see Daddy before he left for his meeting with the DiFiores. Although I was desperate to clean up, I needed him to know how important it was that he co-operate with them and not say anything rash or foolish. I found him in the kitchen, heating up the iron on the stove. His best shirt and trousers were draped over the kitchen table.

He was thrilled to see me, but I didn't feel as if he understood there was still danger ahead, even though he was free. "Just agree to what they say," I begged him. "If they ask for a percentage, don't argue."

He nodded, but his face darkened. "I'll say what I have to, but I hate them for what they did to us. You can bet if I find a way to pay them back, I'll take it."

My head, which had been aching for days, threatened to split wide open. "Please, Daddy. You have no idea what I went through to get you released, to keep the girls safe. I need you to avoid the mistakes you made before. If you want to be in the bootlegging business, you pay up. Either that or find something else to do."

I thought he might argue but he didn't. Instead, he turned from the stove and took me in his arms, kissing my head. "You're so like your mother," he said. "She was no bigger than a minute, but she was smart and feisty and brave, just like you. Thank you for everything you did. I'll make things right, I promise."

Given his temper and his proclivity for gambling, I wondered if that was possible. My throat closed and I took deep breaths to keep the tears at bay. He smelled like himself now—soap and shaving cream and maybe a hint of gasoline. He patted my back. "Don't worry about anything."

Before he left, he told me that Bridget had phoned this morning, frantic with worry. He'd assured her everything was fine and that it was safe to come home.

I nodded, hoping that was true.

Once Daddy was gone, I ate two pieces of toast and phoned Evelyn's house, but her father said she was working. I thanked him and hung up, thinking maybe I'd head over to the bakery after I bathed and dressed. What a story I had for her. I wasn't even sure what I should tell her, or what would be safe for her to know. After trudging wearily up the stairs, I undressed and ran a bath.

Slipping all the way under the water, I held myself there until my lungs felt like they might burst before surfacing again and rubbing the water from my eyes. After washing my hair and scrubbing myself with a bar of Ivory soap, I dried off and dressed in a white blouse and black skirt. When my hair was combed and dry, I put on a little makeup. Checking my reflection in the mirror, I noticed something on my bed that hadn't been there before. I turned around to look more closely, and saw that it was the blue Tiffany box.

I sat down and stared at it. Had I missed it earlier? I lifted off the top, and there it was. Underneath it was a note.

You made it yours the other night.

I scowled.

How dare he give me this after the way he treated me this morning? Who does he think he is? He bought this for another woman!

But within seconds, my blood settled a bit. *Hold on. You got what you wanted this morning, didn't you? He let you go. And he gave you the money to pay Joey back.*

Except I couldn't let it go. Enzo had told me what ultimately mattered to him—power, wealth, control. *I'm just one more cog in the machine he's building to get everything he wants. What about what I want?*

I held up the necklace, watching the diamonds catch the sunlight through my open window. Never in a million years had I thought I'd own a piece of jewelry like this. I went to the mirror over my dresser, draping the necklace around my neck. Then I frowned. Where the hell would I ever wear it? My life was no different than before, was it? I was a still just a struggling nursing student with one short leg, living at home, working for and answering to Daddy. Wasn't I?

Not exactly—you answer to Enzo now too, said a voice inside me. And he'd promised to pay me not only enough for tuition, but more. What would that mean?

Stomach jumping, I clasped the necklace, lowered my arms, and stared at myself. The truth was, I wasn't the same girl at all.

So what did I want now?

Before I could articulate an answer, I heard knocking on the front door. Quickly I ran into Daddy's room to look out the front window. A shiny red Buick Touring was parked on the street, glinting in the sunshine. Clapping a hand to my mouth, I recalled where I'd seen it before—at the boathouse, being driven by Sam Scarfone. Why was Sam here to see me? Should I open the door? What if he knew what I was planning to do?

A voice from below floated through the screen. "Tiny, are you there?"

Joey.

I ran down the stairs and yanked the front door open.

My heart went ka-whump. The car wasn't the only surprise.

He wore a brand new suit, a three-piece dark blue pinstripe, with a lighter blue shirt and a gold silk tie. The coat fit snugly over his broad shoulders and chest, narrowing at his trim waist. And that wasn't all. Gone was his scruffy hairdo and floppy cap. He removed a light brown fedora, revealing neatly styled hair, the curls controlled with pomade. He was clean-shaven, a hint of a smile on his wide mouth—until he saw the diamonds at my throat. Then it slid off his face, as if he knew where they had come from.

He cleared his throat. "Can I come in?"

"Of course." I stepped back. As he passed me I caught his scent—something new, maybe shaving cream or hairdressing. It certainly didn't smell familiar. And he was looking at me so oddly, as if he wasn't sure it was me. I pushed the door shut and faced him again, my fingers twisting together. "Daddy was released yesterday. Thank you for everything—I couldn't have managed without you."

"You're welcome. You got the package then?"

I nodded, reluctant to tell him about the whole ordeal just yet. "Why don't we sit in the front room?" My voice sounded strange in my ears.

Joey waited until I sat on the sofa before lowering himself to the chair across from me. We both sat stiffly, as if we had never been alone together before. *This is ridiculous! It's Joey, for crying out loud!*

"How did it go in Chicago?" I asked.

"Good." He nodded and fooled with his hat in his lap. "Real good. We got the entire load sold and set some connections in place for the future." He didn't mention the opium and I didn't ask. "Actually, I might be moving back there."

"Oh, really?" I fought a momentary onslaught of panic. If Joey left town, my connection to the River Gang was gone. But I was torn, too—Joey would be safer in Chicago. "That's—that's good. I saw in the paper that police are looking for someone who fits your description. Because of the shootings."

Joey focused his attention on his hat. "Yeah. I should lay low for a while." He sneaked a peek at me. "You look good, Tiny. Different."

I rubbed my lips together, although I hadn't put on the red lipstick. "I have makeup on."

"It's not the makeup."

We stared at each other for a few seconds, my face growing hot. "You look good too. I like the new suit."

He sat a little taller. "Yeah?"

"Yeah. You're even wearing a tie. I thought you didn't prefer them."

"Guess I've changed my mind about some things."

I coughed. "And a new car, I see?"

"That's Sam's. I'm just driving it while I'm here. What happened to the window?" He gestured behind me, where cardboard covered the shattered glass. Daddy must have taped it up.

Thinking fast, I said, "Accident. Baseball game in the street."

"Oh."

Unable to hold his gaze, I stared at his shiny brown shoes. "Oh! What's the matter with me?" I stood, and he did too. "I have something for you. I'll be right back." I rushed from the room and up the stairs before he could ask questions. In my bedroom, I gathered together the bills Enzo had given me, pausing to look in the mirror. My cheeks were flaming. *What's the matter with you? Get down there and pay him back. Say thank you. And quit acting like a skittish doe or he'll know something is up!*

When I got to the bottom of the steps, he was standing near the front door with his hat on already, as if he couldn't wait to leave. Was this the same man who cooked pancakes and spaghetti in my kitchen? I handed him the money, and he stared at it.

"Where did you get this?"

"Well... Daddy's back now," I answered vaguely.

"Your pop had this money somewhere?" His expression was suspicious.

"I'm—I'm not sure where he got it."

He tucked the money into his coat pocket and nodded. "That's a hell of a necklace. Diamonds?"

I swallowed as I brought my fingers to the stones at my throat. "Yes."

"Where'd you get it?" A cool tone had crept into his voice and his eyes were downright hard now.

"It was a gift."

"Really. Well, I should get going."

"Aren't you going to ask who it's from?" I blurted.

"I know who it's from." He looked at me one moment longer, and understanding passed between us.

He knows what I've done.

"You're making a mistake, Tiny."

I bristled. "You don't know anything about it."

"I know you. I've always known you."

Suddenly he grabbed me by the shoulders and kissed me. A little squeak of surprise escaped my throat, followed by a soft sigh of pleasure. Joey's lips were so lush and soft, and the way he pressed them to mine was insistent without being demanding. He opened his mouth and gently swept his tongue between my lips. I shocked myself by meeting it with mine, wishing I could feel his chest against me. But he kept my arms pinned fast.

Then he stepped back, breathing hard. "Good-bye, Tiny." He was out the front door and sliding into the Buick before I could even form a coherent thought.

I watched him drive off, bringing my fingers to my lips. My heart hadn't stopped racing since he'd kissed me. *My God, what am I doing?*

I'd thought when Daddy was released, my life would go back to normal. But now I knew that was impossible.

Enzo's words from this morning echoed in my head so clearly I could feel his breath on my ear.

This is only the beginning.

Part Two:

Speak Low

Chapter One

I stood at the door and watched the red Buick tear down the street, my lips buzzing and my head spinning.

Joey had kissed me. Again.

But for real this time.

I brought my trembling fingers to my mouth and closed my eyes. I could still see the barely-suppressed fury on his face as he put everything together—my uncharacteristic nervousness, the thousands of dollars in cash I'd just handed over, the diamonds at my throat.

He knows.

He hadn't said so, not in so many words, but Joey and I had known each other for years. And even though we'd spent most of them at each other's throats, for him to get worked up enough to kiss me like that could only mean one thing: he realized what I'd done with Enzo.

Which was everything.

Twice.

At the thought of Enzo's naked body pressing against mine, my insides went weightless. For a moment I was back in his bed, pulling him deeper. A wave of arousal swept through me, and I leaned against the doorjamb for support, my knees nearly buckling. When my body felt grounded again, I opened my eyes and frowned in the direction of the Buick. Anger pinched off the warmth inside me. *Go to hell, Joey Lupo!*

Not once in seven years had he done anything but tease me and pick fights, and the one time he *had* kissed me, he'd made it clear he was only pretending we were a couple to fool the Prohibition agents who'd spotted our boat full of bootleg whisky on the lake. Now just because someone else had gotten their hands on me—as well as some other body parts—he got proprietary.

And he hadn't even given me a reason! He just announced I was making a mistake and grabbed me, muttering some nonsense about how he knew me, how he's always known me.

Huffing an angry breath, I slammed the door.

Screw you, Joey. I don't care how long you've known me or how much you helped me when my family was in trouble or how tempting your mouth is. That doesn't give

2

you the right to judge me for my choices or tell me I'm making a mistake or kiss me with those perfect fucking lips. Goddamn you!

I stomped up the stairs to my bedroom and slammed that door too. The more I thought about it, the madder I got—mad at Joey for kissing me, of course, but the truth was, I was just as angry at myself for wanting that kiss.

For enjoying it.

Going straight to the dresser, I placed the diamond and pearl choker Enzo had given me into its blue Tiffany box and clapped it closed. Then I grabbed my hairbrush and yanked it furiously through my hair, eyeing my flushed face in the mirror. How dare he make me feel guilty about finally going after something I want for myself! Damn him for waiting so long to show me he felt something for me. *And damn him to hell for making me feel something for him that has me questioning everything right now!*

Hurling the hairbrush across the room, I took satisfaction in the loud thwack it made against the wall. In fact, it felt so good I scanned the dresser for something else to throw. My eyes fell on the blue box, and I nearly picked it up. Instead I braced both hands

3

on the dresser top, stared hard at my reflection, and took a deep breath. And then another.

A memory surfaced.

A few nights ago, I'd stood here in my room wearing nothing but that necklace as I touched Enzo in ways Joey could only dream about. Let him dream, then. *So he's mad, so what?* Served him right. Maybe I'd enjoyed that phony embrace in the boat last week, and maybe the impulsive kiss downstairs had me worked up a bit, but I wasn't the same person he'd known all those years—and if I wanted to make a mistake with my life, it was mine to make.

Because if that mistake was tall, dark, handsome as a movie star and supremely talented with his tongue, then I was willing to risk it.

"You don't know me, Joe Lupo," I whispered to my reflection. "You don't know anything."

I felt superior for exactly ten seconds, which is how long it took me to remember that Enzo was counting on me to stay friendly with Joey so I could get some information from him. Specifically, Enzo wanted a way to get back at the River Gang and its leader, Sam the Barber Scarfone, for hijacking a shipment of booze he'd been expecting from the east coast a few days ago. It hadn't just been any old shipment—hidden somewhere in the cargo was forty thousand dollars worth of opium, which even the hijackers hadn't known about. Briefly I wondered what had happened when they discovered it. Joey worked for the River Gang, and he had just returned from Chicago, where they'd sold the hijacked load, but he hadn't mentioned the drugs.

Then again, he'd only been at my house for about five minutes.

"Shit," I muttered. I'd have to make nice with him again if I had any hope of discovering where the gang's next load of booze would come from and when it would arrive. Fear shimmied up my spine, cold and unwelcome. Enzo had promised not to hurt Joey if I came through with the right information, and though he hadn't given me a deadline, I knew I'd better act quickly.

Trust was shaky between us, to say the least.

I had to think of a way to get Joey to reveal something to me before Enzo decided to take retribution into his own hands. Maybe the best way to do that would be to come clean with Joey and see if we could get back to normal. Our version of normal, anyway, which involved a lot of bickering and frustration, but it was a hell of a lot more comfortable than what had transpired by the front door. I touched my mouth again...had Joey's lips really rested there just minutes ago? How many times had I allowed myself a little fantasy about it?

Too many.

I need a cigarette.

After searching my usual hiding spots and coming up empty, I decided to walk to the small grocery store my older sister Bridget owned to grab a pack. She had taken her three boys and our two younger sisters on a trip to the beach on the other side of the state, so I wouldn't have to worry about a lecture from her, although it seemed ridiculous to me that I was still sneaking around like a child in order to smoke. I smoothed my white blouse over the plain black skirt I wore, found a decent-looking hat in my sisters' room, and locked the front door behind me.

My stomach growled as I headed down the block and smelled a neighbor's dinner cooking. I ignored it and wrapped my arms around my empty belly, frowning at my scuffed oxfords. Last night Enzo had promised to pay me handsomely if I helped him recover his losses from the River Gang—enough to cover nursing school tuition in the fall, and then some.

The damn schoolgirl shoes would go first thing.

I'll get some new clothes. No more stained blouses or skirts I've worn since high school. For God's sake, I'm twenty years old, I survived kidnapping at gunpoint, and I'm sleeping with a gangster. I should dress better. Stretching out my strides, I tried to walk a little taller, which wasn't easy for someone who measured under five feet.

The other luxury I wanted was my own apartment. Daddy would probably put up a big stink since it would mean leaving him to tend to the girls and the house on his own, but Mary Grace was ten and Molly was nearly sixteen—the same age I was when Bridget left home to get married. I'd been keeping house and mothering two girls long enough. Now it was my turn to have a little freedom, a little fun. Even if all I could afford was a little room in a boarding house where I could come and go as I pleased, it would be better than living at home.

I turned left into the alley that ran behind the store, and right away I saw the dark sedan parked behind Daddy's auto repair shop. Narrowing my eyes, I focused on the back door—it was open a crack. The back of my neck prickled. I knew it wasn't Daddy inside, and the nondescript car screamed cops to me. Halting my steps, I debated whether to turn around and hightail it back home or find out who was in there. But I took too long to decide, and when three men exited through the back door, they saw me.

"There she is." Martin, the grocery store's assistant manager, followed two unfamiliar men in suits into the alley. "Tiny, these men are federal agents. They're looking for your father."

He and I exchanged a careful look. Martin knew about my father's neighborhood whisky business as well as the work he did rebuilding cars and hearses for other bootleggers, but his face gave nothing away. I was damn glad he didn't know anything about the events of last week.

"Oh?" I kept an even tone as I walked toward the suits, sizing them up as they flashed badges at me. The one in brown was younger, ginger-haired, and overweight, sweating profusely in the summer afternoon heat. The older one wore blue; he was dark-haired, beady-eyed, and smaller-framed, and he too was mopping his face with a handkerchief. "My father isn't here. Can I help you?"

"My name is Agent Thomas, and this is Agent Janssen," said the one in blue. "We're with the Prohibition Bureau. Your name?" He traded the handkerchief for a small pad of paper and a pencil from inside his coat.

"Frances O'Mara." I racked my brain, trying to remember what damning evidence could be in the garage. All the booze had been removed, and I was pretty sure all the rebuilt hearses were gone too. They'd been sold last week.

"But you go by another name?" The agent glanced at Martin, who'd just used the nickname I'd had since birth.

"Tiny," I clarified through gritted teeth. I really needed to ditch the childhood moniker along with the old clothes, but being called Frances didn't appeal much to me either. Maybe I'd change my name completely. New me, new name.

The cop continued writing, while I imagined *Alias, Tiny* being scratched in lead on the little white pad.

"Excuse me, but what is this about?" I tried to sound girlish and innocent. "May I ask why you were in the garage?"

"We're looking for your father in connection with a crime that took place Wednesday evening of last week: a liquor heist, during which a few men were killed. We have reason to believe Jack O'Mara may have been involved, or at least supplied the vehicles used by the perpetrators. We have a warrant to search the premises." He didn't offer to show it to me.

"Do you know where he was that night?" asked Agent Janssen.

"Yes. He was traveling in Ohio last week. For business." Actually he'd been a hostage of Angel DiFiore last week, and I knew he'd had nothing to do with the crime these agents were referring to—the River Gang's heist of Enzo's shipment. It was *me* who'd sold those hearses to the River Gang, because I'd needed the money for Daddy's ransom.

"Where in Ohio?" Thomas queried.

"I'm not sure exactly. Around Cleveland maybe?" I met his eyes and widened mine slightly as I lifted my shoulders. *You catch more flies with honey than vinegar.*

"And he's still in Ohio?" asked Janssen.

"As far as I know." A hidden drop of sweat rolled down my chest.

"Gentlemen, I think you've taken up enough of Miss O'Mara's time, and I should return to the store. You've searched the garage and found nothing of interest. Why don't you wait for Mr. O'Mara to return and talk to him yourselves?" Martin had an open, honest face, and with his neatly combed hair and polished spectacles, he looked like the dentist he was studying to be, not someone engaged in criminal activity.

Thomas ignored him. "Miss O'Mara, when do you expect your father back?"

"Oh, probably within a day or so. Shall I have him contact you when he returns?" I spoke sweetly, coating the lies with sugar. The sun was at my back, which meant it was shining directly in their eyes, and the brims of their hats weren't keeping their faces too cool. I could tell Janssen wanted to finish with me and get in the shade as quickly as possible.

But Thomas spoke up again. "One more thing. Does this guy look familiar to you?" He reached inside his coat pocket and pulled out a photograph—a mug shot. I leaned forward and pretended to scrutinize it.

"Have you ever seen him around here, maybe talking to your father? Could he be a customer at the garage?"

The young man in the photo was perfectly familiar.

"No," I lied. "I have no idea who that is. Never seen him before."

I had to find Joey. Immediately.

After reassuring Martin that everything was OK —which, in fact, it was not—I swiped a pack of cigarettes from behind the store counter, raced home, and called Joey's mother's apartment, where he was staying. His older sister Marie answered and said he wasn't home but she'd tell him to telephone me as soon as he returned. I replaced the receiver on the hook and chewed my nails, trying to think of where he might have gone. It was warm and stuffy in the house, and my head felt sweaty in the hat, so I tossed it aside and opened all the windows on the first floor. Just as I finished, the telephone rang.

Eagerly, I raced for it and scooped up the earpiece. "Hello?"

"Tiny, there you are!" The voice was my best friend Evelyn's.

"Evvy, I'm sorry we haven't spoken in—"

"Days!" she exclaimed. "It's been days, you naughty girl. You left the club Wednesday night before all the excitement and I haven't heard from you since!"

"I know, I'm sorry. I've been...busy." I actually hadn't left Club 23 before the raid alarms went off—Enzo and I were upstairs in his father's office, where I'd left my virginity, my sanity, and my purse. "Did you make it out OK? I heard it wasn't really a raid, just a false alarm."

"Oh yeah, we were fine. It was all very exciting, actually. Ted and I can't stop talking about it." The lilt in her voice told me she was dying for me to ask.

"Ted? That's the guy you met that night?"

"Yes, and he's wonderful. I've seen him every evening since, and he's taking me dancing tonight," she bubbled. "He's so handsome and sweet and he loves the movies like I do, and he's come into the bakery twice to see me."

"I'm so happy for you, Evelyn. You deserve someone like that." I scratched at a nick in the wooden telephone table with my thumbnail.

"So..." Evelyn prompted. "Tell me what's new with Mr. Dangerous. You were right—he does look like a Hollywood film star. Have you seen much of him?"

Every inch. "Um, yes. It's really kind of a long story, and I promise to tell you all about it when I have time, but I have to do something for Daddy before tonight, and—"

"Is he back, then?" Evelyn was one of the few people who'd known about my father's kidnapping. With Joey's help in negotiating with the River Gang, I'd managed to bootleg enough whisky to deliver the ten grand in ransom, but not without a huge amount of trouble involving men with guns—sometimes pointed at me.

"Yes. He was released yesterday."

"Oh, thank God! Now things can get back to normal."

A rictus smile stretched my lips. "I wouldn't count on it."

"You know what? You need to get another job, Tiny. The bootlegging business is no place for a girl."

I sighed. How often had Bridget said the same thing? But even though our operation was small, the money was too good to pass up, and it wasn't like I didn't have a plan. I'd been trying to pay for nursing school on my own for over a year. Daddy's business ventures brought in decent dough, but he had a weakness for gambling and an aversion to anything that would hasten my departure from the house. "I'll think about it. Let me telephone you tomorrow, all right? Have fun on your date."

"All right." She hesitated before hanging up. "Ooh, Tiny. I just got the shivers! Maybe something big is about to happen."

My stomach plummeted, but I tried to sound hopeful. "Maybe Ted is going to propose."

She squealed with glee. "Silly, it's only been a few days. But if he does, you'll be the first to know."

#

While I waited for Joey to call me back, I sat on the back stoop with my cigarettes and watched the sun turn orange and sink behind the trees in the yard. As I smoked, I decided on a plan of action. When Joey got back to me, I'd do my best to smooth things over between us and explain the situation to him. He had no real allegiance to Sam the Barber or the River Gang, and after all, they never would have known when and where Enzo's shipment was arriving if I hadn't told them.

Joey had probably made pretty good money on the deal, if his new clothes were any indication. And he'd told me this afternoon he was planning on

15

moving back to Chicago. Maybe I could talk him into going sooner rather than later. With the local cops and now feds looking into the heist—not to mention the DiFiores looking to exact retribution—Joey would be safer out of town, and I'd feel better knowing nothing I did could put him in harm's way.

I'd also feel better with some distance between us.

No matter how much I tried not to think about it, Joey's kiss wouldn't leave me alone. And the more I tried to block it from my mind, the more I obsessed over it, analyzing every detail. The shock of his hands on me, the sudden heat of his mouth slanting over mine. It wasn't overly aggressive or demanding, but it hinted at something powerful underneath—as if Joey had been restraining himself, and if we allowed the barriers to fall...

I shivered, imagining the intensity of it. God. I didn't want Joey, did I? No, that was ridiculous. We'd known each other too long, had too much history. No one got under my skin like Joey did. He was distantly related to Bridget's late husband, Vince, and from day one, we'd done nothing but scrap. As a boy, he'd cheated at cards, teased me mercilessly about my height, and never once let me win a footrace. For chrissakes, he'd stolen a pair of my underwear when we were fifteen and made money by offering neighborhood boys a penny a peek! Just because he grew up more handsome than he had any right to be didn't mean he was any different—underneath that fancy new suit, he was still the no- good, pain-in-the-ass delinquent I'd always known.

My stomach growled again, reminding me I still hadn't eaten, and I decided to go in and forage for some supper. As I stood, a low voice traveled through the dusk. "Hey."

Gasping, I searched the shadows and slapped a hand to my chest. "Joey? You scared me half to death! You should know better than to sneak up on me."

"Sorry. I called home, and my sister said you were looking for me."

I lowered my arm, although my pulse still raced. *It's because he startled you, that's all.* "Actually, it's the feds who are looking for you. They were at the garage today."

Joey shrugged. "They don't have anything on me."

"Yes they do, Joey. They asked about the hijacking. They flashed a picture of Sam the Barber at me. Asked me if I knew him or if he was a customer of Daddy's." I twisted my hands together.

"What did you say?"

"I lied! What the hell do you think I said?"

"Don't worry about it. Sam's a big boy. He can take care of himself."

"I'm not worried about Sam." Our eyes met briefly before his gaze dropped to my lips, and I lowered my chin. I noticed he'd removed his suit coat and rolled the cuffs of his light blue dress shirt. His exposed hands and wrists made my stomach flutter a little—I had a thing about Joey's hands. Honestly, I *did* feel something for Joey, but I didn't know what it was or how to put it into words. Was it gratitude? Affection? Attraction?

My plan had been to pretend everything was the same between us. But things weren't the same, and we both knew it.

My eye caught Joey's gold silk tie, which had been pulled askew. Without thinking, I reached up and straightened it. He sucked in his breath, his muscular chest straining against the shirt and vest of his three-piece suit, so different from the workmen's clothes I was used to seeing on him.

"Don't." He pushed my hands away and took over the task.

"Christ, Joey." My voice wavered when I spoke. "Don't be mad at me. You don't know what I've been through. You hijacked that booze and hightailed it out of town, and I had to deal with the consequences."

"What consequences? I left you the remainder of the ransom money. You were supposed to spring your pop from the DiFiores with it and stay the hell out of trouble. Instead you dive right into it, headfirst."

"That's not how it went, dammit! And after the choices you've made, you have no right to judge me. If I want to dive into trouble, that's my business, not yours." I poked a finger into his chest.

He lifted his chin. "You've made that perfectly fuckin' clear."

Bringing the heels of my hands to my head, I exhaled. This was not going well. I was supposed to be smoothing things over with Joey, not making them worse. "I'm sorry. I'm extremely grateful for everything you did for me while my father was... gone."

"He wasn't gone. He was kidnapped, remember? By Enzo's father?"

Stay calm. You'll gain nothing by letting your temper loose. "Yes, I remember. But a lot has happened since you left, and I want a chance to explain it to you without you getting angry with me. Please." I put my hands on his chest. Joey wasn't too much taller than me, but he had broad, thick muscles, and I could feel the warmth of his skin through his clothes.

He took a breath, and I thought he'd swat my hands away once more, but he didn't. When he spoke, his voice was softer, but still had an edge. "Where's your pop?"

Distracted, I answered without thinking. "He's at a meeting with Angel DiFiore, trying to work out the terms of a business arrangement."

"Are you fucking kidding me?" Joey took a step back. "First the guy tries extortion, then when that doesn't work he kidnaps your dad, beats him to a pulp, demands ten grand in ransom—and now your pop's gonna do business with him?" He looked me up and down. "No wonder!"

"No wonder what?"

"No wonder you're crazy enough to jump in bed with the guy's son!"

1Rage burned in my face. "Fuck you, Joey! You got everything you wanted out of this, didn't you?" I gestured toward him. "Look at you in your new blue suit driving a fancy red Buick wearing your shiny new shoes! You wouldn't have any of it if I hadn't helped you! How dare you judge me for getting what I want!"

"That's what you want? Him?" Joey yelled.

"Yes! For once in my life, I have something that's mine, something I'm doing just for me, and if you don't like it, you know what you can do!"

"Fine." He closed his eyes, took a few deep breaths and rolled his shoulders. "So why did you call me today after I left?"

"I was worried about you." Just then my stomach growled again, loud and embarrassing.

Joey's brows went up when the groaning noise refused to stop. "Jesus, Tiny. If you expect to grow anytime soon, you're gonna have to eat a meal every now and then."

A joke. That was a good sign. "I was too scared to eat."

"Have you had a decent meal since I fed you?"

At the memory of the pasta dinner he'd cooked at my house last week, my mouth watered, and I may have moaned slightly. "I think so. I'm not sure. It's been a tough couple of days." I still hadn't told him the whole story.

Joey shook his head and grabbed my elbow, pulling me toward the driveway. "Come on."

"Where are we going?"

"To my house. I'll feed you supper. But this is the last time," he warned, turning back to shake a finger in my face. "From now on, you're his mouth to feed."

Nodding gratefully, I didn't even toss back a sharp response. The thought of eating Joey's cooking again had me salivating.

He opened the Buick's passenger door for me before walking around and sliding into the driver's seat. Then he pulled two cigarettes from his pocket. "Want one?"

I placed one between my lips and he leaned toward me to light it. When its tip glowed orange, I sucked in a lungful of smoke and exhaled. "Thanks."

He glanced sideways at me. "So what happened after I left town?"

I shuddered. "What didn't happen? Things went completely haywire. When Enzo heard the guys who hijacked the load and killed a couple of his men were driving hearses, he knew they had to be the ones he'd seen at the garage the night of Daddy's kidnapping. And since his father had Daddy hostage the whole time, he figured I knew more than I was telling him. Which I did, of course."

"What did you say?"

"I admitted that I'd sold the hearses to Sam the Barber and the River Gang because I needed the money for the ransom, but I didn't tell him I was the one who told you guys about his rum shipment."

"He still in the dark about that?"

I shook my head and took another drag on my cigarette. "I don't think so. When he asked me outright this morning if I knew Sam was planning the heist, I told him I did what I had to do to protect my family."

Joey was quiet a moment, and I thought he might be reflecting on my bravery, but I was wrong. "This morning?"

I shifted in my seat. "Yes."

"Did you spend the night with him?"

Damn it, Joey, don't make me feel guilty! I was glad it was dark, so he couldn't see me blush. "Look, I didn't plan on it. There's another part of the story you haven't heard."

"I'm not sure I want to."

I bit my lip. How the hell was I supposed to be up front with him and ask for what I needed with all this odd tension between us? Did he really have feelings for me? Or was he just angry about what I'd done? "Well, while you were living it up in Chicago, I was—"

"I wasn't 'living it up in Chicago,' you know. It was business."

"Maybe, but all that rum plus the opium must have brought a good load of dough."

Joey studied me but said nothing.

"Well, didn't it?"

"We didn't sell the opium in Chicago."

My jaw dropped. "What? Why not?"

"Sam doesn't even know about it. It was in hidden containers that ended up in the hearse I drove with Angelo. When we found it, we agreed to keep it to ourselves. We sold the rum as instructed, gave Sam his cut, and brought the opium back to Detroit."

My heart hammered in my chest. "Why?"

He shrugged. "Honestly, I'm not even sure what made me do it. It just seemed like the opportunity was there for me to make a move on my own. Like I told you, I'm planning on going back to Chicago, and I could use a little money to get started down there."

"Jesus, Joey. If Sam finds out, he'll kill you." I put a hand on his arm, but when he glanced down, I removed it.

"He won't find out. Unless you tell him."

He might have meant it as a joke, but I couldn't make light of this. "And what about Angelo? Can you trust him?"

"Why shouldn't I? He gains nothing by telling Sam about it."

"So where is it? The opium, I mean."

Joey rubbed his lower lip, as if he was wondering whether to confide in me. Then he looked me in the eye. "This information does not leave the car."

I nodded.

"It's hidden in the boathouse."

"Daddy's boathouse? How the hell did you get in there?" My father had purchased a dilapidated old boathouse on the water for bootlegging purposes a few years back, and although Joey had occasionally worked for him, I didn't think he had a key.

"I took the key off your ring while I was at your house earlier. You were upstairs getting the money to pay me back."

"You stole the boathouse key from me?" Somehow that seemed worse than anything I'd done.

Neither of us had behaved terribly well in the last week, but at least we'd been honest with each other.

"I was planning on telling you. I just got... distracted."

Our eyes met, and I took a drag on my cigarette, fast. "Joey, I—"

"I want to meet with Enzo."

"What?" I coughed, choking on the smoke. "Why the hell do you want to do that?"

"I want to make a deal."

"What kind of deal?"

"I want to know where he was going to sell the drugs and for how much. I don't know anything about that stuff."

"And why would Enzo even talk to you? You just stole thousands of dollars worth of booze and drugs from him!"

"I'll cut him in."

"On his own opium?"

"It's not his anymore, is it?"

"He's not gonna see it that way."

Joey shrugged. "His choice. Thirty percent or nothing. I'm the one that has something he wants."

I brought my cigarette to my lips again, inhaling and exhaling more slowly. If they met in a dark alley, Enzo probably wouldn't hesitate to shoot Joey, but he did want to get his money back. This information could change everything.

"I might be able to set up a meeting," I ventured, watching a ribbon of smoke drift out the open window.

"You can't tell him about the opium beforehand, understand?" Joey pinned me with a hard stare.

"I do, but that makes it a lot harder to guarantee he'll agree to talk to you. He's furious, Joey."

"I have no doubt you'll persuade him, now that you two are so close."

"Stop. Just stop it. If we're going to work together on this, you have to quit harassing me about Enzo at every turn."

He switched his focus to starting the Buick, and the engine came to life. "No promises there."

My jaw jutted forward and I tossed my cigarette out the window. "None here either, then."

Joey looked over at me once more. "You know, I may have been wrong before."

"About what?"

"About you. Maybe I don't know you anymore." As he backed out of the driveway and headed for Jefferson Avenue, I kept my eyes on the road. Why the hell was my throat closing up? I should have been glad he recognized that I was different now. Wasn't that exactly what I'd been saying to myself? And I'd gotten what I wanted—information to give Enzo. If he'd agree to meet Joey without killing him on sight, maybe they could work out a deal. Thirty percent was better than nothing.

The fist of discontent squeezing my throat eased up a little.

I could do this. No one would get hurt. Joey would go to Chicago and stop distracting me with his mouth and his hands and his cooking, and Enzo and I would learn to trust each other.

Of all the lies I told myself that night, the last one was the most foolish.

And the most dangerous.

Chapter 2

Joey's mom ran a restaurant and boarding house near Eastern Market, and the Lupo family lived above it. With Joey's sisters married and out of the house, it was just him and his mother there these days. I hadn't been to the restaurant in years, but it smelled the same when I walked in, like tomatoes and garlic and fresh bread. The dining room was bustling with a noisy supper crowd, and Joey nodded hello to a server setting down a huge plate of what looked like steak in some kind of red sauce. My stomach groaned again, and I cradled it as we took the stairs up to his family's apartment on the third floor.

"How's your mother doing?" I asked.

"Not too good."

"I'm sorry." Bridget had told me his mother was ill, and I felt bad that I hadn't inquired after her very much, but with everything going on last week it had slipped my mind.

The apartment door was ajar, and Joey pushed it all the way open. "Ma?"

"She's in the bedroom." Marie walked through the wide arch in the wall separating the front room from the dining room, wiping her hands on a dishtowel. "Tiny!" She rushed up to kiss both cheeks before hugging me. She looked like Joey, same dark wavy hair and generous mouth, but had little crinkles near her eyes when she smiled and a huge pregnant belly. "It's been so long. How are you? How's your family?"

"Um, good." I exchanged a quick glance with Joey. "We're all well. And you?"

"I'm well too, thanks." She dropped a hand to her stomach. "Just exhausted."

"Go home, Marie." Joey set his coat on the back of the sofa and took the dishtowel from her. "I can take it from here. I don't have any plans tonight, and I promised Tiny a decent meal. As you can see, she needs one."

"Shush, Joey Lupo. She looks just fine." She winked at me, and I wondered if she thought there was something between us.

He turned to me. "Let me just go see how she's doing and then I'll fix us something. I haven't eaten either."

"And I'll say good-bye to Ma and be on my way." Marie attempted to undo the apron strings at her back.

"Here, let me." I untied them for her and she slipped it over her head.

"Put it on, Tiny," said Joey, grinning as he backed through the arch. "I'll give you a cooking lesson. God knows you need one."

I glared at him as Marie dropped the loop around my neck. He was right, I did need a cooking lesson, but I certainly didn't feel like one tonight. I couldn't stop thinking about that opium sitting in the boathouse. Could I convince Enzo to meet with Joey without telling him about it? What would he do if he knew it was there, unguarded? The boathouse was locked and Joey had my key—the rotten thief—but locks were never a problem for Enzo. A smile crept onto my lips and I tried to wipe it off. *Quit thinking about him. Joey will wonder why you're blushing.*

Left alone, I looked around the apartment. I couldn't remember the last time I'd visited here. The wood floors were clean but creaky, and the furniture was Victorian style, with curvy backs and sides and faded burgundy upholstery. Floral-patterned paper covered the walls, on which hung family photos and religious paintings. A crucifix hung over a Brunswick phonograph in the corner, and a porcelain statue of the Blessed Virgin rested on a side table. Sidestepping away from it like a skittish pony, I perched on the edge of the sofa. A photo album rested on the coffee table, and it was open, as if someone had recently been looking at it.

Glancing back at the doorway to the hall, I took the album on my lap and turned to the front of the book. Photographs of the Lupo family were fastened at the corners onto black pages, beginning with a wedding portrait of Mr. and Mrs. Lupo. I studied Joey's father. He looked a lot like Joey, actually, and I wondered how old he'd been when he married. Twenty? Twenty-one, like Joey was now? He and Vince had worked for the Scarfone family, and they were killed the same day, victims of an ambush on the boss, Big Leo Scarfone, right outside the police station.

Neither Bridget nor Joey had fully recovered, although more than two years had passed.

I perused photos of the Lupo family as it grew, quirking a lip at babies in a frilly white baptismal dress and chuckling aloud at the photo of Joey in knee pants, looking miserable and yet adorable in his First Holy Communion portrait.

"Cute little devil, wasn't I?"

I jumped at his voice over my shoulder, and stiffened when he leaned down over the back of the sofa to look more closely. His jaw was so close to mine I could smell his aftershave. If I tilted my head just the right way, my cheek would rest against his. "Devil being the operative word." I scooted sideways and stood up. "But I like the outfit. You should wear knee pants more often."

"Thanks, but I don't think that suit fits me anymore." He grinned as he straightened. "It'd probably fit you, though. You're about the size of an eight-year-old boy."

"Very funny." I pulled the apron away from my white blouse. "Do I really have to wear this? You're not actually going to make me cook anything, are you?"

"I thought you wanted a lesson. Here, I'll tie it." He motioned for me to come forward and turn around, and I felt his hands at the small of my back as he tied the strings. A funny ticklish feeling fluttered through my belly. "There. Now at least you look like you know what you're doing."

I faced him. "Appearances can be deceiving."

Joey looked skyward. "Now she figures it out."

"Is that spaghetti?" I peered over Joey's shoulder at the large copper pot full of boiling water, into which he'd thrown two handfuls of some kind of long noodle.

"No, it's fettuccine. Please tell me you at least recognize the vegetable." He gestured toward a second pot.

I peeked in. "Green beans."

"Thank God. Now go slice the bread and set the table."

While I did that, Joey warmed up some meatballs in the oven and poured some red wine. When supper was ready, we sat across from each other at one end of a table meant for eight, and I quickly devoured the meal in huge, blissful bites. The meatballs and noodles were lightly coated with a savory tomato sauce, and the green beans glistened with butter and lemon. "Oh my God, it's so good." I forked my last bite of meatball and shoved it in my mouth.

"I've heard that about my meatballs."

I narrowed my eyes at him and was about to make a sharp-tongued remark when a face appeared in the hallway leading off the dining room to the bedrooms.

"Ma, what do you need?" Joey jumped up from his chair, throwing his napkin on his empty plate. "Why didn't you call me?" He led her into the dining room by the arm as she took small, unsteady steps in battered house slippers. It was as if she'd aged twenty years since I'd last seen her, perhaps only a year ago.

"Mrs. Lupo, hello. It's nice to see you again."

"Hello, Tiny. Please forgive me for not welcoming you to my home myself. I'm no feeling so well these days." Her accent was still pronounced despite fifteen years in this country. She offered me a rueful smile and let Joey help lower her into a chair at the head of the table.

"Think nothing of it, really. Joey has been a very welcoming host."

Her face brightened a little as she looked at her son. "Like his father was."

Joey cleared his throat. "Are you hungry?"

"No, no. I came out to say hello and finish the dishes."

"I'll do the dishes. You can rest. Would you like to listen to the phonograph a little?"

"I'll help with the dishes, too," I offered, stacking our plates together.

While he moved his mother to the sofa in the front room, I rinsed the dishes and silverware in the large kitchen sink and retrieved the soap from a low cupboard. Soon I heard music coming from the phonograph, which got louder when Joey propped open the swinging door to the kitchen. Wordlessly he took his place next to me, toweling off the dishes I washed and then setting them in the rack to finish drying. I ignored the light hum under my skin at his proximity, but I did steal a few looks at his hands as he worked. When the last dish was in the rack, Joey sighed and shook his head. "I need a drink."

"Sounds good."

He looked at me. "Let's go up on the roof."

#

Ten minutes later we were sitting in the starlight on the building's roof, each with a tumbler of whisky in hand and the bottle between us. Joey tossed back his drink in one gulp and poured another.

I sipped mine, enjoying the way it burned down my throat and warmed my belly. "Thanks for supper. It was delicious. I really should take a cooking lesson from you sometime."

He shrugged. "If there's time before I leave."

"For Chicago, you mean?"

"Yeah. Once I settle things with the cake eater and get my ma moved into my sister's house, I'm going." He glanced sideways at me. "You'll miss me, huh?"

I punched him on the shoulder. "Yeah, what will I do without someone around to call me Little Tomato, make fun of my cooking, and tease me about my size?" But I was unsettled by the realization that I *would* miss seeing him. I'd miss hearing his voice, knowing he was around if I needed him. As we looked at one another, a light breeze ruffled my hair, and the strains of a waltz drifted up from an open window. To break the spell, I sipped my whisky and changed the subject. "It's nice up here."

"I used to come up here with my pop."

"Yeah?"

"Yeah. We'd escape my mother and sisters, and he'd let me smoke while he told me about the stars just like his father did when he was a kid." His voice cracked a little.

"You must miss him."

Joey nodded, took another drink. "Every day."

"I'm sorry."

He was quiet a moment. "I wish I knew for sure who did it. I hate that the bastard got away with it. I'd like to make him suffer, you know? Pay for what he did."

I nodded, although I didn't know what it must be like to have that burning need for revenge inside me. I knew about loss, though. "I miss my mom every day, too."

"It's been rough on you, huh? With those kids at home."

"Yeah. Some days all I want to do is escape it all." Another silence followed, during which I grew increasingly uncomfortable with the way he was running his eyes over each feature on my face—my eyes, my cheeks, my lips. Was he starting to lean toward me?

"So you know about stars?" I looked up at the sky.

"Don't sound so shocked, college girl. You're not the only one with brains around here." Joey drank again and leaned back on his hands.

"Nursing school isn't exactly college. And right now I don't have the money to go back in the fall."

"Ask your pop for the money. He owes you, I'd say."

"Easier said than done. I have no idea what his business will be like from now on. If Angel insists on a high cut, he won't be making as much, especially if he's got to cut the River Gang in too. Are they still intent on transporting all loads across the river for a fee?"

"Yeah. But I still don't get why your dad met with Angel today."

"That's because I haven't told you the final piece of the story." I took a deep breath. "Angel released Daddy and me in exchange for making a business deal that sort of makes him a partner in the bootlegging operation."

Joey sat straight up. "What do you mean, released you?"

"Well, after you left for Chicago with the stolen load, Enzo's younger brother Raymond and his buddy Harry lured me to the boathouse with the ransom money, stole it, and took me to a cabin in the woods, where they'd also taken Daddy."

"What!" Shock rippled through the word. "What the hell for?"

"In their greedy little minds it made sense—they thought they'd use the ransom money to start running dope or something, and Raymond wanted to prove to his father he was a big-time player, like his brother." I took another swallow, grateful for the numbing buzz of the whisky. "But it backfired because Harry kept calling Raymond stupid, so Raymond shot him. Then Daddy and I convinced him we'd go into business with him to show his father and brother how important he was."

"Jesus Christ, are you kidding me?" Joey's mouth hung open.

"Nope. But once he brought me back to town, I managed to escape and get to Enzo."

His eyelids lowered. "Let me guess. He's the fucking hero."

"Not exactly." I ignored his sarcasm. "Angel was furious with Raymond for interfering, and he was already mad at Enzo about the hijacked booze."

"Good." Joey picked up his glass for a gulp.

"So I got Angel to release us both by assuring him Daddy would work for him, or at least pay him the percentage he'd wanted in the first place."

"Fucking brilliant."

I stiffened. "I did what I had to, Joey. I was scared."

He closed his eyes, leaned back on his elbows, and tipped his chin up, exhaling toward the sky. "I'm sorry. I shouldn't have left you alone here."

Right then I made the decision not to tell him that Raymond had wanted me as part of the deal, or how he'd attacked me at the club last night—not only would he feel more guilt, but I'd have to tell him that it was Enzo who broke into the room and fought off his brother before I clubbed him with a heavy lamp. And then later, in Enzo's room...

I shoved the memory of sex with Enzo from my mind. "It's not your fault, Joey. You did everything you could to help me get that ransom money. I'm so grateful to you, and Daddy is too. We have our freedom, at least; the rest is just a business deal."

Joey didn't open his eyes right away. I wrapped my arms around my knees, and we sat in silence for a few minutes, listening to a scratchy piano waltz coming from the phonograph downstairs, before he

41

spoke. "You need to go back to school. Get out of this business. It's not for you."

Tipping sideways a little, I elbowed him. "Look who's talking. Haven't we had this conversation before? I believe it was you who said, 'The movies make you want things. I'm gonna get 'em.'"

He shook his head. "We're different, Tiny. You've got the brains to make something of yourself without being in danger all the time."

"So do you! I was thinking about it earlier, during supper. You could take over here, or use the money you get from the opium to open up your own restaurant or something. You're talented, Joey. You don't need to spend your life breaking laws or skulls to make a buck."

He sat up and rubbed a hand on the back of his neck. "We're not talking about me. It's you who got the good marks in school. I screwed around too much, didn't care enough. If I could go back, I'd do a lot of things differently."

"You mean school?"

"I mean a lot of things."

I thought about that for a moment. *What I would do differently if I could go back and change something in my life?* For the most part, I'd done well in school and stayed out of trouble. Taking care of the house and watching over my sisters took up a lot of time, and I'd worked for Daddy a lot the last few years too. There may have been a boy or two I wish I hadn't kissed, but I had no major regrets so far—unless Enzo turned out to be a big mistake. *Which is entirely possible. Probable, in fact.* A heavy sigh deflated my upper body.

Joey looked over at me. "So why don't you get a different job? Make the tuition money on your own?"

I groaned. "I think I'll have to."

"How much do you need?" His eyes were serious.

"You're not giving it to me."

"I didn't offer anything. I just asked how much." Tipping back the last swallow of my whiskey, I set the glass down next to me and leaned back on my hands again. "It's not just tuition. I feel like there are so many things weighing me down. I want more freedom. I want to move out of my father's house. Get my own place and start living, you know? I'm tired of feeling as if I'm waiting for my real life to start."

Joey nodded but said nothing. He finished his second drink and propped his arms on his wide-spaced knees, looking straight ahead. When he finally spoke, the words stunned me. "Come with me."

"What?" I couldn't possibly have heard that right.

He looked at me over his shoulder. "Come with me. To Chicago."

"Why would I go with you to Chicago?"

"You said yourself you wanted to get out of your pop's house. I'm offering you that chance. You could go to school in Chicago. It would be like going away to college or something."

"That's nuts, Joey! I can't afford that! Where would I live?"

"With me."

"With you!"

"We could find an apartment."

"Together?" I picked up my whiskey glass, found it empty, and tipped it to my lips anyway, hoping to suck up any miniscule drop left at the bottom.

"Why not?"

"Why not? I'll tell you why not. Because we're not —" Frantically I moved my hand back and forth between us. I didn't even know how to put it.

"We don't have to be. I just want you away from here, away from people who...put you in danger. I want you safe, that's all."

Suddenly something clicked. "No, you don't."

"What?" Now it was Joey's turn to be surprised.

"You don't care if I'm safe. You'd be doing the same things down there you're doing up here. I'd still be around the same kind of people breaking all the same laws. You just don't want me to be with him."

Joey shook his head. "That's not true! I'm offering to take you away from all the crummy things weighing you down. I'm offering you a chance to start living your life for you, like you said!"

"Bullshit!" I jumped up. "You're just jealous!"

Joey popped to his feet too, fists clenched at his sides. "He doesn't care about you!" he roared. "You'll never be anything more to him than a good time!"

"Which is more than you can say, isn't it? And that's really what we're talking about. You're mad because he got something you wanted." I poked him in the chest.

Joey breathed hard, his brown eyes flashing with angry fire. "Maybe he did."

Those three words stunned me silent. It was the closest he'd ever come to admitting he felt anything for me, and I had no idea how to react. Weren't you at least supposed to kiss the girl if you were asking her to run away with you?

Before I could speak, Joey went on. "This is the only time I'll make this offer, Tiny. I want you to come with me, but I won't ask you again. You have to tell me tonight."

I narrowed my eyes at him and cocked my head. "An ultimatum. How romantic."

He pressed his lips together. "Forget I asked."

The fight left my body. "Come on, Joey, can't we at least—"

"No. You're right. I don't know what I was thinking. It would never work." He leaned over, picked up the whiskey bottle and his glass, and walked to the stairs before I could argue.

And why would you argue? You don't want to run away with him. What the hell kind of offer was that, anyway? It wasn't like he'd confessed his love and begged me to return it. He was just being a sore loser.

Frowning, I followed him through the apartment, down the stairs and straight into the car.

On the ride home, the tension between us grew thicker and more awkward with every wordless second. It made me realize how comfortable our silences had been before.

Those days were over.

46

I was dangerously close to tears by the time he pulled into my driveway, but the sight of the Ford Model T Daddy and I shared parked next to the house was a relief—he was home from his meeting with the DiFiores.

"Thanks again for supper," I said quietly, one hand on the door.

"Tell nobody about the opium. Got it?" Joey's tone was as cold as his stare.

"I got it."

"Forget I said a word about it. In fact, forget every single word I said tonight." He switched his focus straight ahead, out the windshield.

I stared at his stubbornly set jaw in disbelief. Was he really going to be such a child about this? He'd had plenty of opportunities to admit he felt something for me—not that he was admitting anything now, either. Why couldn't he just say something, anything, about his feelings? Give me some reason besides his jealousy to consider his offer?

But he remained silent.

Chapter Three

"Daddy?" I called the second I got inside the house.

"In here."

I followed his voice into the kitchen, where I found him sitting at the table with a notebook, pencil in hand, and a glass of whiskey. "What are you doing?"

"Just running some numbers."

"Feds are looking for you," I said breathlessly, sliding into the chair across from him and studying his face. We didn't look much alike. I had my mother's Irish farm girl coloring—red hair, fair skin, blue eyes. Daddy was dark-haired and brown-eyed, and even before Raymond DiFiore beat him bloody last week, his face had worn the faint scars and crooked nose of a youth spent boxing in underground fights.

"So I hear. I saw Martin earlier." He didn't sound particularly worried about it.

"Are they going to arrest you?"

"They got nothing on me. Most they can do is bring me in for questioning."

His lack of concern reminded me of Joey. God, men were so exasperatingly overconfident. None of them ever thought anything bad would happen to them. *Maybe that's how they live like this, day after day.* "So how did the meeting go?"

"Uh, good."

"And what's that mean?"

He swallowed some whiskey before answering. "They want me to move my auto repair operation to one of their buildings downtown."

"Why? So they can keep a closer eye on you?"

"It's bigger."

The way he refused to look up from his notebook made me twitchy. "And?"

"And it's got a second floor where I can run a poker game. And maybe a sports book. Might be organizing some fights too."

Aha. I sat back. Nothing was more irresistible to Daddy than an opportunity to place a bet. Didn't matter on what—cards, dice, horses, dogs, fights, ball games...he couldn't walk away. When our mother was alive, her presence had kept the habit in check, but since her death he'd been increasingly susceptible to it. Fear oozed into my bloodstream and my heart thumped a bit quicker. "I'm not sure that's such a good idea."

"It'll mean more money coming in."

"It'll mean more going out too. And don't pretend you don't know what I mean."

His ruddy face flushed. "That's my concern, not yours."

"Bullshit!" I slammed my hand on the table.

"You watch your tongue, Missy. I'm still your father, and this is still my house. Weren't you the one who told me to agree to their terms this afternoon, no matter what?"

"Well, yes—but I meant in terms of the bootlegging business. I wanted you to agree to whatever percentage Angel asked for in order to buy the protection you need to keep operating. That's what he wanted in the first place. If you'd been so agreeable then, we wouldn't be in this mess."

"I'm getting out of the whisky business."

Now I was thoroughly confused. "What? I thought the whole reason—"

"Things are different now. Smalltime bootleggers are done. The mob will eventually control all booze coming in and going out, and I'd have to pay up to somebody anyway. Plus, if I stick to the auto repair business, there's less risk of being caught. And Angel only takes ten percent of the garage."

I narrowed my eyes. "What's he take from the House once you start the poker games?"

"Seventy-five percent."

"Seventy-five. And that's agreeable to you, getting only twenty-five percent?"

"Those places make a fortune, Tiny! Twenty-five percent could be a lot of dough."

Anger spiked my bloodstream. "I see. And what about the girls?"

"What about them? This is good for everybody."

"Not for me. I'm leaving."

"What?"

My voice rose, matching the flare of my temper. "You heard me, Daddy. I can't keep living here and putting off my life any longer. I worked for six months to make enough money to go back to school this fall, and it was gone in a heartbeat last week."

"I'm sorry about that, Tiny. I never should have ignored Angel's letters. That was my fault, and I'll pay you back. You can have money for school."

I shook my head and spoke through clenched teeth. "That's not enough. I want to leave home and be out on my own. Save your money, because you might need to hire some help."

Daddy got to his feet. "You're not moving away from home, Frances O'Mara, and that's final. Your family needs you here." He planted a crooked index finger on the table.

"They need a cook and a housekeeper and a seamstress!" I shouted, jumping to my feet as well. "They need a mother, and I'm not her!"

"No, you aren't!" he yelled back. "Your mother never would have let her family down this way. But when she died, everything changed, and we all have to make sacrifices."

I gaped at him. Was this the same man who told me earlier how proud my mother would have been of my bravery and selflessness this week? "Sacrifices? I sacrificed five years of my life for this family! Ever since Bridget married Vince, I've been running this house and mothering my sisters, and I'm tired of it. Molly is fifteen now—just as old as I was when Bridget left!"

His face went nearly purple. "Your sister left to get married because she'd gotten herself in trouble! I know you're smarter than that." In his eyes I saw all the fury he'd unleashed when Bridget had announced she was pregnant at nineteen. But I wouldn't be cowed.

"I'm going, and you can't stop me."

Daddy closed his eyes and took several deep breaths. If I hadn't just risked my life coming up with the ransom money to free him, he might have slapped me. He didn't often get violent, but since I had a loose tongue and a fiery temper like his, I'd probably been slapped more times than my three sisters combined.

Tonight he managed to keep control. But his knuckles turned white as he pressed his fists on the table. "We'll talk about this tomorrow."

"There's nothing to talk about."

"And how will you support yourself, missy?"

"I'll find a way." But the truth was, I had no idea how I'd support myself. Bridget certainly couldn't pay me enough at the store. It kept her family fed and clothed, but it was just a little neighborhood place. I'd have to apply for a job downtown, and even if I got one right away it would be a while before I'd have enough saved to move out. I was still stuck here for the time being.

Goddamn it. Maybe I shouldn't have said no to Joey so quickly.

#

"Come with me."

Joey's words floated toward me through the dark, whispered in a low voice, raw with need. Masculine scents of smoke and whiskey and aftershave filled my head, and I breathed deeply before a sigh escaped my lips. Then his mouth was on mine, hot and hard and heavy. Too heavy.

Joey, I won't fight you. Take me away.

I tried to murmur words against his lips, but the pressure on my mouth wouldn't let up. *I'm dreaming*, I thought in a haze of confused arousal.

But when I opened my eyes, the man in my room was real.

And it wasn't Joey.

"Shhhh," Enzo whispered, his hand over my mouth. "Come with me. Now."

My pulse, already racing, kicked up even higher at his invitation, at his touch on my lips, at the promise of sneaking somewhere alone with him in the dark. Clothed in only my light summer nightgown, I followed him past my father's closed bedroom door, carefully moving down the stairs in my bare feet. It didn't surprise me at all that Enzo had come right in the front door—he had a way with locks I'd learned not to question.

Outside, I hurried toward a gorgeous cream-colored Packard sedan parked at the curb. Enzo opened the passenger door for me and I slid in, tucking my hands underneath my legs. As I watched his lean, muscular frame move around the front of the car and open the driver's side door, my insides tightened with desire. He wore no coat, no vest, and no collar on his white shirt. The top few buttons were undone, and my fingers itched to pull the shirt from his trousers and undo the rest of them so I could work off some of the tension inside me. I dug my fingernails into my thighs.

As soon as the motor was running Enzo hit the accelerator, speeding down the street and turning onto Jefferson so quickly I had to brace myself against the door. My heart thrummed hard in my chest, and when his right hand slid across the seat and under the hem of my short nightgown, I moved closer to him.

His expression remained impassive and his eyes on the road, although I saw the slightest twitch in his jaw. I held my breath when his hand settled on the inside of my thigh and slowly crept higher. When his fingers brushed against the soft folds between my legs and he realized I wasn't wearing underwear, he glanced sharply at me.

My eyes pleaded with him to continue. I wanted to lose control, lose my mind, lose myself. I wanted the heart-pounding abandon that overwhelmed us when we let ourselves forget who we were and why every moment between us was stolen. Ten days ago I hadn't even known his name, but he'd awakened something in me, something instinctual and insatiable that would not be ignored.

And I didn't want to ignore it. I wanted to indulge it.

With my eyes locked on the exquisite lines of his profile, I put my left hand between his legs. His cock was already hard, but as I rubbed him up and down, it swelled further and strained tighter against his trousers. He slipped a fingertip inside me, sliding it up the slick seam at my center, keeping it torturously shallow, before moving it gently back and forth over the tiny spot that electrified my entire body.

With one hand I slipped the buttons of his trousers through the holes and slid my palm down his hot, tight abdomen. When I wrapped my hand around his solid flesh, he grabbed the steering wheel with both hands.

I said nothing, just moved my hand up and down the hot, thick column, squeezing tight and keeping the rhythm steady, the way I knew he liked it. My lips curved into a smile. The thrill of touching Enzo this way filled me with a sense of power and freedom so intoxicating I often felt drunk when we were together, even when no alcohol had been consumed. The forward motion of the car, the rush of night flying past the windows, the hum of the tires on the road—all of it added to the maelstrom building inside me.

Suddenly the Packard swerved. At first I thought it was accidental, but then I saw that Enzo had turned down a silent residential street with large homes set back from the road. He turned off the engine, looked at me with glittering black eyes, and uttered just one word: "Now."

The keys barely hit the floor before he hauled me onto his lap.

I straddled him, one knee on either side of his hips, and he took my head in his hands, crushing his mouth to mine. We weren't in love, about that I had no illusions, but our desire for each other was volatile and fierce, and we kissed as if we were starved, as if our hunger could never be satisfied. Enzo slipped his arms from his braces and I shoved at the sides of his trousers. Without taking his mouth off me, he lifted his hips and managed to shimmy them down just enough. I grasped his swollen cock in my hand again, anxious to feel it inside me.

But we'd already been careless once the night before. "Wait," I breathed. Do you have...you know..." Without answering, he tilted sideways and reached under the front seat. When he righted himself, he held a small condom tin, and with one hand, he opened it, slipped one from its paper wrapper, and slid it on. I lowered myself onto him, intending to go slow since I was still tender from the night before. But Enzo had other ideas. He grabbed my hips and yanked me down hard, both of us gasping at the shock of it. Bracing my hands on the top of the seat behind him, I turned my face away from his and kept still, allowing my body to push past the sharp twinge of pain.

His mouth, hot and wet, traveled down the exposed side of my neck as the ache inside me eased. He swirled his tongue in an intricate pattern along my throat and down to my shoulder. Instinctively, the muscles surrounding him contracted, and I gasped when I felt his teeth sink into my skin. Then he brushed his lips over the spot, soft as a feather.

Aroused by the whisper of his lips on my neck after the sting of the bite, I began to move, slowly rocking my hips forward and back, and clenching him tight inside me. He picked up his head and our eyes met, our mouths open and breathing hotly against one another.

Then he took control of the rhythm between us, using his hands on my hips, pulling and pushing my body against his, increasingly harder and faster. He cursed and closed his eyes while I smiled and reached up, flattening my palms on the car's ceiling. I let him move me the way he wanted, but I arched my back a little to feel the base of his cock just where I wanted it. A sheen of sweat broke out on his forehead, glistening in the dark, and my back prickled with trapped heat under my nightgown.

Oh my God. Yes, yes, yes...

Pressure built inside me, the powerful need for release a gathering storm at my center, and I wanted to widen my knees even farther to take him deeper. My blood roared, my skin hummed, and every muscle in my body began to tighten.

"Yes," I said, my voice soft and pleading. "Don't stop. Oh God, Enzo—yes, like that. Don't stop..."

He cursed again, and I could feel him start to throb inside me. He dug his fingers into my skin and held me tight to him as he came, and the sight of his gorgeous face and the pulse of his powerful orgasm and even the knowledge that we could be seen through the windows sent me flying over the edge of my own pleasure. I closed my eyes, dropped my head back, and let the waves crash through me.

Breathing hard, I stared at the ceiling of the car as stars swam in front of my eyes. Enzo touched my throat, trailing five fingers down to my chest. "I want you," he growled.

I laughed lazily, picking my head up. "Again? Already?"

He didn't smile. "I want you for myself." His palm flattened over one breast and he squeezed it before sliding his hand to the small of my back. "I don't want anyone else to have what I have."

My body was still tingling, but his words abraded the lingering hum a little. I wasn't interested in being anyone's possession.

And Enzo had no room to talk.

"You're the one with the fiancée, not me."

"I told you last night—that's a business arrangement."

"I remember." Irritated at the thought of the squeaking little twit he was engaged to marry, I tried to get off his lap, but he held me there. His flesh was still relatively hard inside me, but I was no longer in the mood.

"Jealous?"

"No." But my cheeks were burning. "I just don't like being reminded of your goddamn girlfriend while I'm sitting on your lap."

"That's more than just my lap you're on, isn't it?"

"Stop it. You know what I mean. Here you are talking about not wanting others to have me, but I don't even know when we can see each other, between my father and your fiancée, and—"

"Your father won't be a problem. He'll be so busy with his new business venture, he won't even notice you're gone."

"New business venture...you mean the new building?"

"And the gambling. I set that up, you know."

I blinked in surprise. "Your father let you do that?"

"I'm a grown man, Tiny. My father doesn't control me." Anger edged its way underneath his words.

"Sorry, but I thought it was Angel who'd made the deal with my father today. He never said anything about you."

"Well, I was there," he said, irritated. "It was my idea to move Jack to a new building, let him run a few games, and let Raymond take over the bootlegging from Canada on his own."

At the mention of his brother, I froze. "Raymond was there?"

Enzo smiled. "No, he's still recovering from the wrath of Tiny O'Mara."

In my mind I relived the adrenaline-and-terror-fueled blow to his head. I felt no guilt, but I did fear further violence. "Is he going to come after me again?"

"If he does, he'll have me to answer to."

"But he's your brother."

"I don't fucking care who he is—anyone touches you, anyone even looks at you in a way I don't like, I'll kill him."

Unease slithered up my body, wrapping itself around my chest like a boa constrictor. I tried to shake it off. "So it's OK for you to have a fiancée, but no one can even look my way?"

"You know, if your friends hadn't stolen that shipment, I wouldn't be in this position. I could probably even break it off with Gina."

I raised an eyebrow. This was something new. Yesterday when I'd confronted him about the engagement, he hadn't said anything about leaving Gina Meloni, whose father owned a whiskey distillery in Kentucky. "Oh?"

"But now I can't postpone anything until I pay for the fucking whiskey I ordered. It's in Meloni's warehouse, but he won't deliver it until I pay him. And his men won't let anyone else deliver booze to the club, which is a big fucking problem, as you might imagine."

I didn't much care about his whisky problem. "Postpone what? I thought you were already engaged." I tried to recall a ring on Gina's finger, but couldn't. The couple times I'd seen her at the club, I hadn't known about the engagement so I hadn't thought to look for one.

Enzo turned his head and stared out the window. "I asked her father for more time to get the cash for the whiskey, and he offered a deal."

"What kind of deal?"

"If Gina and I get married now, he'll forgive the debt."

The irony that it was now Enzo forced to come up with thousands of dollars on a deadline wasn't lost on me, but I couldn't help obsessing over the word *married*, especially in light of our intimate seating arrangement. "Wait a minute...you're actually going to marry her?"

"I'm trying to get out of it."

My mouth fell open "Jesus Christ, Enzo!" This time when I wrestled my way off his lap, he didn't stop me.

"What's the problem, Tiny? It's not as if you didn't know about her. We discussed the fact that you and I are a secret, remember? That's half the fun."

We had discussed it, sort of—actually it was less a discussion and more his telling me how things had to be. If I wanted him, those were the terms. And while the secrecy did add a certain clandestine thrill to our meetings, I wasn't sure I wanted to be a married man's mistress. Frowning, I looked away as he removed the spent condom.

"Listen to me," he said. "Gina's not important. What matters is that I can't let Meloni see I can be bested by a bunch of fucking upstart delinquents from the Scarfone gang. He'll make my life hell. He'll think he can push me around. That's why I have to go after them myself. Forget what I told you about talking to Lupo."

At the mention of Joey, I froze. "What?"

"I need to handle this now. I can't wait around and hope that he tells you something."

"Can't you just ask your father for the money?"

"I'm not a fucking child, Tiny. I can handle this myself."

"So now what?" Pressing my knees together, I pushed my nightgown down and tucked it around my legs. My thighs were sticky.

"So now I get my money back from those assholes. I can't let it be known that you can steal from Enzo DiFiore. I have to send a message."

Chills swept down my arms. "How?"

He set his jaw and didn't answer, but I knew what he was thinking. My stomach heaved, imagining it could be Joey on the receiving end of that message. "Don't, Enzo. You don't have to hurt anyone—let me help you."

"You can't help me."

"Yes, I can." *What are you doing?* a voice inside me screamed.

But I ignored it.

"The River Gang didn't sell the opium. Joey brought it back to Detroit." I whispered the words, as if the volume at which I betrayed Joey might lessen its reprehensibility.

Enzo fixed his eyes on me. "What? Who told you that?"

"Joey wants to talk to you. Maybe make a deal with you." The words tumbled out quickly.

"Where is it?"

Finally I bit my tongue. "I don't know."

"Oh, I think you do." He leaned closer, slipping his arms around me and dragging me across his lap on my back. My legs extended along the seat, and I pressed my knees together as his right hand slid under my nightgown again. "And you're going to tell me."

"Enzo, please."

He kneaded my thigh, but his touch was gentle, too gentle for how I knew he must be feeling inside. And he was smiling. "Tell me, darling."

I chewed my bottom lip as his eyes searched my face. Despite his warm hands on me, the curve of his lips was as chilling as the calm in his voice. It was the

Enzo I'd first met, the one who could mask his emotions so masterfully that I couldn't tell what he was thinking. He'd let some of that façade slip in the last few days. *But now there's something he wants more than you.* "I can't."

His smile widened as his fingers slid higher and worked between my inner thighs. "You can do anything you want," he said softly, bringing his lips close to mine as he began to stroke me. "You're still wet. I love that I make you this wet." Lowering his mouth, he slid his tongue between my lips and eased one finger, then another, inside me, his languid kiss mirroring the gentle rhythm of his hand.

Somewhere inside my brain was a voice warning me that this was wrong, that I'd made a promise to Joey, that Enzo wasn't kissing me this way because he cared for me. But I silenced it by telling myself I'd done the right thing by revealing Joey's secret—I'd prevented Enzo from hurting anyone. And even if Enzo didn't love me, he certainly loved pleasing me, and maybe that was enough. As his tongue swept mine, my arms snaked around his neck and I widened my knees a little.

"Good girl," he whispered, removing his fingers to caress my tender, swollen flesh before plunging them deep inside me again. "You're going to come again for me."

"Oh God..." I clutched at his neck and turned my face into his chest, but even the smell of him, smoky and masculine, drove me mad with desire.

He rubbed his wet fingers over the most sensitive skin on my body. "I know everything you want. And I can give it all to you, you know I can." His voice was dulcet, the words dripping from his lips like honey. "Your own apartment, money to do as you please, new clothes...the life you deserve. I've been thinking about it all day."

When I moaned, he rubbed faster and harder, and I could only think *yes, yes, yes*. I murmured the words, and he brought his lips closer to my ear.

"Wouldn't you like your own place? Where we can be together whenever we want? I'll make you come all...night...long."

His breath tickled my skin, his words echoing through the roar of blood and the buzz of nerve endings and—oh my God the way he touched me made me feel like nothing else mattered but the moment and the need and the heat and the spiraling climb toward release...

"Yes!" I cried out, lifting my hips against his hand as the second orgasm exploded inside me, no less powerful than the first. When the tightness finally eased, my bones were floating in my skin.

"Mmmmm." He kissed me again. "You'll need an apartment that has thick walls."

I managed a tiny smile.

"So what do you say?"

"I...can't afford an apartment."

"I'll pay for it."

"No." Orgasms aside, I didn't want to him to own me.

"Then I'll get you a job. Would you like to work at the club?"

"Work at the club? What would I do?"

"Whatever you want. Hostess? Hat check Waitress?" He cocked his head. "You don't sing, do you? Or dance? You'd look fantastic on stage in a short little costume."

"Uh, no." Because one of my legs was slightly shorter than the other, the result of a difficult birth during which my hip was broken, I'd never felt terribly natural while dancing—sometimes even walking comfortably was a chore. And my singing made my cooking skills look good.

"Well, you can think about it then. But I'll see to it that you're paid very well, if you want."

I exhaled, closing my eyes. Of course I wanted it. I wanted everything he just mentioned—the apartment, the nights with him, the money to do as I pleased, the freedom to make my choices and own my mistakes as well as my successes. What young woman didn't want to live a flapper's life with all its wicked delights?

But at what price?

If I told Enzo where the opium was and he took it back, Joey would know I'd betrayed him. But if I didn't, Enzo would take matters into his own hands and people would get hurt, maybe even killed.

I opened my eyes. "If I tell you where the opium is, you have to promise me you'll give me a chance to talk to Joey before you take it."

"I can't promise that, Tiny. But I can promise that if you don't tell me, I'll have no choice but to settle this score my own way."

My heart stuttered. "Well...you can't hurt Joey. Promise that."

Enzo stiffened. "What is he to you?"

"A friend."

Silence. "I won't have to hurt him if he cooperates. And I won't have to marry Gina if I get the cash for the drugs."

It was so dark, I couldn't read his eyes. I wanted everything he was offering. And I didn't want him to marry Gina. What had he said to me this morning? *You and I are going to have to trust each other a little bit.*

I took a breath. "It's in the boathouse."

A smile crept onto his lips, slow and sinister. "Shall we take a ride?"

I struggled to sit up. "No!"

He shifted me onto the seat beside him and started the car.

Panicked, I put my hands on his arm and tugged. "Please, Enzo. Just wait, all right?" It occurred to me that I wasn't entirely positive the drugs were still in the boathouse. Even if they had been there earlier today, Joey might have moved them after dropping me off. I hung on as he swung the car around and headed back onto Jefferson. "Listen, I wasn't supposed to tell you anything yet, and now I'll be in trouble."

Enzo laughed. "Trouble is your middle name, darling."

Frowning, I scooted away from him and stared out the window. Enzo rarely used any terms of endearment with me, and somehow this one lacked a certain affection I was hoping to develop between us. Why the hell couldn't I meet a normal fellow like Evelyn had? One who took me to the movies or a dance on a Saturday night?

Enzo turned off Jefferson onto the boathouse drive, and I had to reach out and steady myself again as the Packard bumped and shimmied over the tree-rutted and potholed dirt. Low hanging branches scraped against the windows, and Enzo swore softly. "Fucking trees better not ruin this paint job. I just got this car."

I felt like ripping the new upholstery, and I might have if I weren't so scared.

When we emerged into the clearing where the abandoned boathouse stood, a shiver ran through me. This is where I'd been abducted just a few nights ago by Raymond and Harry, and I didn't much feel like reliving that memory. Beyond the dilapidated old structure, Lake St. Clair loomed, black and silent. I wrapped my bare arms around myself, feeling exposed and vulnerable in my nightgown. "I'll wait here."

Enzo looked over at me but didn't reply. After pulling his braces back onto his shoulders, he got out of the car and opened the door to the back. I thought he might be looking for his coat but instead he reached down and retrieved a pistol from beneath the seat. My mouth hung open as he checked it for bullets.

"What the hell is that for?" I whispered. "There's nobody here!"

"Then there won't be any trouble." His tone was cool and confident—of course it was—but he glanced over both shoulders as he walked past the giant weeping willow to the boathouse door. The waning moon offered little light, so I didn't see how he managed to pick the lock, but within seconds his white shirt disappeared into the shadows of the building.

I swallowed hard, murmuring a quick prayer that the drugs were there, that Enzo wouldn't want to take them tonight, and that Joey would forgive me for this. Before I even got the chance to say Amen, the gun went off.

Chapter Four

I opened the car door and took off running for the boathouse. "Enzo!" I yelled as I crossed the threshold into the cool, dark space. Stopping just inside the door, I was relieved to see him standing there, unharmed. His back was to me, and both his hands were in the air near his shoulders. Neither hand held the pistol.

"Tiny, go back outside please."

I barely heard the words over the galloping of my heart, which felt like someone's fist trying to punch through my ribs. I looked around, confused. The voice was deep and familiar, but it wasn't Enzo's. Inching forward, I scanned the shadows and saw Joey standing next to a large trunk, pointing a gun at Enzo. "Joey?"

"I said, go back outside." He kept his eyes and his weapon on Enzo.

"No! What are you doing?" I tried walking toward him, but immediately someone threw a thick arm around me from behind and pinned my back to his chest—not hard enough to hurt me, but enough to prevent me from moving forward. I tugged at the

Fuck off Joey has every right

74

wrist, to no avail. "Hey!"

"Take her out, Angelo." Joey's voice was colder than I'd ever heard it, which must have been why I hadn't recognized it right away.

"Hold on, just wait a second." I struggled to free myself from Angelo's hairy left arm. Like Enzo and Joey, he wore no coat and his cuffs were rolled. His right arm extended toward Enzo, gun aimed. "What is this?"

"It's a meeting," said Angelo. "Thanks for setting it up."

"What do you mean, setting it up? I didn't do this!" I panicked, imagining Enzo would think I'd sent him into a trap.

"I figured you'd tell him." Joey's voice was devoid of any emotion, but I felt the sting of his words as if he'd slapped me. "And I had a feeling it might be tonight."

"Joey, please," I began.

"Get her out of here," he said.

"Why?" Enzo asked. "If all you want to do is make a deal, why not let her stay? She's hardly going to run away in her nightgown."

Oh God—I'd forgotten I was in my nightgown, and barefoot. Jesus, what Joey must think! And Angelo

— my face burned with shame that a strange man held me so close in my pajamas. Frantically, I wondered why Enzo wanted me to stay. Did he think they'd be less likely to shoot him if I was in the boathouse?

Or did he want me where he could see me?

This was a huge problem with us—we were never sure whose side the other was on. My hands shook, and I tightened them into fists to keep them still. "Let me stay." I forced myself to sound defiant, not defenseless. "I won't be any trouble. I was trying to do as you asked and set up a meeting, Joey, but he insisted on seeing for himself if the drugs were here."

"Of course he did." Joey never took his eyes from Enzo. "He probably wouldn't have met with me otherwise."

"You're right. I wouldn't have." Enzo sounded way too self-righteous for someone with two guns pointed at him. Silently I pleaded with him to show some humility. "You fucked up a huge deal for me."

"Tough luck, I guess," Joey said.

Angelo spit on the boathouse floor, and my stomach turned over at the splat. "You ready to talk business or you want to cry about the past?"

I braced myself for an angry reaction from Enzo, but he stayed calm as he regarded Angelo. "Who the fuck are you?"

"Shut your mouth," Joey ordered. "We came to make a deal. You interested?"

"Can I put my arms down?"

"Be my guest. But stay the fuck where you are."

Enzo lowered his arms. "What's the deal you're offering?"

"You have a buyer lined up for this?" Joey jerked his head toward the trunk next to him. It was large and rectangular, the kind people packed for a long voyage on a steamer ship.

"I might."

"We make the sale together," Joey said. "I'll deliver the product."

"And what do I get out of this deal?"

"A cut of the profit."

"What kind of cut?"

"I think thirty percent's fair."

"I think you're fucking crazy."

"I could just kill you, you know."

A high-pitched sound escaped my throat. Neither Enzo nor Joey looked at me.

"Killing me won't get you what you want."

Joey shrugged. "But it might be fun."

"Please, stop," I begged. Angelo tightened his

grip on me, and I whimpered in protest.

"Let her go," Joey said.

"Hunh?" Angelo was as surprised as I was. "You heard me. Let her go."

The arm around my chest didn't loosen. "What the fuck, Lupo?"

"Just do it."

After a moment's hesitation, Angelo released me and moved closer to Enzo, bringing his other hand to the gun.

"Tiny, bring me the pistol on the ground." Joey's voice was cool and steady, and he still didn't look at me.

I hurried forward, scooping up Enzo's gun from the cement floor and bringing it to Joey. As he took the gun from my hands, the moonlight shining through the high windows revealed the fury in his eyes.

I remembered a night not long ago when Joey and I had been alone in the boathouse, the night he'd kissed me on the lake, the night a storm raged outside and lightning had illuminated his features as he'd moved toward me in the dark, his voice teasing… My throat squeezed shut.

"So DiFiore, you can either agree to what we're offering here, which is an even three-way split—more than anyone else would offer, by the fucking way—or you can kiss thousands of dollars goodbye like a goddamn fool."

Enzo squared his shoulders. "I'm no fool."

"Then make the deal."

Unbearable silence followed. Finally he spoke. "How do I know you've really got the drugs? Could be anything in that trunk."

Joey nodded at Angelo, who grabbed Enzo by the upper arm and put the gun under his chin. They were about the same height, but Angelo was meatier, with a thick neck and a beefy chest that bulged inside his shirt. By contrast, Enzo's frame appeared slender. Angelo led him over to the trunk, which Joey opened. Tentatively, I tiptoed forward and peered inside too.

It was full of tin containers shaped like small bricks with rounded edges, and they were labeled, but I couldn't read the words in the dark. Joey shut the lid. "Well?"

Enzo studied Joey. "What's Sam paying you?"

"This is between us. Sam doesn't know about it, and he's not gonna find out about it, neither, understand?" Joey raised the gun a little higher.

Enzo's lips twitched. "Lupo, you have no fucking idea what you're doing."

My heart skipped a beat—that was exactly what I was afraid of.

But Joey stood his ground. "Deal or no deal, asshole."

Enzo stared at Joey for another few seconds, and then he glanced at Angelo. I might as well have been invisible. "Deal."

To my astonishment, the two shook on it before Angelo marched us out to the Packard at gunpoint. I couldn't even bring myself to glance back at Joey as we left.

#

Enzo was silent on the way back to my house, but he wore an eerily calm expression. He switched off the headlamps once he'd turned onto my street, and slowed the Packard to a crawl before pulling into the drive next to my house.

When the motor was silent, he looked at me. "Are you all right?"

"No."

He smiled, the bastard. "I'd say I was sorry for

taking you out tonight, but I'd be lying."

"You enjoyed this?"

"Well...parts of it. Maybe even most of it." He brushed a finger over my shoulder, but I leaned away from him.

"You could have been killed, Enzo!"

"Those guys were never going to kill me. They need me."

"Well, it frightens me, all the guns and threats and posturing. Not to mention the stealing and the lying and the underhanded deals."

"That's how it works, Tiny."

I crossed my arms in a huff.

Enzo smiled again. "Are you angry with me or with yourself?"

"I'm angry with everyone and everything right now. No matter what I do, I can't get anything right."

"Come on, now." Enzo slipped his fingers up the back of my neck through my hair. When I tried to lean away, he closed his fist, keeping my head where it was and forcing me to look at him. "Everything is going to be perfect, Tiny. You'll see."

"How do you figure? Will your thirty percent cut of the opium be enough to pay off Gina's father?"

His lips tipped up, the smile of an adult

tolerating an ignorant child. "Of course not."

"Well, then—how will everything be perfect? I don't understand." He couldn't mean he was going to steal the drugs—Joey would take them from the boathouse tonight, I was certain, and this time he wouldn't be foolish enough to trust me with their location.

Instead of explaining, Enzo leaned forward and kissed me lightly on each cheek. "Good night, Tiny."

"Enzo, I—"

"Shhh." He put a finger to my lips. "I'm going to take care of you. I'm going to take care of everything."

"But—"

"Leave it all to me."

I pulled his hand away from my mouth. "You can't hurt Joey. You promised."

"I won't have to." He released me and sat back. "If he's smart."

"And you can't go to Sam the Barber with this information. He'll kill Joey himself."

Enzo's voice took on a new edge. "You're awfully concerned about Lupo. I'm not sure I like it."

Be careful. "I'm just trying to prevent people from getting hurt, Enzo." That was the truth, wasn't it? I thought it was, but for me the truth was becoming murkier every day. It was nothing I could cling to for safety.

"I see the way he looks at you," Enzo said icily.

"You're imagining things. Right now he wants to shoot me. I'm surprised he didn't."

"He's not going to shoot either one of us. In fact, I think he's going to negotiate further with me."

"Why would he do that?"

"Because I've done a little research on your friend. And I have something he wants. I'm going to offer it to him." With that he put both hands on the steering wheel. "Now you better go in. I'll see you soon."

After shutting the car door as quietly as possible, I snuck back into the house and crept up the stairs, attempting to avoid the ones that creaked.

Wait a minute, what am I doing? Why am I sneaking around like this? It was probably three o'clock in the morning, but what the hell did I care? What's the worst Daddy would do—throw me out? To hell with it. I walked up the stairs as if it were noontime, actually disappointed that my feet didn't make more noise on the carpeted steps. How I would have liked to show Daddy he couldn't police me anymore! I wasn't his to control—I wasn't anybody's.

In the bathroom, I cleaned up a little before climbing back into bed. My body was tired, but my mind wouldn't rest. I lay on my side, hands tucked under my cheek and knees drawn to my chest. What could Enzo possibly have that Joey wanted? It couldn't be money.

The whiskey? No, he didn't really have that yet either.

But I couldn't think of any other asset Enzo had to offer Joey at this point, so I approached it from the other side.

What did Joey want?

Immediately, my stomach flipped. I curled my toes and squeezed my thighs together, bringing my legs tighter into my chest. *Knock that off. Even if Joey had felt something stronger than friendship for you before, which he'd never actually said, your behavior tonight was enough to splinter it.*

The hideous weight of what I'd done dropped onto my chest like an anvil and stayed there, pressing the air from my lungs. Tears burned beneath my eyelids. Without Joey's help last week, I never would have gotten the ten thousand dollars to free Daddy.

And he'd never asked for anything in return. Yet I'd repaid him tonight with duplicity, giving up his

Exactly bitch

secret to Enzo in exchange for my own pleasure, for promises whispered in the dark. The shame of it rained down on me—I gasped for air as if I were suffocating.

Hold on, just hold on, said a voice inside me. *You did what you had to do to keep Joey safe, right?* Inhaling deeply, I held my breath for a moment and counted to ten before letting it out, slowly. Yes, I did.

Somehow, it didn't make me feel any better.

Weeping into my pillow, I wondered how I'd ever make things right again between us.

#

By the time I left my room the following morning, Daddy was up and out of the house. I'd missed nine o'clock Mass, which I felt some guilt about, but instead of dwelling on it, I dressed and took a streetcar down to Mt. Elliott Cemetery, where our mother was buried. Usually the girls and I did this together on Sundays, and when I entered the scrolling gates and saw other families at grave sites, pulling weeds and sprucing up flowers, or even just holding hands as they strolled or sat on a bench in quiet contemplation, a lump formed in my throat.

Swallowing hard, I walked toward the section where our mother rested, keeping my head down. It was sunny but breezy, and I had to hold one hand on my hat, which was wide with an oversized brim. It wasn't until I was nearly upon her simple Celtic cross that I saw someone already there. I froze, my Sunday dress flapping about my knees in the wind.

Daddy stood, hat in folded hands, feet apart. From the side, I could see his head was bowed, and I had the feeling that his eyes were closed. When I took a step closer, I saw I was right. His lips moved in silent prayer, or perhaps confession or apology—he certainly had any number of things he might have told her in order to unburden himself. I couldn't even imagine what she'd have said back. Would she forgive him his sins and shortcomings as a father, as a man?

And what about your own?

An ache took hold of my heart, and the lump returned to my throat. What would she say to me if she could speak from beyond the grave? Would she tell me I was selfish to leave home? Would she ask me to think of my sisters first? Or would she agree with me that I'd done enough and it was time to move on with my life?

She'd married young, like Bridget, and had a

family almost as quickly. In fact, it was my mother who'd always talked of being a nurse if she'd had the opportunity or the education. She was always so proud of my high marks in school and my determination to go to college. After she died in childbirth with Mary Grace ten years ago, I made up my mind that I'd do as she'd wished she could have.

At the time, I'd had no idea what an uphill climb it would be.

I said a quick prayer for my mother's soul from where I stood and turned to leave, having no desire whatsoever to converse with my father here. My mother deserved peace in her final resting place, and I wouldn't disturb it with another argument. Because I hadn't changed my mind—I still wanted to leave home.

And it wasn't only that I wanted to be with Enzo, although I'd be lying if I said my newfound sexual freedom wasn't influencing my decision. But the longer I stayed at home, the more I feared life was passing me by. I couldn't shake the sense that something was out there for me, and if I didn't try to find it now, I might lose my chance at it forever. Sure, I was only twenty, but I'd seen plenty of unfinished lives snuffed out too soon.

To stay out of sight, I tugged the hat down further over my eyes and made a beeline for the exit. But when I turned to glance one last time at my mother's stone, I saw another familiar figure standing over a grave about ten yards off to my left.

His back was to me, but I knew those wide shoulders that tapered to a trim waist. I'd seen that muscular back naked in my kitchen last week, the night I'd treated Joey's injuries after a fight. Biting my lip, I recalled the way I'd run my hands over his bruised ribs.

He was dressed more in the style I was accustomed to seeing him in—the plain black pants, a cream-colored shirt that even from here I could tell had seen better days, and brown braces cutting into his solid shoulders and making a Y down his back. His head was bare, his dark mop of wayward curls blowing in the breeze, and I figured he was holding his floppy old cap in his hands.

Were his eyes closed? Were his lips moving in silent prayer for his slain father? Was he asking forgiveness of the man who'd taught him about stars and had no doubt hoped for more for his son than the life—and death—he'd had himself? Or was Joey asking for guidance at his father's feet, the way I sometimes did at my mother's? In that moment I felt a kinship with Joey that I rarely felt with anyone other than my sisters, and before I knew it, my feet were stepping through the grass in his direction.

I came up beside him, and although I knew he recognized me from the way his back straightened, he said nothing. Perhaps he, too, didn't want to sully his father's final resting place with heated words.

But I needed to apologize.

"Hello." I braved a sideways glance at him.

Silence. I might as well have greeted the statue on my right.

"Joey, I'm sorry."

"I don't believe you."

I wasn't sure if he meant he didn't believe my apology was sincere, or he didn't believe I had the gall to approach him here. Neither interpretation boded well. "Please let me apologize. I never meant to tell Enzo anything last night."

"Pretty obvious your self-control ain't what it ought to be."

Deep breath. "I thought I was doing the right thing. He was threatening to hurt people in order to get his money back, and I was scared for you. He knows who stole that load."

Joey shrugged. "So you're a hero now too—he saved you, you saved me. Well done. You two deserve each other."

I stepped in front of him so he'd be forced to look at me. "Joey, please. I'm...I'm sorry too about last night on the roof. I wish I—"

"I told you to forget about that," he snapped.

"Have you forgotten about it?"

"It was a mistake. One of many I've made where you're concerned." His glare was more blistering than the sun.

"OK, fine. But I'm worried. I don't know exactly what Enzo is thinking, but I do know that things aren't going to go according to your plan."

"Switching sides already, doll?"

Jesus—I hadn't thought of it like that. Was I? Had I ever really been on Enzo's side? Before I could think it through, Joey went on.

"And what the hell do you mean by that, anyway? He shook on that deal."

A gust of wind threatened to carry off my hat, and I reached up to hold it to my head. "I don't know anything for certain, but I do know that you shouldn't underestimate him. When he wants something, he..." I swallowed hard. "He knows how to get it."

"I bet he does." He slapped his cap on his head. "You tell him I'll be in touch. I want this deal done fast so I can get out of this town. Nothing here but bad memories." With one last look at his father's stone he stomped away, and I noticed he'd traded his new shoes for his old work boots too.

He exited the gates and got into an old Model T parked on the street. Even the fancy red Buick was gone. A pang of regret squeezed my heart. It was the old, familiar Joey in every way except one—he despised me. And he had every right to. Until that moment I had no idea how much that would matter.

I broke into a run.

Chapter Five

Joey was just starting the engine when I reached the windowless passenger door. "Wait," I said breathlessly. "I want to talk about this."

"About what?" Joey spoke loudly over the noisy motor. "There's nothing left to talk about, Tiny. Just go home."

Without being invited—in fact, I'd been dismissed—I opened the door and hopped in. "No." I shut myself in the car, put my hands in my lap and looked at him. "I can't. I won't."

Joey turned off the engine and squinted at me. "Have I told you how annoying you are?"

"Not today."

"And also how weak and impulsive? And for such a smart girl, how stupid you act sometimes?"

I squirmed, but it was no less than I deserved. "Go ahead. I can take it."

"You deliberately betrayed me, Tiny. After everything we went through last week. I told you something in confidence and you went right to him with it." *you tell her*

"I didn't! I swear to you, I didn't. He surprised me by showing up in my room late last night"—and here Joey flinched—"and we went for a drive. We got to..." I flapped a hand in the air, unsure how to proceed. "...talking, and he started in about taking revenge for the heist into his own hands because he owes money to a whiskey distributor. I got scared for you, Joey, I had to tell him!"

"I told you, I can take care of myself." Joey's knuckles were white on the steering wheel.

"I'm sorry. I know I did the wrong thing, but I never meant to betray you. It just came out. Please forgive me." I put a hand on his forearm, and he shrugged it off.

"You should have left it to me like I asked you to."

"You asked me to set up a meeting!"

"No, I didn't! You offered, and if you recall, at the end of the night, I told you to drop it. And I meant what I said."

"I know, but..."

"But nothing." He stuck a finger in my face. "You fucked up. If we hadn't been at the boathouse last night, he would have taken those drugs and left me with nothing."

No point in reminding Joey he'd stolen the drugs to begin with—these guys all played by their own rules. "I wouldn't have let him."

"Ha! You've got no sway over him."

"You're wrong. He listens to me." What possessed me to say such a thing, I have no idea.

Joey smirked. "If you think that, then you're a bigger fool than I thought." He cocked his head, looking more like the old Joey. "What did he do, tell you he loves you?"

My chest and neck flushed with heat. "Shut up."

"Ooh, she's blushing." Joey poked his finger in my side repeatedly. "Did he proclaim his devotion for you, is that it? Is he going to build you a house on Boston Boulevard and buy you a fancy electric car and name his yacht after you? The Tiny." Joey framed the words in the air with his hands. "Hmm, not quite grand enough, is it?" He widened his gesture. "The Frances Kathleen. Eh, a little better."

Irritation bubbled up in me, but I was relieved he was back to teasing. "You remembered my full name. Impressive. Don't worry, I won't ask you to spell it."

He turned to me with murderous eyes and poked my side once more. "Get out of my car, ya no-good, backstabbing floozy. Or do I have to drive his girl around as well as feed her?"

"I'll take a ride home, thanks. Sweet of you to offer."

Joey looked at me a moment and exhaled. "I should put you out at the curb right now."

"But you won't."

A pause. "I guess not. "

I grinned. I couldn't help it.

"Why can't I stay mad at you, anyway?"

Linking my fingers, I tucked them under my chin and batted my lashes. "Because I'm so adorable?"

He scrutinized my face. "Nope. That ain't it."

I dropped the pose. "Just drive me home already."

Rolling his eyes, he started the engine again. "Sure thing, Little Tomato. I only live to serve you."

Crossing my arms, I turned my face to the window so he wouldn't see me smile at his nickname for me, which only a week ago would have made me scowl.

When Joey pulled into the drive at my house, I was reluctant to get out of the car, for some reason. "Have you had lunch?"

Joey looked amused. "And if I said no, what are you gonna do about it?"

95

He's forgive her far too easy but I love him.

"Um...invite you in? Scramble you an egg? I do know how to do that."

He smirked. "Sounds tempting but no, I can't. I have to work the dinner shift at the restaurant today."

"Oh. OK. Maybe I'll see you later this week?" *What the hell are you doing? Just get out of the car.*

"Maybe." His tone changed, as if he was irritated I'd asked about seeing him again. "But this week's busy with moving my ma to my sister's and all. Plus I'm looking to get out of town. You tell your boyfriend to get in touch with me, and fast."

"He's not really my boyfriend." Then I was embarrassed—Joey knew I was sleeping with Enzo. If he wasn't my boyfriend, what was he? "I mean...I don't really know what we are."

Joey switched his focus out the windshield. "It's none of my business. Just tell him."

I nodded as I got out, a funny, prickly feeling in the pit of my stomach, as if a cactus had lodged there or something. Lifting my hand in a stupid little wave, which Joey didn't return, I watched him back out and drive down the street. I was glad he wasn't angry anymore, but I still didn't feel right about things between us. Maybe I was just worried about the deal with Enzo.

That had to be it.

#

Five days later I hadn't heard from either Enzo or Joey, and I was nearly out of my mind with worry. I started checking the newspapers every afternoon to make sure I didn't read about any new gang warfare or heists that took the lives of young mobsters.

Perhaps I should have just left it alone. After all, I was lucky in some regards—the feds I'd seen at the garage had questioned Daddy on Monday but hadn't discovered anything incriminating enough to arrest him. The garage was "sold" to Raymond DiFiore the following day, and I nearly laughed at the thought of the feds constantly breathing down his neck. I hoped they caught him and threw him in the slammer. Sometimes I fantasized about Sam the Barber accosting him in a dark alley, demanding payment for hauling a load of booze across the river, and roughing him up when he refused.

And perhaps best of all, my monthly arrived Sunday afternoon. When I noticed it, I was so delighted I dropped my head in prayerful thanks, offering up a hasty promise that I'd be more careful from now on. Aside from a little fooling around, Enzo had taken precautions, but still—no girl wants to face the hell of discovering she's in a family way before she's married. It had worked out in the end for Bridget, but she and Vince were so in love, I'm certain they'd have married eventually anyway.

Bridget had returned from the beach with the girls and her three sons as well, and we'd all had supper together Monday night at her apartment over the store. Daddy and I ignored each other throughout the entire meal, each going out of our way to avoid even making eye contact. If Bridget or Molly noticed, they didn't mention it. Both of them knew about the ordeal last week, which was why they'd grabbed the younger ones and left town. I assumed they were each so glad to see us all sitting around the table again like nothing had happened, they didn't want to risk any more unpleasantness. It was easy to avoid talking about it, since Mary Grace chattered incessantly about their trip to the beach, showing off shells she had collected, a post card she'd purchased for her scrapbook, and her freckled skin.

Every day that week I worked a bit for Bridget at

the store, and had to tell anyone who came in looking for "maple syrup," our password for whisky, that we were out of business. I mourned the income I'd lose since I wouldn't be making tips on deliveries anymore —finding a new job was a must, but I couldn't motivate myself to look for one.

After work, I'd go home and see to the girls and the house as if nothing had changed, but I just felt like something was off, as if my bones were jumbled up inside my skin. My appetite was nonexistent, I had trouble sleeping at night, and my fingernails were bitten to the quick. For a few days I thought maybe it was related to my monthly—doctors used to say women suffered from hysteria, a particular emotional frenzy caused by disturbances in a woman's body. It was quack stuff, but for a day or so I began to wonder if there wasn't a grain of truth behind it. My bleeding stopped after the usual four days, but the unease lingered.

This is ridiculous, I told myself Thursday evening as I scanned the headlines of Daddy's paper. I've got to find out what's happening or I'll go nuts. Had Enzo and

99

Joey come to an agreement? Was Joey still in

town? And what about the whisky—had Enzo come up with the money to pay Meloni or was there a goddamn wedding next Saturday?

Friday afternoon I went to the telephone and stared at it. Should I call Joey? What would I say? I felt even less comfortable calling Enzo, not that I knew how to reach him. But he would probably be at the club tonight...maybe I could manage to run into him and find out what was going on.

I called Evelyn, whom I still hadn't seen this week. Between her job at the bakery and her nights out with Ted, she'd been much busier than usual, and I'd been keeping to myself. She was thrilled to hear from me, and even more excited when I asked her if she'd like to go down to Club 23 tonight.

"Ted and I were planning on going dancing, so why don't you come with us? That's our favorite spot, since it's where we met. I can't believe it was only ten days ago, I'm so crazy about him." Her voice was thick and sweet.

"I'm happy things are going so well for you," I said, tamping down the jealousy in my gut, "but I don't want to be a nuisance on your date."

"Nonsense! You're never a nuisance, and I haven't seen you in forever. Besides, a whole slew of people are going down there tonight, I was going to phone you about it anyway. Ted says they've got a swell jazz band there from down south somewhere. Real Dixieland music, great for dancing."

"Sounds like fun." And it did, for the most part. Not that I was much of a dancer, but the prospect of being out with a group of young people all having a good time excited me. When was the last time I'd done that? "I just have to make sure the girls are set for the night. Daddy's been working late at the new location."

"New location?"

I sighed. "I'll tell you about it later. What matters is that we get together and have some fun tonight, just like old times."

She squealed with delight. "Perfect! We'll pick you up at nine, OK?"

"I'll be ready." I hung up the phone and took a deep breath.

"Ready for what?"

I jumped at Molly's voice behind me. "Oh! Uh, I'm seeing Evelyn later."

She raised a brow at me. Molly used to swallow my half-truths quite easily, but lately she'd become more perceptive. "Uh huh. And what are you wearing to see Evelyn? That?" She nodded toward my navy skirt and white admiral middy with the faint yellow stain on the front.

"Um..." I looked down as if to examine my clothing, but she caught the pink in my cheeks.

"Aha!" She crossed her arms. "No use lying to me, Tiny. I saw him, remember?"

I bit my lip. How could I forget? Enzo had come to the house to collect me one afternoon last week, and Molly had answered the door. It was the day he'd discovered the connection between the hearses from Daddy's garage and the heist. I shuddered recalling how angry he'd been.

"Are you screwy in the head or what?" she asked. "I know he looks like a movie star and all, but don't be stupid, Tiny. He's dangerous!"

"He isn't," I insisted, although my tone rang false. "He's the one who gave me the money to send you and Bridget and the kids out of town—he's the one who told me it could be too dangerous for you to stay." That was true, at least.

Molly narrowed her eyes. "Men will say anything they have to in order to get what they want, and they usually just want one thing. S-E-X."

"Jesus, Molly. Where do you hear this stuff?"

She rolled her eyes—now that I was used to. "I'm

nearly sixteen, I don't have to hear it from anyone. It's obvious."

"Well, good. Then that's one lesson I don't need to teach you. But as for me, I'm old enough and smart enough to handle myself, thank you very much." I drew myself up to my full height, but I was still shorter than she was by two inches. "Now. I've got a proposition for you. If you help me find something to wear and agree to watch Mary Grace tonight, I'll give you two extra dollars this week and let you go to the movies tomorrow night without her."

She considered it. "And an hour later for my curfew."

"Half hour. I already extended it to ten thirty, remember?"

"You also already agreed to give me two more dollars for helping with laundry and cooking, which I've been doing this week."

That was true. I hadn't eaten much this week, but Molly had made four suppers that looked and tasted much better than my usual underdone scrambled eggs and overdone bacon. "Three dollars, then."

"Deal." She grinned. "Now let's go upstairs and look at our closets, I might even have something you could borrow for tonight—I saved some money this spring and bought a dress I never told you about."

"Why?" I followed her up the stairs.

"Because it's short. And satin. And Rosie told me not to show it to you because you'd never let me wear it."

I stopped halfway up the staircase. Rosie was Evelyn's twin sister, although they looked nothing alike and had opposite personalities. When angel-faced Rosie wasn't breaking hearts or gossiping, she worked at J.L. Hudson's department store. "You went shopping downtown by yourself?"

Molly looked at me over her shoulder. "For heaven's sake, Tiny. A girl's gotta live a little, you know? And I'm not a kid anymore."

I blinked in surprise, and then nodded. "I'm counting on that."

#

At nine on the dot, Ted opened the door to the back seat of his car, and I climbed in next to a young man I'd never seen before. I was about to introduce myself when Evelyn let out a wolf whistle from the front.

"Jezebel!" she cried. "Look at you in that dress, Tiny!"

Settling in, I tried to arrange the ivory satin skirt so that it covered more of my legs. "It's Molly's. I borrowed it."

"Molly's? Your father lets her wear that? It almost looks like a nightgown!" Evelyn couldn't keep the shock from her voice.

"I doubt he's seen her in it. He's not around much." Her comments in front of the men annoyed me a bit, but I could see why she was stunned. The dress did look a bit like lingerie, with thin straps over my shoulders and a low square neck. It probably didn't show as much of Molly's chest as it did mine since she was taller and bigger than I was, but Evelyn's eyes were glued to the lace-trimmed bodice of the dress.

"And where did you get that?" she squeaked, pointing at the choker I wore around my neck. She looked at my hair, which I'd curled and styled, the black and silver headband Molly had lent me—also purchased on the sly—and my red lips. "Gee whiz, Tiny, you look like another person! I'd hardly recognize you as the girl I once knew." She laughed, but I couldn't help thinking she was right.

"It's 1923, Evvy." I took a cigarette from my little mesh evening bag. "And I've discovered I like living dangerously."

The young man next to me quickly offered to light my smoke.

On the way downtown Evelyn introduced me to Ted's friend Walter Lewis, my companion in the back seat. He was friendly and attractive in an Ivy League sort of way, with his natty bow tie and severely parted hair. But I hoped there was no expectation that I would be his date for the evening.

I had other plans.

My stomach flipped uncontrollably as we went down the cement steps into the hidden vestibule that served as the entrance for Club 23. Enzo and I had once shared a kiss in the dark, tight space between the outer and inner doors of the underground speakeasy. My toes curled inside my satin t-straps as I recalled the way I'd been backed up against the brick wall, one hand pinned over my head, one knee hitched up to his hip.

We were granted permission to enter, and walked down the long cement-walled hallway toward the music, our heels click-clacking on the tiles. A Dixieland beat thumped louder and louder as we approached the velvet drapes that opened onto the dark, ritzy club. As usual, the dance floor down in front, as well as all the cocktail tables and large crescent-shaped booths lining the two-tiered room, were packed with revelers. The bar along the back was mobbed as well. The room was hazy with cigarette smoke, and the entire place smelled of perfume, tobacco, and whisky, but underneath it all, I detected the faintest whiff of sex and sweat.

The men checked their hats at the door, and as I looked at the attractive, smiling girl who took them, I wondered again about Enzo's offer to work at the club. Would I be happy here, night after night, working while I watched my friends come to have fun? Watching Enzo as he played host, buying drinks and kissing hands and making deals under the table? I looked around but didn't see him anywhere.

"Hey, there's Rosie. Come on." Evelyn grabbed my hand and the group moved across the room, skirting tables dressed with white tablecloths and low candles. Along the way, Ted stopped a waitress to let her know we'd like cocktails at the end booth on the far wall, and I scanned the club over my shoulder again for Enzo. I was still looking back when we reached the velvet-curtained booth, but I heard Rosie's mocking voice above the music.

"Well, would you look what the cat dragged in. Heya, kiddo, nice dress. You knock over your sister's closet or what?"

Annoyed, I turned toward her. Despite the fact that she was only a few months older than me, she was always calling me kiddo because of my size, and she didn't mean it affectionately. We got along all right, and she was always up for a good time, but I much preferred Evelyn's sweet to Rosie's tart. Nothing Rosie liked more than stirring up trouble, which was why her eyes glittered with pure mischief as she poked at me from where she sat, right on some poor sot's lap.

I was about to bite back when I bit my tongue instead.

Because the sot was Joey.

Chapter Six

"What are you doing here?" I blurted. I couldn't help it. He hadn't contacted me in days and I'd been so worried, assuming the worst, and here he was at Enzo's club with Rosie's round little ass on his lap. What the hell was going on?

"I was invited." He raised his dark eyebrows. "It's nice to see you too."

"Invited by whom? Rosie?" I looked at her, and she smiled at me like a cat looming over the fishbowl, then blew smoke in my direction.

"No, not that it's any of your business," he answered.

My ears were burning hot, and furious energy vibrated throughout my body. But before I could think of what to say, a waitress came over to take drink orders. I requested Canadian Club, straight, and wondered if I'd survive the five minutes it would take to arrive.

"Have a seat, gang," said Rosie, sweet as pie now that she saw my jealous reaction. "Joey and I were just about to dance. You can save our table."

Blustering on the inside, I watched them slide out from the booth and felt like tripping her as she glided by me with a smug look on her face. "Don't look so put out, kiddo," she said over her shoulder. "Your man's around here somewhere, and he looks mighty fine tonight."

I glanced at Joey to gauge his reaction to that, but he kept his eyes on the dance floor and his expression blank. If it bothered him to hear her call Enzo my man, he didn't show it.

Evelyn and Ted decided to dance too, which left Walter and I alone in the dark booth to wait for our cocktails. He tried to make conversation with me, but I couldn't tear my eyes off Rosie and Joey. The band had eased from a hot-tempoed jazz number into a lazy, suggestive blues, and Rosie was draped on Joey like a jungle monkey on a tree. My whisky arrived, and I took two huge swallows.

By the time they were done dancing, my whisky was gone, my head buzzed, and my tongue itched to let loose on Joey Lupo. Exactly why I was so angry I couldn't articulate, but somehow it seemed my right to be mad. Rosie led him back to the table by the hand, and they slid in across from Walter and me.

"Joey, can I speak to you in private for a

moment?" I attempted to look calm and sweet.

"Oh, don't be a spoilsport, Tiny," Rosie piped up. "We just sat down. Let the boy have his fun, why don't you?" She rubbed his arm and smiled at me with the devil in her eyes.

I wanted to kick her under the table, but I kept my eyes on him. "It's important. Please?"

"All right." When Rosie's face fell, he patted her hand. "I'll be right back."

She pouted. "You better. I won't wait around too long, you know."

Detaching himself from her grasp, he stood. "Need another drink?" He gestured toward my empty glass.

"Good idea." I slid out and made for the bar, and Joey followed. When I reached the crowd, lined three deep waiting for the bartenders' attention, I turned on him.

"What the hell, Joey? I hear nothing from you or Enzo all week and then you show up at his club? And with that....that"—I waved a hand in Rosie's direction —"tarantula on your arm?"

"She's more like a peacock, actually."

"Whatever. The point is, what are you doing here and why are you with her?"

Joey looked amused. "You know, your jealousy might actually be kind of endearing if it didn't make your face turn all red like that."

My mouth dropped open but I snapped it shut immediately. "I am not jealous of that two-bit man-eater."

"Oh. My mistake, I guess. Now what do you want to drink?"

"Whisky." I probably shouldn't have ordered a second glass so quickly, but rational thought had been supplanted by confusion and irritation and—yes, fist-clenching jealousy. I could admit it to myself, although I'd be damned before I'd let Joey see it. While he paid for the drinks, I took a few deep breaths, rubbed my lips together to make sure my lipstick was still on, and adjusted my posture to read cool instead of hot.

"Here you go, Little Tomato." Joey handed me a glass of amber liquid and clinked it with his own. "Salute."

I took a small sip. "So if it wasn't Rosie who invited you here tonight, who was it? And why didn't you call me?"

"What is this, the Inquisition? For your information, I was invited here by the cake eater himself, and he told me to come alone."

"What? Why?" I nearly choked on my whisky. In my mind there was only one reason why Enzo would invite Joey here alone. How could Joey be so dumb as to actually show up by himself? Wouldn't he see the trap?

"He said he had some information for me."

"About what?"

"He didn't say exactly, only that it was something I've been looking for." He drank again. "I assume he's ready to finish up the opium deal."

"And Rosie? How'd you end up with her?" I couldn't resist asking.

"I walked in here looking for Enzo, and Rosie accosted me."

I squinted at him. "Accosted you?"

He gave me a crooked smile. "I can't help it if I'm irresistible. It's the hair, you know?" He ran a hand along the side of his brown curls, which had been tamed into submission with hairdressing. "Or maybe the body in my sharp new suit." He puffed out his chest.

It's the mouth, I wanted to say, looking at his full lips, *and maybe the hands.* But I rolled my eyes and took a drink instead. "Well, it's certainly not your modesty, we know that. So Enzo invited you tonight. Well, he didn't say anything to me about it."

Joey shrugged before lifting his glass again. "What he says to you ain't my business."

In an instant his demeanor had shifted from playful to tense. "But—"

"Good evening," said a smooth, deep voice behind me.

I spun around and came face to face with Enzo, whose sleek appearance in a black suit and tie were enough to momentarily steal my breath. *Rosie was right. He does look mighty fine.* "Hi," I said. And then hiccupped, loudly.

Enzo's lips tipped up. "Welcome, darling. I'd buy you a drink but I see you've already gotten started." His eyes moved beyond me to Joey. "Mr. Lupo. You made it. You're alone?"

"As requested."

"Excellent. If you'll just give me a moment with Miss O'Mara here, I'll be with you shortly."

"I'm at a booth down front," Joey said, already backing away from us.

"I know where you are. Enjoy yourself."

It was all perfectly friendly, but something was off about the exchange between them. It wasn't just that they were being eerily nice to one another in a phony way, because even after Joey had gone, I still felt a sense of alarm. "So...you invited Joey here tonight?" Hiccup.

"I did. I have something to discuss with him, and I promised him it would be worth his while. In fact, I invited him a couple nights ago, but this was the first night he said he could get away."

"Oh." Briefly I wondered what had kept Joey so busy. His family? Was his mother OK? Hiccup.

"Shall I get you some water?"

"Yes, please."

Enzo snapped his fingers for the bartender's attention while I racked my brain trying to think up a way to get Enzo to let me come to the meeting he was planning with Joey. A moment later, he took my whisky and handed me the water, watching as I took a few sips. "Better?"

I nodded. "Thank you."

He leaned closer to speak low in my ear. "You look ravishing in that white dress, darling. I can barely keep my hands off you. Is it new?"

Heat bloomed in my cheeks. "I borrowed it."

"Ah. Well, soon you'll have a whole closet full of new dresses, each one just waiting for you to put it on so I can tear it off you. With my teeth."

Enzo giving me the ick lately

"What?" Hiccup.

Enzo laughed as I brought the water to my lips again. "You heard me." Lifting his wolf eyes from my breasts, he glanced over my shoulder and straightened up.

"So what happened with the whisky shipment?" I asked. "Did you get it?"

"You're drinking it tonight, aren't you?"

"Well, yes, but...how did you manage it if you haven't gotten the money for the opium yet?"

"Just leave the business to me." He leaned forward and kissed me lightly on the cheek but seemed suddenly distracted by something. "Now, why don't you join your friends, and I'll try to send for you later."

"But what about Joey?"

His eyes darkened a little. "Leave it, darling. I'll see you later tonight."

He tucked the whisky back into my hand and strode toward the entrance. With dread in my stomach, I turned to see whom he'd rushed off to greet. The dread turned to fury when I saw Gina Meloni making her way toward him, wearing a gorgeous gold and scarlet dress and a feather in her dark hair. She threw her arms around his neck and he kissed her cheek, taking her arm to lead her to their usual table. Spikes of wrath needled my arms and legs, and I finished both the water and the whisky, slamming the glasses on the bar.

If I'd thought I could handle the back and forth between her and me, I was wrong. *Either he wants me or not.* No closet full of clothes was worth feeling so angry and inferior every time he left my side and went to her. So her father owned a distillery and supplied his club, so what? He shouldn't have to marry the guy's daughter if he didn't want to. And he didn't...did he?

As I watched him seat his fiancée and light her cigarette, it struck me what was so unnerving about his behavior tonight. He was acting just like his father— the amused detachment while calling me darling, the cool kisses on the cheek, the shrewd agenda I knew lurked beneath the polite treatment of his enemies. The comparison turned my stomach.

I walked back to the booth, where Evelyn and Ted sat holding hands. On the dance floor, Walter was doing his best shimmy with a black-haired flapper dressed in red, and Rosie had her arms around Joey again. He held her close, spun her out, and they laughed together. When he pulled her in even tighter to his chest and whispered something in her ear, I felt it like a punch in the stomach. No one wanted to dance with me that way.

My hiccups were gone. I ordered another drink.

#

At some point, Joey and Rosie returned to the table, and I did my best to appear unaffected by their flirting as well as by the whisky I'd consumed. It wasn't easy. My head was cloudy, the room wasn't holding still like I wished it would, and my skin itched with irritation. There was plenty of room in the goddamn booth—why the hell did she need to sit on his lap? And why the hell did I care, anyway? I held my tongue, not easy for me, and tried not to stare at them. I even attempted to flirt with Walter, and though my heart wasn't in it, Joey sat up straighter when I put my hand on Walter's arm and laughed at a silly joke he told. It made me feel a little better.

Around midnight, one of the DiFiore goons came to our table and asked for Joey to follow him. Joey excused himself, and I practically elbowed Walter in the face to scramble out of the booth after him. "Joey, wait!"

He turned and grimaced at me. "Go back and sit down."

"No. I'm coming with you."

"You can't. And you're drunk. Now quit acting screwy and go back to the table. I'm sure Arthur misses you already."

"Walter."

"Exactly." He took me by the shoulders, turned me around, and gave me a little shove toward the table.

But I wouldn't go. "I'm coming with you," I insisted, trailing his heels.

Joey shrugged and spoke over his shoulder. "Fine, I'll let the cake eater deal with you."

I hurried behind him, taking two steps for every one of his, stumbling a little in my high heels. When the goon reached the curtained doorway that accessed a staircase to the building's upper floors, I tried to slip through after Joey.

"He didn't ask for you." The goon grabbed my elbow and held me back.

"I promise I won't be any trouble." I smiled sweetly at him, a younger guy with thick eyebrows and a five o'clock shadow. "I stayed here Friday night, and I think I left something in one of the rooms. I'll just retrieve it while I'm here."

"Oh, you work here, eh?" One of his bushy brows arced suggestively.

"What? No! I was sort of—a guest." And sort of a prisoner too, but I left that part out.

"That's a shame," said the goon. Joey bunched his fists at his sides.

"Listen, if Enzo sends me back down, I'll come without any trouble at all." I tried a flirty wink. "What harm could a little thing like me cause?"

Joey coughed, and I glared at him.

"No chance, doll. He didn't ask for you."

So much for my feminine charm. Helplessly I watched them disappear behind the curtain, then spun around and stomped back toward the booth. How dare Enzo shut me out! I was the one who told him Joey had the opium in the first place. Was he keeping me away for a reason? I was torn between being angry and being scared. If he was on the level about his promise not to hurt Joey, why wouldn't he tell me what he was doing? And how dare Joey fail to stick up for me and insist I be allowed to accompany him! I'd put this whole thing in motion.

Bastards, all of them.

I was almost to the table when I recalled another

way to access stairs to the upper floors—the tunnels.

Subterranean passageways led from the club to hidden stairwells as well as to buildings across the street. They were used for escaping during raids or for booze deliveries, but if I could find my way into them, they'd sure be useful to me tonight.

Biting my lip, I scanned the club. There was a door to the tunnels in a room behind the bar, but I'd have to convince the bartender to let me back there, which seemed unlikely. One leg twitched impatiently. It would've been much easier to think through this plan if I wasn't so goddamn tipsy—the room was spinning.

With a loud blaring solo by the trumpet player, the band swung into a hot jazz number, and the crowd rushed the dance floor. I went along, the murky edges of an idea taking shape in the back of my head. I pushed through the dancers as they jumped and flailed to the two-beat rhythm, feeling the thump of the bass drum in my chest. Awkwardly I tried to dance along with them a little, lifting a knee here and an elbow there, hoping it looked like the Charleston, a smile plastered on my face. Thankfully everyone was either too drunk or too exhilarated by the music to notice me. When I'd made my way to the front, I skirted the stage over to the side. An unguarded door led to the backstage area, and I hurried through it without stopping.

I saw no one. Moving quickly, I walked past doors labeled Dressing Room and kept my eyes peeled for one that might access the tunnels. There had to be an entrance to them on this side of the club—if the cops came in the main doors from the street, the room behind the bar wouldn't provide a safe getaway. The logical exit would be in the opposite direction. I congratulated myself on this brilliant deduction, and when I came to an unmarked door, I squealed inwardly and threw it open.

Unfortunately it led to a prop closet where two women and a man were engaged in an activity that was definitely not the Charleston, although it looked just as rhythmic and entertaining, with limbs extended every which way. "Oops, sorry!" I whispered, backing out and slamming the door.

Damn.

I hurried further along the backstage corridor until I came to another door. Crossing my fingers, I twisted the knob and pushed it open, and found myself inside a closet full of cleaning supplies. But at the back of the closet I saw something else—the outline of another door. Stepping around buckets and rags, I prayed the door would open without a key. Who has time to fumble with keys during a raid, right? I pushed the cleaning implements aside.

No lock. Just a baseball-sized hole in the wood, through which I stuck my fingers and yanked.

It opened.

I took a second to pull the outer door shut behind me and ducked into the tunnel, my heart pounding at the sudden darkness. Enzo and I had snuck up to Angel's office twice last week using the tunnels, but he'd had a lighter in his pocket that we'd used to illuminate the way. I fumbled in my purse, where I'd stuck a few cigarettes in a small case along with a matchbook. How many did I have left? My fingers shook as I felt for the number of matches—four. Saying a quick prayer they would last, I lit the first one and started walking.

With one hand brushing along the cement wall for balance, I moved as quickly as my legs would carry me down the dirt-floored tunnel. The music receded until I couldn't hear it anymore, and my breathing got louder. I stopped twice to light new matches and once when the passageway forked and I had to make a choice about which way to go. I stayed to the right, reasoning I was traveling clockwise around the perimeter of the club and wanted to stay close to it. When my third match was nearly burnt out, I came to another wooden door. Crossing myself with my free hand, I pushed it open. Just as the match burned dangerously close to my fingers, I saw stairs.

With a sigh of relief, I blew out the match in my hand and lit the last one.

Then I climbed two flights of stairs and pushed open the heavy door at the top.

Bingo.

Angel's office was just down the hall. Based on previous experience, I knew that office made Enzo feel powerful and confident, whether it was business or pleasure. Pushing the stairwell door closed behind me, I leaned back against it and blew out the match.

"Hey!" bellowed a deep voice. "How'd you get up here?"

I jumped. The goon in the dark suit who'd come for Joey was striding down the hallway toward me. He wasn't that tall, but he was wide and thick-knuckled, and I didn't like the way he was looking at me.

"I want to see Enzo." I planted my feet and stood tall.

When he reached me, his eyes traveled down my

body and up again. "What's it worth?"

"Go to hell." I scooted around him and bolted for the office, but he chased me, catching my upper arm with iron fingers.

"Let go of me, you ape." I tried to wrench my arm from his grip. "Enzo! Help!"

The goon squeezed tighter. "Shut the fuck up."

The door to the office swung open and Joey burst through it. The next thing I knew Joey had thrown a punch so hard it knocked the goon off balance. As he stumbled backward, he let go of my arm and Joey landed a few jabs to his gut before taking a hit in the face. "Joey!" I cried.

With the back of one hand he touched his nose, which was bleeding. He looked at it and then delivered a series of blows to the goon's face and stomach that had him reeling. I flinched at each sickening crack and thump. Finally, the goon went down hard.

"What the fuck, Lupo?" Enzo elbowed his way past Joey into the hallway.

"He had his hands on her." Joey's chest heaved with heavy breaths, and he gingerly touched his nose once more.

Enzo looked at me. "Is that true?"

"Yes!" I snapped.

"Well, she doesn't need you to defend her here."

Enzo took my face in his hands, brushing my hair back with his thumbs. "Are you all right?"

My stomach was roiling a little, but I nodded. "I'm fine."

He pressed a kiss to my forehead, which somehow seemed more for Joey's benefit than my own. "I'm sorry. Go into the office and sit down while I deal with this asshole."

Which asshole? I wondered. But I slipped through the office door and took a seat on the brown leather sofa.

Adrenaline had kept me alert, but once I sat still, I felt the effects of the whisky again. The pattern on the rug in front of my feet swirled like a whirlpool, making me even more sick to my stomach. Snapping my eyes closed, I put a hand over my belly and breathed deeply. The office smelled nice, like leather and tobacco. A moment later, I opened my eyes.

There. That's better.

Now to find out what the hell was going on between Enzo and Joey.

Chapter Seven

Enzo didn't return immediately, so I had a few minutes to myself. The office looked the same as I remembered—oak paneling, gold drapes at the windows, a sideboard along one wall topped with crystal decanters, and two red leather chairs in front of a large mahogany desk.

Oh, the things we'd done on that desk.

I pressed my knees together.

Stop it. This is no time to get distracted by sex. But my body had never listened to my brain where Enzo was concerned, especially once I'd been drinking, and I felt the pull low in my abdomen as I recalled the way he'd set me on the desk, knelt in front of me, and run his tongue along—

"So here we are again." Enzo's voice interrupted my thoughts.

I turned and saw him pouring a glass of something at the sideboard. He'd entered so stealthily I hadn't even heard him.

"Darling, your ability to create chaos among men will never cease to amaze me."

I wasn't sure whether to be flattered or insulted. Glancing at the door, I asked, "Where's Joey?"

"He asked for a moment to clean up."

"Oh."

"He'll be back soon, otherwise I can think of a few things I'd rather do with you in this office than talk." He moved to the desk and sat behind it, looking more like Angel than ever. "Especially at this desk."

"Then you should have told me what you were planning tonight."

"Tiny, this really has nothing to do with you. Why don't you—"

"Bullshit!" I exploded, fueled by whisky and frustration. I wouldn't be brushed off. "You made me a promise and I intend to hold you to it."

He looked amused. "I make a lot of promises. Which one are you referring to?"

I nearly hurtled over the desk to slap his handsome face. Instead I clenched my fists and counted to three. "Tell me why you asked Joey here tonight, alone."

"Leave it, Tiny." I stood as Joey entered the room, tucking a bloody handkerchief into his coat pocket. "It ain't your concern."

I looked from one to the other, seething. "So

that's how it is."

"That's how it is." Joey's face looked pale, and I didn't think it was because of the fight, which was nothing new for him. Something had happened before I'd gotten up here, but neither of them would tell me what it was. The idea that it was now the two of them against me drove me insane.

"Do you know what I went through to get up here?" I stamped my foot like a child. Enzo actually laughed, which only made me angrier.

"How did you get up here, anyway?" He sipped his drink.

"Never mind about that," I snapped.

"I need to go," Joey said. "I'll be in touch."

"Soon," said Enzo.

Joey nodded. "Soon."

"I'll call someone to escort you down." Enzo picked up the telephone on the desk and Joey and I stood in silence. It felt a little like we were two kids in the principal's office, waiting for our punishment. I thought of the time five years ago when Joey'd had the brilliant idea to steal and bootleg the sacramental wine from church. Michigan had just gone dry and he was positive it was a brilliant scheme, sure to make some quick dough. I'd had the brains to turn him down, thank God, but he'd gotten caught. That's when he'd entered the Bishop School, a sort of reform school for kids needing a last chance, and met the future members of the River Gang. He'd been tossed out of *there* for running crap games in the yard.

But he'd once beaten the tar out of this neighborhood bully named Timmy Toos for repeatedly eating out of my lunch box and stealing my milk money. And he'd threatened to cut off Mary McCarty's long hair in her sleep if she didn't stop calling me a dwarf. And when he found out I'd won a prize for mathematics in twelfth grade, he embarrassed me by announcing it at a family dinner at Bridget's that Sunday. At the time I thought he'd just done it to annoy me.

Now I saw it differently.

"Grazi," Enzo said before hanging up. "Someone will be here in a moment to take you both down."

"Me too?" I said, surprised.

"Yes. I have some more business to do tonight. And I can't leave the club just yet—my father is at his new establishment. With your father, actually," he finished, smiling. "I wonder who's having more luck at the tables." His dark eyes sparkled with mischief.

"The house always wins." Joey spoke quietly but

firmly.

"That's true," agreed Enzo. "Now, darling, why don't you go back to your friends and I'll find you later."

"I might not be here later. It's already midnight, and I have to get up early." It was a lie, Molly was ready to handle things at home in the morning, but I didn't want Enzo to think I would just wait around for him.

"Oh? What a shame. Well, I guess I'll be lonely tonight." His tone implied he'd be anything but lonely.

A moment later, a couple moon-faced guys in dark suits showed up and took us back to the club. The music was still jumping, the dance floor was still packed, and the crowd at the bar was even thicker. All of it annoyed me. I marched ahead of Joey on stiff legs and flopped into our booth, across from Rosie, who, despite her threat, was still waiting for Joey.

"There you are!" shouted Evelyn over the music. She rushed from the edge of the dance floor over to the table and fanned her face, which was pink and sweaty. But her blue eyes were lit from within, and the glow in her skin was becoming.

"Here I am."

Her brow wrinkled at my glum face. "Everything

131

I'm really hating Enzo in this book I swear if she ends up with him I'll scream.

OK?"

"I'm fine," I promised her. She deserved a good time tonight. Out of the corner of my eye, I saw Rosie tug on Joey's arm until he sat next to her. "Really," I went on. "Go enjoy yourself. I just have a bit of a headache, so I'm going to rest here a bit."

"All right." She glanced at the table and giggled. "Ted bought a couple bottles of champagne—it's the bee's knees! Maybe that'll cure your headache."

I plastered a smile on my lips. "It might. Go on, dance."

"All right." She tilted her head. "Sure you're OK?"

No. I looked across the table. Joey's face was stony; Rosie's, triumphant. She stroked his arm and whispered something in his ear. "I'm sure."

She patted my arm and hurried back to Ted, who scooped her up close. I didn't see Walter anywhere and figured he'd given up on me altogether. Smart guy.

"So where's that handsome man of yours? He dump you already?" Rosie's shrill voice grated my last nerve. My nostrils flared as I took in her bobbed blond curls, perfectly coiffed around her flawless face, set off by a headband that sat low on her forehead. Her porcelain skin appeared even whiter than usual behind splashes of scarlet on her lips and cheeks, like blood in the snow.

"He's busy." Turning my attention to Joey, I gasped. "You're still bleeding."

Rosie squealed and shrank away from him. "Ew, what happened?"

"Nothing." Joey pulled out his handkerchief and dabbed at his face. "Just a bloody nose." He met my eyes and the secret passed between us. My heart beat a little faster.

"Oh. I've never had one of those." Rosie sounded as if we were talking about a giant wart or a festering wound.

"It's nothing, but I should leave." He braced himself on the table to stand.

"Wait—don't go." I put my hand over his, which was already bruised from the fight.

"Yeah, don't go yet," Rosie put in. "I want to dance with you again."

But I wasn't about to let her take him away. Not when another slow, sexy blues had just started. "Dance with me?" The words slipped out before I realized what I was saying.

Surprise flashed in his brown eyes. "You want to dance with me? To this?" He didn't even bother to mask his shock.

"Yeah." I set my little mesh bag on the table and slid out from the booth. "I do." My heart was pounding now. Would he turn me down? Or worse, dance with Rosie instead?

"All right."

I had to look carefully to be sure he wasn't joking, but his expression was serious.

"Don't be too long, now" Rosie called, a false cheery note in her voice.

We walked onto the dance floor, my knees jittering uncontrollably. What was I thinking, asking him to dance with me to this song? We might have done a tame fox trot or an awkward waltz at Bridget's wedding, but that was in a room full of relatives, and we'd probably kept enough space between us to park a car. This was something altogether different. Where would he rest his hands? Was I supposed to put my arms around him like Rosie had? What if Enzo saw us?

Actually, that thought spurred my confidence a little. *Let him see us. Serves him right.*

In the back of my mind was the dim realization I'd had the same exact thought in reverse just a week ago—I'd wanted Joey to see me with Enzo and be jealous. Tonight...I didn't understand it completely, but

I didn't want Joey to leave, and it wasn't only because I wanted to know what Enzo had said.

We found a sliver of open space and Joey reached for me, slipping his right arm across my lower back, and taking my right hand in his left. I rested my other hand on the top of his shoulder. Despite the crowded floor, he left so much space between us that I was disappointed. *We might as well do the foxtrot*, I thought grumpily.

But when he started to move, he pulled me into his torso, tight. As tightly as he'd held Rosie, maybe even tighter.

My breath hitched and my heart hammered my ribs so hard I was certain he could feel it. He swayed me in time to the lazy, throbbing rhythm, leading me so surely that my feet never fell out of step with his. God, the way he moved his body, and mine along with it...it was slow and sexy and sinuous. Warmth pooled at my center. My breaths started to come faster, and my dress felt heavy on my skin. Had it been this warm in here all night? I could smell the perfume I'd dotted behind my ears and between my breasts and at the backs of my knees, and hoped he could too. My left hand inched along the rough fabric of his coat until my fingers curved around his neck.

His movement slowed.

Rising on tiptoe, I pressed my face into the space between his ear and his collar.

He stopped dancing.

I inhaled deeply, letting the scent of his skin invade me. Soap and starch and aftershave, and the barest trace of something else—something delicious but not sweet, something herbal that brought the memory of cooking with him into sharp relief. My mouth watered.

His turned his head and I felt his lips against my temple. "Move your feet, Tiny." His voice was strained. Oh—right. Was it me who'd stopped dancing? Recovering my senses, I let him lead me again, but I didn't let him pull away. Against my chest I could feel him breathing, and I adjusted my breaths to his so that every part of our bodies moved in tandem, even our lungs. My body hummed with pleasure, warm and decadent. And though I knew it was wrong and misleading and maybe even dangerous if Enzo was watching, I closed my eyes and pressed my lips to the side of his neck.

Immediately I felt him spring to life against my hip. Arousal fluttered between my legs and hollowed out my insides.

He pushed me away. "What are you doing?" His eyes swept the room, as if he was trying to make sure Enzo hadn't seen us. "Are you crazy?"

I found that extraordinarily funny and started to giggle. "Yes. I think I am."

Joey rolled his eyes and grabbed me by the wrist, yanking me back toward the table. "You're drunk," he said through clenched teeth over his shoulder, "and I can't handle this tonight. I don't know why I even bothered to try." We reached the booth and he shoved me in across from Rosie, who was fuming and trying to hide it.

"Well," she said, bringing her cigarette to her lips for a puff. "That looked cozy."

Joey looked around as he adjusted his pants. "Where's your ride home, Tiny?"

I shrugged. "Dancing?"

"I've had it with this joint." Rosie stubbed her cigarette out and looked up at Joey, batting her lashes. "You wanna go someplace quiet, sugar?"

"Yeah. I do."

"See you around, kid." Rosie offered me a smug look as Joey took her hand to help her from the booth.

It was my turn to fume. They walked off without looking back while I pursed my lips and tried not to stare at Joey's ass. Fine, go! Beside the fact that dancing with Joey had me so riled up I could hardly sit still, I hadn't asked him what he and Enzo had discussed, although he probably wouldn't have told me anyway. As usual, the men called all the shots.

The bottles of champagne were still on the table, so I poured the remains of one into a glass and drank it down. Fast. Then I poured from another and did it again. Nothing about this night had gone as planned. I was wound up, I was jealous, and I was alone.

I was also drunk.

Propping my chin in my hand, I scowled at the tilting, swirling room full of happy people dancing to happy music. I hated all of them but Evelyn. I hated Rosie for taking Joey away and I hated Joey for leaving. I hated Enzo for his games and his goddamn good looks, and I especially hated myself.

At that moment, a flash of gold caught my eye, and I forced myself to focus on it. Gina was headed toward the ladies room with a friend. Good idea. I need to reapply my lipstick too. And if I happened to engage her in a little conversation...

Picking up my purse from the table, I stumbled after her.

#

A lot of speakeasies had been men's clubs or saloons in the past, which, of course, were not equipped with bathrooms for women. I had no idea what the history of this building was, but the door labeled Ladies Room was near the hat-check, and when I entered, I almost ran headlong into the sloping ceiling. The room appeared to be tucked beneath a stairway or something. Ducking the sharply pitched angle, I headed through a little lounge area cloudy with smoke, nodded at the attendant, and entered the only unoccupied stall. On either side of me, girls chattered away.

"I still can't believe you're getting married next weekend," said the girl on my right.

"I can," squeaked someone on my left. Fucking Gina. Her voice was like chalk on a slate.

"He's been putting me off all year," she went on. "I would have liked a ring by now, though, or at least some kind of diamonds. Last week he hinted around that he had a gift for me, but I got nothin' to show for it."

The necklace. I brought a hand to my throat, nearly gagging.

I was wearing Gina's engagement present?

"You know he'll get you something. That's how these guys work. They're all down and worried one day and riding high, flush with cash the next."

"He better." The toilet on the left flushed noisily. "I told him I want a rock for each month he made me wait around."

Her friend laughed. "That'll be one a hell of a gift, then."

"No kiddin.'" Gina exited the stall and I heard the water come on at a sink. "I just wish he'd pay more attention to me when I'm here. He's always so busy."

The toilet flushed on the right, and her friend joined her at the sinks. "Well, I guess that's the price you pay for marrying somebody like Enzo DiFiore. I still can't believe he's gonna go through with it."

"For cryin' out loud, Valerie, can you stop saying that?" Gina screeched. "What's so goddamn hard about believing he's gonna marry me like he promised?"

"Don't have a kitten, Gina. All I meant was that he seemed so reluctant to actually say 'I do' before this week. Now all of a sudden it's a rush job."

"Rush job! I been waiting six months for this. I don't know any other girl who had to wait so long. Daddy was getting as anxious as I was."

"Well, I guess he came to his senses," soothed Valerie.

"Yeah. Either that or someone showed him what would happen to his senses if he didn't do the deed." Gina giggled. "I think Daddy might have had a little man to man chat with him."

Her friend gasped. "Really?"

"Yeah. Hey, gimme that lipstick."

I waited in agony as they touched up their lips.

"Why does your father want you to get married so badly? Ouch!"

For a second I was confused and then I realized Gina must have slapped her or something.

"It's not about what he wants, dimwit, it's about what I want! It pays to be Daddy's little girl, you know."

"I know."

"I'm just trading in for a younger, handsomer model." Gina giggled. "One with all the right equipment. And boy does he know how to use it!"

My stomach heaved as Valerie squealed. "You're telling me! He's about the best-looking man I've ever seen. You're so lucky."

"Honey, it ain't luck. I know how to use my equipment too."

"You're so naughty," chided Valerie. I heard the clink of coins and figured they were tipping the attendant.

"At least I'm not boring," said Gina. "You've gotta be naughty to keep a man like that. Otherwise, they'll start running around."

"Honey, they all run around eventually," Valerie said confidently.

"Well, if Enzo does, my Daddy will cut off his balls before he even sees the knife coming. Or I'll do it myself." They laughed again as they exited into the lounge. "Val, you got a ciggie?"

The music got louder when they opened the ladies room door, and then it was muted again. They were gone.

My heart was beating so fast and loud it sounded like a locomotive in my head. Was there such a thing as a heart attack brought on by anger? If so, I was about to suffer one. I shoved the heel of my hand into the side of the stall, hard.

"Miss? Are you all right?" the attendant asked.

I sighed. "Yes, I'm fine. I just...bumped into the

wall." *But I wish it was her stupid face. Or better yet, his.*

I came out of the stall, washed my hands, and tipped her with some loose change from my purse.

What I didn't do was look in the mirror. I dreaded the sight of my stupid, gullible face.

Ducking the slanted ceiling, I left the bathroom and started for the booth. I had to pass by Gina's table, and at first I hoped no one would notice me, but then I happened to look up and notice Enzo lighting her cigarette again.

"Fuck it." I swore softly and turned on my heel, heading straight for them.

Chapter Eight

"Good evening." I greeted the table with a friendly smile. Gina looked at me as if I were a bug to be shooed away but Enzo's face drained of color.

Good.

"Miss O'Mara," he said. "How nice to see you again. You remember my fiancée, Gina Meloni?"

I wasn't sure if the emphasis was because he thought I didn't recognize her, or if it was supposed to serve as a warning to behave myself. Either way, I didn't much care. "Of course. And what a lovely dress you're wearing. I just adore it."

Gina smiled, smoke seeping from her lips. "It's from New York. It was a gift from Enzo. He's always buying me something."

"Mr. Generosity." I met Enzo's eyes. "Got a cigarette to spare?"

"Certainly." He removed a gold case from his coat and opened it. While I chose one, he glanced at Gina, who was staring at the diamonds at my throat. "Allow me to light it for you and escort you back to your table, Miss O'Mara."

I lifted my shoulders. "If you insist."

"Say, that's some serious ice around your neck." Gina pointed at the choker. "Enzo, you see that?"

"I do." He brandished a lighter and flicked the switch, pinning me with a look that said stay quiet. "Lovely."

"That's the kind of gift I want next." Gina pouted as I leaned closer to Enzo and allowed the small flame to light the cigarette between my lips.

I took in a lungful of smoke and exhaled. "You should get her one, Enzo. When is the wedding anyway?"

"Next Saturday," answered Gina. "We just can't wait any longer, can we, darling?"

I feigned a swoon, putting a hand over my heart. "How romantic!"

"What about you? You got a fella?"

"Me? No."

If we were on the playground, the look she gave me might have been accompanied by a bratty little nyah-nyah. "So who bought you those goods?"

I looked at Enzo again, who was gripping the back of Gina's chair so hard, I thought he might break it in half. Oh, how I loved to see him squirm. "Just an admirer," I said airily.

Gina was intrigued. "Is he handsome?"

"Indeed he is."

"And rich?"

"Well..." I pretended to think this over. "He does have a nice new motorcar."

"So does Enzo," she said, smug-faced. "A Packard. Daddy bought it for us as an early wedding gift. Isn't that right, honey?" She glanced back at her fiancé.

I nearly vomited.

"Sure." He cleared his throat. "Tiny, are you ready to go?"

"Absolutely." I stubbed out my cigarette in the ashtray in front of Gina. "Enjoy your evening, Miss Meloni. And congratulations. I'm sure you'll be very happy together."

Enzo grabbed my arm and yanked me sideways before she even had a chance to reply. "What the hell was that?" he hissed in my ear. "Are you out of your mind? Her father will kill me!"

"Good," I snapped. "Saves me the trouble!" I shrugged out of his grasp and tried to run through the crowd, but it was too thick. He got me by one elbow and dragged me over to the booth, which was empty. "Stop acting like a child," he demanded, shoving me onto the bench. "Give me a chance to explain."

I looked up at him angrily. "Why should I?"

"Because... I have something for you."

I lifted my chin higher. "Not. Interested."

A knowing smile snuck onto his lips. "You will be when you see it. Meet me out front in ten minutes."

"You don't really expect me to go somewhere alone with you, do you?"

"I'll make it worth your while."

"You want to take me somewhere, you have to tell me what you said to Joey tonight."

Anger darkened his complexion. "I don't have to do anything."

"Then I'm leaving. Alone." I stood and tried to get past him, but he blocked my way, gripping me by the upper arms.

"No. You're going to stay here and wait for me."

Something in his tone made me clam up instead of making a sharp-tongued retort or kneeing him in the balls, which was another compulsion I occasionally had around him. I froze, my gaze sliding to one of his hands squeezing my skin.

He must have realized he'd gone too far, because he let go and glanced around to make sure no one was watching us. "I'm sorry," he said, softer now. "I know this sounds crazy, but I'll make it up to you."

"You hurt me." I rubbed my upper arms.

"I *said*, I'm sorry."

"Fine. You're sorry. I'd still be crazy to go anywhere alone with you."

"Tiny, please." He brought his fingertips to his forehead. "I'm sorry I grabbed you that way, but you just do something to me, something I can hardly control, and it drives me crazy when I see you and can't touch you. That's all."

"That doesn't excuse your behavior tonight. And there is no way I'm going to sit in this club any longer and watch you fawn all over the future fucking missus."

He groaned in frustration and closed his eyes. "What do you want from me?"

"I told you. I want to know why you asked Joey here."

He opened his eyes and stared hard at me. "Fine. Meet me outside in ten minutes."

#

When Enzo went to make his excuses to Gina, I tugged Evelyn off the dance floor just long enough to whisper my plans to her and tell her not to worry.

"Now if only you can ditch Walter somewhere, you could have the back seat of Ted's car all to yourself." I tried to keep my tone bright.

She shoved me playfully but gave me a conspiratorial wink. "The front seat's just as comfortable, you know."

Yes, indeed I do. I made my way to the exit. But I wasn't going to let him touch me that way tonight. Not a chance. *I just have to be strong, that's all. I have to let him know that he can't expect me to sit idly by while he chauffeurs Gina around in his shiny Packard during the day, and then expects to fool around with me in it after dark.* The nerve of him!

Last Saturday night it had seemed glamorous and exciting, but now the experience had lost its allure, and I wasn't even thinking about the way the evening had ended in the boathouse. How dare he come for me in the car her father bought for them? As a wedding gift!

By the time he pulled up, I was fuming again.

I got into the Packard, and the familiar interior gave my surging temper a boost. After slamming the door, I slapped his face. Hard.

"How could you? This car was a wedding present from her father? You fucked me in the front seat!"

Enzo held a hand to his cheek and grimaced. "You didn't have any complaints at the time."

"Because I didn't know, Enzo! And this necklace —take it back!" I unclasped it and threw it at him, then I crossed my arms and thumped back against the seat. "I don't even know what I'm doing in here right now. I must be crazy."

He set the necklace aside and reached for my hand. I snatched it back, but he took it again. "Listen to me. You're not crazy. You're here for the same reason I am—I can't stay away from you, no matter how much I want to."

Something occurred to me. "You knew. You knew that night that you were going to marry her next weekend, and you lied to me."

"I said I was trying to get out of it, and I am. But I had to agree to marry her, Tiny. The club was low on booze and I have a business to run. But listen—it's all gonna be OK, I know it. I won't have to marry her."

I looked at him incredulously. "And why not?"

"Because I'll be able to pay off Meloni with the

cash I'm getting from all the opium. That plus what the club brings in this week, now that I've got good booze to sell."

I shifted in my seat to face him. "And what makes you think you're getting all the opium again? I'm still confused about that part."

"I'll tell you. But first...your surprise." He dropped my hand and pulled away from the curb. I sat ramrod straight, wanting as little of my body as possible to touch any part of this car.

"Where are we going?" I asked as Enzo drove north on Woodward toward Grand Circus Park.

"You'll see."

In a few minutes Enzo pulled up at the ritzy Statler Hotel, and my temper flared again. If he thought we were going to enjoy a quick romp here, he was mistaken. "A hotel? That's what you wanted to show me?" I set my jaw. "Well, you can forget it. I'm not going to a hotel room with you."

"It's not a hotel room. Just trust me, OK?"

Trust him. Ha. "No."

Enzo sighed as attendants rushed to open the passenger door. I was tempted to refuse to get out of the car, but figured that would embarrass me more than Enzo, so I allowed the uniformed man to help me

151

out. He led me underneath an awning, where I waited with tapping toes and a scowl for Enzo to give instructions for parking the Packard. In a moment he took me by the elbow, and we entered the lobby.

My bottom lip dropped open. I couldn't help but be awed by the sheer size and splendor of the hotel. One of my secret dreams was to travel to big cities and stay in romantic, luxurious places like this. My childhood scrapbook was filled with advertisements and post cards from lavish hotels whose lobbies looked just like the one before me. Now that I was actually inside one, I felt like a child again, small and wide-eyed and dazzled by the opulence.

The room ran the entire width of the hotel and was two stories tall. The night air had been hot and humid but inside the lobby was cool and airy. Gooseflesh broke out on my arms, and I was instantly sorry I had not worn gloves, both for modesty and for warmth. As we crossed the marble floor, our heels clicking elegantly, I craned my neck and looked around. The wall facing the park had five huge arched windows and opposite these were balconies with wrought iron railings. The cavernous space was mostly empty of people at this late hour, but still I chewed my lip and dropped my eyes to my clothing. The dress I'd so loved for its daring earlier tonight seemed inappropriate here in the well-lit luxury of the Statler Hotel lobby. Enzo sensed my discomfort and put an arm around me.

"You're a vision," he whispered in my ear.

"I—I'm...just a little bit chilled," I stuttered. Warily I eyed the five huge chandeliers looming over my head.

He squeezed my arm, and I thought he might offer me his coat, but he didn't.

Maybe there's a rule about men's dress, I thought. In which case there may be one about women's dress as well, and I doubted my bare shoulders would pass muster. Along the east wall was a massive oak counter, from behind which two pairs of eyes watched us intently. I glanced at Enzo, but he didn't appear concerned, not even bothering to look their way. We walked by potted palms and elegant spindly-legged furniture toward the back of the room, where a short corridor led to a bank of four elevators book-ended by two marble-lined staircases.

As we waited for a car, I kept my legs pressed tightly together and tried to keep my knees from knocking. Precisely what had me so nervous was hard to say. Was I afraid that I wouldn't be able to fend him

Yep he's out of here Book 1 Enzo would of offered her coat. I don't like character changing just to fit with where me book is going.

off if he tried something? Was I scared that my willpower wouldn't be enough to resist his physical overtures? Or was there, beneath it all, an actual fear for my safety? After all, no one knew where I was, and I was allowing a man I knew to be obsessed with power and control to lead me to an undisclosed part of a huge hotel.

"Enzo," I began nervously. "I'm not sure this is a good idea. Maybe if—"

"Hush now, darling." The elevator car arrived and the doors opened before us. He nudged me in front of him, took me by the arms where he'd grabbed me before and whispered in my ear. "You and I have never been a good idea." He steered me into the car and told the operator to take us to the ninth floor.

As the elevator began to ascend, Enzo kept his hands on me. We stood behind the operator, who kept his eyes on the doors in front of him, and a few seconds into the ride, Enzo's right hand slid from my arm across my chest, slowly, possessively. His palm, fingers spread wide, came to rest on my left breast, and he snaked his left arm across my stomach, pulling me back against him.

"I want you." His lips formed the words right at my ear, barely a whisper. He was hard already, his solid erection pressing into the small of my back.

Oh, God.

This might be more difficult than I thought.

Gina. Wedding. Packard. Secrecy. Lies. I reminded myself of the myriad reasons I had to be angry with Enzo, and it worked. When the doors opened, he released me and I stepped out of the car. He followed me into the hall, and when the elevator doors closed, he reached for me again.

"No." I held up one palm toward him. "First, tell me what we're doing here."

"All right. Follow me."

I trailed him down a long carpeted corridor, passing doors on both sides. He finally stopped at a set of double doors straight ahead of us and pulled a key from his pocket. After unlocking the door on the left, he pushed it open and gestured for me to enter first. "After you."

I walked into a dark room, but a moment later Enzo flipped a switch and an overhead light came on. As he shut the door, I moved deeper into an elegantly furnished parlor with a large window opposite the door. I went to it and pushed the filmy white curtains aside, peering down onto Grand Circus Park. Spinning around, I took in the sofa and chair upholstered in gold and brown stripes, the end tables and their lamps dripping with rust-colored fringe, and the low coffee table, upon which sat an amber glass ashtray. The carpet felt thick under my feet.

"Well, what do you think?" Enzo asked.

"Is this your apartment?" A glance to my left revealed another doorway, through which I glimpsed the shadowy outline of a double bed.

"It was." He walked toward me and I backed into the windowsill. When he reached me, pressing his body flush against mine, he leaned back slightly at the waist and dangled the key between us. "Now it's your apartment."

"My apartment!"

"Mmhm." He braced his hands behind me and I leaned back. His face hovered above mine, and I looked at his lips. They weren't as full or sensuous as Joey's, but their fine edges and sharp peaks were beautiful, and he was an expert at using them on my body. My insides heated up quickly, and when he lowered his mouth to mine, I let him kiss me. But I didn't put my arms around him, and I kept my lips closed.

"Want to see the bedroom?" He toyed with the straps of my dress.

"No." I elbowed my way out of his reach and put some distance between us.

Sighing, he faced me with an exasperated look on his face.

"Don't give me that look, Enzo. I'm still angry with you. I only came here to hear what you have to say about Joey."

He pressed his lips together. "Why are you always so worried about him?"

"Because he's my friend, and I dragged him into this mess to begin with."

"Really. You instructed him to hijack those trucks and later advised him to steal the opium from the load?"

"No, but..."

"Lupo's a grown man, Tiny. He makes his own decisions, and now he's got another one to make."

An alarm pinged in my head. "About what?"
"Come into the bedroom and I'll tell you."

I scowled at him. "You're impossible."

Enzo smiled and disappeared into the bedroom, and I followed a moment later when he switched on a lamp. The room was even more impressive than the parlor, with two big windows on the left, a large closet with a full mirror on the door, and a private bathroom with a claw-footed tub. The bed, with its scarlet-hued spread and curvy high-backed frame, looked especially inviting. And it wasn't just because I could imagine myself and Enzo naked underneath that coverlet, although that was easy to do—I was exhausted.

"All right. I'm in here. Now tell me."

He took my purse from me and laid it on a chair in the corner. "Do you like the apartment?"

I loved it, but there was no way I would live here at his beck and call. Not when he had a wife living with him somewhere else.

I turned away from him. "I'm not doing anything else until you talk."

"You don't have to do anything," he murmured, coming up behind me. He brushed my hair off the back of my neck and rubbed his lips on my nape. His breath sent shivers down my spine, and I willed myself to be strong, even though it felt *so good*. He kissed his way down one side of my neck and slipped one strap from my shoulder. "I simply told him..." He kissed that shoulder. "That I had some information..." He slipped the other strap from my shoulder and pressed his lips there too. "I thought he'd be interested in." He brought his hands to my shoulders and trailed his fingers down the insides of my arms. "Interested enough to trade for the opium."

"What kind of information?" I whispered, my arms tingling.

He bracketed my hips with his hands and pulled me into him. "Well," he said, bending at the knee to grind against me before whispering in my ear, "I know who killed his father."

Chapter Nine

"What did you say?" Pulling the straps of my dress back on my shoulders, I stared at him in disbelief.

"I know who killed his father," he repeated, as if we were discussing the weather. "I know who pulled the trigger outside the station and I know who ordered the hit on Big Leo that killed him."

"But—but how?"

"Nobody keeps a secret for that long in this business. It's been a few years now—eventually you find someone disgruntled with a particular faction and willing to talk, for the right price, of course."

"Of course." My mind was spinning. I knew how badly Joey wanted to find out who'd killed his father—he'd just told me so when we were on the roof. Undoubtedly he'd give up the drugs to know who pulled the trigger. But would he stab Angelo in the back? "So...so did you tell him?"

"No. I simply told him I had the information. If he wants the details, he'll have to decide what they're worth." He moved toward me again, but I backed up.

"Just wait." I put my hands out. "I'm a little flustered right now."

"I like you flustered." He kept coming at me and I thought he might back me right into the closet but instead he swept me off my feet and carried me over to the bed.

"Enzo, please."

He set me down and slipped my shoes off. "Please what? I'll do anything you want me to." Running a hand up one leg, he paused at different places—my knee, my thigh, and finally my hip. "I'll kiss you here. And here. And especially here." He slipped his fingers inside the loose edge of my step-in and brushed them against my tingling skin.

Oh, God. He was so handsome and the room was so beautiful and the bed was so inviting and I knew it would feel so good, but—

"No." I pushed his hand away, brought my knees together, and propped myself up on my elbows. "I'm not doing this with you. You're about to marry some other girl, and—"

"Jesus!" he exploded, pounding a fist into the bed. "How many times do I have to tell you? I'm not going to fucking marry her!"

"You lie!" I shouted through gritted teeth.

"You're always telling me just what I want to hear and nothing that's actually true. Until you prove to me that you're not stashing me in this apartment just so your wife won't see us together, we're not doing this."

He eyed me angrily. "You knew about her last time we did it. And you knew we had to keep our time together a secret. What's changed?"

"I don't know!" I yelled. "But something has."

"Within one week?"

"Yes!"

Enzo breathed deeply through his nose. "What the fuck do you want, Tiny?"

I had no idea. What had actually changed? It was a fair question, in a way—I had known he had a fiancée the last two times we'd slept together. True, I hadn't known about the wedding date, but if I was honest with myself, I had to admit there wasn't much of a difference between sleeping with a man who had a fiancée, and sleeping with one who had a fiancée and a wedding date. Both were pretty despicable, separated perhaps by a scant few degrees on the scale.

"I don't know, Enzo. I guess...I guess I'll wait until next Saturday and see if you manage to dodge your own wedding. " Slapping a hand over my face, I groaned. "God, that sounds so ridiculous."

"That's a long time away, Tiny." He trailed his fingers along my shin. "I don't think I can wait that long. I don't think you can, either."

"It's one week, Enzo. You can't go seven days without having sex?"

"I just want you so badly." He rubbed my hip, staring at his hand against the ivory material. "Can't we come up with a different plan?"

"No." I got off the bed and located my heels on the floor. "We can't."

"Is this about him?" He watched as I slipped my feet into my shoes.

My cheeks flushed, and I bent over one leg as if I needed to concentrate on the buckle. "No."

"I don't believe you. You have to decide, Tiny. You can't be loyal to two people in this situation."

I straightened so quickly I got dizzy. "Ha! Look who's talking!"

"Gina means nothing to me. In fact, she annoys the hell out of me, and it's pretty clear I am not loyal to her. I never claimed to be."

I bent and buckled the other shoe. When I straightened, Enzo was reaching for the lamp, and a second later the room went black. "I need my purse," I said.

He picked it up from the chair brought it to me. "Are you sure you won't stay?" His voice was lilting and soft again. "I can come back later and stay with you. All night."

I felt a quick tug of arousal, but it disappeared at the thought of him coming straight from Gina's side to my bed. "No. Not until I know for sure that you're not going to marry her."

"How do I know for sure that you're not fooling around with Lupo?" he asked testily. The light coming from the parlor illuminated only one side of his face, leaving the other half dark.

"I'm not."

Silence. "I saw you dancing with him."

My stomach flipped. "So what? It was just dancing. There's nothing between us."

"What if I want you to prove it?"

"How would I do that?"

A smile appeared on his half-shadowed face. "By keeping a secret."

"What secret?"

"This one: The gunman outside the prison was a hitman named Legs Putnam. And the hit was ordered by Sam Scarfone."

I gasped. "Sam Scarfone! But Big Leo was his

uncle! Why would he do that?"

"Because Big Leo was the boss. And if you don't like the way things are being run, and you think you deserve more than you're getting or you been screwed one too many times, that's one way to fix it. Take him out."

"Oh my God." I brought a hand to my mouth.

"It was especially smart because Scarfone must have known everyone would blame Provenzano, since that was the big rivalry at the time. But it backfired, because none of the old guard under Big Leo wanted to take orders from pissant Sam and his hot-headed buddies."

That part wasn't new to me—Joey had told me about Sam and his friends leaving the Scarfone faction to start the River Gang. He'd known some of them from school and thought they were decent guys just doing what they could to make a buck.

I swallowed hard. "But...it was family."

Enzo shrugged. "Sometimes blood is cheaper than whisky."

\#

Out of the apartment. Down the hall. Into the elevator. Through the lobby. Under the awning. One thought held my mind hostage the entire time.

I know who killed Joey's father.

And I couldn't tell him.

Could I?

No. Stay out of this.

> So you'll tell Enzo about the opium but not Joey about his family..

As the attendant pulled up in the Packard, Enzo put his hand on my arm. "I need to see someone at the desk a moment. Just wait in the car, OK?"

Another attendant opened the passenger door for me and I got in, my earlier distaste at riding in the wedding gift eclipsed by my anxiety over the information I now had. I knew exactly why Enzo had told me—he wasn't sure he could trust me and this was the test. Enzo wanted to see if I would run to Joey with the knowledge of who killed his father, which would mean I was loyal to Joey over him. Not that I had any guarantee Enzo had given me the truth— when had he ever done that? Giving me false information was just as effective a test as giving me the real names.

I thought of Joey, agonizing over the decision to give in to Enzo's demands in exchange for the information he'd wanted for years. If he did, he'd betray Angelo, who might then be tempted to put Sam wise to the scheme. Sam, whose nickname was The Barber because of his skill with a razor, who'd ordered the murder of his own uncle in order to gain a bigger share of the black market spoils.

What would he do to Joey if he found out about the opium?

"God, Joey," I whispered as my eyes filled. "What a fucking mess. Why didn't you just stay in Chicago to begin with?"

My nose began to run a little, and I sniffed, wiping at it with my hand. I needed a handkerchief, but I'd forgotten to put one in my purse. Maybe Enzo had one in here somewhere. I checked the glove compartments in the doors. Nothing. Twisting in my seat, I glanced into the back and thought I saw a bit of white peeking out from under the seat. Enzo was always tossing his coats in the back, so maybe one had slipped out. I opened the door, waving off the attendant who came immediately to assist me. Pulling the rear door open, I leaned into the back and slipped my hand under the seat. My fingers closed around a piece of cloth, and I pulled it up. It wasn't a handkerchief.

It was a pair of women's silk underwear.

I dropped them as if they had scorched me and backed out of the car.

Heart racing, I slammed the rear door and jumped back into the front, tucking my hands between my knees. What the hell was going on? Some girl had been in the back seat of this Packard and left without her knickers? That meant at some point, she'd removed them—or they'd been removed, I thought, scowling—and there was only one reason a girl doffed her underwear in the back seat of an automobile.

Bastard. WHY SHE MAD IT COULD BE GINA'S

Seething, I crossed my arms over my chest. I had no idea what to say to him—part of me wanted to claw his eyes out and tell him he could go fuck himself in his nice apartment because he'd certainly never fuck me there. I recalled the one physical flaw on Enzo's body, a crescent-shaped scar at the top of one sharp cheekbone near his left eye.

Maybe I'd give him a matching one on the right.

Thank God I didn't sleep with him tonight.

The moment he got in the car and turned to me, I slapped him again. "You bastard!" I shouted. "Want to tell me what a pair of women's underwear is doing in the back seat?"

"What?" Enzo grabbed my wrists so I couldn't smack him again, but he struggled to look into the back seat. "What the hell are you talking about?"

"I'm talking about the lacey little panties on the floor back there."

"I don't see anything."

"You're not denying anything either."

"I have no idea what you're talking about."

"You've never gone parking with Gina in this car, like we did the other night?" My blood boiled as I imagined Enzo in here with me one night and her the next.

"No!"

"Then how do you explain it?"

"I don't know, Tiny! Maybe she had some clothing in here or something. Yes, that must be it. She's been moving some of her things to a new place."

"A new place at the Statler?" I snapped. "How *convenient* it would be to have your wife and mistress in the same hotel!"

"No." He dropped my arms and rubbed his face with his hands. "Jesus Christ, Tiny. I brought you here tonight because I thought it was what you wanted. You told me it was what you wanted. Your own place. Where you can come and go as you please. Where you can do what you want." He looked at me. "Am I wrong? Isn't that what you want?"

I struggled to reply. "Yes. But no. I mean—not like this."

"You don't want the apartment?" He held up a key. "Because that's what I was doing in there. Getting you your own key." When I didn't take it, he dropped it into my lap. "It's yours, Tiny. You want to get out of your father's house? Here's your opportunity."

I stared at the gold key, linked to an oval plate that said Hotel Statler, Detroit, Michigan. "I can't afford it."

"I'll pay the rent."

"I'm not your charity case, Enzo."

"I'll get you a job at the club. I just want you to ICk stay here, so I can see you when I want. When you want. It'll be fun, just like we said."

I sighed, exhausted and overwrought, physically and emotionally. Did I really want to continue fighting him? What did we owe each other, after all? Fidelity? Or just a good time? I played with the key in my lap. "I don't know, Enzo. I need to think about it. Can you take me home now, please? I'm tired."

We went back to the club, where Enzo put me in a different car and instructed one of his men to drive me home. As usual, I had no idea when or where I might see him again, but I was so worn out I didn't much care. I nodded off several times on the way home and fell asleep the moment my head hit the pillow.

#

The next morning I woke up around eight, the sounds and smells of breakfast drifting into my room. The scent of coffee made me whimper a little, and I licked my dry lips. Actually my entire mouth was dry, and my tongue felt swollen. Dammit, who told me to drink so much? Every one of my teeth felt as if it was covered in wool. I tried to sit up and promptly fell back when the sunlight stabbed my eyes. Was it always this bright in here in the morning?

I flung an arm over my face. I didn't want to wake up. I didn't want to move. I didn't want to think.

But over the clink of plates and cups downstairs, I heard Enzo's voice telling me who killed Joey's father again. *The gunman outside the prison was a hitman named Legs Putnam. And the hit was ordered by Sam Scarfone.*

I couldn't remember all the names of the men

brought to trial for the ambush at the police station, but there were several, and Putnam might have been one of them. A few had been held but released for lack of evidence, and the trial had been a joke. I vividly recalled the day the jury reached a verdict—not guilty, of course. No witness had been willing to testify, and every member of that jury was well aware of the danger involved in deciding against a gangster. They'd reached a verdict in less than an hour.

I swallowed hard. Had the same hitman shot Vince too? What would it do to Bridget, knowing the name of the man who put the bullets in her husband, robbing her children of their father, robbing her of the love of her life? She told me repeatedly she'd never remarry. *It only happens once*, she always claimed, *falling in love that way. I'm grateful I had it at all. Some people never do.*

While I liked the idea of that once-in-a-lifetime love, I wanted her to be wrong too, so she could love someone again. But what did I know? I'd certainly never been in love, and I'd never had anyone say he was in love with me. Given the two offers from men I'd had in the last week, it didn't seem as if love was on the near horizon, either. Joey had invited me to run off to Chicago with him without even so much as a kiss, and Enzo had offered me a luxury apartment, for free, with the idea that we could use it for uninterrupted nights of illicit pleasure. But despite telling me how much he wanted me all the time, he wasn't murmuring any words of real affection. Once, he'd even admitted to wanting to kiss me one minute and strangle me the next.

And what about my own feelings?

Last week I'd been willing to overlook the fact that Enzo had a fiancée—it had almost seemed like a fun little twist in the game. I'd sort of convinced myself that it really didn't matter, and a few fiery hot sexual escapades with a gangster seemed like the perfect way to kick off my new life.

But was it?

I slapped my hands over my face. What was wrong with me? I was getting everything I'd wanted, wasn't I? Enzo had made good on his promise and come through with the apartment, that beautiful apartment at the Statler with a view of the park, my own bathroom, my own space. Would I take my meals in the dining room there? Order breakfast in my room? At the thought of food, my belly rumbled, and I knew I'd feel better if I ate something.

Swinging my legs over the side of the bed, I

counted to three and righted myself. My vision clouded a bit, so I closed my eyes and counted again. When I opened them, the room was still. Getting slowly to my feet, I shuffled toward the dresser and looked at myself in the mirror.

I couldn't help groaning when I saw my reflection. Not only was my red hair tangled and matted, but I'd neglected to remove my eye makeup, which was smudged around my eyes like a raccoon mask, and I'd put my nightgown on backward. As I pulled it over my head, I remembered wearing it the night I'd been with Enzo in the Packard. I tossed it into my hamper. It needed to be cleaned.

#

I spent the day doing household chores with Molly, who was glad to help me out as long as I kept my promise to her about going to the movies without Mary Grace. Daddy had disappeared after breakfast, saying he was emptying the office at the garage of his things and moving them to his new space, and not to hold supper for him. My sisters said goodbye, but I ignored him. We still hadn't exchanged more than two words since he'd forbidden me to move out.

All afternoon Molly and I laundered the linens, scrubbed the bathroom, mopped the kitchen floor, washed the windows with newspaper and vinegar, and took the rugs outside to beat them. With each swish of the mop and pillowcase pinned on the line, I fretted about Joey. What would he do? What would I do in his place?

More important, what should I do in mine?

I had the power to allow Joey to keep a third of the drug money and discover who'd taken his father's life—assuming Enzo had told me the truth. The problem was, Joey didn't just want to know who killed his dad; he wanted to act on it. He wanted revenge. Did I want to be responsible for what he would do with the knowledge? He could go to jail for the rest of his life. Actually, Joey going to jail might be the least painful result—if Sam the Barber heard what he did, there would be consequences. Not to mention what friends of Legs Putnam would do, assuming he had friends. And what price would I pay for betraying Enzo's confidence? I didn't think he'd send me to the bottom of the river, but he'd be plenty mad.

On the other hand, I could just say nothing. Let

Joey make his own decision. Let him decide what the information was worth. I hated the idea of keeping something he wanted so badly from him, but it seemed like the safest option.

Between the agonizing and the hangover and the household drudgery, I was totally miserable.

If I accept Enzo's offer, I'll be free of these chores. In my mind I saw that apartment once more. *I bet the Statler has maid service.*

"Molly." We were hanging sheets on the line in the back yard, and she had to pull a clothespin from between her teeth to answer me.

"Yeah?"

"If I moved out, would you help Daddy with Mary Grace and the house?"

She stuck her neck out so far I almost laughed. "Move out? What are you talking about?" She shrank back, eyes wide. "Are you pregnant?"

I smiled, unable to help it. "No."

"Then why move out? Where are you going?"

I continued pinning a sheet and tried to explain without telling the whole truth. "I'd like to move downtown...into an apartment."

"With Evelyn or something?"

"No. By myself."

She burst out laughing. "How are you going to afford an apartment downtown by yourself?"

"Well, I'm going to get a job. And the place belongs to a—a friend, so the rent is reasonable." Briefly, I wondered what that suite actually cost.

"Oh." She went back to her sheet. "I guess it would be OK. Yeah. Actually, I know it would." Her tone was more positive with each word, and I imagined she was getting excited about the prospect of one less adult breathing down her neck. "I mean, I'm a better cook than you are, anyway, and Mary Grace is certainly old enough to take over some chores." She stopped and looked at me. "Does Daddy know about this?"

I sighed. "Kind of. I mean, I told him I wanted to move out, but he didn't take the news too well."

"You're an adult. You should be allowed to do as you please."

Grimacing, I reached for another damp pillowcase from the basket. "He doesn't see it that way."

"Well, I support you. If you want to move out, I think you should do it. I know I'd do it if I were you— in fact, I will do it. As soon as I'm out of school, there's no way I'll stay here. A girl's gotta get out and live a little, you know?"

I nodded. It would mean more work for her in the short term, but her support made more sense now that I realized she wanted to do the same thing when she was old enough. And if I did it first, Daddy couldn't stop her. At least, that's the way she saw it. "Well, we'll see. I haven't made my decision yet. Lord, my head is pounding."

"You don't look too good. Your face is a little green. Why don't you go lie down or something? I can finish this." She took the pillowcase from my hands and nudged me toward the house.

"Actually, I prefer the fresh air. Maybe I'll just stretch my legs a bit. Take a walk."

"OK. Just don't be gone too long—I'm leaving right after supper, remember?"

"I remember."

I headed down the driveway and turned right. The sun was hidden behind clouds, so the day had taken on a gray pallor that suited my mood. I sniffed the air and caught a whiff of something strange, almost metallic. Maybe I wouldn't walk that far—it smelled like a storm might be coming.

Chapter Ten

Without really thinking about it, I walked to Bridget's. I stuck my head into the store, waved hello to Martin at the counter and took the back stairs up to her apartment. The scent of roasting potatoes hit me just outside the door, and I breathed deeply. Her place always smelled so good.

I walked into the kitchen without knocking. "Hello?"

"Hello." Bridget stood over an ironing board at one end of the kitchen. It folded down right out of the wall, which was handy, but when the stove was on it made for some hot, sweaty ironing in the summertime. She wiped her forehead with a sleeve. "What are you up to?"

"Just taking a walk. Smells good in here." I wandered over to a chair and dropped into it.

"Thanks. Stay for supper?"

"I can't. I should make something for the girls and Daddy, although God knows when he'll return."

"He's busy with the new shop, huh?"

I pressed my lips together. No good would come

of blabbing to Bridget about the gambling if Daddy didn't want her to know. "Yeah."

"And what about you? Now that everything is... settled, are you thinking of returning to school this fall?"

"If I can afford it, perhaps." Clearing my throat, I went on. "I'm actually thinking of moving downtown. Getting a job that pays a little better so I can save up easier."

I figured she'd protest right away, but she just nodded, dropping her eyes to the blouse she was working on. "Oh?"

"Yes. I'm...I just... It's like I told you that day before all that other stuff happened. I'd like some independence."

"I can understand that."

I looked at her, surprise. "You can?"

"Sure I can. I was your age once too, you know. Not that long ago, in fact."

"I know, but you were always so in love with Vince. I never knew you wanted to live on your own." Bridget tilted her head this way and that. "Well, it wasn't so much that I wanted to live on my own. And I *was* in love with Vince. But we certainly had very few opportunities to be alone without Daddy lurking or you three monkeys hanging all over us, not to mention Vince's overprotective mother, who never thought an Irish girl was good enough for her Italian boy."

I smiled. "Really?"

"Really. *Oh*, she gave us such a hard time. So did Daddy." She set the iron on its stand and fanned her face. "Jesus, Mary, and Joseph, it's hot in here."

"Why did Daddy give you a hard time?"

"Well, Vince and I wanted to get married and he didn't want us to. Not because Vince was Italian—he was Catholic, at least—but because he didn't want to be without me at home. Same reasons he'd give you if you announced your intention to leave. I was doing the lion's share of the work and had been since Mother died."

"I never knew you asked permission to leave and marry Vince. I thought you got pregnant and had to marry him."

Bridget selected a handkerchief from her laundry basket and laid it flat on the board. "I did."

I scrutinized her closely. Was she blushing? After all this time, she was still ashamed of it? Or was there another reason?

It struck me hard.

"You did it on purpose."

The color in her cheeks deepened to purple.

"You did it on purpose!" I gasped. "Bridget, I don't believe it!" My mouth refused to close, and I slapped the table with my palm. "You asked Daddy if you could leave home to marry Vince and when he said no, you got pregnant on purpose so he'd have to let you go!"

"Shhhhhhhh." Bridget glanced out the window behind her. "Do you want the whole neighborhood to hear you?"

"I just can't believe it." Blinking in surprise, I stared at my older sister, seeing her in a new light. "Was it Vince's idea?"

"No, it was mine." She shook her head as she smoothed out the wrinkled in the white cloth. "And I'm not sorry. I'll never be sorry. The years we had together were worth it. The children are worth it."

I nodded, sadness squeezing my throat.

"And I knew you were able to handle things at home without me." She looked at me then. "And you have. You've been wonderful, Tiny. You kept that house running and those girls in line and made good marks in school too. You deserve a life of your own."

Sighing, she dropped her eyes to her ironing again. "I just don't know that Molly is as capable as you were at her age."

We'll see, I thought. My mind was still whirling, and I wanted to know one more thing. "Bridget...can I ask you a personal question?"

"Might as well. But if you're going to sit there, would you mind folding some laundry? There's a basket of the boys' things in the front room."

Nodding, I retrieved the basket and used the kitchen table to fold and sort the little items of clothing. "You once said that you got pregnant with Vince the first time you ever did it. Was that true?"

The color deepened in her cheeks. Slowly, she shook her head.

I set a little pair of overalls on one stack. "So you'd been sleeping with Vince before?"

She nodded. "We'd done it a fair amount of times, and we were always careful. We only had to do it a few times without any, you know, precautions, for me to get pregnant."

Dropping my eyes to the basket, I selected a white cotton undershirt.

"Tiny, what's this about? Do you have feelings for someone?" A note of concern crept into her voice.

"I don't know." Chewing my lip, I finished with the shirt and set it down, staring at the stains on its front. I was dying to confide in her. "I might."

"I know you said it wasn't, but...is it Joey?"

I looked at her sharply. "What makes you ask that?"

"I told you last week. It was the way he was talking about you. And the way you two constantly had your heads together. Seemed obvious to me." She grinned. "And you weren't that convincing when you claimed to be just friends."

"I wasn't?"

She shook her head. "No. And neither was he. You know, Vince always used to tease Joey about you. Said he was positive you'd end up together."

"And what did Joey say?"

Bridget's smile deepened, and her eyes glittered wickedly. "A lady should not repeat those words."

Rolling my eyes, I flopped back into the chair. "I don't know, Bridget. I'm confused. I feel something for Joey, but I don't know what it is. And he's completely frustrated with me right now. Then there's this other guy too, and he's handsome and wealthy and he's... taken quite a shine to me." That was one way of putting it.

"Oh? Quite the popular girl, you are."

I grimaced. "Anyway, this other man has made

me sort of—an offer."

Bridget froze and stared at me. "What kind of offer? A marriage proposal?"

Ha! "No. He's not exactly free to do that."

"He's married?"

"Not yet."

"My God, Tiny, that's the last thing you need. Whatever offer he's made you sounds a bit less than honorable."

I threw my arms up. "What's so fun about honor?"

Her eyes went wide and she returned to her ironing. "Well, if all you're looking for is fun, then be my guest. You just be sure you know how to protect yourself."

"I do. I'm not completely foolish." *Although I act like it sometimes.* "One more thing."

"Jesus, Tiny. You want to join the circus or something?"

"Ha, ha. No. I have a question for you." I stood and began folding another little shirt. "If you had some information that you knew a friend had been searching for, that in fact this friend had been obsessed with finding for years, but that might cause that friend to commit violence, would you tell him?"

Bridget parked her hands on her hips and stared at me. "What is this about?"

"Just answer me. Would you?"

"I don't know. I'm not much for violence, that's certain."

"Let's say the violence would harm only bad people."

A look of understanding flashed on Bridget's face. "But would there be potential consequences for my friend?"

I nodded glumly.

"Then no, I wouldn't."

"Thanks. That's what I thought."

#

I ate supper with the girls and did the dishes myself, since Molly had done the cooking. As expected, Daddy didn't show. At seven o'clock there was a knock on the door, and Molly flew down the stairs to answer it. She introduced me to a tall boy with wavy blond hair and a friendly smile whose name was Chet, and asked permission to ride in his car to the movies. He looked like a safe enough kid, so I gave it, and she rewarded me with a grateful hug before they left. I wanted to remind her about her curfew, but I bit my tongue, tired of acting like a mother.

Mary Grace and I played tiddlywinks and snacked on a box of Cracker Jack she'd bought earlier in the day, and later she asked to look at my scrapbook. We were upstairs lying on my bed with it when I heard the first roll of thunder in the distance. A moment later, a gust of wind blew in through my open window, ruffling the white curtains.

"We'd better shut the windows." Rolling off the bed and onto my feet, I pulled both my bedroom windows closed and instructed Mary Grace to shut those in the room she shared with Molly, Daddy's room and the bath. I went downstairs and shut them in the kitchen, where rain was already beginning to slant through the screen. Another clap of thunder echoed from the west, and I heard Mary Grace's fast footfalls on the stairs.

"Tiny? Are you down here?" Her voice shook a little.

"Yes, I'm here." Mary Grace got anxious during thunderstorms, and I tried to think of something that would comfort her until this one passed. "Do you want to play another game? Checkers, maybe? Or a card game?"

"Maybe." Rain began to rattle the windowpanes and a few gusts of heavy wind made the house creak. Her worried eyes peered out the front window. "Do you think the storm will be over soon?"

"Sure it will, these summer storms never last too long." I put my arm around her and walked toward the stairs. "Tell you what. How about we go upstairs and I read a little Ruth Fielding aloud to you and let you sleep in my bed. Does that sound good?"

She brightened. "Can we put rag curlers in our hair?"

"Absolutely."

Upstairs, we put on our nightgowns and I tied up Mary Grace's hair in rags. Then I sat on my bed while she stood behind me and did her best to tie mine up too. We giggled at our reflections in the mirror, brushed our teeth in the bathroom, and slipped beneath the covers in my bed. The steady, drumming rain on the roof was soothing in a way, but I'd read only a few pages when the lights began to flicker. Mary Grace tensed beside me. I patted her arm and kept reading, and the electricity winked a few more times before it went out altogether.

"Oh no!" She grabbed my arm.

"Don't worry so much, poppet, it's all right. This happens all the time when the wind is rough." I patted her arm again and got off the bed. "I'll go down and find a candle and we'll read by candle-light, like in the old days."

"No, don't go!" She scrambled to her feet and grabbed onto the back of my nightgown. "I'll come with you."

It was hard to move with her tugging on me, but I managed to feel my way down the stairs in the dark, moving along the wall in the front hallway into the kitchen, and from there into the dining room, without stumbling. In the built-in corner cabinet, I located two candles in small silver holders that had probably been a wedding present, and from a kitchen drawer I dug a box of matches. Striking one against the side of the box, I lit both candles and saw the worry in Mary Grace's expression.

"Honey, it's all right," I assured her. "Come on, you want to carry one? I'll carry the other and we'll go back upstairs and finish the chapter, OK?"

"OK." She was trying hard to be brave, but her hand shook so much that I felt better holding on to both candles and letting her hang on to my arm. As we ascended the stairs, guilt over leaving home pounded my heart as hard as the rain against the windowpanes. If I left, who would be left to comfort her on a night like this? Molly? I swallowed hard. Would she take the job of mothering a ten-year-old girl seriously? Could I ask her to? Granted, both Bridget and I had done it at her age, but Molly was a different sort of person, and I wasn't convinced she would handle the responsibility well. Maybe leaving home was a bad idea.

We made it up to my room, set the candles on my night table, and crawled back under the covers. The thunder and wind let up a little, and though the lights didn't come on, I was able to read by the glow of the candles, and we even laughed a little that this was probably how our mother had read at night as a child. When Mary Grace's eyelids began to droop, I lowered my voice to a hush. When I was certain she'd fallen asleep, I closed the book and checked the clock. It was just after ten. I was exhausted, but I blew out one candle, and took the other one downstairs to wait for Molly to get home. I set the candlestick on the coffee table and curled up on the sofa, chin on my knees, but I kept dozing, so I blew out the flame and waited in the dark. Soon the drizzle on the roof lulled me into a deeper sleep.

The sound of the front door opening and closing woke me with a start, and I picked up my head. The electricity must have been restored, because a lamp in the corner was on. Wiping a bit of drool from my lips, I held my breath until my eyes adjusted and I saw it was Molly, back from her date.

And trying to sneak up the stairs.

"What time is it?" I demanded in a whisper, jumping off the sofa. My muscles and joints felt stiff, as if I had been curled in one position for hours.

"Oh!" She whirled on me and put a hand to her heart. "You scared me! What are you doing down here?"

"Waiting for you. You were supposed to be home by eleven. What time is it?"

"Uh, about midnight?"

"About?"

"Maybe a little after?" She started laughing and clapped a hand over her mouth. "I'm sorry, I know I'm late and you're mad, but you look so funny with those rags going every which way on your head. Did Mary Grace do it?"

"Yes. Now, where were you? And don't tell me you were at the movie theater all this time."

"I—I wasn't."

"So? Where were you?"

"After the movie, we were going to go out for ice cream but the shop had closed early or something. The entire block was dark."

"Electricity went out."

"Right. So we just drove around a bit and then... parked."

"Parked?" Immediately the image of Enzo and I in the front seat of his Packard lodged in my mind.

She sighed. "Yes, OK? Parked. Please don't lecture me. I had such a wonderful night and I didn't do anything to be ashamed of, and for once, I didn't have Mary Grace around to bug me or tease me or tattle. Daddy's car isn't here, so he's not home and he doesn't have to know."

"Unless I tell him."

She gripped the banister with two hands. "Please don't, Tiny! I'm being honest with you, aren't I? I could lie and say we were at someone's house or at a party... but I'm not. I was alone with Chet, in his car, and I was safe."

I held back a sarcastic response, because it wouldn't do any good. I didn't want to argue with her about what was and wasn't safe when you went parking with a boy. And based on our conversation yesterday, she knew more than I thought she did about what boys want from a girl in the dark. *And what girls want too.* I took a deep breath.

"Listen, Molly. I'm glad you had a nice time, and I appreciate knowing the truth about where you were. I'm going to trust that you know right from wrong and that you're aware of what can happen if a girl gets a reputation. I know it's not fair, the boy should have the reputation too," I said when I saw her about to protest, "but that's just the way it is. The more important thing is, you had a curfew and you disobeyed it."

"Not on purpose! We just lost track of time," she whined. "Please don't punish me for it, Tiny. Just let me have this one night, please. I'll never do it again, I promise. I'll—"

At the sound of a light knock on the front door, we both gasped. She rushed off the steps and we clutched one another's arms. "Who could that be this late at night?" she whispered.

"I don't know. Maybe Daddy forgot his key?"

Whoever it was knocked lightly again, and then pushed the door open.

"Hello?" The voice was deep and familiar. A face appeared.

"Joey, you scared us half to death!" Molly

scolded.

"Sorry. I was out this way, and I saw the light on." He came in and shut the door behind him. His suit and hat were wet, but even so, the sight of him quickened my pulse. He took off his fedora and met my eyes. "I wanted to talk to you."

Frantically, I tried to position my arms so they covered as much of my bare skin as possible. My usual nightgown wasn't dry, so I'd put on an old eyelet-trimmed chemise, which had thin straps, a low neckline, and didn't even reach my knees. I crossed my arms and legs and covered one bare foot with the other, but not before I noticed Joey stealing a glance at my chest.

"What were you doing over here at this hour?" I asked.

"Dropping Rosie off."

"Oh." Jealousy flared in my gut. "Molly, you go on up," I said to my sister. "We can continue our discussion tomorrow."

"Or not." She scurried up the stairs. "We could just forget about it. That's fine, too."

"Sounds like I came at a bad time." Joey tried to make a joke, but I could tell something serious was on his mind. I was pretty sure I knew what it was.

"She was late for curfew."

"Ah. You trying out a new hairdo?" He gestured toward my head with his hat. "Looks like flapper meets Medusa."

Wincing, I brought a hand to my hair and felt the rags there. "Mary Grace did it. I'll take them out so you don't turn to stone when you look at me."

Unbuttoning his coat, he wiped his feet before entering the front room and taking a seat on the sofa while I began tugging the rags from my hair. At first I tried to keep one arm across my chest but gave up on modesty when I realized I needed two hands to untie the knots Mary Grace had fashioned. *Jesus, what did she do? A sailor couldn't have tied these things tighter.* And she'd gotten half my hair inside the knots too—it was hopelessly tangled. Joey watched me silently for a minute, during which the rain picked up again. "Weather keep you in tonight?"

I angled away from him a little. "I had enough fun last night to last me a while."

"I'll say. You drank too much."

I glared at him over one shoulder. "What do you care how much I drink?"

He put up his hands. "I didn't come here to argue."

195

"One of us always says that, and we still end up arguing."

That brought a little smile. "Yeah. I guess we do."

"So what did you come here to do in the middle the night?" I yanked at a particularly stubborn rag, but only succeeded in pulling the knot tighter. *If I had a mirror, this would be easier.*

"I told you, I came to talk to you." Joey scratched his head. "Do you need some help with those or something?"

"No. Go ahead. Talk."

"I can't talk to you with those things hanging off your head. It's bad enough that you're in your pajamas."

"What did you expect I'd be wearing when you show up at my house at this hour?" Exasperated, I dropped my arms, leaving a few rags dangling in my hair. "Fine, help me."

Joey shrugged out of his coat. "Come sit on the floor here in front of me."

Moving the coffee table out of the way, I dropped onto the floor and backed up against the sofa between Joey's legs. His pants were damp from the rain and felt cool against my bare arms. Gooseflesh prickled across my skin, and a dozen admonishments flickered through my head. *Go up and put a robe on. Joey shouldn't be here. Don't sit so close to him.*

And even though I knew he was going to touch me, I jumped when he put his hands in my hair, unprepared for the buzz that swept from my scalp down my arms and over my legs. It lingered as his fingers carefully worked the knots from the rags.

Neither of us spoke.

It probably only took him a few minutes to remove them, but with each passing second I was more aware of him, of everything around us. Colors and scents and sounds were sharper. The low golden glow of the lamp. The thrumming of the rain on the roof. The tick of the clock on the mantle. The scent of Joey's wet gabardine trousers and leather shoes. My breaths came faster and deeper as I imagined what his hands looked like in my hair, how difficult it must be for masculine fingers to work the thin strips of cloth from my tangled tresses. But his touch was gentle.

Too gentle.

"There. Done." He held the scraps of cotton over my right shoulder, his hand suspended near my collarbone. Beneath my chemise, my nipples peaked against the thin cotton.

Those hands. Those fucking hands.

Even though his knuckles bore the angry red evidence of the fight last night, his hands still had the power to arouse me. Would I never know the feel of them on my skin? Desire and jealousy twined their roots deep inside me. What had he done with Rosie tonight? What affection had he shown her? What physical pleasure had he experienced with her, with any girl, that he never would with me? My heart pumped hard.

I reached up with my right hand, telling myself to simply take the rags, but instead, I wrapped my fingers around his solid wrist. With my other hand, I took the scraps and let them fall. Twisting at the waist, I looked over my shoulder at him, my mouth falling open. Joey's olive skin appeared golden, his eyes almost black. His expression spoke of restraint and frustration, but also undeniable hunger. For so long something had simmered between us, threatening to erupt, and now I had to know, or I'd go crazy.

He pressed his lips together and his fingers tightened into a fist, the muscles tensing beneath my grasp. He tried to pull his hand away, but I held on.

Biting my lip, I used my other hand to unbutton the top of my chemise and slip one delicate eyelet strap off my shoulder.

He didn't move.

Oh God, Joey. Please don't say no.

With my heart thumping wildly, I looked down at his fist, unfurled his fingers, and slipped his hand beneath the cotton. Taking a deep breath, I pressed it to my skin and shivered with pleasure when his warm palm covered my breast.

I looked back at him again. For one agonizing eternity of a second, he struggled with his decision.

Well, maybe it was half a second.

Then he bent forward, grabbed my head with his other hand, and crushed his mouth to mine—oh my God that mouth, those full, luscious lips I'd stared at so many times—how was it possible for them to feel and taste even better than they looked? He kissed me hard, his tongue plunging between our open lips, stroking and sucking. Lust ricocheted throughout my body and centered between my legs. Reaching up to take his face in my hands, I kissed him so deeply and desperately I couldn't breathe, but I cared less about consuming oxygen than I did about consuming Joey.

He lunged off the couch at the same time I struggled to get up on it, and our bodies came together before we tumbled to the floor, frantic to climb inside each other's skin. We ended up on the rug between the sofa and the coffee table, a tangle of twining limbs and searching hands and hungry mouths. Joey's leg slid between my thighs and I squeezed it, lifting my hips. It felt so incredible I nearly exploded right then and there. *My God, it's Joey,* I kept thinking. *It's Joey and me and it's finally real and it feels so fucking good.*

Passion for him surged through me like a lightning storm. My heart pounded against his chest, or was that his pounding against mine? *I have to get closer, there has to be a way to get more of him.* The image of him shirtless in the kitchen popped into my head. I remembered eyeing the muscles in his back, how hot and hard his chest felt under my hands when I checked for bruises. I recalled the way his abdominal muscles rippled down his taut stomach. Oh, God, I wanted to touch him there, touch him everywhere, with my hands, my lips, my tongue. I wanted him naked, next to me, on me, under me, inside me. My head fell back, my jaw dropping in disbelief at the way I wanted Joey.

He moved down my body and took one nipple in his mouth, sucking it through the cotton, and I had to bite down on my own hand to keep from crying out at the pleasure it wrought from deep inside me. Desperate to feel more of his weight on me, I shimmied underneath him, claiming his mouth again with my own and wrapping my legs around him. And then I couldn't help smiling against his lips because I could feel the way he wanted me. Moving my hands around his sides to his round, muscular ass, I pulled him into me, gasping at the huge, hard feel of the bulge in his trousers. *Oh my God, I could come just like this, just feeling his cock rub against me through our clothing, because it's him and this is crazy and my heart is going to burst out of my chest and he feels so good and I never want him to stop and —*

"Christ, Tiny." Joey braced his hands above my shoulders and looked down at me, breathing hard. "What are we doing?"

"I don't know," I whispered, digging my heels into the backs of his thighs. "But don't stop." He groaned, and I lifted my head off the floor and kissed his lips, his chin, his jaw. "Please don't stop." I pressed my lips to his throat and felt his pulse on them. "I want you."

"Since when?"

"Since when?" I panted.

"Yeah, since when do you want me?"

I dropped my head to the floor. That was not the anticipated response. "What do you mean?"

Lifting himself off me, he knelt between my

knees. "Last time we talked about this, you said you wanted him, not me."

I propped myself up on my elbows. "I never said that."

"You certainly did. You accused me of judging you for getting what you want. I asked you if you wanted him, and you said yes."

Had I said that? Sighing, I closed my eyes. "I know, but..." God, this was so maddening—my feelings were so twisted up inside me. I had wanted Enzo, and everything he'd promised me. But now that he was offering, I wasn't sure I wanted it anymore. Why was that? Was I simply that fickle? Or had I changed my mind because of Joey? I wasn't sure, and I knew the worst thing I could do right now was say something I didn't mean.

I opened my eyes. "I don't know what I want anymore. I'm confused."

"Well, that makes two of us." He got to his feet and snatched his coat off the sofa, shoving his arms through the sleeves.

"And what about you?" I demanded, sitting up. "You're the one who was out on a date tonight, not me!" It was so irritating having to whisper when I wanted to shout. I scrambled to my feet. "Where did you take her?"

"Nowhere, I just gave her a ride home."

"Did you kiss her? Did you?"

"No." Joey ran his hands through his hair. "Why the fuck do you even care?" He tried to push past me and go for the front door, but I didn't let him. I caught him by the elbow, spun him around and threw myself at him, grabbing him by the back of his head and pressing my lips to his. He groaned in frustration but slanted his mouth over mine, and I sucked his tongue into my mouth. He tasted so good, like the rain, and oh my God I wanted to taste every inch of his body. His arms looped around my lower back, lifting me off my feet, and held me tightly to his chest. But when I tried to twine my legs around his hips again, he set me down and gently pushed me away.

"I can't do this," he said, picking up his hat from the sofa. "I just wanted to say goodbye."

I twisted my hands together. "Where are you going?"

"Chicago."

"Tonight?"

"No. There's something I have to do here first, but I'll have to leave fast after that."

"Something with a gun?"

Joey looked at me carefully. "He told you."

I nodded.

"Then you understand."

I saw the pain of his father's death in his face, and it squeezed my heart. "I do, but...this won't help, Joey. It won't stop here. You kill somebody, his friends retaliate. More death isn't going to solve anything."

"I gotta do it, Tiny. I feel it in my bones."

I tried a different tactic. "So you're giving up the drugs to Enzo? Letting him win?"

"It's already done."

My heart fell to my heels. "What about Angelo? When he finds out, he'll go to Sam, won't he?"

"I'm gonna talk to Angelo, try to make a deal by cutting him in on my first few whisky hauls in Chicago. As for Sam..." Joey fidgeted, and I knew he was struggling with what was safe to tell me. "Look, the less you know, the better," he finally said. "But stay away from Sam, and if he tries to contact you, you should tell Enzo right away."

My mouth fell open in disbelief. "You're telling me to go to Enzo?"

Joey grimaced. "I don't like him, and I don't know what kind of games he's playing with you, but I do believe he'd protect you if you were in harm's way."

I nodded, battling a fierce urge to cry. He moved for the door. "Joey, wait."

He turned to me and sighed. "This is useless, Tiny."

"I'm scared. And I don't want you to go."

With one hand on the door, he said, "Give me a reason to stay."

I felt like the wind had been knocked out of me. *Give him a reason. Something, anything. Don't let him walk out that door, because if he's killed trying to avenge his father's death, you'll never have this chance again.*

"You could be arrested. Or shot."

"I don't care."

"Killing the gunman won't bring your father back," I said, desperate to get through to him. "And your father wouldn't want you to die for him—he'd want you to live for him."

Joey set his hat on his head. "I wasn't asking for a reason from him," he said quietly. "I was asking for a reason from you."

With that he moved quickly for the door and disappeared into the rainy dark.

Joey is too good for her

#

Upstairs, I crawled into bed next to Mary Grace and cried myself to sleep.

Chapter Eleven

The next morning, I woke with puffy eyes, a sore throat, and Mary Grace's stuffed bear tucked underneath my arm. Her small hand was resting on my shoulder.

Love and gratitude washed over me. I tried to move without waking her, but her round blue eyes opened as I sat up.

"Hi," I said. "Thanks for letting me have your bear last night." I held him out to her.

"You're welcome." She took the bear and hugged it close. "You were sad about something. Was it the storm?"

I smiled and shook my head. "No."

"Was it because of Mother? Because I cry about that sometimes too, and I don't even remember her."

"No, it wasn't that either." I tugged on one of the rags in her hair. "You look like her, you know that?"

"Yes. But I like hearing it."

I lay down again, propping my head on my hand. "She had red hair and blue eyes, just like we do."

She squeezed her bear. "It makes me feel close to her, even if I didn't get the chance to love her."

If I'd had tears left, I might have shed them. "Oh, honey, you can still love her."

"Don't you have to know a person to love them?"

I continued stroking her hair, and it reminded me of Joey taking the rags from mine last night. "I guess you do, poppet, but loving your family isn't the same as loving someone else."

She was quiet for a minute. "How do you know if you love someone?"

"Well..." I tried to think of a good way to explain it, but I couldn't. "I'm not really sure. Maybe it's different for everybody."

"I always know if I love someone, because I miss them when they go away," she said. "It makes my heart hurt."

My hand stopped moving. "I think that's a good way to tell, Mary Grace. As good a way as any I've heard."

#

After Mass, my sisters and I went to the cemetery, and I couldn't help looking over at the spot where I'd seen Joey last Sunday. But he wasn't there. Disappointment made my feet heavy as we trudged through the wet grass to our mother's grave.

"Where's Daddy?" Mary Grace asked. "How come he didn't come with us?"

"He never comes with us," answered Molly.

"Yes, he does. Sometimes," Mary Grace defended. "And sometimes he comes alone, he told me."

"Does he?" Molly looked at me as we walked.

"I've seen him here once," I admitted. "But he's been busy this week with the new location and moving out of the garage." Why I felt the need to make excuses for the man, I didn't know.

"Daddy says we'll have more money now that he's got the new place," Mary Grace said. "Maybe even enough to hire a housekeeper or a cook."

"What? When did he say that?" I stopped walking and turned Mary Grace to face me.

She shrugged. "I don't know. A few days ago, maybe? He said maybe it will even be Mrs. Schmidt who used to work with mother where she was a maid, at that big house."

Molly and I exchanged a surprised look. "That would be nice," I murmured, starting to walk again. We let Mary Grace run ahead of us and moved to walk shoulder to shoulder.

"Does this mean he's letting you move out?" she wondered.

"I haven't the slightest idea. Daddy never tells me his plans."

We walked silently for a moment, our shoes squishing in the soggy ground. "Are you going to tell him about last night?"

I sighed, lifting my skirt so the hem wouldn't get wet in the tall grass. "I guess not. But if it happens again, I will. You understand?"

She grabbed my arm and tilted her head to my shoulder. "You're the best sister ever. Thank you. I hope Mary Grace is right and Daddy is letting you go."

Of course you do. Then no one will be around to catch you coming in late! It was not a very nice thing to think, but I wasn't in a nice mood. I hadn't slept well, I was worried about Joey, and I still hadn't decided what to do about Enzo. At Mass that morning I'd prayed for clarity, but I didn't feel any closer to it than I had last night. My feelings were a jumbled mess.

When we reached our mother's site, we pulled some weeds that had sprung up and stood silently together in prayer. Closing my eyes, I folded my hands together and lowered my chin.

Please, Mother, I begged. Help me to do things right. I know I don't always act the way I should. I know I've been reckless and self-indulgent and unwise. I know I've had unkind thoughts about my family. I want to be the kind of person you'd be proud of, but I don't know where to go from here.

Sniffing, I wiped a tear from my cheek with the back of my hand.

For years I've been telling myself that all I want is to get out and live life, because all I've known of it is our house and our family and our neighborhood. Since Bridget left, I've been mother, housekeeper, cook—yes, I know I've been remiss in that area—and I tried not to resent it, but I suppose I did sometimes. And I suppose I went a bit crazy because I've felt trapped, and misbehaving made me feel free and full of life.

I took a deep breath, inhaling the scent of wet earth. Exhaling, I made one last plea.

And Joey...dear God, Mother, please help him. We've made such a mess of things between us, and now he's planning to do something foolish and dangerous, and I didn't know what to say to talk him out of it. Please watch

over him—I promise to be a better person and stop
tormenting him if you'll protect him the way he protects me.
I promise to stop doing things that confuse him, like showing
my jealousy over girls he dates, or looking at him with
wicked thoughts, and I especially promise to stop kissing
him.

Even though I want to. I really want to.

As I crossed myself, a strangled sob escaped my
throat, and then another. Saying nothing, Molly and
Mary Grace each took a hand and led me away. I saw
tears on their cheeks too.

#

I managed to pull myself together for the
streetcar ride home, dabbing at my face with a
handkerchief and tilting my hat low over my eyes so
no one would see how swollen and red they were.
From the stop we walked to Bridget's for a visit, and
the second I saw her, I burst into tears. My loud
keening bounced off the walls in the kitchen as she
shooed her wide-eyed boys into the front room with
Molly and Mary Grace and dragged me back to her

bedroom.

"Stay here," she said. "Let me just get everyone a little lunch and I'll be right back."

Tossing my hat to the floor, I threw myself onto her bed and wailed into the spread. I wasn't even sure what I was crying about exactly. Joey? My mother? My father? The situation with Enzo? My dying dream of independence? Because I knew now I had to say no to Enzo's offer. How could I move into his apartment when I didn't trust him? Gorgeous looks aside, I hardly knew him, and most of what I did know scared me.

And what if I moved in there and felt ashamed of myself? What if he never managed to break things off with Gina and we could never be seen in public together? What would happen if what we felt for each other now died out as quickly as it sparked? Or what if I wanted to leave, and he didn't want me to? I cried harder, knowing that Enzo would not be a man who gave up his possessions without a fight.

Because I saw quite clearly that's what I would be—his possession.

The door flew open and Bridget opened her arms to me. She sat on the bed and I crawled into them, weeping on her shoulder, a little more quietly. After a few minutes, she squeezed me and stood up, going to her dresser. Pulling a clean white handkerchief from the top drawer, she returned to the bed and touched up my face.

"There, there," she soothed. "Nothing can be all that bad. What's happened, love?"

I took the handkerchief from her and swiped at my eyes and nose. "It's a lot of things. I'm scared and exhausted and overwhelmed, and I don't know what to do, and I feel as though I've made such a mess of my life and Mother would be horrified with me."

"Oh, come on now. She wouldn't, either. She'd be so proud of the way you've handled things at home, Tiny. I know she would. And I think she'd want you to have the chance to get out on your own if that's what you want for yourself."

"You don't think she'd tell me to stop being selfish and stay home where I'm needed, like Daddy did?" My words came out between halting breaths.

"No, absolutely not. If anything, she's up there feeling horribly guilty for leaving us girls to take care of things and be a mother before we were ready."

"She didn't leave us by choice."

"No, of course not. But trust me, motherhood has a way of making you feel guilty about many things you have no control over. You'll see, someday when you have your own children."

I sniffed. "If I have children."

"Why wouldn't you? Don't you want a family?"

"I guess so. I've always been so busy with this one, I've not really thought about my own."

"Never? Not even about getting married?"

"Why would I? I've never been in love the way you were with Vince. I don't even know what love feels like." Fresh tears welled in my eyes, and then spilled over.

"Oh, honey." Bridget circled my shoulders with her arm. "You'll know when you find it. It fills you up, so many good feelings, from your toes to the top of your head, until you think you might burst from it. You won't be able to keep it inside of you—you'll want to shout it and share it and give that person everything you have to give. And it still won't feel like enough, but you'll want to keep trying to show him how much he means to you. And the way he'll love you back..." She sighed. "You'll think it's impossible that he loves you the way you love him, but he'll do everything in his power to convince you otherwise. And love makes you do drastic things—look at what Vince and I did!"

I tried to smile. "Love sounds like a lot of work."

She laughed. "It does take work, I won't pretend it doesn't. Both people have to be willing to make themselves vulnerable, to open up. It's not easy to put your heart out there, to offer it up and ask for another's heart in return. Especially for men—they never know exactly what to say, and sometimes it comes out terribly wrong."

I thought of Joey asking me to come with him to Chicago without even telling me how he felt. Was that what she meant? Should I have recognized unspoken affection in his words? How the hell could I be expected to know? I closed my eyes, sighing. It was hopeless.

"What now?" she asked.

"Joey's leaving."

"And you don't want him to?"

I shook my head. "No, but I had no idea what to say to stop him. He asked me last night for a reason to stay, and I couldn't give him one."

"He asked you to give him a reason to stay? And you couldn't think of one?" She looked at my tearstained face incredulously.

I could. I could think of one, and I had—maybe I hadn't been willing to admit it yet, even to myself.

But things change.

"I couldn't then." I stood and walked to the mirror over Bridget's dresser, taking in my puffy, splotchy face. "But I think I can now." I turned to face her. "Can the girls stay with you tonight? There's something I have to do."

#

After leaving Bridget's, I went home and took a bath, lingering for a long time in warm water I'd scented with a little vanilla extract. I'd thought about something fancier, like rosewater or lavender, but decided Joey would find vanilla harder to resist.

I needed to be irresistible.

I washed my hair with Cocoanut Oil shampoo and combed it out, then I pinned curls to my head and let it dry. Choosing an outfit was a bit of a problem, since I didn't want to wear anything too fancy, but my day dresses weren't romantic at all. After agonizing over it for two hours, I chose a simple navy dress with white piping that had been at the back of my tiny closet all summer since it had a tear near the hem and I hadn't felt like mending it. Locating a needle and a spool of navy thread in my sewing kit, I sat on my bed in my black stockings and white chemise and stitched up the tear.

It wasn't as bad as I remembered.

See, broken things can be repaired. Torn cloth can be mended. Apologies offered.

Feelings declared.

As long as I had the guts to do it.

Around three o'clock, I walked to the streetcar stop and took a car heading downtown. As I hurried on foot to the restaurant, I tried to calm my swirling stomach by reminding myself it was just Joey I was going to see. There was no reason to be scared.

But there is, worried a voice inside me. He could turn me away, he could tell me I'm too late, or worse— he could tell me I was mistaken about what I felt, or what I imagined he felt.

But I hadn't imagined it last night, I knew I hadn't. When we'd finally come together on the sofa— well, on the floor near the sofa—it was just as Bridget had described. I'd felt so full of passion and relief and want and need and shock and happiness—so many feelings I couldn't even name them all.

But it added up to one thing, and I couldn't stop thinking it.

I was in love with him.

I was in love with him.

I was in love with him.

And I wanted to say it to his face.

My stomach tightened. Would he kiss me when I told him? Would he pull me to him like he had last night? Would he let me tear the clothing from his body? Will he throw me down and ravage me the way I want him to, and let me ravage him in return?

The thought was enough to make the muscles in my lower body seize up, and I stopped walking. Closing my eyes, I whispered a prayer.

Dear God, please avert your eyes tonight. Because I'm going to do things to Joey Lupo I have never done before, things I've never even imagined doing before.

Licking my lips, I walked two steps before stopping again and glancing up.

And you might want to cover your ears too. Amen.

#

By the time I opened the restaurant door, I was more than ready to confess my love to Joey and beg him not to follow through on his revenge plan. Pulse racing, I walked past the hostess at the entrance to the dining room and took the huge central staircase up two flights, two steps at a time. By the time I reached the third floor I was winded and my hip hurt, but I didn't care. The hallway smelled delicious, and I hoped I wouldn't be interrupting dinner. My hands shook as I knocked on the door.

No one answered.

I put my ear to the door and heard conversation. It actually sounded as if a lot of people were in there. Crap, now what was I going to do? What if his mother had company? The scene I imagined between Joey and I could not take place in front of an audience! Disappointed, I nearly turned around and left, but suddenly the door opened.

"Tiny!" Marie shouted. "I knew I heard a knock! Are you alone? Come on in, honey."

Taking me by the arm, she shepherded me into the living room, where, to my horror, the entire Lupo family was gathered. Adults were sitting on the furniture and young children scuttled around underfoot. A quick scan of the room told me Joey wasn't among them.

My heart fell.

"You all remember Tiny? She's Bridget's sister...."
Marie switched to Italian and I caught the words
sposata and Vincenzo, so I figured she was introducing
me as the sister of the woman who was married to
Vince.

Several people crossed themselves; others
nodded and smiled. Marie went on with introductions
but I knew I'd never recall anyone's name. I only cared
about one person, and I didn't see him here. Just as I
was about to ask if he was home, Mrs. Lupo rose from
her seat on the sofa and kissed my cheeks. "*Cara*, good
to see you. You stay for Sunday dinner."

"Oh, I don't want to intrude on your family
dinner, I just—"

"Nonsense, Tiny, you're family," insisted Marie.
"And if you've never had Joey's *arancine*, you're in for
a treat."

"Joey's what?"

"*Arancine*. They're rice balls," she said. "And
they're delicious."

"No one make them better than me but my
Giuseppe," Mrs. Lupo said proudly. "He don't even let
me come in there today."

"That's right, Ma. You just rest. Joey can handle
the cooking today."

A ball of rice didn't sound that appealing to me, but I would've eaten anything they asked me to in order to stay. *He's here!* I glanced at the kitchen door, which was closed. Would it be strange if I asked to go in there? "Can I help with the meal?"

"Absolutely not, you sit down with us." Marie led me to a dining chair, which had been brought out to the front room. Perhaps she'd heard about my cooking somehow? Helplessly, I sank into the seat and looked around. There were three or four older women, one old man and two younger men that I thought might be Joey's brothers-in-law, and probably five or six kids. I didn't see Joey's other two sisters, Joanna and Therese, and I guessed they were in the kitchen with him.

"I'll let Joey know you're here, Tiny. Can I bring you a cup of coffee?" Marie asked.

"Thanks. But no thank you on the coffee. I'm fine."

She smiled at me and went into the kitchen, and my stomach knotted itself worse than the rags in my hair last night. What would Joey do when he heard I was out here?

A moment later, he pushed open the swinging kitchen door and stood in the frame, staring at me through the arched threshold between the dining room and front room. My heart thumped three times in quick succession. My God, he was so beautiful—his face took my breath away. He had a dimple on his chin. Had I not noticed that before? And the lightness in his brown eyes. The lashes so dark and thick I could see them across the room. The mouth. Dear Lord, that mouth. My bottom lip fell open as we locked eyes, and my breath was stuck inside me.

He wore an apron over a blue shirt with his sleeves rolled up and dark trousers. He'd removed his collar and tie to work in the kitchen, and the top button of his shirt was undone. He held a dishtowel in his hands.

I felt paralyzed by the sight of him. How had I ever thought he wasn't the one? I wanted him so badly —I felt it in every nerve ending in my body. But now what should I do? I could hardly take off running, hurdle the sofa his mother sat on, and throw myself at him, which is what I wanted to do. And Joey's face was unreadable; I couldn't tell if he was angry at me for coming or glad to see me. I smiled and raised my hand in a pathetic little greeting, and he nodded grimly and backed into the kitchen again, the door swinging shut behind him.

Shit! That reaction was not in the fantasy of how this moment went.

Maybe he didn't want me here. My throat threatened to close up, and I took several deep breaths. Conversation went on around me, but I barely heard it. It was half in Italian, anyway. I'd have to learn some more words if Joey and I were going to be together.

The thought sent chills cascading down my spine.

Joey and I were going to be together.

The more I thought about it, the more certain I was that it was right. I knew him, and he knew me. He was part of my history, and I was part of his. We had a lot to learn about each other, still, but I knew at the core of his being was devotion to family, a sense of duty, and a huge heart. I had no doubt he had a vast capacity to love someone, and I wanted to be her.

I have to be her.

Staring at the kitchen door, I wondered how insane his family would think it if I just got up, walked through it, and announced to Joey I was in love with him. It wasn't ideal, but if I had to sit here one minute longer, I was going to go mad.

I stood up.

"Tiny? Can I get you something?" Marie asked.

"Uh, would you excuse me for a moment?"

She smiled and pointed toward the hallway off the dining room. "The bathroom is just down the hall there."

"Thanks."

With a longing look at the swinging door to the kitchen, I went through the dining room and down the hall to the bathroom. Once inside, I shut the door and stared in the mirror over the sink, arguing with myself.

Coward! Just go in there and tell him! He probably thinks you're here to berate him for his choices again.

I know, but I'm scared! And his family is here...

Figure it out. You're not leaving until he knows how you feel. If he rejects you, so be it, but you're going to tell him. Tonight. Now.

I racked my brain for another minute trying to think up a plan. Then it hit me—a note, I could bring him a note, or ask Marie to take one to him. It wasn't as good as face to face, but it was something. My heart tripped excitedly as I dug through my purse for paper and pencil. No luck.

Shit! What could I use? I dumped out the contents and studied them.

I had a lipstick and a handkerchief. It would have to do.

Kneeling on the floor, I spread out the white square and clicked the red color up the tube. Biting my lip, I printed carefully. There was no room for error—I only had the one handkerchief. The words would not have the same effect on toilet paper.

I love you.

Should I add an apology? Ask for forgiveness?

No, something told me to just go with one simple message. Joey was intuitive where I was concerned. He would know from those words what I was asking for.

Standing, I clicked the lipstick back down, capped it, and tucked it into my purse again. I folded the note, careful not to smudge my letters.

Deep breath. Now to deliver it.

Be brave, be brave, be brave, I told myself as I walked down the hall into the dining room. Instead of returning to my chair in the front room, I squared my shoulders and pushed open the swinging door to the kitchen.

Chapter Twelve

"Tiny!" Joey's oldest sister Joanna greeted me with surprise. She stood at the center table putting together a huge tray of meats, cheeses, vegetables and olives. "What are you doing in here?"

Joey, who was stirring something in a pot on the stove, spun around and stared at me.

I stared back, unable to speak. He was just so handsome—my stomach whooshed at the sight of him only five feet away from me. God, I'd rolled around with him on the floor last night and then let him leave?

"Are you staying for dinner?" Joanna asked. "Joey's making *arancine* one last time before he abandons his family again for Chicago."

She was teasing, but Joey glared at her over his shoulder before turning back to the stove. Either he was really angry or he just didn't know what to say to me.

"I heard," I said, growing bolder. "In fact, Joey promised me a cooking lesson before he left town, and I'm here to see that he makes good on it."

Joey's body stilled and Joanna laughed heartily.

"Wonderful," she said. "I keep telling him he should stay on here and run this place. He's got the knack for it, and it needs someone like him to give it some new life."

"I've got other plans." Joey's voice was firm, and he spoke without turning around. "And today's not the best day for a lesson."

"Joey, don't be rude," scolded Joanna.

"I won't get in your way." I walked over to him. With a glance over my shoulder to make sure his sister wasn't watching, I took one of Joey's hands and pressed the tiny white square into it. "And if it's not the right time for a lesson, that's OK."

Joey looked at me with a confused expression. "What's this?"

"Read it." I pleaded with my eyes before backing away.

"So, Tiny, how's your sister Bridget? I haven't seen her in a while," said Joanna.

"She's well," I answered with a shaky voice. From the corner of my eye, I saw Joey unfold the handkerchief and my heart threatened to bounce out of my chest right onto the olives. *Oh God, oh God, oh God. He's reading it.*

And then he looked at me, his lips parted. We

stared at each other for a few seconds, and hope rose in me like a hot air balloon.

But he turned away and faced the stove again, and all I could do was blink back tears in disbelief. *He doesn't want me. I'm too late.* My eyes dropped to the floor before closing.

"Bridget was such a good card player," Joanna went on. "I remember how she and Vince used to beat Tony and me at—"

"Tiny." Joey's voice had a new energy to it. I looked up to see him yanking the apron over his head. "I forgot, I need something from the restaurant pantry downstairs. Will you help me bring it up?"

"I can get it," Joanna offered. "What do you need?"

"No, we'll get it. You watch the sauce," Joey said quickly, rushing over and grabbing me by the wrist. "Come on."

He pulled me out the kitchen door and we flew down the back steps, our feet thumping on the wood as quickly as my heart was beating.

When we got to the bottom of the stairs, Joey pushed open the door to the restaurant kitchen and yanked me through it. I had to run to keep up with his strides and we rushed by several cooks and servers who stared after us in confusion, but Joey didn't stop. "Just grabbing something in the pantry," he called out, pushing open a thick wooden door at the back of the kitchen and pulling me into the pitch-black space. He slammed the door shut.

As soon we were alone, what he grabbed was me.

First he pulled me into him, his glorious mouth on mine, his tongue driving between our lips. Then he boosted me up with his hands beneath my bottom and pushed my back against the door. "Wrap your legs around me," he demanded, his breath hot against my mouth.

Heat rushed my lower body as I moved my dress out of the way and locked my ankles behind his hips. He put his hands on the door at either side of my head and pushed against me, and I could barely breathe it felt so good. If it was this incredible with our clothes on, I was going to lose my mind once we were naked and pressed skin to skin. How long would I have to wait? Could we get naked in the pantry?

I was honestly considering it.

"Did you mean it?" Joey asked between frantic kisses. "What you wrote?"

"Yes," I breathed, reluctant to take my lips from

his even for a moment. "Yes, I meant it. I mean it. I love you. And I'm sorry."

"Shhh." He trailed kisses down my neck. "We don't have time for apologies. God, I love your neck. You smell good enough to eat." He licked and sucked a spot below my ear that made my nipples tingle.

"That feels so good. You feel so good." *The pantry it is.* I reached down between us and rubbed my hand over the erection straining at his trousers. "I want you inside me. Now."

He made a strangled sound, the vibrations tickling my throat. "We can't, Tiny."

I ignored him, undoing buttons, slipping my hand inside his underwear and wrapping it around a cock so big and hard my mouth fell open in shock. "Jesus," I whispered. "Maybe you're right. I'm not sure you'll fit inside me."

Groaning, he kissed me again. "You are a little bit of a thing." He brought his lips back to mine. "But I've spent too many hours thinking about you for it not to happen."

"Hours, really?"

"Probably more like months, if not years."

"Mmmm, you should have told me sooner." I slid my hand up and down his impressive length.

[handwritten marginal note: I hate how often this is in books]

Maybe it was because Joey wasn't very tall, but I had never imagined he'd be so big. "Oh my God, Joey. How do you keep this hidden?"

"Around you, it's an effort," he managed, clearly struggling for control. He dropped his forehead onto my shoulder and gasped. "Fuck, that feels good. I shouldn't say fuck in front of you. Sorry."

"We don't have time for apologies, remember? And you can say fuck in front of me. Better yet, you can just fuck me, how's that?" I squeezed him tighter in my fist.

He picked up his head. "Oh, Christ. Listen, I'm gonna be sorry for a whole lot more than that you if you don't stop doing...what you're doing," he said, alarm in his voice. "I'm going to make a mess of our clothes, and then we'll have some explaining to do."

I laughed, withdrawing my hand and dropping my feet to the floor. "Ok, then we'll save that for later. But I don't want to leave yet..." I pushed the braces off his shoulders and shoved his trousers down at the sides.

"Jesus, Tiny, now what are you doing?"

"Shhh. Just let me." Dropping to my knees, I ran both hands all over his cock. It felt firm and thick and hot. I gripped him with one hand and rubbed the silk-smooth tip with the other. Immediately it was slick with a few drops of liquid warmth. *I want to taste him.*

The moment I put my lips on him, Joey braced himself against the door with two hands again. "Oh, fuck. Oh my God."

I rubbed my lips back and forth over the slippery tip before sliding it into my mouth and swirling my tongue along its velvety surface. I wasn't sure, but I thought Joey's knees might have buckled a little. Then I sucked on it as I rubbed my hands up and down his solid length. Joey inhaled sharply.

"You better stop, Tiny." His voice held a warning.

But I didn't want to stop. Taking him out of my mouth, I held him in two hands and licked him like an ice cream cone, all around. Then I slipped my wet lips over the top again and took him in as far as my throat would allow, but I was still able to wrap my hands around the base. My mind raced ahead to the way he could tear me apart, and my own legs trembled. Slowly I lifted and lowered my mouth again and again, while he breathed heavier and harder and said fuck more times than I'd ever heard anyone say it. Placing one hand on his hip, I braved pulling him into me a bit, not too fast, but at a quicker rhythm. I loved feeling him hit the back of my throat.

"Jesus Christ, Tiny. If you don't stop now—"

I pulled him from my lips with a little pop. "I won't stop, so you might as well enjoy yourself. It's my first time, you know. How am I doing?"

"Oh, fuck," he said again as I slid his hot, hard cock between my lips once more. Joey must have given up on bringing things to a halt because he began to thrust into my mouth, tiny little stabs that sent bolts of lust straight between my legs. My underwear was damp and I imagined how fucking amazing it was going to feel to have Joey's unbelievable cock pounding into me. The thought of it had me moaning, my mouth and throat vibrating with sound.

Joey stiffened and gasped, his erection throbbing as he swayed forward. Immediately my mouth was filled with pulsing hot liquid, but I'd been expecting it and didn't stop. I waited until his body had shuddered and stilled and only the sound of his labored breathing could be heard over my fast-beating heart, and then I slipped him out of my mouth and swallowed.

"God, that was incredible. I wish I could've seen you," Joey said when he could speak again, "although it probably would have been over even faster."

"Guess I'll have to do it again sometime."

"Oh, Christ." Joey dropped to his knees in front

of me and took my head in his hands. "I've thought about you so many nights, but even my fantasies didn't get this good."

"Really?"

"Really. That was...oh, forget it. There are no words to tell you how that was for me. I'm sorry, I wish I could find some."

"We need to stop apologizing to each other."

He kissed me hard on the mouth. "You're right. We do."

"But we might have to apologize to your mother for ruining Sunday dinner if we don't get back upstairs."

"Just wait. One more minute won't hurt." Joey pulled me in close, laying my cheek on his chest and wrapping an arm around my waist. As he spoke, brushed the hair back from my face with his other hand. "Thank you for coming here today. For writing me that note. For taking a chance on me."

I picked up my head but pressed me to his chest again. "Let me finish. The day I saw you after I got back in town, even before all the stuff with your dad, it hit me how I felt about you. Remember when you pushed me into the dirt at the boathouse? I think I fell in love with you that moment."

I laughed. I did remember that—he'd made me so angry that day, but when I'd pushed him and he'd pulled me down with him, something had stirred within me at the feel of our bodies pressed together. At the time it had just made me angrier.

"And I wanted to tell you, but I just couldn't. I thought you'd laugh in my face, maybe even spit in it."

"I probably would have. Just to spite you."

"But every time I was near you, I felt it like a punch in the gut how bad I wanted you."

"You hid it well," I said. "After that kiss in the boat, I thought there might be something happening between us, but you acted so aloof, as if you weren't even affected. It drove me crazy."

"I've got a good poker face," he said seriously. "That kiss fucking terrified me."

I smiled. "Good."

"You terrify me."

"I do?"

"Yes. Because in all my life, I have never wanted to be as close to someone as I want to be to you. I've never wanted to make someone happy the way I want to make you happy. I've never wanted to protect someone the way I want to protect you." He dropped his head to speak low in my ear. "And I've never wanted to do to another person the things I want to do to you. Oh my God, the things I'm going to do to you..."

My stomach fluttered at the gravelly intensity in his voice. "What's so terrifying about that?"

"It's terrifying because I think I'm a pretty tough person, but I had no idea how...unprotected you would make me feel. That probably doesn't even make sense."

"No, it does." Wrapping my arms around his torso, I thought about what Bridget said, how you make yourself vulnerable when you love someone, and I knew that's what he meant. "But you don't have to worry. I feel the same. I thought I was going to die of fright on the way over here."

"Why?"

"I had no idea what to expect, after last night. All I knew was that I had to see you and tell you how I felt. Then it would be up to you." I paused. "But I did have a few fun things in mind to persuade you if you gave me any trouble."

Joey laughed. "I was too easy, then."

"I got to do one of them anyway."

He groaned with pleasure at the memory. "That's true, you did. And next it's my turn." His tongue flicked at my earlobe before he took it in his mouth, sucking gently. "But I need more light," he said, kissing down my neck as I arched back slightly. He moved a hand to the other side of my throat and held me against his mouth as he whispered hot words against my skin. "I want to see your body while I worship every inch of it with my tongue. I want to look in your eyes when I get inside you. I want to watch you lose control, over and over again..." He circled the flat of his tongue on my neck before closing his mouth over it and sucking hard.

I think I whimpered.

With a low laugh, he released me. "So now, I'm going to button my pants and we'll go back upstairs, suffer through what is sure to be the longest fucking Sunday dinner in the history of men, and then I will spend the rest of the night—and hopefully a hell of a lot more nights in the future—doing and saying things to you I've only fantasized about."

My belly flipped. "Should I be scared?"

He helped me to my feet and leaned in close. "Terrified," he whispered.

Oh. My. God.

How the hell was I supposed to get through dinner?

Giggling like schoolchildren, we raced out of the pantry, avoided meeting anyone's eyes in the kitchen and scurried back up to the apartment. Joanna eyed us suspiciously when we entered.

"I thought you said you were just going to the pantry, Joey Lupo. What did you need there again?" She transferred a huge plate of what looked like meatballs coated with breadcrumbs from the table to a counter near the stove, tossing him a knowing look over her shoulder.

"Uh..." At the sink washing his hands, Joey looked over his shoulder and met my eyes. I had to clap a hand over my mouth to keep from laughing. "I forgot," he said.

"What? What on earth has gotten into you two?" Joanna looked back and forth between us, scrutinized my neck for a moment, and shook her head. "Forget it. I don't want to know." She took the apron she was wearing and threw it at Joey. "Finish these up, the oil is hot. I always overcook them. And Tiny, why don't you

239

help me set the table?"

"I'd be glad to." I couldn't stop smiling. Joanna must have thought we were crazy. "Just let me wash my hands."

In the bathroom, I noticed Joey had sucked my neck so hard a bruise had formed. I slapped a hand on it and laughed silently as I looked at my rosy cheeks in the mirror. After trying unsuccessfully to arrange my collar to cover the red and purple spot, I gave up and went back to the kitchen. When Joanna's back was turned, I flashed Joey my neck and he burst out laughing. I slapped his shoulder and Joanna turned to us, rolling her eyes. "Honestly. We have company for dinner. Pull yourselves together!"

But pulling myself together was out of the question. Just watching Joey prepare Sunday dinner for his family was enough to make my legs quiver and my insides clench. Whenever he turned around and I got a glimpse of his gorgeous face, flushed with heat from the stove or maybe from what we'd done—I nearly swooned.

Had I never noticed the way he moved? Joey didn't have Enzo's height or lithe grace, but his muscular body brimmed with caged aggression, more feral than feline. Even doing mundane things like bending for something low in a cupboard or reaching high on a shelf, or moving from the stove to the icebox to the table, his physicality spoke volumes about the way he'd move when unrestrained by clothing or convention.

I lost track of how many times I licked my lips and crossed my legs, tight.

Somehow we made it though dinner, although I was fairly certain we weren't fooling anybody. We sat next to each other, and neither of us did a very good job of paying attention to conversation. When we weren't sneaking glances at each other or sharing secret smiles, we were just staring at our plates, grinning like idiots, and several times I caught both of us eyeing the clock, willing its hands to move faster so this dinner would end and we could be alone. I don't think I ate more than three bites, although the food was delicious.

"Tiny, how old are you now, dear?" Joey's oldest sister Therese smiled at me from across the table, which had been extended to accommodate all the adults.

"Twenty. I'll be twenty-one next month."

"And are you working or going to school, or does your father keep you busy at home?"

"Well, I've been working for Bridget at the store and I attended nursing school at the University of Detroit for a bit over the last year or so. I'd like to go back, if I can save up tuition money."

"Oh." She took another bite from her plate and chewed thoughtfully. "So you'd like to work a while then, before you have a family?"

"I'm sorry?"

Therese exchanged a look with Joanna. "Do you plan on having a family?"

Joey and I locked eyes for a second. "Uh, I... haven't really thought about it. Not too much, I mean. My own sisters have kept me pretty busy."

"Oh, they should be plenty able to care for themselves by now, shouldn't they? You should start thinking about your own."

"Therese. Leave her alone," Joey scolded. "Tiny can make her own decisions." He scooped another helping of roasted zucchini onto his plate and turned to me. "Can I get you some more?"

I shook my head—I still had a full plate of food. Joey's sisters exchanged another look.

"So, Joey," Therese said. "Going back to Chicago now that Ma is settled at Marie's, I hear?"

Joey sipped his wine. "That's the plan."

I set down my fork and picked up my wine as well.

"I wish you wouldn't go," Joanna piped up. "I've been trying hard to convince him to stay and run this place, Tiny, but he won't listen to me. Maybe you'll have more luck."

"*Basta*, Joanna." Joey's voice held a warning.

She put her hands up. "Don't get mad, I'm only saying it because I think you'd be so good at it. And it's breaking Ma's heart to have to sell." She lowered her voice to a whisper and gestured toward the other end of the table, where Joey's mother sat with the older adults.

"Nice. Pin Ma's broken heart on me now, too." Joey forked a rice ball with vehemence.

"Well, anyone can see she doesn't want to give it up. It was her dream to run this place. And Papa's too."

He glared at her and she dropped the subject. But from that point on, something in Joey was less than it had been. He still smiled at me affectionately, and in his eyes was a promise of what was to come later, but I knew that he'd been bothered by the mention of his father. We hadn't even spoken about what he planned to do with the information Enzo had given him. And what about Chicago? Would he still go? Dread settled in the pit of my stomach. I'd just gotten him. Would I lose him already?

Over cannolis and coffee, I brooded a little. As thrilling as falling in love was, Bridget and Joey were right—it left you vulnerable, unprotected. Had I offered my heart to Joey only to have it broken when he left? Was he still bent on seeking revenge for his father, or would I be enough to convince him to leave the past alone?

Then there was the other kind of danger—the kind that might occur once Enzo realized I'd been less than truthful about Joey and me. And even though I hadn't exactly lied, I knew he wouldn't see it that way. Fear seized me, and my coffee cup clattered against the saucer in my hands.

Joey put his fingers on my wrist, and I looked into his concerned eyes, which made me hot through the center all over again. Lord, when would his family leave? I was desperate to get him alone. At the same time, we both glanced behind us at the clock on the mantel. When we realized it, we shared a genuine grin, and my hands steadied.

And when his relative finally gathered their hats, purses, and children to leave, my pulse began to race.

Chapter Thirteen

Goodbyes in Joey's family were endless. Endless! Just when I thought he'd hugged and kissed the last relative goodbye, there was another one standing with open arms. All of them hugged me and kissed my cheeks as well, and his mother made Joey promise to send me home with a big plate of food for my father and sisters. She and Marie's brood were the last ones out the door, and she looked around longingly at the front room before going.

Her eyes were shiny with tears, and I understood. It must have been hard for her to move out, leaving all the relics of her past here. She pointed a finger at Joey. "You take her right home. I don't want her father to think I don't raise a gentleman."

"Ma, for cripes sake." Joey turned her by the shoulder and steered her out the door into the hallway. He looked back at me. "I'll be right back. I'm just going to see them off."

Nodding, I watched Marie's two young children scurry out after them, which left only Marie and I in the front room.

"I'll be down in a minute," she called, securing her hat to her head. Then she turned to me, a smile on her lips. "He's crazy about you."

I dropped my eyes to my shoes. I'd worn my nicest ones, the black heels, even though they were a bit much for Sunday dinner. "Oh, I don't know."

She laughed. "Yes, you do. I could see it last time you were here, but today it's even more obvious. I think even Uncle Manny could see it, and he's half-blind!"

A smile took over my face. "Well, maybe we won't have to hide it anymore."

"Oh, I hope not. You'd be perfect together. Just don't let him go running off to Chicago, for heaven's sake. What's that boy thinking? He should stay here. Then Ma wouldn't have to sell this place."

"We...we haven't really had a chance to talk about that yet." And I really wasn't terribly interested in doing a lot of talking tonight.

Swoosh went my insides.

I crossed my legs at the ankle and stood with my thighs pressed tightly together, as if Marie could read my mind. On a small table to my right, the statue of the Virgin Mary eyed me suspiciously.

"He's just always been so stubborn, you know.

He gets an idea in his head and thinks he has to follow through with it, even if it's the dumbest idea ever. And we all know he's had plenty of those!" She shook her head. "*Madonna*, the things he put Ma through... Some days I know she's just glad he's still here." She crossed herself and put her hand on my arm. "If he loves you, and I believe he does, then he'll stop all that gang nonsense and settle down."

"I don't know that I'm—"

She waved a hand in the air to stop me. "Forget I said anything. Honestly, my mouth runs away from me sometimes. And I'm terribly emotional these days." Dropping her hand to her pregnant belly, she laughed. "I fall apart at the drop of a hat. Just you wait and see —oh, for Pete's sake, I'll stop pestering you now—"

"Impossible." Joey appeared at the door. "You'll never stop pestering. But unless you want to walk home, you better go down and get in the car."

"I'm going, I'm going. Good night!" She waved and disappeared down the stairs.

Joey shut the door after her and leaned back against it. "They know."

I smiled. "They know."

He reached into his trousers and pulled out the handkerchief with my lipstick confession on it. "I left this on the counter by mistake. Joanna found it."

My eyes went wide, and I clapped my hands to my face. "What!"

Grinning ruefully, he said, "I was just so excited to get you alone, I thought I put it in my pocket, but I guess I didn't. She gave it to me just now."

"After showing the rest of your sisters, no doubt." My cheeks were searing hot under my palms.

"No doubt."

"Does it bother you?"

"Not at all. I want to tell the entire world I'm in love with you"—and here my breath stopped—"but not tonight."

My insides went from simmer to full boil. *We're alone.*

Inside a heartbeat we lunged for each other, locking together from mouth to hip. Joey lifted me right off my feet, and I twined my legs around him. Walking backward, he tried to move us around the sofa and into the dining room, but since neither of us was willing to break off the kiss and look where we were going, we kept bumping into things. First we pushed the sofa and coffee table out of place. My leg knocked a lamp off an end table and his elbow nudged a painting of Jesus off the wall. We thumped the china

248

cabinet and the contents rattled precariously.

We didn't care.

Finally, we got through the dining room into the hall and Joey was able to walk forward and get us to his bedroom. He kicked the door shut with his heel as I cupped his jaw in my hands and kissed his top lip, then his bottom lip, running my tongue along them, sucking them into my mouth, rubbing my lips back and forth against them. "God, I love your mouth," I murmured. "I can't stop thinking about it. And your hands—I've never told you how much I love your hands."

Heading straight for the bed, he crawled up on it with my arms and legs still wrapped around him. When he finally lowered his weight onto me, kissing me long and deep, I thought I would scream if I couldn't have him naked, fast.

I tugged at his sleeves and he knelt, one knee on either side of my hips, to free his arms from his braces and wrest his shirt from his body. Then he grabbed his white athletic tank from the back and yanked it over his head as I watched, mesmerized by the rough masculine movements, the twitching muscles in his arms and chest, the way the lines on his abdomen undulated as he breathed. My fingers flew to them and

I sat up, running my palms over his hot, tight skin. Grabbing his hips, I brought my mouth to his stomach and brushed my lips across it. Planting soft kisses on hard muscles, I placed a hand between his legs, thrilling at the feel of the bulge there. He sucked in his breath, and I looked up at his dark eyes and tousled hair, my heart pounding.

"Should we draw the curtains?" I asked.

"No. I want to see you." He moved backward on his knees and stepped off the end of the bed. "Come here."

I crawled to the edge.

He reached for me. "Stand up."

I did as I was told, feeling the damp heat between my legs as I stood.

Taking me by the shoulders, he turned me around, and I felt his hands at the back of my neck and then working their way down the row of buttons to the sash at my hips. When the dress was loose, I slipped my arms from the sleeves and let it drop to the floor. I turned to face him wearing just my chemise, step-in, and black stockings rolled thigh-high.

The sight of him shirtless and hungry-eyed was too much for me to bear. I reached for his trousers. "Wait," he said, grabbing my wrists. "I want to look at you."

"I want you to do more than look."

"I promise you, baby, I will. Raise your arms." Reaching for the bottom of my chemise, he lifted the simple white garment over my head and set it aside. Then he crouched in front of me and pulled down my step-in. I held his shoulders and lifted one foot from them, then the other. But when I went to remove my stockings, he took my hands again. "Leave them on."

I stood before him, naked except for my stockings and shoes. I'd worn less in front of another man, but somehow this felt like the most naked moment of my life. Every inch of my skin was sizzling as he swept his ravenous eyes over my body. The tension inside me pulled tighter. My nipples grew harder under his stare, and when he licked his lips, I felt a flutter between my legs as if he had licked me there.

"You're so beautiful," he whispered, bringing his hands to my hips and guiding them to the bed. Then he dropped to his knees and slid his hands down my thighs, pushing them apart.

My mouth fell open.

Moving his hands to the small of my back, he pulled me toward him, closing his mouth over one breast. I inhaled deeply when he dragged his tongue around my nipple in lazy circles and flicked it with tiny strokes. When his teeth closed on it, I grabbed his head, filling both hands with his thick, wavy hair. Heat rushed my center, which was cradled against his stomach. "Now, Joey. Please."

He switched his mouth to the other breast and ran a hand up my ribcage to the first, torturing me with his thumb and fingers in a way that made me pant.

"You're making me crazy," I whined, looking down at his lips closing over my nipple. Leaving the drapes open made everything he did even more arousing because I could see it.

"I'm just getting started." His breath tickled my wet skin. I shivered at the cool tingle on my breast and the nearly unbearable hum between my legs. He moved a hand to the top of my thigh, his thumb brushing my sensitive outer folds, and then softly circling over my clitoris.

"Yes," I whispered. "Yes, yes."

"Now lie back." He brought his hands to my shoulders and gently laid me back. Standing for a moment, he leaned over me and kissed my neck, a moan rumbling from his throat. "Mmmmm, I can't get enough of the way you smell." He kissed his way down my chest, stopping to take each breast in his mouth again before continuing down my stomach. "Or the way you taste." Planting a kiss on each of my hips, he licked a circle around my belly button before trailing his hot, wet tongue in a line straight south. "I want to taste you everywhere."

He took a moment to slip my heels off my feet. Then he dropped to his knees between my legs again, hooked his arms beneath my thighs and pulled me to him.

When he put my knees over his shoulders, I flung my arms over my head.

At first, I felt only cool air at my center, and then warm air as he exhaled. My body was coiled so tight as I waited for his mouth on me I thought I might explode the moment I actually felt it.

I nearly did.

Slowly he licked his way up my center, and my legs trembled. When he reached the top, he lingered there and swirled circles with the flat of his tongue before flicking lightly with the tip. Then he did it again, and I felt the telltale tightening of my muscles in my lower body. I'd never fought an orgasm before, but now I knew the exquisite torture Joey had experienced in the pantry. Soft, tender strokes every which way, barely-there flicks that left me panting, loops and lines and curves...Jesus, he could write poetry with his tongue.

"Joey," I whispered. "Please..." But then I couldn't even form a coherent sentence, because he chose that moment to take the tiny bud, tingling with heat, into his mouth and suck, and at the same time he slipped his fingers inside me. My heels dug into his back. My toes pointed like a ballerina's. My hands flew to the bedcovers next to my hips, clawing them in tight fists. He pushed his fingers deep inside me and somehow twisted them to press upward on some magnificent spot I never even knew existed. Working me with both fingers and mouth, he brought me to a peak so high, so hot, so deliciously fraught with tension that I thrashed my head from side to side, my mouth open in a silent scream. When he moaned against my throbbing center, I couldn't hold on any longer. Letting go completely, I was rewarded with an orgasm so powerful, my body went completely stiff with ecstasy as I yelled his name between gasps.

For a moment afterward, I didn't move or speak or even breathe. Joey kissed each of my inner thighs before standing and removing the rest of his clothes.

When I propped myself up on shaky elbows and saw him naked before me, I nearly cried with need to feel that body on mine. In the light of the setting sun that crept in through the open drapes, his skin was golden, and every muscle was etched in line and shadow. He had the kind of body immortalized in marble by Italian sculptors four hundred years ago.

Plus an erection that would rival the leaning tower of Pisa.

He picked up one of my legs, set my foot on his chest and removed my stocking. Then he kissed each of my toes, my instep, the inside of my ankle, the back of my knee.

Oh, dear God—how had I never imagined how good his lips would feel at the back of my knee?

He picked up my other leg and repeated the process.

I was shaking. "Joey, inside me. Now."

He grinned crookedly. "You're always so bossy." Leaning down to kiss me, he hooked an arm around my back and dragged us up the bed. "But I'm going to give you what you want." He stretched over me. "Just the way you want it. I promise."

I felt like screaming at how good his skin felt against mine, how blissful his weight was on my body.

Our lips and tongues molded, sucked and stroked, and my hands traveled all over him—his back, his arms, his face, his hair. His cock pushed into my thigh and I wanted it pushing into me. I scooted down, knees wide, putting him exactly where I wanted him.

"Tiny." Joey braced himself on his hands above my shoulders and looked down at me with serious eyes. "Are you sure?"

"Yes, yes, yes." I punctuated the words with kisses pressed to his chin, his jaw, his neck.

"I wasn't planning for this, so don't have anything to, you know...stop things from..."

"I don't care. I love you, and I've never wanted anything more than this. We can be careful."

"I'll go slow." Reaching between us, he guided himself to the entrance of my body, and I bit my lip. Would it hurt? I closed my eyes and willed myself to open up to him. *It's Joey*, I kept thinking. The first couple inches slid in, tight and hot with friction. *Oh, God. More. Now.* I put my hands on his ass and pulled, panting with frustration.

Joey let out a strangled groan. "I'm trying really hard to be a gentleman here."

"Fuck being a gentleman." I opened my eyes and dug my nails into his skin. "I want you all the way inside me, and I want it now."

At that his eyes blazed with heat and he rammed into me. I gasped and threw my head to the side, crying out at the sudden shock of being stretched so tight and filled so completely. He pulled out and then slammed into me again, hitting a place so deep inside I was rendered soundless, if not actually mindless. Then he slowed down, and with several long, deep thrusts, he taught my body how to take him in, how to surrender completely to being pushed to the limit.

When I could finally breathe again, I looked up at him. His eyes were open, and in them I saw the battle between how much he loved me, which meant he didn't want to hurt me, and how badly he wanted to pound his cock into me until I screamed for mercy. And even though a sliver of fear still lingered that my body wouldn't be able to handle it, I knew what I wanted. When he hit the deepest spot again, I held him there; then I tilted my hips so I could feel pressure exactly where I needed it.

"Right there, baby?" he whispered, rocking into me with smaller movements.

"Yes," I breathed, closing my eyes as pleasure triumphed over pain. Staying deep within me, he circled his hips in a slow, steady rhythm. Within seconds I grew wetter and hotter and the buzzing tension began building again at my center.

"Fuck, you feel so good," he said. "I had no idea, no fucking idea..."

"Me either," I breathed. "I used to dream about your hands on me, and even that was enough to make me crazy."

"I used to think about exactly what I'd do to you if I had the chance. All the ways I'd touch you. How you'd feel wrapped around me. How you'd smell, how you'd taste. There isn't one fucking inch of your body I haven't dreamed about. And now you're here," he said, his voice going hoarse, "and you're so fucking beautiful." He began to move faster, harder, and I wanted it, I wanted everything. My lower body hummed and coiled, and the euphoria began to overtake me again. "Oh my God," I panted, completely lost to him. "Oh my God, you're so good. You're so gorgeous and big and hard and you feel so fucking good."

Over and over he pounded into me, hard and steady and deep. His mouth came close to mine but we were so out of our minds with rapture we couldn't even kiss—our eyes locked and our breath mingled and our bodies moved together in an unceasing, savage rhythm.

"Christ, I'm gonna come," he said through clenched teeth. "So if you don't want me inside you—"

Gripping him tight to my body, I lifted my head and pressed my mouth against his. "Don't leave me."

With powerful, primal sounds coming from deep within his throat, he pumped himself into my body even harder and throbbed inside me, over and over again. Powerless against the torrent any longer, every cell in my body burst open in a glorious fireworks of light and sound and color. I turned my cheek to the bed and cried out, short, repeated screams of pleasure beyond belief that echoed through my head and were probably loud enough to burst Joey's eardrums.

The moment our bodies stilled, Joey propped himself on his elbows and dropped his head to mine, pressing his damp forehead to my temple. "Tell me this is real." His chest rose and fell from exertion.

I finally closed my mouth and licked my lips. "I hope it is."

He put his lips on my cheekbone and held them there, and inexplicably, a lump jumped into my throat.

What the hell? I was perfectly happy and my body was totally sated. What on earth could I possibly have to cry about? But the tears were coming, and there was nothing I could do about it. Completely mortified, I felt one slip from the corner of my eye, and a sob wrenched itself from my chest.

Joey picked up his head. "What's wrong, baby? Oh God, I should have pulled out."

I grimaced through tears. "No, no, it's not that. Nothing is wrong, I swear to you, nothing." Sniffing, I squeezed my eyes shut. "This is so dumb, I don't know why I'm crying because I'm actually really happy right now."

Laughing gently, he wiped a tear from my cheek. "Doesn't look like it."

"I know! That's why it's so dumb!" Incredibly, I continued to sob, and even though Joey must have thought I was crazy, he wrapped his arms around me and flipped us onto our sides, keeping our bodies joined.

"Come here. It's OK."

I circled his torso with my arms and buried my face in his chest, loving the warm feel and smell of his skin and detesting myself for ruining this moment. Weeping like a child, I let him hold me. Joey kissed the top of my head and rested his chin there, rubbing my back with slow, soothing strokes.

Thankfully, my insanity passed and I was able to

stem the tears after a minute or two. "Sorry." I sniffled. "I suppose I'm just emotional."

"You? Emotional over me?" He squeezed me tight. "Then go ahead. Cry all you want, doll."

I slapped his chest and picked up my head to look at him—messy hair, smiling mouth, and best of all, eyes full of content and adoration. No one had ever looked at me that way before. "No, I'm done now."

"Oh. Well, in that case..." He deftly slipped underneath me so I was sitting on his hips, my hands propped on his chest. We were still connected, and I felt him stirring inside me again. "God, you're so beautiful. Even with a red nose and puffy eyes."

I slapped my palms over my face. "Don't look at me."

He took my wrists and brought them to his chest again. "Let me." As his eyes took me in, they warmed with unmistakable intention.

I wouldn't have thought we had anything left.

I was wrong.

Chapter Fourteen

"I said sprinkle, not pour!" Joey rolled his eyes when he saw how much sugar I'd dumped over the apples in the pan. "That looks like an avalanche."

"Well, sorry," I said, laughing. "I thought I was sprinkling. And you never said how much to sprinkle so I just guessed." He was teaching me how to make a dessert called Brown Betty Pudding, but I wasn't a very good student. Who could blame me? We'd been in his bedroom for hours working up an appetite, and Joey was still shirtless and barefoot, wearing only a pair of black pants that sat low on his hips. He'd offered me one of his shirts to wear, and I insisted on the one he'd worn today. I couldn't stop sniffing it.

"Jesus. Give me that." Joey took the canister of sugar and spoon from my hands. "Go into the pantry and get cinnamon and bread crumbs."

"You're supposed to be giving me a lesson. How am I going to learn to cook if I miss what you're doing?"

"I'm just adding the butter and salt. Did you at least manage to heat the water?" He looked skeptically at another pan on the stovetop.

"I think so. Even I can't screw that up."

Joey didn't look convinced of that, but I was in too good a mood to bicker so I went to the pantry. I found the cinnamon pretty quickly, but didn't see any bread crumbs. "Joey?"

"Yeah?"

"I need help."

A moment later he appeared in the pantry doorway. "Geez, Tiny, I'm beginning to think even lessons from me aren't going to help you. Maybe you should stick to rum running."

"Ha, ha. I found the cinnamon but I don't see any bread crumbs. Are they in a box?"

"Oh. No, they're probably in a container but it might be labeled in Italian." He glanced up at a shelf and pulled down a canister with something handwritten on the front. Flipping the lid, he peeked in, a curious expression on his face. "Aha."

"Bread crumbs?"

"Nope." He reached in and pulled out...a gun?

I jumped back. "Jesus, Joey! What is that and why is it in your pantry?"

He set it on the shelf and closed up the container. "It's a pistol. My dad's. He used to keep it in there just in case, and my mom probably forgot about it. Don't worry. I won't shoot you, even if you ruin dessert."

I stuck my tongue out at him, and he swept me up in one arm and kissed me. "But if you stick that tongue out at me again, I might have to end this lesson early."

I grinned and kissed him back. When he let me go, I couldn't resist hopping from one foot to the other out of pure joy. Joey laughed at me as he set the empty canister back on the shelf and took down the bread crumbs.

"What are you doing, dancing?"

"Why not?" I skipped out of the pantry and twirled around in the kitchen on my toes. "I just realized on Friday night how much I love dancing. I never knew it before I danced with you."

Joey followed me out, groaning and shaking his head. "You have no idea how hard that night was for me. First of all, seeing you there, in that dress, and thinking you were there for someone else." He set the bread crumbs on the counter. "And then when you asked to dance with me, I couldn't resist saying yes even though I knew it would be a bad idea."

"What are you talking about? It was a great idea!" I bounced around some more and sniffed the inside of his shirt again.

"I didn't think so at the time. I wanted to throttle you for getting me so worked up and thinking it was all a big joke."

"I didn't think that at all." Coming up behind him, I wrapped my arms around his waist and laid my head on his back.

"I didn't know that at the time. Move for just a second, OK, baby?"

I let go of him and watched as he added more butter, sugar and cinnamon atop the bread and poured the hot water around the edges of the pan. He stuck the whole thing in the oven, closed the oven door and took me in his arms again.

"I figured you'd only asked me to make Rosie mad. But even then, I couldn't resist the chance to get that close to you."

I snuggled into his chest. "I'm glad you couldn't. But I didn't ask you only to make Rosie mad— although that was an added benefit, I'll admit. I asked you because suddenly the thought of you leaving the club was unbearable to me."

He kissed the top of my head. "Well, I'm glad you asked, although keeping my hands to myself during that song was the hardest thing I've ever done.

No—I take it back. Leaving your house last night was the hardest thing I've ever done."

Squeezing him tighter, I shivered. "I can't believe I let you go. After you walked out the door, I cried myself to sleep."

"You slept?"

I looked up at him and smiled. "Maybe just a little."

He swatted my backside and I yelped in protest. "Hey!" I said, scooting backward with my hands on my butt. "You were the one out with someone else. What went on with Rosie after you left the club? And why were you out with her again last night?"

Joey's eyes lit up. "Jealous?"

I shrugged. "Maybe a little."

"You've got nothing to worry about. I took her straight home both nights, and dancing at the club was the closest I got to her."

"It was close, all right." I sniffed, crossing my arms in front of me. "I thought I'd have to peel her off you."

"Well, you didn't. And *you're* here now, not her. In fact, you're the only girl I've ever had here."

"Really?"

"Really."

"But there were...other girls before me?" It was the kind of question no girl should ask, but I had to torture myself a little.

Joey shrugged. "No one like you."

"What's that mean?"

"It means no, you're not the first girl I've ever been with, but you are definitely the first girl I've ever loved."

I took a deep breath. I'd assumed I wasn't his first—and I hadn't been a virgin before seven o'clock tonight, either—but it was still hard to hear. I didn't want to think about his hands or lips or any other body part on any other girl. And I didn't want to be with anyone else again either. Ever.

Suddenly Bridget's scheme to marry Vince made perfect sense to me. Now that I knew what it was like to love someone this way, I understood the desperation they'd felt to be together. *And Joey is planning to move away.* We hadn't even talked about that yet. But before I could bring it up, he took me in his arms and kissed me, slow and deep and sweet.

"I promise you," he said, resting his forehead on mine. "I've never loved anyone the way I love you. I never will."

And then my throat closed up too tightly to talk

anyway.

When the pudding was ready, we sat at the table and ate right from the pan with one spoon. The combination of apples and butter and sugar and cinnamon and shirtless Joey was enough to make any girl moan.

As we neared the bottom of the pan, Joey began smearing it on my lips and licking it off. Then he got more creative, unbuttoned my shirt, and dripped some on my neck, down my chest and onto my stomach, all of which he ate off my body with great relish. He was just licking some from my inner thigh when we heard the front door open and slam.

"Which rosary, Ma? There's more than one here. Well, I don't know, so you might as well come up and get it. Cripes, Joey didn't even turn off all the lights before he left. Is he still here?"

Joey and I exchanged a panicked look. His mother and Marie were here, and we were stuck in the kitchen, nearly naked, and I was covered in sticky Brown Betty sauce! If they caught us, there was no possible way to explain ourselves, and we couldn't get to the bedroom without coming out of the kitchen.

"Come here!" he whispered. Grabbing my hand, he pulled me into the pantry and shut the door silently.

I saw nothing but blackness and heard nothing but the canon blasts of my heart.

"I'm scared," I whispered.

"It's OK." Joey put his arms around me from behind. "She just forgot her rosaries and made Marie bring her back to get them."

"This late at night?"

"She's religious. Something must have been keeping her up. They'll be gone soon."

I hoped he was right. We heard nothing for a few minutes, and I began to relax.

So did Joey. "Your neck is sticky," he said. "Mmmmmm." He began licking the back of my neck, and within seconds, I felt him hard against my lower back. A quickening in my stomach made me close my eyes and squeeze my thighs together.

"Joey, no."

"Yes." He took his arms from me for a moment and I heard him unbutton his pants. Then he lifted the bottom of the shirt I wore. I had nothing on underneath it.

"Spread your legs," he said in my ear. My resolve splintered.

I widened my legs and he pushed up into me from behind, lifting me onto my toes and nearly off the floor. Gasping, I had to bite down on my lip to keep from crying out. My hands braced against a shelf.

I would never look at a pantry the same way again. Ever.

Leaning forward slightly, I whimpered softly as he began to move in and out of me, slow and rhythmic. I moved my hands to a higher shelf and my right fingers brushed something cool and metal—the pistol. *Oh my God, sex and guns in the pantry. This is my life now.* Somehow the thought of it spiked my desire even more.

Then he reached around and rubbed me from the front with wet fingers, and I forgot about everything else but his magic hands.

"Does it feel good, baby?" he whispered.

I nodded, unable to speak and terrified I was going to scream with pleasure before we were through. The way Joey moved, it was as if he could read my mind, or at least my body. He knew exactly where I wanted to be touched and how. He knew the perfect way to angle himself inside me and how fast or slow I wanted him to go. He knew just what words to whisper in my ear to rattle my insides and make me clench around him. Grabbing the shelf harder, I sucked in my breath and willed myself not to yell or moan or even squeak.

Suddenly we heard voices in the kitchen.
Joey put his other hand over my mouth.
"What is all this mess? Dear God, Ma, don't even come in here."

Oh my God oh my God oh my God. This it is. This is my punishment, isn't it? This is the consequence of all my awful behavior, my sins, my criminal activities. I'll be caught fucking Joey in the pantry by his mother and she'll faint from the shock and never let us be together again and Joey will hear her call me all sorts of names and oh God he's still hard, how is that possible and why don't they just leave, I'm so hot and tight and tingly and yes, yes, yes—just like that...

At the slam of the front door, Joey started moving again. "They're gone," he said. But he kept the hand over my mouth, and I sucked two fingers between my teeth and ran my tongue along them. He groaned, shoving into me deep and hard and driving me to insanity with his other hand. "God, you're so wet," he breathed. "And so tight, and so hot, and I never want to stop fucking you, ever..."

Neither of us lasted another ten seconds.

"You have perfect toes," Joey said. We were in the bathtub, leaning back against opposite ends, and Joey held my foot up near his face. We'd locked the heavy wooden bathroom door, of course, but we'd also been smart enough to throw the deadbolt on the apartment's front door as well. No need to invite further calamity.

"Thank you." I bowed my head graciously, and rubbed my hands along the backs of his calves, which were alongside my hips. We'd already soaped and rinsed each other, and now we lingered in the warm water, pruney and damp-haired but happy.

"And your feet are so small," he went on, holding up his hand to compare the size. "Do you have to shop for shoes at a children's store?"

I pulled my foot from his hands and kicked water at him. "Still with the jokes about my size? Are you ever going to let me be?"

Joey laughed deep and loud, the sound echoing off the black and white tiles. "I'm sorry, I'll be nice." He fished underwater for my foot again. "Let me have it back."

I let him, and he brought it to his lips and kissed it. "I love your toes." He sucked on each one, sending a frisson of delight up my leg. "I love every perfect part of you. Except maybe your temper."

I sat up and pushed a huge wall of water at him, which soaked his face and splashed over the edge of the tub. Sputtering with laughter, he wiped his eyes and grabbed for me. "You got water in my mouth!"

"Serves you right."

Grinning, he got me by the arms and traded places with me, pulling me against him, stomach to stomach. His skin on mine felt so warm, so good, it melted every other feeling but contentment. I kissed his collarbone and rested my head there, tracing the letters of my name on his chest with one finger. His arms wrapped around me, and I closed my eyes. We were back to our comfortable silences.

But in a moment, icy fingers of fear crept beneath the warmth. How could I let him do something I knew might get him arrested or killed?

"Joey, please don't do it." The words slipped out before I had an argument prepared.

He said nothing.

"Don't. Please. I'm scared."

"I have to, Tiny. I have to do it—I promised

myself."

"But things are different now."

"Between you and me they are. But that situation hasn't changed." His voice had a harder edge to it than I'd heard all night.

"If you kill that man, Joey—"

"When I kill him."

I picked my head up. He looked at me, but his eyes were cool.

"You're scaring me."

"This is who I am, Tiny. This is part of me."

"That's not true—who you are is not what you do. You're so much more than that."

He was silent a moment, staring into the water. "If you think I can let this go, you don't know me very well."

"But I do! I do know you well." Agitated, I got to my knees between his legs. "I know you love your family more than anything in the world, and I know you would do anything for them. I love that about you." Taking his hands in mine, I squeezed them tight.

"And I know you were hurt when your father died, but—"

"I was in the car. Did you know that?"

Confused and sad, I just looked at him.

"I was in the car waiting when my father came out of the station."

"Oh, honey." My heart broke for him.

"I heard those bastards come around the corner and start firing. I heard my pop yell for me to get down, and you know what I did? I fucking ducked. I covered my head and ducked down below the window like a frightened kid."

"You were scared! Anyone would've been scared. And you did what your father wanted you to do—you stayed safe!"

He shook his head, his jaw protruding. "His gun was on the seat. I could've grabbed it. I could've shot back. I could've done something. But I didn't."

"You might have been killed yourself, Joey!" Slamming my eyes shut, I lowered my chin, my lower lip trembling. "Is this how it's always going to be?"

"I promised myself. I promised myself that day that I would never be a coward again. That I would stand up for myself and my family the way he would have. I can't let it go."

"Not even for me?"

He met my eyes, and I saw how hard it would be for him to actually say it. "I love you. You know I do."

"But not enough."

"Don't say it like that."

Sighing, I toppled forward onto him again, fitting myself against his body as tightly as possible. "I love you too. But I don't know if I can live like this...I'll be constantly worried about your safety, wondering if today's the day your luck will run out." I snaked my arms behind his lower back and ran my palms along his solid muscles.

His arms locked around me, and he brought his lips to my head as he squeezed me close. "Don't give up on me. Please."

I didn't want to. Bridget said love was work, and I was willing to work hard at loving him. And I'd never felt as cherished as I did lying there in Joey's arms—I knew he loved me too. But the fear that he could be taken from me at any moment on any average day was enough to give me pause. "Are you still going to work for Sam Scarfone?"

Joey's body stiffened. "I don't want to. But I have to tread carefully. I didn't get a chance to talk to Angelo today, but he's gonna be looking for me. If he goes to Sam—"

My eyes flew open. "I thought you said he wouldn't!"

"I said I didn't see how it would do him any

good—but I don't put anything past anyone, and you shouldn't either."

Biting my lip, I kept rubbing Joey's back. Between Sam, Angelo, and Enzo, there were going to be a whole hell of a lot of gangsters unhappy with us. "And after that? Are you still going to Chicago?"

"I was planning on it. But that was before."

"Before what?"

He kissed my head again. "Before I got your note."

I couldn't help smiling at the memory of that. "I'll never forget the look on your face when you turned around."

"I'll bet it was something else."

"It was."

I felt him swallow. "Come with me. To Chicago."

"I thought you said you wouldn't ask me again," I teased, but my heart was pounding.

"This is different. That was a stupid thing to do that night. I should have told you how I felt but I was mad and jealous and I didn't know what to do. But now I do."

"You do?"

"Yes." He took me by the shoulders and held me away from away from him slightly. "Marry me, Tiny."

My jaw fell open. "What?"

"Marry me. I love you, and I want us to live together."

I stared at him with wide eyes. His hair was wet and disheveled, and his jaw was shadowed with whiskers, but his eyes were serious and I saw no sign of a teasing smile on his lips. But still, this was Joey. "Is this a joke?"

That brought a smile. "No! I'm serious. I've never been more serious. Will you marry me? Please?"

"Oh my God, Joey." All I could do was stare at him in disbelief. He was proposing to me? *In the tub?*

He shimmied my shoulders lightly. "You're starting to make me nervous here. I've asked three times now."

"I'm sorry, I'm just so surprised—I never imagined—I mean, I love you, but—"

"But what? You think that will change?"

"No, but—"

"You want to keep living with your father and sisters?"

"Definitely not."

"You didn't enjoy yourself in the pantry—I'm sorry, pantries?"

My cheeks flushed. "I did, but—"

"Then say yes! You're killing me."

The look in his eyes was equal parts love and torture. God, he was so handsome. And strong and sexy and loyal and hard-working and funny and sweet and smart.

He adored me. I adored him.

I chewed my lip. "I want to, Joey. I want to say yes."

"Then say yes. Vince always said we'd end up together."

A rueful smile stretched my lips. "I heard." Yes was on the tip of my tongue.

He'd be a great father someday.

Our own apartment.

And the cooking. My God, the cooking.

But then I thought about other things. Guns. Bullets. Coffins.

Vince was hardly older than Joey was now when he was killed.

I took a breath. "I have to think about it." At his devastated face, my heart ached. "It's not that I don't want to marry you, Joey." The words *marry you* made my stomach flip.

"But you're not ready? You think you're too young?"

"Not exactly. I mean, yes, we're young, but my parents were young. Bridget and Vince were young."

"Then what? You think I don't love you enough?" he went on, getting more worked up. "Because I do—I love that you've spent your life taking care of your family. I love that you were willing to risk your life to keep them safe. I love how smart you are, how brave you are, how beautiful you are. I love that you want to get out and see the world—I do too. You want to go to school? I'll find a way to pay for it. I love that you want to be a nurse."

"Joey—"

"Let me finish. I love that you can't reach the high shelf in the pantry. I love that you can't cook worth a damn. I love the expression on your face when I catch you staring at me. And I love the way you came here tonight, ready to fight for me. Now I'll fight for you." He kissed my lips. "Say yes."

My throat was so full. "I can't."

His face fell. It hurt me not to give him the answer he wanted, but I didn't want to end up like my sister, widowed at twenty-three with three children.

"Look at Bridget, Joey," I said softly. "She asked Vince to do something else with his life, but he wouldn't. He said nothing would happen to him."

"When you came here tonight, you knew all this about me," he said sadly. "And yet you still came."

"I had to come." Of that I was positive.

"And we haven't been careful tonight."

I grimaced. "No, we haven't."

"So what happens now?"

"I don't know, Joey. I need to think." Laying my head on his chest again, I shivered. "We should get out. The water's getting cold."

#

I spent the entire night in Joey's bed, wrapped in the warm comfort of his arms. We didn't talk any more about Chicago or getting married. I slept a little, my body spooned in the curve of his, his right arm tucked securely around my chest, our right hands clasped. From time to time, I brought my lips to his fingers and kissed them. And more than once I awoke to find him brushing the hair back from my face or rubbing his lips against my shoulder. Countless times, my throat tightened and tears threatened, but there was no point in crying.

Toward dawn, Joey rolled onto his back and I turned over, propping my head on my hand. With his features in repose I could see the little boy he'd been in that First Holy Communion picture. I saw the devil-eyed mischief-maker who'd stolen my underwear. And I saw the full-grown man who wanted to spend the rest of his life making me happy, if only I'd let him.

My gaze wandered down his body, exposed to the waist, and my belly tightened at the sight of his chest, his stomach, the line of dark hair trailing from underneath his belly button. My hands itched to touch him again. My insides felt hollow with need again. If I'd been wearing underwear, it would've been damp again.

I sighed. There was no use pretending I could stay away from him—I knew better.

Joey was who he was. And he was offering himself to me, everything he had. His heart, a home, a family, a life together.

What more could I ask him to give?

By sunrise, I'd made up my mind.

Chapter Fifteen

"Joey," I whispered, gently shaking his shoulder. "Wake up. The answer is yes."

"Hmm?" Joey's brow wrinkled and he sniffed but didn't open his eyes.

"The answer is yes. I'll marry you." Saying it out loud made my entire body radiate with excitement.

His eyes opened and he turned his head to look at me. "Did I hear that right?" He sat up and shook his head in disbelief. "Did you say yes, you'll marry me?"

I nodded. "Yes. I'll marry you. I'll marry you, can you believe that?" I slapped his shoulder. "After all the years of your mean old short jokes and my giving you lip?"

Pure elation lit his features, and he tackled me, throwing me down and raining kisses all over my face. "I love your lip. You can give it to me any time you want."

I rolled my eyes. "That's not what I meant."

"God, Tiny, do you really mean it?" He stopped and looked down at me, and I threw my arms around his neck.

"Yes. I really do. I want to marry you. I want to be your wife." I laughed. "That sounds so strange—your wife. You're gonna have a wife!"

"You're damn right I am." He kissed my lips. "I knew you'd come around."

I circled his neck with my hands and pretended to choke him.

He flipped to his back and set me on top of him, straddling his stomach. "Tell me again that you'll marry me."

"I'll marry you. Now enough talking." Reaching behind me, I took his cock in my hand—it was already hard. I raised an eyebrow. "Already? I just woke you up thirty seconds ago!"

He grinned. "Better get used to that. Every morning."

"Every morning? Yes, please."

Grinning, he shimmied down so my knees rested on either side of his head, and without further warning, buried his tongue inside me.

I tipped forward, clutching the headboard with white knuckles, and wondered how I'd ever thought I needed anything or anyone else to feel alive.

A couple hours later, we sat in the kitchen—dressed properly, this time—drinking coffee and eating eggs and toast. *This is what it will be like*, I thought, staring at Joey's hands as he brought his coffee cup to his lips. I grinned involuntarily.

"Happy?" he asked.

"Yes. But I still can't believe how much things have changed in just one day."

"Or one month," he said. "A few weeks ago, you couldn't stand me. I lost track of how many times you told me to go to hell."

I lifted my chin. "I make no apologies. You can be very exasperating sometimes."

"Well, I suppose enduring your temper is a fair price to pay to have you for breakfast—I mean, at my breakfast table."

I brought a forkful of eggs to my mouth. "And I'll put up with your teasing if you'll cook for me. I've decided I'm not going to learn how."

"That, my sweet, is a relief to both of us."

I glared at him, but my gaze softened when he glanced at the clock. It was going on nine, and we'd have to part soon. "So what will you do today?" I set down my fork.

"I need to talk to Angelo first thing, convince him I can pay him off in whisky hauls."

"Will you tell him the truth?"

"I don't have a better story, so yeah. I guess so."

I nodded. "I can help you with the whisky."

Joey shook his head. "You're done with the whisky business, doll. You're going back to school, remember?"

"Telling me what to do already?" I arched a brow at him.

"Sorry. But I'll be the bootlegger in the family, OK?" He stood and carried his dishes to the sink to rinse them.

"What about...the other thing?"

Without turning around, he said, "What about it?"

"Are you still going to do it?"

He didn't answer right away. "I don't know."

"Really?" Hope surged within me.

He turned off the faucet and stayed where he was. "I'm reconsidering."

I jumped out of my chair and rushed to him, circling his torso with my arms and pressing my entire body to his back. I didn't say anything else, didn't want to push further. Just knowing he was having second thoughts was enough.

"I had a dream this morning, after we fell back asleep. After you said yes."

"You did?"

"About my dad." He swallowed hard before continuing.

"Tell me about it."

"We were sitting up on the roof like we used to do, like I did with you that one time."

"Oh?"

"And he was smoking a cigarette just like he used to, and he gave one to me and told me not to tell my mom. But I was grown, and I knew he was dead, so I told him, 'You're not supposed to be here.' And he said, 'I have to tell you something.'"

My arms prickled with gooseflesh. "What did he tell you?"

"This is the weird thing. I thought for sure he was going to say something about killing the man who shot him, tell me not to do it or something. But he didn't."

"He didn't? What did he say?"

"He said, 'Teach them about stars.'"

"Teach who about stars?"

"Well, at first it wasn't clear who he meant, and I was confused. The dream ended there, but ever since I woke up, I've been thinking about it, and I think I know what he meant."

"You do?"

"Yeah." His voice caught, and he turned in my arms to face me. Brushing my hair back from my face, he said, "I think he meant my children. Our children."

I couldn't have spoken even if I wanted to.

"And I got to thinking, if anything were to happen to me..." He struggled to finish the thought. "Anyway, I understood better what you meant when you talked about Vince and your sister. I don't want that to be us."

"Me either."

"I haven't made up my mind completely yet, but that promise I made to myself seems less important today than it did yesterday. And I know I gave up all that money just to find out who it was, but you know what? It doesn't matter. What matters is you."

I smiled up at him. "You mean it?"

"Yeah. I do. I can't promise to get out of the business right away, but I'll do everything I can to make things right with Angelo and get out clean. It'll be hard, and I'll miss the money, that's for sure—"

"I don't care about money."

He smiled. "You don't want a nice ring?"

"No." I pursed my lips. "Wait, yes I do."

Laughing, he hugged me close. "Don't worry. I'll find a job that makes decent money. Who knows, maybe my sisters are right and I should stay here take over this place."

My heart thumped happily. "You should! You should!"

"I'll think about it. Right now I should take you home and then settle up with Angelo." I couldn't see his face, but I heard the dread in his voice. "God, I wish I'd never hijacked that stupid shipment and stolen those drugs."

"No sense thinking that way." There were plenty of things I wished I hadn't done either, but regrets never helped anybody. "Let's look ahead, OK? We've got a lot to do."

We finished the breakfast dishes together before Joey drove me home. We were quiet on the way, each of us thinking about the conversations we had to have today and dreading them. But I wasn't one to wait around chewing my fingernails when there was something unpleasant to be done. I wasn't looking forward to turning down Enzo's offer and explaining the sudden existence of a fiancé in my life—especially since I'd made such a big deal about his—but it had to be done. No use putting it off.

And maybe he wouldn't even be that angry. After all, he didn't love me. Ours had not been an affair of the heart, only of the body. We barely knew each other. Certainly, we had enjoyed each other physically, but he could have any woman he wanted— it wasn't as if I was the only one who could please him. And half the time I drove him crazy anyway. By the time Joey kissed me goodbye and promised to call me later, I was certain I could explain things to Enzo in a way that would have him positively glad to be rid of me.

#

The house was empty when I got home, and I skipped up the stairs to my bedroom humming a tune. As soon as I was cleaned up, I walked down to Bridget's. I couldn't remember the last time I'd walked with a spring in my step, but I practically bounced along the sidewalk toward the store. It was sunny and hot, and even though I knew the humidity would do awful things to my hair, I didn't care. I was still wearing my navy blue dress, which was perhaps a bit wrinkled from spending the night on Joey's bedroom floor, but I had clean undergarments on and anyway, each little crease in the skirt reminded me of him. I started humming again.

When I turned the corner into the alley, I noticed Daddy's sign above the garage door was gone, the one that read Jack's Auto Repair. I saw no sign of activity and wondered if the Prohis that had questioned him had given up on the case or still lurked around town trying to investigate. It was an impossible job. Nobody I knew obeyed the dry law, and I was certain there were very few people who wanted to risk the ire of the big mobsters who now bootlegged most of the booze around here. Too many stories in the papers these days about where you might end up if you ratted on them.

Spying a produce truck behind the store, I grinned like an idiot. The day I'd first heard Joey was back in town, he'd helped Bridget unload produce at the store. He often helped her out if Martin wasn't available, and for free too, or maybe just for a sandwich or bowl of soup. Bridget said he wouldn't take money from family. At the time I'd rolled my eyes and declared him a dope, but now I understood him better. Family meant everything to him.

I'd be his family soon.

I may have squealed just a little at the thought.

Letting myself in the back door, I headed through the stock room and into the front, where Molly was teaching Mary Grace to use the cash register, and Bridget's boys were stacking candy behind the counter. "Good morning, everyone," I chirped gaily, stopping to ruffle the dark hair on my nephews' heads.

They both blinked as if they didn't recognize me. My grin widened and I patted Molly on the shoulder and tweaked Mary Grace's turned-up nose. "Bridget upstairs?"

"Yeah," said Molly, her brow furrowed. "Where were you?"

"At Joey's," I answered. My body felt lighter than the air around it. I'd nearly forgotten what it was like to tell the truth.

"All night?" Molly's eyes were wide.

"Uh huh."

"Tiny, guess what?" Mary Grace either wasn't surprised at that or it didn't faze her. "Molly's teaching me to work the register and Bridget says she'll pay me if I work some hours at the store each week!"

"That's great, poppet. You'll catch on in no time." I ruffled her hair. "I'll be down in a little bit." Tossing them one last smile, I sailed back into the stock room and up the stairs to Bridget's apartment, leaving Molly in open-mouthed stupor.

The back door was open and music drifted into the stairwell from her radio, a piano waltz that took me back to the night Joey and I sat on the roof.

Teach them about stars.

The world tilted, and I grabbed onto a chair back for balance. We would. We would teach our children about stars and planets and history and geography. We'd have a map of the world and show them where their Daddy was born, where their grandparents had immigrated from. Joey would teach them to cook meatballs and tomato sauce and *arancine*, and I'd teach them—

I frowned for a second. Well, I'd think of something to teach them.

And I didn't want children yet, anyway. Quickly I put a hand to my stomach, closed my eyes and mumbled a prayer asking God to forgive Joey and me for throwing caution out the pantry door—and the bedroom door, and the bathroom door, and the kitchen door—and to grant us some time together before starting a family. Not that we deserved much pardon; we'd been completely reckless. And if it happened, it happened. I was stunned to realize I'd be all right either way.

"Bridge?" I called, fighting the maniacal grin that seemed to have taken up permanent residence on my face.

"In here," she hollered from the boys' bedroom. I wandered back and found her stripping the sheets from the beds. "Monday. Laundry," she reminded me. "Although I don't know how I'm going to get these sheets to dry, it's so darn humid outside." She was sweaty from the exertion of housework and wiped the back of her wrist across her forehead. Finally she eyed me curiously. "You look happy."

"I am."

"You're positively glowing." She came around the bed to examine me with shrewd eyes. "What happened with Joey?"

"I told him I was in love with him."

She gasped. "You didn't!"

I smiled even wider at the shock on her face and rocked back on my heels. "I did."

"What did he say?" The grin on her face nearly

matched mine.

"He said he loved me too."

Bridget clapped her palms to her cheeks. "I don't believe it."

"And," I went on, twirling around before backing up to the dresser and leaning back against it dramatically. "He proposed."

She gasped again. "I don't believe it!"

"Believe it." I had no ring to show her, but I didn't care. "I accepted."

She sank onto the bed, her hands still splayed on her face. "Of course you did." She shook her head. "I don't *believe* it. Vince was right all along."

"He must have seen something we didn't."

Finally she dropped her hands and lowered her chin to shoot me a look. "Everyone saw something you two didn't. Mary Grace saw it, for cryin' out loud."

"She did?"

Bridget nodded. "Yes. You weren't fooling anyone but yourselves." She fanned her face. "Well. Well. I just can't seem to think straight."

"I know the feeling."

She smiled. "Have you told Daddy?"

It was the one thing capable of turning my smile into a grimace. Well, that and the thought of the conversation I had to have with Enzo. But I wouldn't think about that now. "No. I wanted to tell someone who'd be happy about it first."

"I think he'll be happy," Bridget said carefully. "He likes Joey. Always has."

"He likes me at home better, though."

She stood. "Leave Daddy to me. If he's anything less than glad for you, I'll take him to task. The girls are old enough to manage the house and themselves at this point, and you deserve to be happy."

"Thank you." I rushed forward and threw my arms around her so forcefully, she staggered backward. "I'll need all the help I can get."

She laughed and squeezed me back. "Want to wear my wedding dress?"

"Oh, Bridget, really?" I held her at arm's length as my excitement soared. Bridget's wedding dress was beautiful.

"Of course. It'll have to be hemmed of course, but I think it will fit you." Her lips tipped up. "We got married fast so no one would notice an expanding waistline."

I groaned. "Hopefully I won't have that problem."

"Hopefully?" Her face went white. "Does that

mean—Frances Kathleen O'Mara, have you gone crazy?"

"Never mind about that." I breezed toward the door. "Let's pull your dress from the trunk so I can try it on."

#

Twenty minutes later I stood before the cheval mirror in Bridget's bedroom wearing her wedding dress. She brought a hand to her mouth, fighting tears. "It's beautiful on you, Tiny. It really is."

I caught her eye in the mirror and smiled. "Thank you. I loved it on you, and I'm so grateful you're letting me wear it. You're sure it's OK to alter it a bit?" The fit wasn't terrible, since Bridget was small-framed too, but the length would need to be taken up and the side seam taken in. It was a simple gown, made by a friend of our mother's. Cream-colored lace, three quarter sleeves, rounded neckline. A wide peach-colored satin sash emphasized my small waist and slight curves, and the lovely skirt fell in three fluttery lace panels to the floor. On me the final tier puddled a bit, but Bridget knelt at my side and examined the seam where the bottom panel was attached.

"This won't be too hard to fix, Tiny. If I can't do it, I'm sure Mrs. Hobbs would do the work for a reasonable price. She'll like knowing it's being worn again." She looked up at me. "Want to try on the veil?"

I clapped my hands together. "Yes!"

Bridget got to her feet and dug in the trunk we'd lugged from the back of the cedar closet. The veil was boxed and wrapped in tissue paper, and I gasped when she pulled it out. From a thick crown of beads and lace hung a floor-length swath of lace-trimmed tulle. Bridget stepped behind me and settled the crown on my forehead; it rose to a peak in the center. The tulle fell over my ears and shoulders, flowing down my back to the floor. I wouldn't be able to trim it, but that was all right. When I walked it would drift behind me like gossamer, just like it had on Bridget.

I turned to her with tears in my eyes. "I'll take good care of it all."

Fussing with the veil, she blinked back her own tears. "I hope you and Joey are as happy as Vince and I were the day we married." She met my eyes. "And I beg you to convince Joey to choose a different path than his father."

I put a hand on her arm. "I'm trying. I am."

"Good." She went behind me to begin undoing the column of looped buttons running up my back. "And I hope he's more patient than Vince was trying to remove this dress—he tore three button loops trying to get it off me!"

I grinned at my reflection in the mirror. "I wouldn't count on it."

Chapter Sixteen

Joey called that afternoon around four. "Hello," I said, my insides warming at the sound of his voice.

"How's my girl?"

"Good. Busy."

"Oh?"

"Monday is laundry day," I explained. "The girls are helping me get it all done."

"Good. Make sure they know how to do it because pretty soon you won't be there to show them."

"You sound awfully confident about that, Mr. Lupo."

"That's because I know something you don't, Mrs. Lupo."

My belly turned completely inside out and the floor seemed to rumble beneath my feet. "I'm not Mrs. Lupo yet, you know," I said with the widest grin imaginable. "You shouldn't count your chickens and all that."

He laughed. "These particular chickens, I'm gonna count."

"Tell me what you know that I don't."

"Uh uh, that's no fun at all. You'll just have to wait."

"Joey!" I stamped my foot on the hallway rug. "Tell me, please!"

"And what will I get in exchange for this information?"

I blushed, peeking out the kitchen window to make sure the girls were still outside hanging things on the line. "I'll do that thing," I whispered into the phone.

"What thing?" He whispered too, although he was probably alone.

"You know..." I wobbled one leg. "The thing I did in the restaurant pantry."

"Oh, that thing! In that case, I'll tell you—I went down to the garage and spoke to your father."

I stopped fidgeting. "What? You did?"

"Yes. I know you're not the old-fashioned type, but I know my pop would've wanted me to ask your dad for his blessing."

"And did he give it?"

Joey paused, and I closed my eyes, imagining the difficulties we'd face if my father put up impediments to the marriage. I wouldn't care—I was going to marry Joey whether Daddy said it was OK or not.

"He gave it."

"Oh, thank heavens," I breathed. "One less thing to worry about."

"He was surprised but not entirely shocked. And he grumbled about you leaving home a little, but in the end he shook my hand and wished me luck putting up with your sharp tongue and foul temper."

"He did not say that!"

Joey laughed again. He'd probably never stop teasing me, but I could live with it—in fact, I'd learned I couldn't live without it. "So should I come over now?" he asked.

"Now?"

"Yeah. You know. So you can do that thing."

I clucked my tongue. "Good-bye, Joey Lupo. I'm going now and I don't care if you ever call back." He was still laughing when I hung up.

#

Within the hour, the doorbell rang. *Joey, you fiend.* I was upstairs putting some clean clothing away and raced down the stairs to answer it, smoothing my hair and my blouse. Just before reaching the door, I slowed down as if I'd walked leisurely and put my fingers on the handle. *Relax. He doesn't need to know you're out of your mind with need for him.*

I pulled it open and blinked in surprise—it wasn't Joey. It was a delivery man from a Gianni's Flowers, and he was carrying a long white box. Over his shoulder I spotted his truck, painted dark green with white letting on the side.

My heart tripped with excitement. My first flowers from Joey!

"Miss O'Mara?" the man asked. When I nodded, he held the box forth. "These are for you."

"Thank you." The box was thick and heavy, and I didn't bother trying to hide my grin. "Have a good day."

He tipped his cap at me. "You too, miss."

He jogged back to his truck, and I shut the door, squealing inwardly. Rushing into the living room, I set the box on the coffee table. When I pulled off the lid, I gasped.

Joey had send me a dozen gorgeous red roses. My hands rose to my heart and then reached to finger the thick, velvety crimson petals, the emerald stems dotted with thorns, even the crinkly white paper. They were the most beautiful flowers I'd ever seen—so pretty they didn't even look real!

Peering closer, I noticed an envelope nestled among the blooms. When I reached for it, I saw that something else was in there too. Lying at the bottom of the box was a smaller parcel wrapped in white paper. I gasped again—had Joey gotten me a wedding gift already? The box looked too big to be a ring, but with Joey, you never knew...he might be teasing me somehow. Maybe he'd placed the ring in a bigger box just to fool me. But wouldn't he want to offer something like that to me himself?

Immediately I glanced out the front window. Was he lurking in the bushes, ready to pop out and surprise me?

Grinning like mad, I pulled the envelope from the box and tore it open. Inside was a plain white card, upon which words were written in spidery black script. As I read, the smile faded from my face, my lips going slack.

The flowers weren't from Joey.

Dear Miss O'Mara, I'm delighted to find that you are excellent at keeping a secret. I hope you have had time to consider my offer, as I am anxiously

awaiting your acceptance, and I hope the flowers will help persuade you to give it sooner rather than later. I am also returning something that belongs to you, as you mistakenly left it in my motorcar the other night. Wear it tonight when you visit me at the Statler, just the way you wore it in your bedroom. Telephone the number below to reach me so we can arrange a time...although I believe you still have the key.

Until then, E.D.

Enzo DiFiore. I didn't even have to open the smaller box inside the flowers—I knew it contained the diamond choker. The one he'd bought for Gina as an engagement gift. The one Raymond had stolen from his brother's room and sent to me as a misguided attempt at affection. The one I'd worn in my bedroom, naked everywhere else, when Enzo had snuck in and surprised me. My face burned.

You can't think that way. What's past is past, and the escapades with Enzo are part of your history. It was just a bit of fun, just a girl reacting to being responsible her whole life, and finally getting a taste of freedom.

A taste?

OK, more like a meal.

A really attractive five-course meal, served

searing hot.

But I wasn't the type to wallow about my mistakes, even if Enzo was the biggest one I'd ever made. No sense in it. What made sense was that I needed to tell him right away that I wouldn't be accepting his offer, that what was between us was done, and he should focus on Gina or switch his attentions to some other girl he could control easier than me. But not tonight. Not when we were alone in that apartment with darkness pressing at the windows. I was in love in Joey and trusted myself not to give in to Enzo, but I didn't trust that Enzo would be a gentleman. I'd barely managed to put him off last time we were there together, and he was not a man who liked being told no.

I needed to phone him right away. But I felt that I'd have more success in person than on the telephone convincing him not to be angry, and I had to return the key and choker. A daytime meeting would be best, or one in a crowded location. Would he agree to see me on my terms?

Chewing my lip, I went to the telephone and dialed the number. I wondered if it was the number to the apartment at the Statler and got my answer when the hotel switchboard operator came on the line.

"Mr. Enzo DiFiore, please," I requested.

"One moment, thank you."

While she made the connection, I wondered briefly what a switchboard operator made. If I didn't return to school right away, I'd have to get some sort of job. I didn't much relish the thought of sitting in a small room plugging wires all day long, but maybe as something temporary, it would do.

"Hello, darling." Enzo's deep, smooth voice sent a chill down my arms. This wouldn't be easy.

"Hello. Thank you for the flowers."

"You got them."

"Yes, they're beautiful."

"They'd better be. And the necklace was inside?"

I glanced nervously at the box on the coffee table.

"Yes. It's there."

"Good. Otherwise I'd have to have a word with the florist."

I laughed uneasily.

"Will you come tonight?"

"Actually, I can't tonight. I have to...stay with my sisters."

Enzo clucked his tongue. "You see, darling, this is why you need to accept my offer. No girl as tempting as you should be alone in her bed at night."

"I—I can't tonight. I'll be with my family."

He sighed. "Tomorrow, then?"

"All right. Tomorrow."

"I'll be at the club."

"I'll come there." The club—perfect.

"Wear the necklace, Tiny. And plan on staying."
The connection went dead.

#

That night we ate together as a family for the first time since the day Bridget and the girls returned from vacation. She came over a bit early to give me a hand in the kitchen, while Molly and Mary Grace took the boys outside to play in the yard.

Actually, Bridget did most of the work in the kitchen. I sat at the table doodling my name and Joey's on a piece of scrap paper when I was supposed to be writing down Bridget's method for frying pork chops.

Tiny Lupo.

Frances Kathleen Lupo.

Mr. and Mrs. Joseph Lupo.

Huh, what was his middle name?

"Are you writing this down?" she barked at me for the tenth time when she caught me staring into space.

"What? Oh, yes. Egg. Bread crumbs." I scribbled it down. Bread crumbs... Of course, my mind wandered to the pantry and nothing Bridget said got through after that. Eventually, she gave up.

"You're not listening to a word I say," she complained over the hiss of frying meat.

"I'm sorry, I'm too distracted. And besides, I think Joey will be doing the cooking for us."

"I hope so, otherwise you're going to starve." She shook her head. "Just set the table, will you?"

Happy to oblige, I set eight places around the table and even hummed a tune while I worked.

Bridget laughed. "My, my. Such a difference in you, Tiny O'Mara! Just look what love does!"

I stuck my tongue out at her, but even my tongue reminded me of Joey and I got lost in dreamy thoughts again. Would he come over tonight? I'd gone almost twenty-one years without seeing him every night, but now the prospect of a single night without him seemed unthinkable.

When Daddy came in I held my breath. But he said nothing unusual, just poured his customary evening whisky and poked his head out the back door to wave at the boys. Bridget and I exchanged a glance. I'd told her what Joey told me, and she was thrilled that Daddy wasn't giving me trouble like he'd given her. But he wasn't exactly jumping for joy either. I couldn't help being a little disappointed—it wasn't that Daddy was the type of father to be effusive with praise or affection. But when he felt strongly about something, he got worked up, and it seemed to me this was something he should feel strongly about, one way or another. I'd almost rather have an argument than silence.

Bridget called everybody inside and they took turns washing up at the sink. We sat down and Daddy started to say grace. With my eyes closed and head lowered, my mind began to drift again, but it snapped to attention when Daddy said, "And now, Lord, a word about my Frances Kathleen."

From the corner of my eye, I saw Bridget peeking at me from the corner of hers.

"She's borne the load around here for a while since her dear mother departed, and today I gave my blessing for her marriage, even though it will be a struggle without her. Please be with her and Joseph in their marriage and help us get along without her here.

And, Lord, let her know that I'm proud of her and if her mother were here, she'd want nothing more for Tiny than the good man she's chosen. Amen."

"Amen," everyone echoed. Everyone but me—I couldn't speak quite yet.

"Tiny," breathed Molly, staring at me from across the table. "Are you and Joey getting married?"

I looked at Daddy but he was already reaching for a pork chop. Evidently that was all the fanfare my news was going to get, but it was enough for me. I'd take quiet approval and a reluctant admission of pride over his blustering any day. Flashing Molly a smile, I nodded.

"But—but..." she stammered. "It's so soon."

"Sometimes, Molly," I said, reaching for the potatoes, "you don't realize a thing is staring you in the face until you're hit over the head with it."

"Joey hit you?" Mary Grace asked, her eyes wide. "That doesn't seem like him."

The three older sisters at the table burst out laughing. "Not really, poppet. It's just a way to say Joey had been there all along but I didn't realize how we felt about each other until now."

"Oh." She gave me a smug face. "Well, I could have told you how you felt about each other. It was positively obvious to me all along."

I grinned and reached for a pork chop. It was the nicest supper we'd had as a family in a long time. We talked a little about the wedding, although I didn't have any details the girls cared about yet but for the dress I'd wear. Daddy said business was going well at his new location, and I tried to read his face, wondering if the gambling arrangement was working out, but he kept his eyes on his plate. When he was finished, he retired to the front room with his whisky to read the paper, and I left him alone. If he was satisfied with his life working for a man like Angel DiFiore, so be it. I wanted nothing to do with it. My only hope was that he'd bring home enough money to take care of the girls, and when they were ready, pay for their schooling. I might have to enlist Bridget's help to convince him to do it, but I'd worry about that later.

Molly and I did the dishes after supper, and I was still drying when there was a knock on the front door. Mary Grace pulled it open, and a moment later I heard Joey's voice.

"Hi." I rushed into the front hall. He looked even more handsome than I remembered, if that were possible, even though he only wore work clothes and the old floppy cap.

"Hi." He removed the cap and came forward to kiss my cheek. Mary Grace elbowed Molly and the two of them stood there beaming like idiots.

"Scram," I told them. "Go finish the dishes."

"Oh, just a minute," Molly scoffed, stepping toward Joey and offering a hug. "We heard the news, Joey, and we're really happy. Congratulations."

Joey hugged her, giving me a surprised look over her shoulder. Mary Grace, not to be outdone, threw her arms around Joey and Molly's waists.

"Well, thank you." Joey laughed as he embraced both girls. "Just what I always wanted—more sisters."

"OK, you said your congratulations, now away with you. Finish the dishes." I pointed a finger toward the kitchen.

"Sure will be nice not to hear that anymore, won't it?" Molly said to Mary Grace as they headed down the hall.

Rolling my eyes, I turned back to Joey. The way he looked at me—like he was barely able to keep his hands to himself—sent my heart pounding. Before supper I'd changed into a peasant blouse and an old blue skirt, but he looked at me as if I wore diamonds and silk. Or maybe nothing at all. Simultaneously, we glanced to our left, where my father sat reading the paper only ten feet away.

Then we grinned at each other. "Can you come for a ride?" he whispered.

"Maybe." I raised my voice and called to Daddy. "Is it OK if I go for a ride with Joey?" Daddy nodded without lifting his eyes from the paper, and my excitement ratcheted up ten notches. "Thanks."

I grabbed my purse off the hall table and followed Joey to his car. It wasn't quite full dark yet, and the warm air was filled with all the sounds of a summer night. Soft breeze, noisy cicadas, tinny music from a phonograph drifting through an open window. Joey opened and closed the door for me before getting in on the driver's side. The moment his door was shut he grabbed my face and pressed his lips to mine, his tongue sliding into my mouth in a way that told me exactly what he was thinking. Blood rushed to my center.

"God, I've been thinking about you all day," he whispered, putting our foreheads together. "And I can't go another hour without your body next to mine."

I put my hands to the back of his head and pulled him to me, my pulse racing faster and faster as the kiss grew more frenzied. I lavished the attention on his lips and tongue I wanted to lavish on other parts of his body.

After a moment, he groaned. "We can't do this here."

"Let's go to your house," I said breathlessly.

He grimaced. "Can't go there either. My Ma and Marie are there packing up come things she forgot in the attic. She keeps coming back," he whined.

I thought fast. Where could we be alone? "The boathouse. You still have a key?"

Without a word, he started the motor and tore down the street. My head was thrown back against the seat and the wind rushed to meet me, and I laughed, the air around me crackling with energy.

On the short drive to the boathouse, I didn't bother to keep my hands off him. Unbuttoning his pants, I freed his hot, hard erection and tantalized him with my fingers and palms, the backs of my hands and the inside of my wrists.

"Jesus, Tiny. I can barely drive." Joey gripped the steering wheel hard.

With a wicked grin, I lowered my head and licked him like a lollipop.

"Oh, fuck, now I really can't drive. Oh my God. Oh Christ. Where the fuck is that boathouse, I can't even remember the way right now."

I laughed with him inside my mouth, the hum from my lips making him even harder. Tasting the salty sweetness of his imminent release, I took him deeper, relishing the feel of him at the back of my throat.

He must have remembered where the driveway was, because my head thumped the steering wheel as the Ford traversed the pocked dirt road that led down to the dock. Giggling again, I sat up. "Ouch. Guess I better stop for a minute."

He parked under the willow tree and grabbed my hand, hauling me out of the driver's side and racing for the boathouse without even shutting the car door. At the boathouse entrance, he fumbled with the key.

"Hurry," I whispered, wrapping my arms around his torso and kissing his back.

Finally the lock gave. The moment we were inside we tore frantically at each other's clothing, our lips and tongues and teeth colliding hungrily. The short amount of time that had elapsed since we'd last had our hands and mouths on each other was completely out of proportion with the appetites we'd built up. With impatient fingers I pushed the braces from Joey's shoulders and shoved the buttons of his shirt through their holes. He managed to get my skirt off before shrugging off his shirt and pulling his undershirt over his head. Giving up on the tiny buttons on my blouse, he bent and yanked my underwear to my ankles. I kicked it off and jumped up, twining my stocking-clad legs around his waist.

When he licked his fingers and reached low, I opened my mouth to tell him he needn't bother, I was already wet, but then his fingers were rubbing me, inside and out, and all I could do was sigh with pleasure.

Satisfied he wouldn't hurt me, he moved toward the door. I cried out as he shoved his cock inside me, slamming my body against the wood. My eyes rolled back in my head and I dug my nails into his skin. But he didn't stop. Again and again, he drove me into the wall with powerful, deep thrusts, shocking me with his violent need to fill me so completely.

When I regained the capacity to respond, I covered his face with feverish kisses. Between gasps, I breathed his name, pulled his hair, licked and sucked his neck, his mouth, his tongue. And when he put his hands on my ass and altered his angle just enough so that I rode him tighter to his body, the rock hard base of his cock rubbed me just the right way. I clutched him hard with arms and legs. "Right there," I whispered against his lips. "Fuck me right there. Yes, yes, yes." Something deep inside me was tightening and coiling in a way I'd never experienced. It wasn't only just the delicious friction between our bodies; it was some hidden place in my body he was able to reach this way, and I had no words, no thoughts, no voice for what he was doing to me.

Higher and higher I climbed as he moved with utter abandon, until my muscles clenched and pulsed around him. Starbursts of color exploded in front of my eyes and I moaned his name over and over through the shimmering waves of bliss.

"Fuck, I can feel you," he whispered. "Oh my God, I'm gonna come so hard."

"Do it," I panted. "Now, Joey. I want to feel it, now."

Slamming me back into the door again, he groaned long and hard as he poured into me. I felt his shuddering release as deeply as I'd felt my own and exploded once more, the delicious rippling at my center lingering even longer than before.

Joey dropped his forehead to my shoulder. I hadn't even realized my eyes were closed until I opened them and the colors disappeared. One by one, my senses returned. Beyond Joey's dark hair, I saw the glow of the moon through the high windows. I felt the damp heat of his shoulders under my hands. I heard our heavy breathing as our lungs recovered and smelled the musty wood of the boathouse walls. Lowering my lips to his neck, I slipped my tongue through them and tasted the salty warmth of his skin.

"You keep doing that, I'm gonna have to pound you into the wall again." Joey's voice was muffled in my shoulder.

"Promise?"

He turned his face into my neck and inhaled deeply. "Mmmmm. Yes."

"Good, because I liked it."

Joey chuckled before picking up his head. "I used to wonder what you'd be like. I had a feeling you'd be a firecracker."

"And? Am I a firecracker?"

"Doll, TNT's got nothing on you."

I laughed. "I'll take that as a compliment."

"You should."

"I used to wonder what you'd be like too."

"Yeah?"

"Yeah. And I used to touch myself all over, imagining my hands were yours," I whispered.

I thought his eyes would pop from their sockets.

"Really?"

"Really."

"Maybe you'll show me sometime."

"I'll show you right now."

Joey staggered backward as if he'd been shot. "Oh my God, Tiny. You're killing me." Keeping me hoisted around his waist, he dropped to his knees on the cement floor, and then onto his bottom. My knees came to rest beside his hips and he leaned back on his elbows. "Show me," he said.

I bit my lip. Was he serious? Down on the floor, the shadows were thick, and I could barely make out his expression.

But then I felt him stir inside me. "Show me," he said again.

Oh, what the hell.

Slowly I unbuttoned my blouse while he watched. When it was undone completely, I did the same with the tiny row of buttons down the front of my chemise. With each new inch of my skin exposed, he grew harder. I let the blouse slip from my shoulders, but kept the chemise on, open at the chest. My thighs were pale above the tops of my black stockings. When I looked down, I saw the place where our bodies were joined, and a rush of arousal swept over me. My skin tingled. Involuntarily, I clenched around him.

He grew harder.

I brought my hands to my breasts, kneading them as I began to rock my hips a little. "First I'd do this," I whispered, keeping my eyes on his. "And I'd pretend it was your hands on me."

Joey's mouth fell open and he made no effort to close it.

My breasts were small but responsive, and as I played with my nipples they tightened and peaked. I brushed my fingers over the taut pink skin, pinching and pulling them. His cock continued to swell, and I closed my eyes as I circled my hips.

"Oh my God," Joey moaned.

"And then," I said, sliding one hand down my body, "I'd do this." When my fingers reached the warm, slick spot just above where our bodies were connected, I rubbed myself slowly.

By now Joey was fully hard and I could feel him moving his hips, trying to push up inside me. "Christ, you are so beautiful," he said. "I'm dying to touch you but I don't want you to stop."

I laughed, luxuriating in not only the compliment, but the intimacy of the moment and the erotic pleasure of the act. "Remember the night you slept on the couch at my house?" I asked. "I could barely sleep that night, knowing you were downstairs." Taking my other hand from my chest, I leaned back slightly, placing it on his leg behind me. The new angle increased the pressure to that place inside me that made me gasp and arch.

Joey groaned as if in agony. "Me either. God, I wanted you so badly that night."

"And then the next morning, you stayed to cook breakfast and I went upstairs to take a bath."

"Yeah?"

"Yes, and this is what I did while I thought about you. Your hands on me, your mouth on me, your cock inside me."

"Oh my God." Joey sat up fast and took a nipple between his teeth. Crying out at his bite and the uncontrollable urge raging through my body, I held on to his thick, muscular shoulders and rocked against him. Nothing had ever felt so good in my entire life, and as the frenzy inside me hit the tipping point, I flung myself forward, knocking Joey onto his back and pinning my hands on his chest. Bucking wildly on top of him, I thrilled at the sound of his rasps and strangled grunts and the sight of his gorgeous jaw dropping open as another climax hit him. He gripped my hips hard as we came together, our bodies pulsing in perfect synchronization.

When I could move again, I brushed the hair from his forehead. "You know, that was actually even better than it was in my fantasy."

"Mine too," he whispered, eyes closed.

"Now you'll have to show me how you touched yourself when you thought about me. It's only fair."

He opened one eye and looked at me. "You're killing me."

"Not right now, silly. Maybe next time."

"Deal." He shut his eyes again and sighed. "God, I love you. And I don't want to go, but I promised to meet Angelo at ten. I should get you home."

I couldn't bring myself to release him yet. "How much will you owe him?"

He grimaced. "Probably about ten grand. I'll have to run booze from Chicago to keep Sam's nose out of it. Or maybe New York. But don't worry about it."

"Ha."

He squeezed my hips once more. "Come on, let's go. Better pull yourself together, though. I don't need your dad after me at this point."

Reluctantly I got to my feet, my knees aching a bit from the cement. "At this point, what would it matter?" I checked for holes in my stockings. "We're getting married, aren't we?"

Still on his back, he lifted his hips and pulled his pants up, a masculine maneuver that somehow made my belly tighten even after I'd already come three times in the last half hour. "Yeah, the sooner the better. Because I want to do this all the time now."

Smiling, I buttoned my blouse and pulled on my skirt. "Me too. Any idea where my underwear went?"

Joey squinted into the shadows. "I think I see something white over there." He walked over and picked them up. "These belong to you?" he asked, swinging them around on one finger.

When I grabbed for them, he held them out of my reach. "Now, hold on just a second. I once made some pretty good dough charging the boys to peek at your knickers. I might be able to afford a ring if you let me keep these."

"Joey Lupo! You give me back my underwear this instant!" I jumped for them.

"Last time you threatened to tell my mother." He held them way over my head.

"Don't think I won't, mister. Or better yet, I'll

punish you myself."

He stopped moving and considered that before handing them to me.

"That's what I thought."

On the way back to my house, I asked Joey if he'd told his family about us planning to marry.

"Not yet. I thought we could do it together." He took my hand and squeezed it. "Maybe dinner one night this week over at my apartment?"

His apartment? "So you're going to keep it?"

"For now." He glanced at me. "We can live there after we're married. But I'd like a house eventually. Once I save up the money."

"I'd love that. All of it."

"Good." He kissed my hand. "When do you want to get married?"

"As soon as possible."

"Me too. Let's go see the priest tomorrow, OK?"

"OK." God, there was so much to do—I hadn't even told Evelyn yet! "Where will we do it?"

"Well, if you don't mind, I'd like to get married where my sisters did, at Holy Family."

"That sounds nice." Bridget had been married there too.

"And then maybe luncheon at the restaurant? We

could close it for the day. Would you like that?"

"That's perfect!" Inside my chest, my heart thumped a happy rhythm. "Hey, you know what? Drop me off at Evelyn's—I want to tell her the good news if she's home."

"Sure." He turned onto her street and chuckled a bit. "Hope Rosie doesn't throw something at you. She was coming on pretty strong."

"Yeah, I saw that. Looked like it was really tough on you."

He grinned. "I liked that it made you jealous."

"Of course you did. Well, not to worry, I'm sure she's on to the next sap by now."

"Swell. She can bring him to our wedding."

"As long as she keeps her hands off the groom, it's fine by me."

"Could be tough. Especially if I wear my nice suit."

I sighed in disgust as he pulled up in front of Evelyn's house. "You know, just when I think you're a nice guy..." I opened the door and started to get out, but he grabbed my arm.

"You know how much I love you, right? How happy we're gonna be?"

"Beat it, Joey Lupo. You're a troublemaker, that's

what you are." I leaned closer and lowered my voice. "And if you didn't have such perfect lips and hands, or such a nice big"—I glanced down at his crotch —"apartment, I wouldn't even talk to you."

He laughed out loud, and I pulled my arm away. "No kiss goodnight?" he asked.

"You've had enough kissing. Now go." I slammed the door.

Grinning, he threw me a kiss and took off down the street.

Chapter Seventeen

Later that night, I walked home, my cheeks sore from smiling and laughing so much with Evelyn. Other parts of me were sore too, but even that made me happy.

At the news of my engagement, Evelyn had been stunned, then ecstatic, then envious, and then thrilled when I asked her to be a bridesmaid. After a lot of squealing and hugging and misty eyes, she got practical, going over all the details I'd have to attend to before the wedding took place.

"You'll need bridesmaids dresses—you'll have your sisters, of course—and flowers. You'll have to plan the menu for the party and have Bridget's dress altered and get a license and oh! You will let me throw you a bridal shower, won't you?"

I'd winced and shook my head, telling her I wasn't really the bridal shower type, and anyway, we were moving into Joey's apartment, which already had everything we'd need, assuming his mother let us keep it all. Did I really need my own china or silver tea service to sit unused on a shelf like Bridget's?

Eventually, Evelyn got smug and told me she'd seen it between Joey and me all along, and how even Rosie had admitted that he hadn't laid a finger on her and in fact he had talked about nothing but me the two nights he'd driven her home. When we imagined her sitting next to him in the car, getting huffier and huffier at his inattention, we laughed out loud.

As I rounded the corner onto my block, I thought about Joey's meeting with Angelo. Twisting my hands together, I prayed that everything had gone smoothly. Why hadn't I made him promise to call?

Daddy's car was still in the driveway. I was surprised that he was taking a night off, although it was a Monday. Perhaps the club was closed. I let myself into the house, which was dark and silent. Everyone must have gone to bed already. I knew I should too, but I was antsy. I wouldn't be able to sleep worrying about Joey. So when my eye caught Daddy's keys on the front hall table, I swiped them into my hand and went out again.

I wanted everything settled. No point waiting until tomorrow.

I'd talk to Enzo tonight.

"Floor, miss?"

"Nine, please." My voice was shaky, and I cleared my throat. "Thank you."

The operator at the Statler pushed nine and the doors closed. As we ascended, my stomach churned incessantly. What would his reaction be? Had I made the wrong decision to come here tonight? I hadn't told anyone where I was going. By the time the elevator pinged and the doors open, I was close to nausea.

But I stepped out, nodding at the operator behind me and taking a few deep breaths. *Come on. You faced Angel down when you were hundreds short on the ransom. You tricked Raymond into all sorts of things, even when you were at gunpoint. You can end things with Enzo without falling apart.*

I put one foot in front of the other and began the walk down the hall to the front apartment. But my knees wobbled. What if Enzo didn't see it my way? What if he tried to change my mind?

No, impossible. I straightened my shoulders and lengthened my strides, confident I wouldn't be seduced by him ever again. *Maybe I won't even find him attractive.*

Somewhere deep in my brain I heard a peal of laughter.

OK fine. But even if I find him attractive, there is nothing he can do or say to make me change my mind about Joey.

Positive of that, I approached the door to his apartment, lifted my fist, and knocked.

No answer.

Maybe he wasn't here? He'd said he would be. I put my ear to the door, and sure enough I heard his voice. It was too muffled to tell what he was saying, but it was definitely his.

I knocked again, louder.

Nothing.

Shifting my weight from one leg to the other, I debated using the key he'd given me. I'd brought it to give back to him, along with the necklace. I raised my hand to knock one more time when suddenly a rhythmic thumping began. I cocked my head—it sounded like it was coming from inside the apartment.

Then laughter. Female.

That's it—I was using the key.

I rummaged in my purse, pulled it out, and slipped it into the lock with trembling fingers. Bursting into the apartment, I took in the low light, the women's heels on the floor near the window, and an evening bag on the coffee table.

Half furious and half elated, I slammed the door loud enough to interrupt.

Sure enough, a minute later, Enzo appeared in the bedroom doorway wrapped in a sheet, and holding a pistol.

"Tiny? What the fuck are you doing here? You said you couldn't come tonight."

"Clearly I was the only one. Who's in there?"

"Enzo? What's going on?" The squeaky voice from the bedroom was unmistakable.

I raised my eyebrows. "Your fiancée. How refreshing."

"Just wait a minute." Enzo disappeared into the bedroom for a moment and returned without the gun but wearing pants. Only pants. He ran a hand through his disheveled hair and pulled the door shut behind him.

I was delighted to find that in fact I did not find him as attractive as I feared. Yes, he still had the face and the body, but underneath lurked deception and a darkness I'd never again find beautiful. I threw the apartment key at his head, and he caught it before it struck his cheekbone.

"Tiny, what the hell? Why are you doing this?"

"What a laugh. Why are *you* doing this?"

"Doing what?"

My eyes popped. "Doing what? Fucking another girl in the apartment you just offered to me!"

"It's my apartment!"

I folded my arms. "And it's going to stay your apartment."

"Don't be like that," he said quietly, moving deeper into the front room. "This doesn't have anything to do with you."

He probably believed that. "You're right, it doesn't. Because I no longer care what you do."

"I don't understand you. I thought we agreed about exactly what we could be and what we couldn't." He moved closer to me, too close. I could smell Gina's perfume on his skin.

I took a step back. "Maybe we did. But I'm no longer interested in it."

"Oh no?" A seductive smile crept onto his lips and he came toward me again. "Bet I can change your mind."

"No." I tried to take another step back but bumped into the sofa. "You're insane. Your fiancée is in the other room. Probably naked."

"And she's going to stay there if she knows what's good for her."

From my purse I took out the necklace box and slammed it into his waist. "Go back to her, Enzo. You don't care about me or anyone else. You just want what you want when you want it."

"Until now you felt the same way. That's why it worked between us."

"Not anymore."

"Tiny, I want you," he breathed, tossing the box on the coffee table and reaching for me. "I've wanted you since the moment I saw you. You know that."

I put my hands out to stop him from touching me. "And I wanted you. And we had each other, and it was fun for a lark, but now it's done. You've got everything you want—the drugs, the whisky, the club, the car, all of it. I just want you to let me go now."

"What if I don't want to let you go?"

"You have no choice."

His eyes flashed with anger. "It's Lupo, isn't it?"

"I didn't tell him what you told me," I said quickly. "I kept the secret."

"Bravo, darling. You passed the test."

"Damn right I did. I never lied to you."

"You told me there was nothing between the two of you. That was a lie."

"There was nothing between us then."

"And now?" His breaths were controlled.

"And now..." I swallowed. "Now there is something."

To my surprise, he laughed. "You want that fucking boy?"

Rage exploded inside me, and I shoved his chest. "Go to hell! It's none of your business who or what I choose! It never was."

"You'll change your mind. You'll want what I can give you—I know you, Miss O'Mara. Don't forget that."

"No, you don't. You knew a girl who chased danger for a while, that's all." I backed toward the door.

"You chased more than that, darling."

My face burned. "Maybe I did. But that's done."

He moved toward me, slow and sleek, unfairly handsome. Before I knew it, he had me up against the wall, a hand on either side of my head. "And I say, it isn't done. I still want you."

"You'll find another girl."

He moved a lock of hair off my face. "I don't

want another girl. I want this face, and these lips, and this body."

I turned my cheek to prevent him from kissing me. "You can't have me. Leave us alone."

He slammed a hand into the wall and backed away from me, rage radiating from his body. "Go, then. But if you thought I'd let him go unpunished, you were mistaken. He stole from me."

Panic screamed through my veins. "Enzo, please don't do anything to hurt him."

His lips tipped up. "You're too late. It's already done."

It was the smile that frightened me most.

#

I drove straight to Joey's. The restaurant was closed, of course, and the block was dark and deserted. As I parked along the street, I glanced up to the apartment. No lights were on. I had no idea if there were any guests staying in other rooms or renting other apartments, but I wasn't going to be able to get into the building if no one was inside. Chewing my

336

thumbnail, I looked up and down the block. This area was not well lit at night, and I had no weapon of any kind.

Or did I?

Frantically, I looked around inside Daddy's car. Nothing on the floor, nothing under the seat. Standing on the seat, I leaned into the back and checked the secret compartment in the floor, used for hauling whisky.

Nothing.

Dammit, Daddy, you were a bootlegger. Couldn't you at least be the kind that carried a gun? But he wasn't. Bootlegging hadn't been violent until recently, and Daddy's favorite weapons were his fists, anyway. Slumping back down in the front, I looked at my own fists. Pathetically small. I had nothing to fight back with.

But I had to find Joey.

Exiting the car, I gritted my teeth and took the steps up to the double doors at the recessed entrance. I was completely in shadow. My teeth chattered as I rang the buzzer.

No one came.

Cupping my hands over my eyes, I peered inside and saw the silent lobby, the dark wood staircase. I pounded on the glass pane with the heel of my hand.

No one came.

Tears welled. Where was he? Had Enzo done something to him? Why did one man have to be so greedy? I knew it was futile but I tried opening the door before I pushed the buzzer again, three times. Now don't get hysterical. He's probably just still out. But I wasn't going to feel better until I saw him, held him, safe and sound. Weeping openly, I rushed down the steps and around the side of the building. Maybe I could climb the fire escape.

In the alley, dark and silent and smelling of rotting food, I held my breath and said a prayer I'd be tall enough to pull down the ladder.

But it was already down.

Something about that seemed off, but I climbed it and then raced up the steps to the third floor—oh, shit.

The back door was open.

"Joey?" I peered into the kitchen, my heart knocking painfully against my ribs. It was dark, but my eyes adjusted fairly quickly—no one was there. I entered and crossed to the swinging door to the dining room.

But before I pushed it open, I heard Joey's voice. "No! Just let her go, Sam, she has nothing to do with this." His words sounded muffled and strange, as if he had a mouth full of cotton.

"Shut the fuck up, Lupo. I should cut you right now for hiding that dope from me."

I pulled my hand off the door as if it had burned me, backing up until my butt hit the kitchen cabinet, which rattled noisily.

Shit!

In a panic, I grabbed a butcher knife from a block on the counter, darted into the pantry and shut the door almost all the way. In a moment someone swung into the kitchen.

"Nobody in here!" I heard a voice say over the galloping of my heart.

But it would only be a matter of seconds before whoever it was checked the pantry, and I begged God for the strength I'd need to plunge the knife into human flesh. I didn't want to kill anyone, but I'd need to injure him badly enough so he couldn't hurt me. *Aim for his right side, maybe a shoulder.* My hand shook horribly, and I tightened my grip lest the knife clatter to the floor.

And then I remembered the pistol. I swept my left hand along the shelf.

It was still there.

I dropped the knife, swiped the gun into both hands, and screamed as the pantry door opened, revealing the stocky, thick-necked outline of a guy. More than either of the weapons, I think it was the scream that stunned him. He faltered a little at the noise, and I took advantage of his surprise to draw back one foot and kick him in the balls as hard as I possibly could.

Grunting, he went down hard, his own gun clattering to the floor. I couldn't bring myself to shoot him, even though he might have been willing to shoot me, but I did kick his gun away and clock him over the head with my own.

A few times.

When I was positive I'd knocked him out, I burst into tears and shoved open the door to the dining room.

"Tiny, get out of here!" shouted Joey. But his words still sounded muffled.

Disoriented, I looked through the archway into the front room, where one lamped burned.

My knees nearly buckled.

Joey sat on a chair, the same chair I'd sat in before Sunday dinner, while Sam Scarfone stood to his side, holding a straight edge razor to his throat. His face, his beautiful face, was bruised and bloody, and his wrists and ankles were tied with rope. *Just like Daddy.*

Instinctively, I tucked the pistol I held behind me.

"You heard him. Get the fuck out of here," said Sam. "Where the fuck is Freddy?"

"I..." My voice stuck in my throat. Fear had totally paralyzed me. Somewhere in my mind, a voice said shoot him, but I wasn't sure I could do it. I locked eyes with Joey, who silently begged me to go. I could see the desperation in his face, but I wasn't about to leave him. My fingers tightened on the pistol.

Sam glared at me. "Get the fuck out of here, I said, before I show you the way myself."

"You lay one finger on her, and I'll rip you to fucking shreds," Joey said, the clearest words from him yet.

"You got a lot of nerve talking to me like that, Lupo, after what you pulled. I ever hear you held back again, I'm gonna lay more than my finger on her and make you watch."

I saw the rage erupt in Joey and he vaulted out of the chair and hurled himself at Sam, butting his head into Sam's chin.

"Joey, no!" I cried.

Sam was easily able to shove Joey down to the floor, and he grimaced, touching his tongue to one bloody corner of his mouth. "You're gonna pay for that," he said. "I thought you were smarter than Angelo, but I guess I was wrong." He brought the blade to Joey's cheek, and I snapped.

Rushing forward with the pistol out in front of me, I took aim at Sam's chest.

And pulled the trigger.

Chapter Eighteen

Turns out, I did have it in me to shoot someone.

It also turns out that I'm a horrible shot. I missed his chest by a mile, putting a bullet in his leg instead. But it was enough to knock him backward, and as he staggered I pulled the trigger again. This time I caught him in the shoulder, and he dropped his blade, groaning in pain. I raced into the room and scooped it up.

To my utter shock, he actually stumbled for the kitchen door and disappeared through it.

"Oh no!" I cried. "Should I go after him?"

"No!" Joey struggled to sit up. "Let him go. Just let him go, he won't get far."

I rushed over to him. "Oh my God," I said, breaking down again. "Are you OK?"

"I'm fine, baby. Where's the other guy—Freddy?"

"He's in the kitchen. I kicked him in the balls and knocked him out with your dad's gun."

Joey actually tried to smile. "He'd be proud of you."

I untied Joey's wrists and ankles. He threw his

arms around me and I wept into his chest, relieved and grateful. "Shhhh, it's OK now. It's OK, *cara*." Then he murmured something in Italian, I had no idea what, but his voice was soothing and the lilting, rhythmic words were so beautiful, I grew calmer immediately.

Joey took one of the guns and went into the kitchen, where he discovered Freddy had disappeared as well. However, he must have been too cloudy-headed to handle the fire escape because the police found him in a heap of broken bones beneath the iron staircase as if he'd fallen. Either that or Sam had pushed him.

Turns out there had been someone else in the building, and though she'd been too scared to answer my knock after hearing the shouts from Joey's apartment, she'd called the police. Freddy lived through the fall and was promptly arrested after being released from the hospital.

Sam Scarfone was not so lucky—but it wasn't my bullets that killed him.

Joey once told me that friendships and rivalries change with the wind in organized crime. You can never be sure exactly who your allies or enemies are at any given moment. Someone might shake your hand one day and sign his name with your blood the next.

That summer, there were a lot of shifting alliances as the top figures in Detroit's underworld sought to position themselves to make the most money and gain the lion's share of the criminal rackets.

Enzo, unable to handle his jealousy of Joey and seeking to punish him for the hijacking, had extended an offer to Sam Scarfone, unbeknownst to me. If Sam would run booze for Enzo's clubs, Enzo would tell him about River Gang members who'd screwed him out of thousands of dollars on a drug heist. Sam responded by confronting Joey the evening I showed up, and might not have killed him, since they had been friendly before, but I don't know for sure. In their business, there was no greater crime than not paying up.

However, earlier that day Joey had reached out to the old guard of the Scarfone faction, the men who'd split with Sam over control of the Scarfone territory after Big Leo's death. To get even with Sam for ordering the hit that had killed his father, Joey spilled what he knew about Sam's role in his uncle's death, and the old guard agreed—Sam had to pay.

His bullet-riddled body was found in the river a few weeks after the incident at Joey's.

No one was convicted.

Angelo, who had agreed to Joey's offer of a cut of

his bootlegging spoils, had been roughed up pretty good by Sam and wore a necklace of scars the rest of his life, but he survived. The River Gang disbanded once Sam was gone, and the leaders of the various powerful outfits in Detroit and the rest of the Midwest got together and agreed on a distribution of territory to cut down on violence. Eventually, even the outfits on the East Coast reached out to make a deal that would set up mutually beneficial smuggling operations.

Joey and Angelo decided to partner up and bought a boat together, and they ran whisky from Canada across the river on a regular basis for ten more years under the protection of the Scarfone outfit—until Prohibition ended. Eventually, they had enough money to buy an airplane, and they partnered with a few Canadian farmers who agreed to let their fields be used as landing sites in exchange for some booze and a fee. I wasn't crazy about Joey staying involved in organized crime, but he promised me it would only be bootlegging, and he'd stay out of trouble. After all, he wanted to dedicate most of his time to running the restaurant and raising a family with me.

As soon as his injuries healed, we were married at Holy Family and feted by friends and family at a reception at the restaurant. The morning of the wedding, a beautiful September Saturday, my sisters and Evelyn helped me dress in my old bedroom.

Bridget, dressed in soft blue, fastened the row of buttons at my back and we exchanged a look in the mirror remembering what she'd said about Joey getting them undone later. Molly and Evelyn, also in blue, settled the veil's crown on my head and adjusted the tulle to fall around my shoulders. Mary Grace, in a sweet white dress, brought me my satin shoes and helped me into them. Bridget and Evelyn were teary-eyed, but I felt nothing but pure joy.

At the back of the church, I stood with Daddy, waiting for the processional to begin. He'd been mostly silent throughout the wedding preparations, grumbling at the price of things here and there, but never denying me something I really wanted. Now, we stood aside in the vestibule with our arms linked, my fingers tight around the stems of white roses.

"Tiny," he said, his voice gruff, but soft. "I need to say something."

"Now?" I whispered, glancing nervously toward the aisle.

"Yes, now." His jaw was set.

"All right, Daddy."

He swallowed. "I'm not good with words or

affection like your mother was."

"It's OK."

"Let me finish," he said as the organ bleated the first notes of my processional music. The church coordinator began sending my sisters up the aisle as Daddy tugged me back. "When your mother died I did the best I could, but I know most of the raising fell on Bridget and then you. I could've done better to help."

His voice caught, and I squeezed his arm. When he looked at me, I was stunned to see tears in his eyes. My throat immediately tightened.

"Of all the girls, you're the most like me, Tiny. You're the spittin' image of your mother, but you've always been the most like me and I suppose that's why I've let you get away with more, the whisky and everything, and why I've been harder on you."

"I understand." I shot a nervous glance up front. Was Joey there yet?

"I'm sorry for the things I've done that have hurt you or put you in danger, and I'll always remember how you—did what you did for me. I might not've come through without you."

"I'd do it all again. And you'd do it for me." "I would." And he put a hand over his heart.

I knew he meant *I love you*, and I leaned over to

kiss his cheek. "I love you too, Daddy. We are who we are, and the people who love us have to take us as we are. But now you gotta get me to the front of the church, or Joey's gonna think I changed my mind."

He sniffed. "Let's go, then. I need a jar of whisky, and there ain't anything like it in this church."

I smiled, the lump in my throat dissolving, and we stepped into the center aisle. Mary Grace was just reaching the altar, and we paused a moment, allowing the guests to rise. I was briefly stunned at how many people were there, perhaps more than a hundred, but then I remembered how large Joey's family was. His mother and sisters were so thrilled with our plans to marry, they'd insisted on inviting every last person on the family tree with breath in their body.

For a second, nerves knotted in my stomach, but then Joey walked to the altar, and they unraveled into a thousand butterflies taking flight. Daddy and I began walking toward him at a quick clip, so quick that some guests hid smiles behind gloved hands and handkerchiefs. But I didn't care—Joey was waiting for me. It wasn't just his gorgeous face or the beautiful dark blue suit, or the strong body beneath it. It was that I knew that body now, every inch of it. I knew his mind. I knew his heart. I knew his history and his hopes for the future. I knew that he loved me and wanted me and understood me. He wanted to see the world with me. Some people might see marriage as a thing that trapped a girl in her home, but I knew life with Joey would never be dull, even if we never left the house.

In fact, as my eyes traveled from his slicked back hair to his lips and down his torso, I thought never leaving the house sounded like a pretty good idea.

I forced myself to keep my mind as pure as possible—we were in church, after all—and looked Joey in the eye. His were wet, and as I got closer, he blinked and then brought a hand up, thumb rubbing at one eye, fingers at the other. I smiled at him, full to bursting.

Daddy gave me away, Joey took my arm, and the rest of the ceremony was a blur but for the moment Joey slipped the ring on my finger. He'd wanted to surprise me, and he did—my mouth fell open and I didn't stop staring at my hand for a full ten seconds, so long the guests began to chuckle. It was unbelievably beautiful—a large rectangular diamond surrounded by delicate filigree work in a silver band. Later he would tell me the diamond was emerald cut and the metal was platinum. The ring reminded him of me, he said—

350

lovely and strong all at once. I had no idea how he afforded such a ring, and I never asked. Some things I just learned not to question.

We shared a chaste kiss when the priest pronounced us married, and Joey squeezed my hands. "Mrs. Lupo," he whispered in my ear as our guests cheered.

I loved every moment of our reception— especially one particular moment when I caught Joey watching me from across the restaurant. Rather than smile, he simply locked eyes with me and jerked his head toward the kitchen. I had a feeling I knew what he meant, and my belly tightened with desire. He excused himself from whomever he was talking to with barely a glance, and he came over and grabbed my hand. Moving quickly, he pulled me through the kitchen door and we flew by the surprised staff. I laughed out loud, glad I'd already removed the veil from my head. I'd have tripped for sure.

The moment the pantry door slammed shut, he kissed me for real, wrapping his arms around me and lifting me right off the ground. "Mmmmm." He teased my tongue with his. "I can't wait any longer."

"Me either," I said. "But we can't leave yet."

"Who said we had to leave?" He set me down

and ran his hands up my sides.

I laughed. "Joey, this dress!"

"It's beautiful." He kissed his way down my neck, setting my skin on fire. "You're beyond beautiful."

I shivered, cradling his head at my chest. "I still can't believe it. We're married. We're actually married."

"I know." His words were muffled as he kissed my breasts through my dress. "So even if they miss us, they can't say anything. And I can't wait to taste you one more minute."

He dropped to his knees, lifting the long tiers of my dress up to my waist. Holding them aloft, he pressed his lips to my thighs above the white stockings clipped by garter to my corselette. Moaning again, he brought his mouth to my center, covered by the thinnest layer of loose silk that snapped between my legs. "Back up," he said.

I did, bracing myself against the pantry door.

"Good. Now put your leg on my shoulder." I rested the back of one thigh on top of his shoulder, gasping as he nibbled and sucked at me through the silk. "Now the other." His breath was hot on my skin.

Since his hands were holding up the front of my

dress, only his shoulders would hold my weight. But I was so needy for him, I plastered my hands on the door next to my hips and swung my other leg up.

Sometimes being small was a blessing.

Joey easily held me suspended on his shoulders, burying his face between my legs. Unsnapping the step-in with his teeth, his magnificent mouth worked the damp silk aside and he slipped his tongue inside me, eliciting a long sigh of pleasure from deep in my throat.

Eventually he let my dress fall over his head and reached under my backside to hold me to him. I had no idea how he managed not to suffocate, but I was so deliriously aroused I didn't give it more than a passing thought. He absolutely devoured me, licking and sucking and fucking me with his tongue until I was panting and digging my heels into his back and pounding my hands on the door behind me. When I finally came, I yelled his name so loud I was positive the entire reception heard. He moaned into my pulsing wetness, making me throw my head back, and it banged the door, hard.

I'd have a lump. I didn't care.

As I began to breathe again, he kissed each of my inner thighs before helping me stand. "God, I love that." He hugged my legs from his kneeling position. "I want to do that every day. Twice a day."

I laughed. "We'll never leave the house."

"Fine with me, Mrs. Lupo."

The name sent a ripple of joy through me. I looked down at him and wished I could see his face in the dark. Smoothing my hand over his hair, I marveled at how we'd ended up here. "I love you."

He stood and pressed his lips to my forehead before pulling me into his chest. "I love you too."

I breathed in the scent of him, knowing how lucky I was to be in that moment. So many things could have prevented it—from outside threats to our own stubbornness. "Isn't it amazing how much has changed this summer?"

"Definitely. Just think about how much you disliked me before now."

I squeezed him tighter. "I didn't dislike you. You just drove me crazy with all your teasing."

"That's how I showed I cared."

"Well, you have better ways now."

He kissed my temple. "Yes, I do. But I'll probably still tease you."

"How would I know I married the real Joey Lupo if you didn't?"

He released me slightly and tipped up my chin. "I'd do anything for you." He kissed me. "Anything. You want me to leave bootlegging behind, I'll do it. You want to move away from Detroit, I'll do it. You want ten kids, I'll do it."

I laughed. "Uh, let's start with one—eventually. And you don't have to leave bootlegging behind, not completely. Just promise me you'll be careful and smart, and if it gets dangerous, you'll quit."

"Promise."

"And there is something you can do for me."

"Name it."

"I want to go to New York and stay in a big hotel like the Astor or the Plaza."

He kissed me again. "Done."

I hugged him close. "So how much longer do we have to stay at this reception? I'm dying to get these clothes off you."

"Say the word and I'll carry you out of here."

"Now."

"That is a word you like, I've noticed." After one last kiss, Joey pulled the pantry door open, and led me back through the kitchen. We ignored the knowing looks among the waiters, who elbowed each other and guffawed, keeping our heads up as we re-entered the restaurant. As always, Joey's family said the longest goodbyes in all Creation, each person hugging and kissing us and wishing us well. I endured more than a few jokes about having children soon, and rolled my eyes at Bridget, who was laughing at me from across the room. I knew she understood.

We said goodbye to my family too, Daddy actually kissing my cheek and then Joey's wordlessly. My sisters hugged and kissed us both, and Bridget clung to me for a long moment. "I know you'll be happy together," she whispered. "Vince would be so glad." I squeezed her back and turned to Evelyn, who embraced me while Ted shook Joey's hand.

"I can't believe it, Tiny. You're married. To Joey!" She released me but kept my hands in hers.

"I know. I can't believe it either," I admitted. I'm glad you and Ted aren't as stubborn or blind as Joey and I were."

"Me too." She leaned in again to whisper in my ear. "Cross your fingers for me. I think we might be next."

"Crossed," I whispered back in hers.

She giggled. "Now go. Any fool can see how impatient you two are to be alone." Glancing at the ceiling, she added, "And if the chandeliers start shaking, I'll know why."

I gave her one last hug and took Joey's hand, and we walked out the main doors into the lobby. It was there Joey swept me into his arms and carried me up two flights of stairs. I laughed when he started skipping steps on the second flight. "Take it easy. I don't want you worn out before we even get inside."

He grinned. "Never."

Without setting me down, he turned the knob and opened the door to his apartment.

Our apartment.

Inside, he went straight for the bedroom, setting me down at the side of the bed. I grabbed him by the tie and pulled his mouth to mine, tipping backward onto the mattress. He laughed as he fell on top of me, then propped himself up slightly on his hands, pressing his lower body into mine. My breath hitched at feeling him hard on my leg, and I wiggled impatiently beneath him. "Too many clothes between us," I whined. "Get them off, now."

He laughed, and my insides filled with longing again as I looked up at him. I'd never get enough. "Relax, Mrs. Lupo. We're just getting started."

It's only the beginning, I thought as I brought my hands to his face. When he lowered his lips to mine, I remembered thinking the exact same thing the day he'd kissed me in the front hall, only that day the words had filled me with trepidation.

Today, I just felt alive, bursting with life and love and hope, and it was everything I wanted.

Epilogue

Joey and I spent a week in New York after we wed, and a more romantic honeymoon I could not have imagined. Soon after we returned I discovered I was in a family way—of course I was, we were terribly careless about precautions from the start—and we began planning for our family. I thought I might feel some regret at expecting so soon, but I never did. Joey still said he'd support my going to school if I wanted to, and I did, in fact, take a few classes before the baby arrived. It was a good thing I was interested in science, because I was only permitted to take classes where the long white lab coats would hide my condition.

But once the baby was born, a girl we named Vincenza Kathleen, I realized school would have to wait. I didn't mind—taking care of Vinnie and keeping accounts for the boarding house kept me busy, although Joey, true to his word, did all the cooking for us. How he managed that plus the restaurant and his bootlegging operation was a mystery to me, but he was smart, hard-working and ambitious, although never so much that ambition overshadowed his devotion to his family.

Unlike Enzo DiFiore.

We didn't cross paths with him for a while, but I heard he married Gina and took over her father's distilleries after Vito Meloni's mysterious death—shot one day while exiting a diner, the victim of a sniper across the street whom no one seemed to notice. The sniper even entered a woman's nearby apartment and called a cab, explaining that his car had broken down, and waited in her front room for twenty minutes before the cab showed up.

Yet she was unable to identify him.

Evelyn told me Rosie was Enzo's mistress of choice for a few months the next year, even staying at his apartment at the Statler. But he grew tired of her and eventually took up with someone else, leaving Rosie to move back home until she married a divorced executive at Ford, moved into his house in Grosse Pointe, and never set foot in J.L. Hudson's dress department again.

As for Evelyn, she married Ted that winter and had twin girls almost as quickly as I had Vinnie. We often met for walks with our babies, pushing the buggies and laughing about how much our lives had changed in just one year. For the most part, it felt like my life began when Joey and I fell in love, and I never even thought about those insane weeks during July of 1923.

Until one day when Enzo showed up at the restaurant with a blond on his arm that was not his wife. Sometimes I helped Joey down there if he was short-staffed, and I happened to see them at a corner table. Immediately, my stomach filled with dread and I sought out Joey in the kitchen.

"It's OK," he assured me. "He came in about a week ago demanding payment. Apparently, territory has been renegotiated once more and this is his block now."

"And?" My heart was pounding with fear. *Not again.*

"And I paid him. And I'll keep paying him as long as he stays out of our lives and doesn't interrupt my bootlegging. We settled on a number and agreed to put the past behind us."

I relaxed a little. "And you trust him?"

"I wouldn't go that far. But I don't think he'll bother us," he continued, his eyes going dark. "Because I told him if he comes near you or our family, I'll fucking kill him."

"What did he say?"

361

"He said, 'Congratulations,' and he handed me a hundred dollar bill."

It didn't surprise me at all. Doling out favors on the street was part of Enzo's vision of himself as an all-powerful, benevolent mafia don, just like the men he'd seen growing up in Brooklyn. "God, what an asshole."

"Yeah. I told him to keep it. We don't need his money."

"No, we don't." I wrapped my arms around Joey's waist.

When I went back into the restaurant, I looked at Enzo, and he raised his glass to me in a silent toast.

I nodded. *That's right, asshole. Here's to me. I have everything I want, and you'll never be happy. Life isn't about owning things or people or money, but you'll never understand that.*

The next time I saw Enzo's name, it was in the newspaper—he'd been arrested for shooting his brother in an argument over who was stealing money from Club 23.

It didn't even faze me.

As for the rest of my family, Bridget surprised us all by marrying Martin after he graduated from dental school, and they sold the store, bought a home on the east side near Daddy, and raised the boys there, as well as their own two girls that followed. Eventually, Joey and I bought a house in that neighborhood, and our eight children grew up playing with their cousins, just as it should be.

Yes, eight.

Four of each, within ten years.

We never did get very good about precautions, and we couldn't keep our hands off each other.

Molly and Mary Grace both went away to college—paid for by Daddy, who finally put some money away—but both of them returned to the Detroit area to raise families. In fact, we rented our apartment to Molly and her pharmacist husband Jeff, and they lived there happily for many years.

I did become a nurse, eventually. It took me a while, what with eight children and all, but by the time the second world war broke out, I was working for the Red Cross. Two of my daughters followed me into medicine—one became a nurse; another, a doctor.

Prohibition ended, of course, and with it went a large portion of our income. But Joey had saved a good deal of cash, and at that point he and Jeff invested in a chain of drug stores that took off, and while we were never overly rich, we were certainly wealthier than either of us had been growing up.

And as the years went by, the summer of 1923 took on an unreal quality—as if it had been the plot of a movie or a book, the events so dramatic it didn't seem as if they could've happened to us in real life. But then Joey would dig out that handkerchief, the one with the words still written on it in red lipstick, faded but still legible. And we'd know it was all real.

The beginning of us.

Thank you for reading!

If you enjoyed this series, please leave a review where you purchased or borrowed it! Reviews, even short ones, are a wonderful way to spread the word about books you love and help other readers find them!

I love hearing from readers! Please feel free to email me if you'd like to share your thoughts about the book or just say hello.

Cheers,
Melanie

AB°UT THE AUTH°R

Melanie Harlow likes her martinis dry, her lipstick red, and her history with the naughty bits left in. She's the author of the Speak Easy historical duet as well as the Frenched Series, sexy contemporary romance. Find her sipping cocktails at cool places in Detroit, or look for her online…

Website: www.melanieharlow.com

Facebook: www.facebook.com/AuthorMelanieHarlow

Twitter: @MelanieHarlow2

Email: melanieharlowwrites@gmail.com

Pinterest: www.pinterest.com/melanieharlow2/

Tumblr: http://melanieharlow.tumblr.com/

Printed in Great Britain
by Amazon